Fallen buildings, ash heap[...] roads, black stone, all remain[...] How? Ross had never understood how the Ancients could waste such good land, covering it with stone and trees that bore no fruit. If the Ancients could waste the best land for miles, then perhaps the old legends were true. Only the fabulously powerful could conjure food from a valley of stone.

The Moon rose steadily, and there were blue witchlights on Mount Wilson to the east. Sorcerers lived there on the mountain towering high above the Dead Lands. They had built a great stone palace, larger and stronger than Kenyon Keep, stronger even than the Mayor's Palace in Los Angeles. They had neither lands nor religion nor army, but their fortress had stood for five hundred years, since before the Burning and the Plagues—or so they said, who could dispute it? They lived in uneasy peace with the Highlanders, and demanded little from the lowlands, though farmers often took them tribute and heard the Oracle tell them of the weather to come. The sorcerers lived well.

Yet they were only men. They could not fly, not even as well as the Highlanders of the Sierra. They knew things that others did not, of events that happened far away, but they were only men. They could be killed, and had been, when the tribesmen penetrated into the Valley and the Civilized lands beyond . . . and the tribesmen were coming again.

—From "Kenyons to the Keep!" by Jerry Pournelle

**AFTER ARMAGEDDON—
THERE *WILL* BE WAR**

CREATED BY

J. E. POURNELLE

AFTER

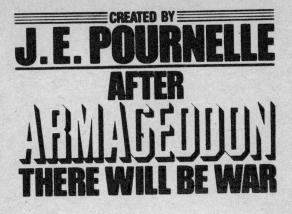

ARMAGEDDON
THERE WILL BE WAR

A TOM DOHERTY ASSOCIATES BOOK
NEW YORK

AFTER ARMAGEDDON

Copyright © 1990 by J. E. Pournelle

A TOR Book
Published by Tom Doherty Associates, Inc.
49 West 24 Street
New York, NY 10010

Cover art by Tony Roberts

ISBN: 0-812-54967-8   Can. ISBN: 0-812-54968-6

First edition: March 1990

Printed in the United States of America

0 9 8 7 6 5 4 3 2 1

ACKNOWLEDGMENTS

The editors gratefully acknowledge that research for some of the nonfiction essays in the book, including "After Armageddon: New Beginnings," was supported in part by grants from the Vaughn Foundation. Responsibility for opinions expressed in this work remains solely with the authors.

CONTENTS

AFTER ARMAGEDDON:
NEW BEGINNINGS
J.E. Pournelle

HAVE YOU EVER WISHED YOUR HOUSE WOULD BURN DOWN? I have. Not really, of course; but there could be advantages. We'd get to start over. All that furniture: it's okay, but it isn't what we really want, and we can't change over to a new style because of all the older stuff that wouldn't match. The machinery, adequate but obsolete: not old enough to scrap, but you can get appliances that are so much better now.

It would be tough going for a while if we had to start over, but it might be worth it . . .

Our house of state has a number of *national* problems. Trash and sewage: our waste management systems were designed to dispose of them, not treat them as valuable resources, and now we have this huge investment in the wrong philosophy. City plans, where they exist at all, were framed when energy (particularly gasoline for cars) was cheap. Office buildings and factories were designed with the assumption of cheap and inexhaustible energy supply. Now there's so much sunk investment involved that we can't start over, although we have a much better idea of the crucial factors we ought to consider.

How might we design America if we had a clean slate, given

1

what we know now? After all, it's obvious that the United States has better technology than industry. One of the less obvious advantages of World War II was that it smashed up Europe's obsolete industries, forcing them to rebuild from scratch—thus making them vastly more efficient.

Suppose we in the United States had such an opportunity. We would begin by designing collection systems to make use of "wastes" so that sewage and garbage and much of the cellulose could be fermented into methanes and fertilizers. Metals could be collected for re-refining, while the low-grade combustibles would become an energy source for processing these "urban mineral resources." The result would be to reduce the volumes to a manageable size, cut down on the transportation costs, and very greatly reduce the land costs involved in creating "sanitary landfills."

All this would save something like five percent of our national energy budget—not the Earth, but certainly worth striving for—and make waste management a source of profit to cities, rather than another burden on taxpayers.

We could revise building codes and tax assessment rules to require that residences be built with sufficient insulation and elementary solar heating. The combination could save as much as forty percent of the energy now used in space heating—and space heating is one of the major components of our energy budget. We'd avoid taking high-grade energy, such as coal and natural gas and electricity, and turning it into low-grade energy (warm air in habitations) as we presently do.

Sure, that's possible for new structures now. But consider the vast number of present dwellings and office buildings and factories; they were designed in such a way that just altering the piping to shunt the hot-water intake across a simple flat plate collector on the roof would generally cost more than the total hot-water bills for many years. If we could just start over, though—redesign—solar preheaters and solar room heaters could be put in at break-even prices for the buyer, with consequent benefits to the national balance of payments.

We could design cities with industries around the power plants, thus making use of high-grade steam as *steam*, rather than turning much of it into electricity (with losses in generation), transporting it across country (more losses in the transmission lines),

2

and finally turning it back into steam and heat at the other end. With proper design of industrial parks and residential areas would come real rapid transit—not something forced on people against their will (the major problem with present-day transit schemes), but a system actually more convenient than automobiles—again with consequent savings in energy.

Doing that would have enormous effects; after all, space heating and transportation are two of the largest chunks of our energy budget, and transportation consumes a very great part of the imported oil. (I know, I know: usually I give the exact numbers, rather than speaking in broad generalities. Give me time, and have a care for the newcomers who don't know how painlessly I can insert numbers into these discussions.)

Somehow I have trouble getting interested in this scenario . . .

An alternative would be to suppose Earth were struck by a giant comet. With any luck there's no one out there who hasn't at least heard of *Lucifer's Hammer* by Larry Niven and Jerry Pournelle (Fawcett, 1978). The results were described in our book, and it could be fascinating to assume you have nothing left but electricity while facing the depleted resource-base of Earth: a sort of *Challenge of Man's Future* (Harrison Brown, circa 1950) from the 1978 viewpoint.

Brown's *Challenge*, for those not familiar with it, made the point that the easily exploited resources are gone; the near-surface oil, the shallow-mine coal, even the forests; thus, once we lose technology (Brown was concerned about war, but a natural disaster would do the job as well) we can never regain it. It takes a high-technology society to exploit deeply-buried energy and mineral resources; without high technology, you can't get enough high-energy sources to construct your power sources.

However, Brown wrote in the '50s; could things have changed since then? Not really; you do need a high-energy technology in order to construct a high-energy technology when starting with a depleted resource base. However, given electricity—in *Hammer* there is at least a chance that a 2000-megawatt nuclear plant could survive, giving the survivors somewhat more electrical energy than the entire United States had prior to 1940—something might be done after all. The how of it could be fascinating and certainly would make a good essay . . .

Except that I can't get interested in that one either.

No: I am not going to go on for five thousand words on what I can't do. I'm about done with that. But I do want to say something about why I have trouble playing the "new beginnings" game.

It's too deadly serious. In some ways it is terrifying. Not in the obvious one. I have spent a great deal of my professional life "thinking about the unthinkable," and I have no real difficulty with intellectual exercises that assume fifty to seventy percent of the Earth's population is dead, most of the industry destroyed, etc., etc. Nor am I concerned about "becoming callous to disaster," or any of those other old saws; in my judgment the cruelest people are those who take no thought for the morrow, and who act without a shred of prudence and forethought, no matter how noble their intentions.

No, the frightening part about universal disaster is its attractiveness.

It would make things so easy. Clear off the deadwood, chop down the surplus population in one sweeping tragedy. The result would be horrible, but a billion dead is not a billion times more tragic than a single death: and we could build such a beautiful world on the ashes!

Think of it: a world with few comforts and luxuries, to be sure, but one in which all work is meaningful; a world without rat-races and monkey-motions, a world of hard work simply for the sake of survival, but one close to nature, with really magnificent goals for the future; a world with few regulations and rules and paperwork and all the other frustrations that make us psychoneurotic.

Look at the other effects. The genetic pool would be (by definition) composed of survivors. If there's any truth to the cliché that what's good for individuals *en masse* is bad for the species, then the bigger the disaster (up to the point of extinction of the race) the better. And if the disaster were a war which largely employed neutron bombs so that the destruction of physical resources was minimal . . .

It is morbidly attractive. Not that we'd *choose* it, of course (well, a few who are really far into "ecology" might), but still, we could live with it, and it does have advantages over the present, and we could be *so* kind to the Earth while rebuilding . . .

That's what's so terrifying: when I find myself thinking that

4

way; because if I, with all my commitment to technology and man's vast future, can get into a mood in which the only way out seems to be through destruction of some large fraction of the human race, then there must be very many more out there who see no hope for the future at all.

And that's senseless.

Anything we can do after a disaster can be done now. Can't it? Given the resources left over from an unprecedented disaster wiping out a very large part of humanity, we can certainly accomplish more with our total resource base—and yet it is easier in many ways to imagine starting from scratch.

Why is that? How have we got ourselves into such a box that disaster looks attractive?

Well, we haven't. We've got the resources and capabilities not for mere survival, but "survival with style," as I put it in another essay: to build a world in which Western civilization is not an island of wealth in the midst of a vast sea of poverty; in which all the world has access to at least the wealth we enjoyed in the '50s; and to sustain that level of wealth practically forever. We need only exploit what's available to us; to abandon the notion of "Only One Earth" and realize that we live in a system of nine planets, thirty-six moons, a million asteroids, a billion comets, and a very large and benign thermonuclear generator we call "the Sun."

Yet—we aren't doing it. As I write this, the Shuttle program is limping along in the wake of the *Challenger* disaster. Certainly the Shuttle was not an optimum design; certainly it was justified on the basis of missions which could be performed more cheaply by unmanned boosters (we'll never recover the cost of the Shuttle program through salvage and repair of satellites, or even through the "cheap" launch of dozens, yea hundreds, of "black box" satellites). But the Shuttle is the only game in town: it is our access to the space environment, the truck we can use to begin real exploitation of space—and without it, we have *nothing*.

Well—since I wrote those words we have come up with new hopes. The SSX, Spaceship Experimental, has been proposed to the Vice President and the Space Council. But it's not funded; so it's still true that without the Shuttle, we have nothing.

Instead of an energy program, we have a taxation system;

5

instead of research and development, we have a myriad of rules and regulations, while the R&D budgets are pared to the bone. We play about with windmills, but neglect solar power satellites; we dither about conservation, learn that everyone is in favor of it so long as somebody else does the conserving—and neglect new energy sources.

We have an aging work force and a bankrupt Social Security system. Social Security always depended on growth: the younger workers taxed to support the retired. Now, with low birth rates, the work force decreases relative to the number of retired people, and therefore we must increase productivity per worker to avoid disaster. (You can't much increase the work force for the next twenty years even if you begin breeding the workers now—and expanding population is probably not an optimum method anyway.) We can only get increased productivity by providing more energy per worker; to do that requires more power plants; and we aren't building them.

Two options open: coal and nuclear; and neither can be constructed. The U.S. nuclear energy industry is dismantling itself; it turned out to be a marvelous way to produce power (during the Great Freezes, the only power sources operating in much of the nation were nuclear) but a better way to subsidize lawyers. As to coal, it's just great. There are only two things you can't do with coal: mine it or burn it.

Item: the "Natural Resources Defense Council" has "won" a judgment against the U.S. Department of the Interior that provides, among other things, for no new coal leases for about three years; and restricts the United States to release of lands approved by the NRDC. The NRDC is a private organization of "concerned" people.

The interesting part is who the Carter administration chose as U.S. attorneys to defend the Department of the Interior: John Leshly, who a year before had been employed by NRDC to prepare NRDC's case against the government; and Deputy Assistant Attorney General J. Moorman, whose previous employment was as Executive Director of the Sierra Club's Legal Defense Fund.

And after (surprise!) the United States lost the case came an even more remarkable development: on February 25, 1978, the U.S. Dept. of Interior signed away its right to appeal the case.

You may draw from that any conclusions you want, but surely we will have some difficulties developing new coal resources.

Item: as I write this, they're laying off scientists and engineers from the fusion research program; delaying construction of electron-beam fusion research devices; stretching out studies of the ocean-thermal system; chopping more out of the space budget; ignoring the potential of geo-pressurized zones (superheated water deposits supersaturated with methane, about three kilometers below Louisiana and Texas, with estimated energy potential greater than the entire known U.S. coal reserves); refusing to deregulate the price of natural gas; and doing nothing about simplifying the present tangle of sixty-four permits required to build nuclear fission power plants.

The U.S. of A., home of "know-how" and "Yankee ingenuity," inventor of most of the technology being deployed in the Soviet Union and the rest of the world, has firmly backed away from government-sponsored research and development, while keeping a tax structure that makes it nigh impossible for private R&D to work on big projects such as space and fusion.

Why?

The usual answer is that we can't afford big R&D programs. That, of course, is nonsense. When your energy system is to pay $50 billion a year to the Arabs; when you rack up in a single year a trade deficit larger than the cumulative deficit balance of payments from George Washington through and including Richard Nixon; when you're selling the nation on the installment plan to Japan and the Sheik of Araby—when that's your system, you can afford any alternative.

You don't even have to worry about whether the alternatives have a high chance of payoff: given what we're doing now, it makes sense to pursue a number of alternatives simultaneously.

Moreover, we have the money. Item: the Occupational Health and Safety Administration (OSHA) has consumed about $4 billion in direct costs since its inception, and the total cost of OSHA has been in excess of $14 billion. Maybe that would be worth it, but in fact the accident rates at present are not measurably different from what they were before OSHA began. There's a large part of the Apollo program right there.

At its largest, NASA took about two cents from each tax dollar. Few would argue that we haven't been repaid many times over for the investment. Not in Teflon frying pans, but in new technology: carbon-filament materials, weather forecasting, communications, Landsat and Earthsat data for prospecting, crop management, ecological and environmental data available only from space; management techniques, firefighting techniques, medical technology, food processing, automated checkout procedures, quality control systems—the list of benefits from space research is nearly endless.

It would only take about two percent of the national budget to bring about what Harry Stine has called "The Third Industrial Revolution": to usher in an era of plenty; to make it possible to be really concerned about pollution and damage to the environment; to put the really messy industrial processes into space; and to ensure plenty of raw material for ourselves and our posterity for at least 50,000 years.

The argument that we can't afford space and energy research just won't hold water. We can't afford *not* to have vigorous research in those areas.

Item: on November 11, 1977, prominent physicists from the USA, USSR, Canada, France, and Japan issued a statement from their meeting in Fort Lauderdale, Florida, noting that the world's living standards and the size of "disadvantaged populations" would continue to rise throughout this century. Thus, they said, demand for resources would continue to increase, and "failure to meet this demand will result in extensive evils such as poverty, starvation, unrest, epidemics, riots, and wars." What's the cost of a small war compared to a decent R&D program? A lot more than two percent of the national budget, anyway.

At that same conference Nicholai Basov, Soviet Nobel Prize winner, announced several breakthroughs in laser-simulated fusion, and gave the technical details in an unclassified briefing.

The U.S. promptly classified his data. From whom is the government keeping it secret? Nor was this the first time: when Leonid Rudakov (Soviet electron beam expert) came over to the U.S. to tell of his experiments in fusion, U.S. officers put a blanket over his blackboard! (See *Science*, Oct. 8, 1976, p. 166.)

What is going on here? The U.S. is acting as if we are deliberately rejecting technology; it almost seems as if we are determined to try Rousseau's return to nature—a suicidal policy indeed.

The Soviets offer cooperation—they need energy resources as much as we do—and we turn them down. The British, French, and Japanese use U.S.-developed technology to build breeder reactors, while we stubbornly dismantle our nuclear industry.

No wonder that a "new beginning" can be superficially attractive.

There is another type of new beginning: one that starts with our present situation and moves ahead.

It should begin with a revolution in our social science. Nearly every major political philosophy was generated at a time when our "understanding" of the universe was scarcely worth the name, and at a time when scarcity was seen to be an inevitable fact of life. The latest of the most influential political philosophies was Marxism, which attempted to integrate the industrial revolution into political thought; and Marx wrote before the airplane and automobile, before electronics or radio or the telephone; before the real effects of the First Industrial Revolution (steam) could be seen.

There has been at least one major industrial revolution since Marx: call it electronics, or servomechanisms, or feedback, or cybernetics. The effects have been at least as profound as was the steam engine.

But Marxism, outdated as it is, is the latest of the political philosophies. Most political theories were familiar to Aristotle; indeed, graduate students in political "science" literally read Aristotle—as primary source material.

True, there have been a few attempts to deal intellectually with the modern world. Peter Drucker, Herman Kahn, Galbraith, Prehoda, Possony and myself, a few others, have tried to investigate the effects of modern technology on political and social theory; but there has been little real impact. In the grade schools and high schools, in undergraduate colleges, indeed in graduate schools, the academic community still teaches social theory based on a very false picture of the physical world—theories derived from a world without electricity, a world in which agriculture was primitive, transportation was limited by the speed of the horse and wind-driven ships, law was an arcane science

9

because most of the population would never learn to read—and, most importantly, in which the "goods of fortune" (Aristotle's phrase) were necessarily limited; a world in which wealth-for-all was not possible even in theory.

We don't live in such a universe any longer.

The United States annually produces about 400 million tons of metals each year: 1.7×10^{15} grams of metal. Assume ore at three percent and a density of 3.5 gm/cm³, and we find that in 1977 the USA processed ores equivalent to a sphere a little over three kilometers in diameter.

That's in the United States. Suppose, though, that we want the *world* to be wealthy; one measure of wealth is usable metal. U.S. population, about 250 million; world population, about 4 billion. Thus the U.S. had some 6.8 million grams of metal *per capita* to play with; multiply by the 4 billion world population and we need a total of 2.7×10^{16} grams of metal to make everyone as rich as we are.

Once again assume three percent ore and that's a sphere some eight kilometers in diameter.

There are 40,000 asteroids larger than five kilometers in diameter, and 3.5 percent ore is probably a severe underestimate of their useful metal content: the random samples from the Moon ran eight percent. Asteroids are now thought to be fragments of larger bodies, many of them large enough to have been differentiated (heavier elements such as metals sinking to the core), after which they were battered over the eons, with the rocky outer layers knocked off to leave the metal-rich core exposed. It is thus possible that many asteroids will run fifty percent and above useful ore.

Note the potential: Even with a population of 30 billion on Earth there is enough raw material to keep everyone rich for millennia.

About that population: is it not obvious that through history there has been one and only one effective means of limiting population? Not war, of course: birth rates rise in wartime. But wealth has always lowered birth rates. Catholic or Protestant or Shinto or Buddhist, it makes no difference: when nations get wealthy, their populations stabilize.

Wealth requires only raw materials and energy. Raw materials are available in plenty.

So is energy. Solar power satellites (SPS), as an example, could furnish the world far more energy per capita than is presently consumed in the USA—and do it forever. Now it may be that SPS is not the best way to go. It may be that fusion will do it cheaper and more conveniently. Who cares? My point is that the energy is there, that we know how to get it, that we have the technology to do it, and we have the investment resources right now. If fusion doesn't work, SPS will.

Isn't that expensive? Not compared to $50 billion paid for Arab oil, it isn't. A full SPS program couldn't possibly cost what we're already paying for energy.

Given energy, we can take care of pollution; if need be we can take pollution products apart to their constituent elements. Given energy, we have solved the food production problem: on Abu Dhabi, a desert island, they grow in greenhouses a fantastic crop per acre, and all they have to work with is sand and seawater—and energy, of course. Given energy we can make the world wealthy.

Given energy and space mining we could, if that became desirable, turn the Earth into a park; vastly increase the wilderness areas; put all the contaminating industries out there where—were we to devote the gross world product and vaporize the Earth in the bargain—we couldn't manage to "pollute outer space" for more than a few decades.

That's my idea of a New Beginning: a political philosophy that recognizes the vast potential of mankind; that recognizes that if there are limits to growth, they are so far beyond our comprehension that they may as well be infinite; that recognizes Gödel's theorem (the number of mathematical theorems is essentially infinite: i.e., there is no limit to the potential growth of knowledge).

The major political and social philosophies were generated in a time when mankind didn't even know how many stars there are.

It is a time for such a New Beginning.

Aye. And past time.

KENYONS TO THE KEEP!
Jerry Pournelle

EDITOR'S INTRODUCTION

I began this story about fifteen years ago when I was hikemaster for a troop of local Boy Scouts. Los Angeles is a unique environment for a city in that within its borders it encompasses beach, desert, and wilderness. We hiked through a lot of different terrain in and around Los Angeles; it wasn't hard on some of our trips to imagine all that passes for modern civilization wiped clean away.

From these hikes came the inspiration for several works, including *Lucifer's Hammer* and "Kenyons to the Keep!" When the retreat from civilization begins, it can be as hard to stop as erosion on a mountain top—one of several lessons Ross Kenyon learns in this story.

———————————— •¡• ————————————

I

THE LEGENDS SAID MAN HAD ONCE WALKED ON THE MOON.

Ross Kenyon didn't believe it, but the Moon rising full and blood red over Griffith Castle seemed close enough to touch. He knew that Sierra tribesmen flew. They soared like the great condors. Ross had heard of other aircraft that could lift themselves from the ground, although he had never seen one. If men could fly, surely they could go to the Moon? Perhaps when it was only rising, not so high above and far away . . .

The Sun had fallen into the Pacific, but dusky twilight hung across the great battlements of Kenyon Keep. Out ahead, directly in front of Ross, torches and campfires dotted the San Fernando Valley. They stretched north, then ended abruptly. Ross could not see the ruins that marked the northern boundary of Kenyon lands, but he had seen them often enough to know where each stood.

For three hundred years the northern San Fernando and the Newhall Valley beyond had been battlefields in an endless multi-sided war. The Highland and Sierra clans of the mountains, the Oxnard outreaches of Santa Barbara, desert nomads, Ekofreak and Greenpeace, all contended with the divided forces of the Civilized Lands of the South, and none could hold the valleys. The Kenyons had pushed farther than most, but even they had been driven back. From the day of his birth Ross had been at war.

Ross hated it. The Kenyons held the northern keep of Civilization, and always they tried to push forward, to take and hold the San Fernando and Newhall Valleys. Ross Kenyon was fifteen; when he was ten his father had laid Kenyon boundary stones westward past Topanga. When Ross became El Señor Kenyon it would be his turn, and in his lifetime he might take five more miles. Five more miles for a lifetime probably cut short. It did not seem a fair exchange.

The Valleys were good land; but were they worth endless war? Ross imagined them in the darkness. Valleys covered with ruins, except where the nomad tribes had leveled them. If those lands were cleared they could be held with a new keep at the top of the Newhall Pass, a lesser keep to guard the Big Tujunga canyon; two strong places, and the Valleys could be held. Ross had designs for the keeps, and there would be plenty of stone for building. The Valleys were covered with stone.

Fallen buildings, ash heaps, flat stone in slabs, white stone roads, black stone, all remains of what the Ancients had built. How? Ross had never understood how the Ancients could waste such good land, covering it with stone and trees that bore no fruit. If the Ancients could waste the best land for miles, then perhaps the old legends were true. Only the fabulously powerful could conjure food from a valley of stone.

The Moon rose steadily, and now there were blue witchlights on Mount Wilson to the east. Sorcerers lived there on the mountain towering high above the Dead Lands. They had built a great stone palace, larger and stronger than Kenyon Keep, stronger even than the Mayor's Palace in Los Angeles. The sorcerers had neither lands nor religion nor army, but their fortress had stood for five hundred years, since before the Burning and the Plagues—or so they said, and who could dispute it? They lived in uneasy peace with the Sierra Highlanders who held the Angeles Mountains. They had little enough contact, demanding nothing from the lowlands, but farmers often took them tribute, and sometimes received gifts, or heard the Oracle tell them of the weather to come, and the proper time for planting. The sorcerers lived well.

Yet they were only men. They could not fly, not even as well as the Sierra. They knew things that others did not; sometimes of events that happened far away, or the coming rains long before anyone in the City or the Hills or the Valley could see any cloud; but they were only men. They could be killed, and had been, when the tribesmen penetrated into the Valley and the Civilized lands beyond . . . and the tribesmen were coming again.

They knew much, these witchmen, but they seldom spoke to anyone not their own. Sometimes their stewards, led by officers with strange titles—Grad, and Postdoc—came to the lowlands to trade. Sometimes they bought women. Young girls, orphans of good family, whose ancestry was known. "Not slaves," the Postdoc had told Ross's father. "Never slaves. The girls will marry." Flintridge Kenyon had made the Postdoc swear . . .

Ross Kenyon's private reverie was interrupted by galloping hooves. Three horsemen, riding fast up the winding road from the Valley to the ramparts of the Keep. Kenyon touched the thick walls with reverence. Ten feet thick, built of stone quarried from the ruins below, they circled the brow of the hill, enclosing a large horseshoe-shaped ridge. The central courts were large, more than ample to hold the Kenyons and their retainers and their flocks. There were enormous cisterns, kept always full from rainfall and water carried from the Los Angeles River below.

14

There were the long cannón, with a range of over three miles, and the smaller guns which could fire grape and canister. The fortress had been started by other families, driven out so long ago their names were forgotten; but since Ross Kenyon's great-great-grandfather had taken the hill and strengthened the walls, it had killed every army that marched against it. Highlander, Eko-freak, Sierra, Santa Paula, Berdoo, Greenpeace, Apache, the Mayor of Los Angeles himself; all had tried, and still the Ken-yons held. Three horsemen were no danger.

Ross heard the shouted challenge from the gates, and the re-sponse; the creaking gates, just shut for sundown, now opened again; and hooves clattered on the cobblestones of the outer courtyard. Now there were other sounds: running men climbing the great stone stairways to the high rampart tower where Ross stood. Five men at least. Two carried torches.

The flickering light showed two of the Kenyon household guard, dull reflection from the links of their mail armor, crimson sash of the officer of the watch. He was not much older than Ross: John Stephenson, a cousin. When they were younger John had been a good friend. Now the differences between the heir and a relative came between them. Behind the officer ran two vaqueros. Ross recognized Wenceslas, *vaquero jefe* of the Ken-yon herds and another in the blue and gold Kenyon livery. The fifth man wore dark robes with no flash or ornament.

"Don Ross," Wenceslas shouted. He spoke rapidly in the San Diego patois, part Spanish, part Mexican, part ancient English and part nothing ever heard before the Burning. The Kenyon family had never spoken anything but Anglic until Ross's father had, in his youth, gone on a diplomatic mission to the Alcalde of Escondido and returned with the daughter of the house. The Alcalde had insisted that his daughter should go to the North in a way fitting to her ancestry, and sent fifty vaqueros and their families as her dowry. Now the Kenyon house was bilingual. Ross could not remember a time when he did not speak both Anglic and Sandiegan.

"A message from your father," Wenceslas was saying. "A message from Don Flintridge. Padre Guitierrez has brought it, *hijo de mi patrón.*"

Ross interrupted the rapid flow of words. "And what is so urgent that you have brought Padre Guitierrez to me before of-

15

fering him the hospitality of Kenyon Keep?'' he demanded. ''You have brought him with the dust of the road on his feet and in his throat.''

''It is urgent, Don Ross,'' Guitierrez said. The voice was younger than the man. Guitierrez seemed withered, bent with age, although some of his weariness would be from the ten-mile ride from the Abbey San Francisco de Chatsworth to Kenyon Keep. Ross had never seen Guitierrez without robe and cowl, not even in the heat of the day, and often wondered if the clothing concealed deformities. There were monsters in the world, and some of them grew to be men, and the Church was a natural refuge for them. Celibacy kept them from breeding more monsters . . . Ross became aware that Guitierrez was silent.

''Prepare rooms and dinner for the Padre,'' Ross ordered. ''And ask my uncle and my mother to join me in the Library.'' He said the word proudly. There were few great families who collected books, and the Kenyon collection was magnificent, almost five hundred volumes.

Ross waved dismissal to his retainers. John Stephenson hung back for a moment, eager to hear the news, but he caught the displeasure in Ross's eye and went with the others. Ross regretted sending him. John was a loyal officer, not eager to grasp more than should come to him, and probably could be trusted with any news; but it was too late. Stephenson had turned angrily away.

A vaquero put his torch into a niche on the rampart, where it added its smoke to the soot of countless torches that had burned there before. The high ramparts were a place of meditation for five generations of Kenyons. When all had left, Ross said, ''My father is well?''

''Don Flintridge lives,'' Guitierrez said.

Ross kept his face impassive. ''That is good news, but you would not come to tell me only that.''

''He is badly injured. An arrow, and he fell from his horse. He is now in the Great Keep at Ramona. The Alcalde is with him.''

''I will go immediately.''

''You cannot, Don Ross. You could not enter. The Mexicali forces, with many mercenaries, have the Keep under siege. It

16

was while cutting his way in to aid his father-in-law that Don Flintridge was wounded.''

Padre Guitierrez did not say that Ross would be unable to take more than a tenth of the forces that his father had led south. He didn't have to. Kenyon Keep was stripped of its professional soldiers. Flintridge Kenyon took his family obligations seriously, and had ridden immediately to the Alcalde's aid; if his household guards had a difficult time entering the Ramona Keep, the vaqueros and other mobile troops available to Ross would have no chance at all.

"The Abbot has ordered perpetual prayer for Don Flintridge," Guitierrez said.

Ross kept his face in shadow, careful to show no emotion in his eyes. "You're a Kenyon!" his father had thundered. Countless times: when Ross had fallen from his horse; when his brother had died; when the mamacita of his infancy lay with blackened tongue and the bursting pustules of plague; when the tribesman's arrow had pierced his shoulder; and when a favorite pony had broken a foreleg and Ross himself had to take the loaded musket to the stable . . . "You're a Kenyon. We command, and command shows no fears."

But his father was hurt, besieged more than a hundred miles to the south. In these times men lived and died quickly, and Flintridge Kenyon had lived more than his share of years; but Ross was only fifteen. His feeling for his father was a mixture, love and duty and fear and respect; and always there was the knowledge that when Flint Kenyon was laid with his fathers in the vault below Kenyon Chapel, Ross would be El Señor Kenyon, Master of Encino, responsible for a thousand families . . .

"There is worse news, Don Ross."

"What can be worse?"

"The tribes are gathering in the Mojave. Yesterday they held a Great Council at the Palmdale Stone Field. Chiefs of the Sierra were there. Among them the Mahons of Solamint. The Sierra Chiefs returned safely to their mountains."

And that said it all, Ross thought. If the Mojave tribesmen sat at Council with the mountain clansmen and the clansmen went home alive . . . then the way from the Mojave into the Newhall and San Fernando Valleys was no longer closed to the tribesmen. "How do you know this?"

17

Guitierrez shrugged. "The Church has her miracles."

Ross nodded. On Mount Wilson they called it sorcery. The Church said miracles. Master Yorumma, Ross's tutor, called it "science" and said that certain Ancient devices had survived. Some of the books in the Kenyon Library said the same thing, but there was no point in discussing it. Who would listen? Certainly not Guitierrez; the Church had not since time out of mind let anyone who knew the secret of the farspeakers go outside heavily defended walls.

However they did it, everyone knew that some of the monasteries and episcopal palaces—but not all of them—learned of distant events long before messengers could ride with news. But although the Church *could* know, this message might not be true. His Most Holy Excellency Don Jaime O'Riley Cardinal Diego, Archbishop of Western Noramerica and secular prince of San Diego, had his own political plans. Abbey San Fernando de Chatsworth was strongly allied with the Kenyons and wouldn't deliberately lie, but the message was no more reliable than those who had sent it.

But to what purpose? Ross wondered. "Does the Mayor know?"

Guitierrez shrugged again. "Not from us. My instructions were to inform you. I have done so."

And to the devil with the Protestant Mayor and his Council and people, Ross thought. The padre's attitude was natural. More than one Mayor of Los Angeles had led armies against the Abbey before Ross's mother brought it under Kenyon protection, and the Church in the City proper had been despoiled, reduced to a tiny diplomatic mission existing within the Mayor's palace, not even granted its own quarters.

"But you have no objection if I tell His Honor?" Ross asked.

"I repeat my instructions, Don Ross. Dom Julian sent me to inform Don Ross Kenyon. I have done so. And now, if I may, I will accept the hospitality you have offered."

"Yes. Certainly. Thank you, Padre. I will show you to the dining hall. If you wish anything else, you have only to ask." Automatically Ross led Padre Guitierrez to the lesser hall, not the Great Hall; for although the Church was always welcome, and Padre Guitierrez had ridden hard to carry his message to Kenyon Station, there were, after all, proprieties to be observed, and Guitierrez *was* only a priest—and probably hunchbacked at that.

II

The Library was a hard room, as hard as the men who had held Kenyon Keep for generations. It was stone, with an oak council table, and the books which stood behind locked glass doors could not soften the effect of massive granite and splintered concrete blocks. Even the tapestries with their battle scenes looked hard.

Doña Estella Almoravez Kenyon had borne nine children and buried four of them. There were deep lines in her face, lines that all the expensive creams and ointments Flintridge Kenyon bought couldn't erase. She had grown thin with age, so that she seemed very tiny in the enormous chair at the end of the great council table, dark blue gown and black shawl with silver trim; her eyes peered brightly from the lace folds. She waited expectantly for Ross to speak.

"Father is alive," Ross said. "But—"

"How badly?" Ross's mother asked.

"There was no word. An arrow, and a fall from his horse. And now he is besieged in the Great Keep at Ramona, with Grandfather. Dom Julian had ordered perpetual prayer."

She sat very still for a moment, then held up her arms, and Ross ran to her. He knelt beside her and she drew his head to her chest. He blinked back tears, then sniffed loudly.

"We must both be brave," his mother said. "But the walls will not fall if we cry, a little, before your uncle comes . . ." She held him, and whispered in the border language of her childhood, and then they were both very quiet for a while. "And now you take your place at the head of the council," she said. "You must not shame your father."

"We can't hold them." Jeremiah Weigley, Colonel of Cavalry in the service of the City of Los Angeles, drained his wine glass and stared moodily into it. "Most of the City's army has gone east, to Berdoo. We've sent riders, but it will be three days before much of our strength gets here. We all know what the raiders could do in that time."

19

They all nodded. Everyone at the council table had seen the results of nomad raids. Women taken into slavery, if they survived. Men thrown into the blazing wreckage of their houses, or dismembered alive, buried under the works of man . . .

Ross traced the route to Berdoo with his finger. Hand-drawn, his chart was a copy of a copy; the original lay in a keg in the donjon of Kenyon Keep. The scribe who had copied the ancient road map had worked well. He had left off a hundred roads that time had ground into dust, and added new symbols. The map showed a peculiar patchwork, of lands dotted with fields and irrigation ditches and ranchos; great stoneyard areas, the ruins of Ancient cities; and the great highways that stitched across the land like seams on a garment made from scraps of cloth. The highway to Berdoo was broken in many places. "Why did the Mayor take the City troops to Berdoo?" Ross demanded.

Before Weigley could answer, a smooth voice interrupted. "A hurried call for help, Don Ross." Councilman Letterman's voice was reassuring. A politician, who kept his seat through the favor of the Mayor, not because he had the support of any powerful family. "There were reports of tribal invasion through Cajon Pass. Better to stop them at Cajon than to allow them into civilized lands. And there wasn't time to call a Council meeting."

Ross said nothing, but he looked down the table and saw his own anger reflected in the face of his uncle, Colonel Amos Yaegher. The Kenyons owned two seats on the City Council, and it was one point of dispute that Mayor Dortmund more and more acted without the Council's advice. He hadn't called a meeting for six months. One day there would be trouble over that, but City politics could wait. There was a more immediate danger.

"They'll be here tomorrow. Day after at the latest." Amos Yaegher's voice fit the hard room. It was a voice that could be heard in the thickest battles. Ross thought sometimes that Amos Yaegher could bring down the high rafters with their banners and trophies if ever he shouted; he seemed to shake the walls when he only spoke.

Yaegher didn't need the map. He had it memorized. Certainly he had risen to his post as Colonel of the Kenyon forces through influence: he had married Flintridge Kenyon's only sister. Even so, he was respected as a fighting man, a soldier who spoke

20

bluntly and shared rations with his troops; the men would follow him. "They'll be here, and what do we have to stop them?"

"Household troops," Weigley said. "City Council guardsmen. Bits and pieces. Not a proper regiment in the lot. We will call up the militia, but you've got the best troops right here."

"The hell we have."

"Amos." Estella's voice was soft, almost inaudible, but it brought silence to the room and a blush to Amos Yaegher's face. She was the daughter of the House of Escondido, and two hundred years of command was in her manner. She did not need to raise her voice to be obeyed in her own house.

"Your pardon, Doña Estella. Colonel, you know that most of the Kenyon troops are south. There are plenty of other households in the city that can stand in the way of the tribesmen—"

"We're sending for them," Weigley said.

"The City has enemies," Councilman Letterman added. "You face barbarians on this frontier. The southern families must keep guard against Civilized armies—"

"Bah." Amos Yaegher didn't try to hide his contempt. "They fight mercenary troops. Pitched battles, and nobody killed—unless they fall off their horses! Big men in big armor riding in circles all day, and when it's over a few dozen prisoners are ransomed, and you call it war! If you want the problems of the south taken care of, send us. We'll show them war."

"Which is what Don Flintridge has gone south to do now," Letterman said. "And meanwhile, the southern landholders must stand guard. We will send for them, Colonel Yaegher, but it will take time to summon the City militia—and as you have said, the tribesmen will be here tomorrow."

"Amos, we are Masters of Encino," Ross's mother said.

"Aye." Amos Yaegher's booming voice fell low—a soldier's trick, to speak so low that everyone had to listen carefully. "The last time the tribes gained free access to the Valley we took the field," Amos said. "We blunted them. Ross wouldn't remember."

Not remember? I was only six years old, Ross thought, but you do not forget a day such as that . . .

"We went out to meet them," Yaegher said. "The first Ross Kenyon, young Ross's grandfather. He was Master then. The tribes came into the Valley and we met them at that big stone

21

field in the east Valley. I'll never forget that. Ruins everywhere around, and those long stone strips on the ground. The plainsmen's horses didn't like it. Shod horses are always better on stone.

"We beat them, damned well we beat them, but a regiment rode north out of Kenyon Keep that morning, and we brought a corporal's guard back. I say we don't do that again. I say we pull into the Keep, and hold Laurel Canyon, and let the Mayor's troops hold the Cahuenga Pass."

"But the Master of Encino guards all the passes from the Valley," Ross's mother said. "And there are settlements north of the Cahuenga."

"Not ours."

"Civilized people," Councilman Letterman said.

"It's your job," Colonel Weigley said. "You hold here as officers of the City."

"No!" Amos Yaegher's voice thundered to the captured banners hung high above the table. "The Kenyons are Masters of Encino because we hold Kenyon Keep! We took our lands and we hold them. We owe no lands to the City."

"Pride." Colonel Weigley stared into the fire. "Pride. The Ancients were here no more than two hundred years ago, no more than that, and they built Civilization across all of Noramerica. In five hundred years since the Burning we have not been able to reunite Los Angeles. And we won't for a thousand, because of pride. Amos, I'm a soldier. Like you. Can you hold your forces in this Keep and look out on slaughter? And do nothing?"

"If I have to. What is it you're asking for?"

"March with us. With what I have of the City Guard. Stop the tribesmen north of the Los Angeles River, before they can reach City lands and houses—and people."

"And if we lose? Who holds the Keep?"

"Your guns will hold," Weigley said. "Councilman Letterman. You are in charge for the Mayor. Will you send gunpowder for Kenyon Keep?"

Letterman looked distressed. "I don't have the authority—"

"Then by God we won't march," Amos Yaegher said. "We'll not risk the Keep—"

22

"The Mayor would have my head," Letterman said. "That powder costs— The cost is unbelievable. And we have so little."

The room fell silent. Not silent, though, Ross thought. Outside were the sounds of frantic activity. Vaqueros driving the stock into the Keep. Outlying detachments of Kenyon retainers and landholders riding in. The armed ranchers assembling at the walls, as they had done at Kenyon summons for a hundred years and more.

"We're ranchers and farmers," Ross said quietly. "You're asking us to fight your battles for you, but you won't pay the costs. If we had our own powder mills—" He fell silent at the look of alarm Letterman showed. The Mayor didn't want the Kenyons getting into industry. Los Angeles and her Guilds had an effective monopoly on ironworks, with the rich mines opened in what had been refuse heaps for the Ancients; but even more precious was the monopoly on gunpowder. It was through the powder supplies that the Mayor kept even a loose hold on the great families who owed allegiance to Los Angeles.

"I'll do it," Letterman said. "Twenty— All right. Thirty tons. By noon tomorrow."

"And if you do not ride with us, you will have much blood on your soul, Don Ross," Colonel Weigley said. "You've seen what the tribesmen do. They kill for sport, worse, for religion, and they do not let their victims die easily. Your pardon, Doña Estella, but these things must be said."

"We will consider." Ross got up from the table and went to a crimson cord at the wall. He pulled it, and two officers came into the room. "Please entertain Councilman Letterman and Colonel Weigley," Ross said.

Once again the room fell quiet except for the sounds that came in from the outside. A bell tolled: the timekeeper guildsman was striking the twenty-third hour. Ross imagined the crippled old man and his crippled apprentices, turning sand glasses and filling water clocks.

"We have defended the north borders of civilization for a hundred years, Amos," Estella Kenyon said.

"Yes, Estella, and while we held off the barbarians the Mayors have played politics," Yaegher said. "Instead of building more keeps as he ought to do, our present mayor pulls down the ones we have. Tears down keeps so that no bossman can resist him.

23

The Mayor would rather the tribesmen burned out half the City than give up one ounce of power! Unification, Mayor Dortmund calls it. I can think of better words. And Weigley has the infernal gall to accuse *us* of pride!''

''But we do have pride, Amos,'' Estella Kenyon said. ''It is our conceit that since the Kenyons have been Masters of Encino, no tribesmen have passed without war to the death. We have never taken bribes to look the other way while they ride into the City. We are the outpost of civilization.''

''So Ross's grandfather said,'' Amos thundered. ''I carried him off the Field of Stone myself. I lashed him onto his horse and watched him bleed to death while we rode for the Keep. That's pride and honor for you.''

''Do you think I am anxious to send my only remaining son into battle?'' Estella demanded. ''Ross, you must decide. Your father left you master here. I do not think he would wish you to forget the duty of this house. Duty to God and to civilization.''

III

Trumpets sounded in the dawn light. Trumpets and drums, the bandsmen of Kenyon Keep, sending men to battle; and as always there were the women, silent on the walls and along the winding road down into the Valley. They had said their farewells, and now there was nothing more but silent prayer.

The Kenyon troops rode proudly, but there were not many of them. A hundred men in armor, half of them regulars, and others armed landholders. Another three hundred men with leather jackets and helmets, muskets and sabers. The vaqueros with their short hornbacked bows waited below, falling in with the other cavalry as they rode past. There were also infantrymen, none of them regular soldiers. The Kenyons crossed the river on the great stone bridge, a relic of Ancient days. The other bridges across the Los Angeles River had been torn down to make the line more easily defended.

The City troops waited on the other side. They fell in with the Kenyons.

''Look sharp there,'' Sergeant Major Highbee growled. ''Show the City bastards what real troopers look like. Number five, Loris, get that lance higher! Line up the banner!''

"He doesn't look retired," Ross said. He nodded toward Highbee.

"A good man," Colonel Yaegher said. "But it's still a fool's errand. One we'll regret."

"You don't have to come," Ross said.

"Nephew, I'll forget you said that," Amos Yaegher said. He didn't say that Ross could stay behind. When the regular guardsmen rode out they might be led by any of their officers, but when the Kenyons summoned the vaqueros and relatives and friends and tenants they were always led by a Kenyon.

"I'm sorry, Uncle," Ross said. He got a curt nod in answer. I'm scared, Ross thought. Does everyone feel this way? They can't. They wouldn't be going.

But you are, he told himself.

The troops nearest him were a personal guard. Five vaqueros, led by Guillermo, oldest son of the vaquero jefe. Guillermo was nearly thirty, and had been in danger most of his life; the vaqueros held the northern reaches of the Kenyon lands and were often sent into the desert as scouts. Behind Guillermo was Sergeant Keeler, another old regular guard, long past time when he should be retired to the walls, and the five regulars who rode with him were not much younger—except for Harry Benton, trumpeter, barely twelve years old.

Tension showed in their faces, and in the easy remarks they made to each other. They felt something too. Premonition? Ross wondered. The Old Woman at the Keep had no Sight, or at least none that she admitted to. That was an evil omen, to be kept secret, but soldiers find these things out.

A wave from Yaegher sent Wenceslas and thirty vaqueros galloping ahead, fanning out as scouts. The desert tribes had been known to send in advance parties in the night, but the vaqueros were as good at *ambuscado* as the tribesmen.

The rest of the Civilized force, Kenyons and City Guard, rode straight up the San Fernando Valley. At first there were many stone ranch houses, homes of hardy families who dared live in the Valley because they had faith in the Kenyons—and, Ross admitted to himself, in the hostility of the mountain clansmen who usually kept the passes into the Mojave sealed.

Usually, but not always. The mountain clans were not allies of Civilization, but they did live in uneasy truce with the City

25

dwellers. They stayed to their mountains, and the City stayed to the plains, and the tribes stayed in their high desert—until, suddenly, the tribes would make common cause and burst into the hills, and the clan chiefs would let them through the passes rather than endure the raids themselves.

But every effort to cooperate with the clan chiefs ended in disaster and distrust. The Highlanders did not have the feral hatred of Civilization that drove the desert tribes, but they had no love for its cities and politics.

The ranchlands ended abruptly. Beyond were the ruins: twisted hulks of Ancient buildings, crumbling bridges over nothing at all, vast fields covered with black stone, flat and level and useless. No one could protect this land. The Highlanders came down to salvage the ruins, and war parties of nomads burst through the passes—but that was not why the land was never reclaimed. The Kenyons would never allow anyone else to fortify the north Valley—and the Mayor wanted no expansion of Kenyon lands and power. For a generation and more that stalemate had kept the ruins intact, with no one to profit from it.

The ruins ended a mile after they began. Beyond them was the strange area cleared by Ekofreak and Greenpeace tribesmen in the years when they held the north Valley. The land was broken by mounds and hills, and the remains of the underground dwellings the tribesmen built themselves. There was no other sign of human activity. It was the tribal religion, to remove Man's defilements from their Mother Earth, and they did the work well. They broke up walls, removed the remains of burned buildings, pried up the stones from the roads, and heaped them into mounds which they covered with earth and sod. They planted trees and vines, creating artificial laurel thickets and cane patches. No one knew what they would do if they held the entire basin. Their ecologists and lesser leaders did not disclose their plans.

The Kenyon forces rode on, northwards, hoofs pounding. Ross held his head high. He wanted to run, to go back to the keep, but he sat proudly and rode north.

Ross Kenyon wasn't a warrior by nature. His father had been, and his grandfather as well. The Kenyons had always been warriors, although there had been something else as well, a strain of builder and administrator, and, sometimes, even a dreamer.

26

Rumor had it that three generations before a Kenyon had gone up to the fortress atop Mount Wilson, sent his servant back with the message that he was well, and was never heard from again. But mostly the Kenyons made war.

Perhaps it was Doña Estella's influence, but Ross could admire the deeds of his ancestors without wanting to duplicate them. Fighting and killing, eternal war and battle held no glory for him. They were necessary, and he would do what had to be done, but he took no joy in it. Let the others sing war songs. Ross would rather read books. Few books had survived the Burning, of course, but there was one on building and another on agriculture, copies of copies, with words he did not understand, but he worked at them patiently anyway. He learned the skills of a warrior because he had to; but he studied what little was known about growing crops and breeding cattle because those were skills he wanted.

But they were no use now, as he rode north through the Valley, into fields that his family had coveted for generations, and the hot California sun beat down on helmet and armor.

They halted at noon, with the Sun high overhead. The Valley was clear, the morning haze all burned away. Up ahead was a small cloud of dust—the scouts returning—but their message was already known.

The tribesmen were coming over the San Fernando Pass. They threw up no betraying dust cloud, because they stayed on the splendid roads the Ancients had thrown through the Pass. Their vanguard was in sight, then over and down into the Valley, and behind them an endless column of light cavalry.

"Mount up," Yaegher called. It would be an hour before the battle. No more.

Condors and vultures wheeled high above the Valley. Do they know? Ross wondered. They should. When men ride in large numbers, there is always food for the vultures.

And for vultures of another kind. High up on the hills ringing the Valley was another warrior host—the Sierra tribesmen. Ross looked for the telltale triangles in the sky, the flying men of the Sierra, but there were none there. Not yet. But up above, on Mendenhall Peak, on the ridges to the east, there were flashes of bright color: Sierra clansmen. On foot, as always. They seldom rode. They did not hold the Angeles Mountains, and all the highlands north to the High Sierra itself, with horses. Cavalry for the valleys, mules for the highlands, both for the desert. And other creatures, camels, in the Mojave. They hadn't brought camels with them on this raid; at least Ross hadn't seen any.

Weigley and Yaegher clustered around him. "With your permission, Nephew," Yaegher said, "here's the battle plan. Kenyon regiment will take the right wing and press forward. The City forces will cover our left flank and hold back a few hundred yards. When there's enough of the tribe force committed we'll roll down toward the City troops with the vaqueros to cover our right. We'll blood them, and fall back toward the River. That might be enough."

It might be. The tribesmen were a superstitious lot. They believed in their luck. Medicine, some tribes called it. Luck. Fortune. Ross didn't know much about the nomads. No one did. They never met Civilized people in peace. All that Ross knew came through the Highlanders, who sometimes made truce with the City, and sometimes made truce with the Mojave tribes.

But everyone knew the tribes didn't take defeat well. Inflict losses on them early, and their chiefs—what did they call them? Ecologists—their ecologists might take an early defeat as a sign of disfavor from whatever gods the tribes worshiped, and then the whole horde would run back to their desert and cast their spells . . .

But the Old Woman had no vision, no sight, and it all came down to the decision of a fifteen-year-old boy who had never before in his life seen two thousand enemies gathered together.

Yaegher was Colonel—but a Kenyon commanded. Always.

"What else might we do?" Ross asked.

"Nephew, we could hit and run. Fall back toward the River line. But somewhere we have to make a stand, and better up ahead where the ground's clear than here among the ruins. Open ground favors heavy cavalry . . ." Yaegher's voice trailed off. This was no classroom, and no time to teach Ross something the boy had learned years before. "At your orders, Nephew."

Weigley was listening silently. Ross looked into the City colonel's eyes, trying to understand what he saw there. Something. Fear? But it seemed to be more, and Weigley wouldn't meet his gaze. Do we trust this man? Ross wanted to ask, but it was too late; he couldn't ask that while Weigley listened. That would certainly make him an enemy.

And the plan made sense. Part of the City force was infantry. Crossbowmen, good at defense. They could hold the north edge of the ruins. With cover like that to shoot from they could hurt the tribes, while the Kenyon cavalry rolled through them, breaking them—

And whatever we do, we must do it *now*, Ross thought. He looked up at the wheeling vultures, looking for a sign, but there was none. "Forward. Uncle, command the regiment."

"Sir."

"Where do you want me, Uncle?"

"With the vaqueros on the right wing, Nephew. You understand them better than me. Better than any of us." And, Yaegher didn't add but could have, they are only loyal to your mother, and thus to you; not to the Kenyon name, but to Estella Trujillo Kenyon, infanta of the house of the Alcalde de Escondido. "It won't be the safest place in the battle. You'll have to move fast, to cover our right when we wheel west and south. God go with you."

"And with you, Uncle." Ross waved to his guards and cantered off to join the returning vaquero scouts. The dust of the valley stuck in his throat, and he felt the knot of fear tearing at his stomach. At least it will soon be over, he thought. Soon. One way or another.

IV

The battle was a screaming confusion of dust and trumpet calls, the bark of musketry and the clatter of horses. It was the smell of blood, the moans of dying men, lamed horses thrashing in the dirt. It was half-naked men charging with lance and bow, to be met by armored riders with lance and musket and saber. It was men firing their muskets and holstering them to draw thirsty sabers because there'd never be enough time to reload. And through it all it was trumpets and the smell of blood.

It was John Stephenson, only two years older than Ross, leading an insane charge into the thick of screaming savages, lance shattered and then saber flashing until his horse was down, and still Ross's cousin fought, screaming his defiance and rallying

29

the shattered remnants of the score of men he'd led. It was Hyman Silverberg, tenant on Stephenson land, swinging a great axe and rushing to his young officer's defense. It was heads severed by Silverberg's axe until an arrow grew between his shoulder blades and the giant yeoman went to his knees with a puzzled expression in his eyes, dying without knowing he was dead.

It was Ross Kenyon leading his vaqueros to aid his cousin. It was a blond man with long hair and painted shield charging Ross, and Ross spurring his stallion forward, lance cocked as he'd been taught in a hundred mock battles, and the lance piercing the leather shield and ramming home in the nomad's throat, and the man's weight hanging horribly on the lance, bright blood spurting, and the lance coming free but too late, and Guillermo coming from nowhere to fling a javelin and rescue his master.

It was Ross coming to his cousin's aid and seeing the white ropes of intestines trailing in the dust, and the bright blood, and John Stephenson screaming for his mother before falling to the ground with a dozen hostiles in leather breeches rushing to count coup before he died, and the trumpets sounding again, commanding the vaqueros forward and to the left to aid the faltering right wing of the Kenyon forces, leaving Ross no time to recover his cousin's body. It was Guillermo, at a nod from Ross, throwing one more dart, straight and true into Stephenson's heart, then Ross and his guard with sabers cutting through a new wave of tribesmen to answer the trumpet's imperious call.

It was two hours of madness, and it was disaster.

"Retreat," the trumpets sang. "Kenyons to the Keep!" Ross had never heard that call sounded except for practice. "Kenyons to the Keep!"

"But who?" Ross demanded. "Who?"

He reined in, gathered his guardsmen around him. They were a small island of calm for a moment. Dust lay thick across the Valley. Ross stared south at the hills in wonder. There, above the battlements of Kenyon Keep, flew the Red Ball. It was the most urgent summons known. *The Keep was in danger!* Yet—yet they were miles from the Keep, and the tribesmen had not broken through, couldn't have broken through.

"Retreat," sang the trumpets. "Kenyons to the Keep!"

"Who?" Ross demanded again. Guillermo and Keeler gave him only blank stares. "Ride, then. To the Keep."

The horses were exhausted. The left-wheeling maneuver had carried Ross and his vaqueros far to the west, beyond the old highway and far toward the Santa Susanna hills. The horses could never gallop all the way to the Keep.

And as they rode, the Red Ball fell, and then, incredibly, the blue and gold Kenyon banner wavered, and fluttered down from the high battlements a lifetime away across the Valley. There was an eternity of time, then another banner climbed in triumph to stand out proudly in the wind above Kenyon Keep.

"Green and gold," Keeler growled. "Green and gold."

"The Mayor," Ross screamed. "But—"

There was no time to say more. Another knot of nomads, white men, brown men, black men, all on the small unshod horses of the desert; screaming men with blood lust in their voices. They charged, and Ross's tiny command was surrounded, their horses too exhausted to fight on, but they fought. Keeler was down, his left arm severed by an axe blow meant for Ross, and then trumpeter Benton who wouldn't live to see his thirteenth birthday.

He woke in darkness. There were the sounds of activity around him. He lay with his eyes half open, not daring to move, not even to test whether his hands were bound. Captured! He had only one thought, to gather his strength and find a weapon, to die fighting before the tribesmen could give him to their gods.

But slowly the voices around him began to make sense. Anglic and Sandiegan. Not the gutturals of the Mojave dialects.

"Don Ross. Don Ross."

No tribesman would call him by that name. Ross opened his eyes.

Darkness, with flickering firelight. Rough homespun wool cowl hovering above him. The crinkled face of Padre Guitierrez, and from somewhere nearby Guillermo endlessly repeating his name.

"You are awake?" Guitierrez asked.

His head swam in confusion. Ross struggled to move. His hands were not bound. He was free. "Where—" he croaked.

"You are in the Abbey." Ross heard without comprehension.

A hand lifted his head, another put a cup to his lips. Cool water trickled into his mouth. He swallowed eagerly.

"More—"

"In a moment."

Slowly the memories came back. The Red Ball. And—"The Keep! To the Keep!" Ross shouted.

"No. It is too late." The voice held both sadness and finality. It had come from beyond Padre Guitierrez, and it took moments for Ross to recognize it. Dom Julian, Abbot. "The Keep is in the hands of the Mayor."

Ross tried to speak again, but the cup was put to his lips. The taste was bitter. Herbs of some kind, steeped in water and wine. The oddly bitter taste was pleasant. Ross drank, and again felt the world reeling, and sank back into darkness.

It was daylight when he woke again. Padre Guitierrez still sat beside him.

Ross struggled to sit up. He was in a small room, no more than a cell. Bright sunlight streamed in through a narrow window. Again the memories came, and Padre Guitierrez saw terror in his eyes.

"How?" Ross demanded.

"After you have eaten. You have much to do before dark. Come. I'll help you walk."

The monks cleaned him and fed him, but they would not answer his questions. He was given new clothing: rough wool clothing, no fine fabrics, and none of it with the Kenyon colors. Still they would not talk to him. Finally he was led into the Abbot's study.

Dom Julian sat at a large desk. He motioned Ross to a chair nearby. "You have eaten?"

"Yes, Dom Julian."

"And you look well."

"I am all right."

"A miracle. I have seen the dent the war hammer put in your helmet."

"What happened, Dom Julian?" Ross demanded. "How—"

The Abbot's lips were tightly pressed together. "I scarcely know how to begin. The Mayor holds Kenyon Keep—"

"I saw the banner hoisted. It was nearly the last thing I ever saw. For that I thank God, that my last sight was not—"

The Abbot held up his hand. "Be careful. God has spared you for some great purpose. You should be dead. The Mayor has placed an enormous price on your head."

"He wouldn't dare."

"He had dared. Your retainers are scattered or dead, Don Ross."

"Mother. What has—"

There was pain in the Abbot's eyes. He looked away, then back at Ross. "Dead also," he said bluntly. "The Mayor's troops despoiled her chapel. She died defending the altar. Defending the Faith."

It was too much. His home lost, his mother dead— "You're a Kenyon! Command shows no fears!" His father's voice rang in his head. Ross sat tight-lipped, his hands clinched into fists, the nails digging into his palms. He spoke carefully. "That is war. The Alcalde—"

"Your grandfather is in no position to send aid," Dom Julian said. "Escondido is under siege. This is no ordinary rising. Guillermo brought in arrows and other signs. At least five tribes, a dozen septs here, and as many more have risen in the south."

"But they were also raiding San Berdoo—"

The Abbot shook his head slowly. "No. That is what Mayor Dortmund said. But he did not ride to Berdoo. He kept his troops much closer, and when you rode out into the Valley they stormed the Keep. There is more. The tribesmen plundered Kenyon lands freely. Then they turned and went back. They are camped at the head of the Valley now."

"And they never raided the City at all," Ross said wonderingly. "Was it planned all along? The Mayor and the tribesmen together—"

"We think so," Dom Julian said.

"But why? Why would the tribesmen aid the Mayor?"

"Perhaps they are less in fear of Kenyon Keep held by the Mayor than by Kenyons," Dom Julian said. "I would be. The advantages to Dortmund are obvious, and he is too proud to believe the tribes might deceive him." The Abbot looked uncomfortable. "What will you do now?"

"I don't know."

33

"If you ask for sanctuary, we will give it. I want that understood," Dom Julian said.

"But you don't want me to ask."

"Frankly, with you here we might not be able to hold the Abbey. I do not think Mayor Dortmund will storm this place soon. It has held too often, and the Highlanders around us would not care to see the Mayor in possession here. It would be a dangerous game for the Mayor, one he will not play unless he has a powerful motive. You would be such a motive."

Ross said nothing.

"So long as you are alive, you are witness to his treachery," Dom Julian said. "I do not know what stories Dortmund will tell. He will need powerful lies to justify himself. Other Masters and bossmen will not be pleased to hear that Kenyon Keep has fallen into the Mayor's hands. But with no one to deny his tales . . ."

"He will expect me to go to Escondido," Ross said.

"Yes. You may be certain he will be watching the roads."

"I can't stay here and I can't go to Escondido. Where?"

"I point out that you will be safer if I do not know," Dom Julian said. "More: if I do not know, you cannot suspect the Church of aiding the Mayor if—"

"If he finds me, I won't be able to suspect anything," Ross said.

"Even so, I would not care to have my name in your dying curses," Dom Julian said.

"Your miracles," Ross said. "Can you get word to Escondido? I need instructions from my father."

Before Dom Julian spoke, Ross knew the final horror to come. Don Flintridge was dead, and the remains of his guard besieged in Escondido. Ross was El Señor Kenyon, the last of the Kenyons, but he was not Master of Encino. He was utterly alone.

But a Kenyon. Now and forever.

HOLO-CAUSTIC
Peter Dillingham

EDITOR'S INTRODUCTION

In the *There Will Be War* series we have published as much poetry as any other non-poetry anthology in science fiction. There are several good reasons for this: one is that we receive a lot of excellent poetry submissions, another is that it gives us the excuse to publish some of the best war poetry ever written. Another reason is Peter Dillingham: we believe that Peter writes some of the best poetry published today—whether it's called science fiction or mainstream.

Not only does Peter's poetry contain arresting imagery, but often it is visually moving as well. Such as this poem, "Holo-Caustic," which we present here for the very first time.

Holo-Caustic

"It was visible by day,
like Venus;"
Yang Wei-te,
Chief Computer of the Calendar,
told the Emperor
in July, 1054:
"pointed rays
shot out from it
on all sides;
the color was reddish-white . . ."

In November, 1572, Tycho Brahe,
Astronomer of Florence,
"saw,
with inexpressible astonishment,
near the zenith,
in Cassiopea,
a radiant star
of extraordinary magnitude."

Right Hemisphere

the cell reacts
a glorious
sacrificial blossoming
at 10,000 km/sec
phagocytic . . .
triggered by
contagion's spread
a malignant thrusting forth
of virulent sentience
from long containment
the cell reacts
a glorious
sacrificial blossoming
at 10,000 km/sec
phagocytic . . .
triggered by
contagion's spread
a malignant thrusting forth
of virulent sentience

COLLECTOR'S PIECE
Edward P. Hughes

EDITOR'S INTRODUCTION

No society could endure if, as is sometimes implicitly assumed, its members became hostile to it by reason of and in proportion to their lowly status within it. Should you so plan a society as to establish and maintain equality in every respect you can think of, there would naturally be a restoration of scarce, desirable positions, by nature attainable only by a minority. You can allot equal time to each member of an Assembly: but you cannot ensure that all will command equal attention. You can chase unequal (more or less log-normal) distributions out of one field after another: they will reappear in new fields. Nor are men so base as to be disaffected from any order in which they are low-placed: they are indeed lavish in the precedence they afford to those who excel in performances they value. What exasperates them is a system of qualifying values which seems to them scandalous, a social scaling which jars with their scoring cards.

—*The Pure Theory of Politics*
Bertrand de Jouvenal

Civilization is a fragile thing; once gone, it is not easy to rebuild. Harrison Brown long ago showed that if our civilization falls far enough, it will be exceedingly difficult to rebuild. Social structures are delicate.

The late H. Beam Piper postulated two different ways for societies to "de-civilize": attack by "barbarians" from within and attack by Barbarians from without. It has happened enough in our own history: the fall of Athens after the Peloponnesian War, the fall of the Macedonian Empire after Alexander's death, and in more recent times the decline and fall of the Ottoman Empire.

Social institutions, work skills, knowledge, and culture—far too often taken for granted—once lost can take untold generations, if ever, to reinvent.

In the small world of Barley Cross children are no longer being born; not in small towns, not in cities, not anywhere. All know the magnitude of the disaster; it has brought most of what we know as civilization crashing down everywhere on Earth. To men without hope there is no future and the present can be of little or no value.

Commerce and industry have come to a halt in the large cities, but life is closer to normal in the small hamlets and villages, where change of any kind has always been slow. Yet, even in the hinterlands, marauders and bandits make the roads dangerous to travel and bring trade to a standstill.

For all that, the inhabitants of Barley Cross are determined that life shall remain normal—no matter what the cost. In their quest for order, they have decided to follow Patrick O'Meara, onetime sergeant of Her Majesty's Forces, now Master of the Fist. As Lord of Barley Cross the O'Meara has taken it upon himself to lead the town militia in raids to recover aspirin, antibiotics, and other vital supplies.

In past volumes of There Will Be War we have chronicled the adventures of Barley Cross and its Masters; now many of these fine stories—and some new ones—have been collected together into Masters of the Fist (Baen Books, 1989) by Edward P. Hughes. We encourage all of you who enjoy this latest episode in the ongoing saga of Barley Cross to purchase a copy.

━━━━━━━━━━━━━━━ ∎ ━━━━━━━━━━━━━━━

THE LORD OF BARLEY CROSS PROWLED THE ECHOING CHAMBERS of his future home, pondered the naked floors and peeling walls, and wondered if someone was making a fool of him. The place was supposed to have been furnished and decorated. Beside him, General Larry Desmond waxed eloquent on the advantages of O'Flaherty strongholds.

Patrick O'Meara spoke, tight-lipped. "I thought it was furnished."

"Och, so did I," admitted his general. "Thim Higgins folk must have moved their stuff out while me back was turned."

Patrick O'Meara examined a blotchy ceiling. "And it leaks."

"True," conceded the general. " 'Tis probably the roof. I heard thim Higgins put on new tiles. But the pitch ain't very steep. And there's a gully behind the battlements that traps the rain. And, no doubt, the boyos have been stealing your lead flashing."

"No doubt," agreed his lord. "But it's not my lead flashing yet. I'm quite content with Mooney's place."

The general registered alarm. "Och, me lord!" he protested. "Ye can't remain there. Ye have a position to uphold. We have a castle, and the villagers will expect ye to live in it. Haven't they already christened this place 'O'Meara's Fist'? And didn't I hear ye say yerself that ye intended to make a real stronghold of it—where yer people could take refuge in times of trouble?"

A shrewd blow. Patrick O'Meara raised a suspicious eyebrow. "You trying to con anyone, Larry?"

Larry Desmond shut his eyes for a moment, a gesture meant to give his lord the impression that he sought strength from a divine source. Then he produced a smile, wide and guileless. "In no way, Pat. Why worry about a leak? Seamus Murray can knock a bit o' fresh lead over any holes he finds up there . . ."

Patrick O'Meara envisaged the height of the O'Flaherty tower, then counted floors in his head. "If the leak is in the roof, there's at least three ceilings marked," he pointed out.

"I'll get the lads in," promised the general. "We'll have the whole place cleaned up, replastered and painted for you. Ye won't know it."

"Will you now?" murmured the O'Meara. "And the broken windows? And the lock you forced to get in?"

" 'Twill all be fixed, Pat. Don't worry about a thing."

"And how about furniture? Don't I get a few chairs? Something to sleep on?"

Larry Desmond grew cautious. Pat O'Meara might be josh-ing, but finding furniture could be a problem. Many shops in Galway—a city rapidly being wrecked by gang warfare—were already burned out. And, anyway, who cared to shop with bul-lets flying about their ears! The general of Barley Cross's Vol-unteer Militia commanded a pool of labour. As unofficial Minister of Economics he could probably talk someone into pro-viding lead, paint, glass and plaster. But furniture? No doubt Tom O'Connor was skilled enough carpenter to build what they needed. But it would take time. And General Desmond wanted his lord up the hill as soon as possible.

"Some of the villagers might be persuaded to part with a few bits and pieces, me lord," he murmured. "Would ye settle for second-hand stuff?"

Patrick O'Meara, who had abandoned a truckle bed in a Bel-fast barracks for the hard interior of a Chieftain tank, and cur-rently inhabited a cramped apartment above Fechin Mooney's taproom, decided to go easy on his general. "I'll settle for any-thing softer than the floor of my tank," he grinned.

Larry Desmond inflated his chest with relief. "Leave it to me, me lord. I'll have ye up here, snug as a bug in a rug, in no time at all."

Patrick O'Meara wasn't listening. He rapped the newel post at the bottom of the staircase, peering closely at it. "No wood-worm, Larry?"

General Desmond jumped in with both feet. "'Tis sound in wind and limb, me lord. Thim Higginses took out a set of stone steps to put in these stairs. Sure, they only need a lick of paint."

Patrick O'Meara decided he had been soft enough for one morning. He eyed his general amiably. "Let's have the wood-work sanded down, stained and revarnished, Larry."

Larry Desmond eyed this man who had put fire in the bellies of Barley Cross's citizens. Who had frightened off the most per-sistent of the rogues who regarded the village as their legitimate prey. The general sensed a certain lack of respect for the opin-ions of the village's more influential citizens. Was the new Lord of Barley Cross going to be difficult? He sighed inwardly. No doubt, a drop of stain and varnish wouldn't be hard to find. And if it got the fellow installed in this draughty hole a wee bit sooner,

41

it would be worth the bother. "Leave it to me, me lord," he mumbled. "I'll put it on me list."

Later that morning, over a glass of the black stuff in Mooney's bar, the Chief of Barley Cross's Armed Forces confided his troubles to the village doctor.

"I'm having a divil of a job getting him up there, Dinny. The whole place has gone to rack and ruin since the Higginses left. There's not a full pane of glass left in the windies, nor a decent lock on the front door. And right now, that felly is poking about upstairs, looking for more work for me lads."

Doctor Denny Mallon smiled. "Sure that's why we've renamed them a Temporary Service Unit. Every one of those lads has agreed to do whatever he can to make our new Lord and Master comfortable."

General Desmond choked on his stout, spilling a drop—a near tragedy, since Fechin Mooney had warned his clientele that they were drinking the last barrel, and couldn't expect to see further deliveries of the darlin' stuff. The general coughed and snuffled. "I'd been hoping to get me gutters repainted while the lads were willing . . ."

The doctor studied the ceiling. "I didn't hear that last remark, Larry." Then he smiled. "But if your gutters change colour, I don't think I'd notice."

It was doubtful whether the general appreciated the doctor's duplicity. He continued. "Trouble is, when he's not finding work for them, he's got 'em out on exercises—learning 'em to shoot, and take cover and the like."

"Very commendable, too," commented the doctor, who didn't always share the general's prejudices. "Especially in these dangerous times."

Larry Desmond peered gloomily into the depths of his glass. "I fear we may have got ourselves a tiger by the tail, Dinny."

"But a friendly tiger," Denny Mallon reminded his friend. "Just think—we've not had a single attack on the village since Patrick O'Meara took over."

"That's true," mused the general. "Give the divil his due."

"He's no devil," said the doctor sharply. "And don't forget—he's carrying fertile genes. We're lucky to get a trained soldier, as well as fecund male, to rule the village."

42

The general clapped a hand to his forehead. "There ye go, Dinny, using fancy college words to confuse an old soldier."

The doctor cocked an eyebrow. "An old copper, you mean. You served with the *gardai* in Limerick. You've never worn a military uniform."

The general drained his glass, then crooked a finger at the bartender. "Ye've the memory of an elephant, Dinny—"

"And while we're on the subject of the law," interrupted the doctor, "there's a character in your cooler you should take a look at."

Among his various hats, Larry Desmond wore that of Justice of the Peace. Normally policed from Galway City, Barley Cross had seen neither sight nor sound of the *gardai* for months; and until Patrick O'Meara's arrival, Larry Desmond, by virtue of his *gardai* service, had been regarded as the law's representative in Barley Cross.

"What's he done?" he demanded.

Denny Mallon waited until the bartender had placed two pints of stout on the table. "I'll be asleep all afternoon after drinking this," he complained, sipping the dark liquid. "The fellow's a vagrant. I had Seamus Gallagher lock him up in your greenhouse."

Larry Desmond's wife had been a keen gardener. Since her death, her flowers had also died, and her greenhouse had become a handy place for holding suspects, criminals, and characters of ill repute until the law had time to examine them. In many ways it made an ideal jail, being warm, isolated, and allowing constant scrutiny of its tenants.

The general raised the fresh glass to his lips. "Och, I'll get round to him," he said. "Did he made a statement?"

"Only that he wasn't going to make no trouble."

The general wiped his lips. "Just as well. That's my conservatory he's enjoying."

Later, after being persuaded that the bar was positively shut, the general made his way home, recalling belatedly that he hadn't asked Denny Mallon if he knew of anyone with furniture to spare.

A small crowd had gathered at his gate, their eyes on the exhibit in his garden.

Larry Desmond recalled his duties. He waved a hand, while

searching his pockets for a key. "Into the courtroom with ye all," he commanded. "I'll pick a jury inside if we need one."

Unlike that of the cooler, the Desmond front door was never locked. While his audience trooped in, the general opened the lockup.

The prisoner was thirtyish, undersized and dirty, his clothes torn and travel-stained. He cowered under the Desmond glare.

"Out ye come!" ordered the general. "Into me house . . . where those people are going. I want a word with you."

Most of the audience had found seats in his front room. The latecomers propped themselves against the wall behind the settee. The general's coffee table had been pulled in front of an armchair awaiting his posterior. The Barley Crossers knew how to set up a court.

The general pushed his prisoner into the centre of the room. "Stand there while we look at you."

He took his seat, seized a poker from the fireplace. "The court will come to order," he intoned, rapping the table with the poker.

When the outbreak of coughing had ceased, the general addressed the prisoner. "Your name?"

"Michael Terence Dooley, yer honour."

"No kin of mine," snapped Claire Dooley promptly from the settee.

Larry Desmond noted the prisoner's form of address, and recognised an old lag. "Where are you from?"

"I was born in Drogheda, yer honour—the town Cromwell burned to the ground."

"Man, ye've a long memory!" called a voice from the wall.

"Silence!" roared Barley Cross's Justice of the Peace. "If ye want to crack jokes, go outside." He addressed the prisoner. "I didn't mean 'where were ye born,' I meant 'where have ye come from?' "

"Westport, yer honour," responded the prisoner.

"And what did ye do in Westport?"

The prisoner grimaced, looked quickly round the room as though seeking a familiar face, then said, "I worked for a gang of criminals, yer honour."

The audience ceased fidgeting, and paid attention. Larry Desmond's eyebrows alerted Maggie Pearce. Maggie acted as clerk

44

of the court when the general wanted notes taken. **Maggie got out a stub of pencil and the notebook she used for bread orders.**

Larry Desmond resumed his interrogation. "Which **criminals** did ye work for?"

The prisoner responded without hesitation. "A gang working for a felly called Garvey. They've took over Westport. They threw the *gardai* in the Carrowbeg—tied up first so they couldn't swim."

Maggie Pearce tutted, and wrote rapidly.

"Get it all down, Maggie!" crowed a voice.

The general turned on the culprit. "If ye think ye can do it better—?" he warned.

All eyes swivelled towards Jemmy Boyle. Jemmy was a Volunteer, and presumably could be disciplined for smart aleckry.

Jemmy shrank. "Apologies for interruptin', gineral."

Larry Desmond returned to the prisoner. "So, ye are a criminal?"

The man seemed surprised. "No, yer honour. I only worked for them."

Larry Desmond frowned. "There's a difference? What was yer job?"

The little man put his hands behind his back. "I was cook."

The general gnawed a thumb. It was a moot point. Shouldn't cooking for criminals make the cook a criminal too? Larry Desmond sighed. Sometimes he regretted the lack of a decent law book. He decided to ignore the question for the moment. "And why did ye leave these criminals?"

The little man shrugged. "I'd had enough of grafting for ingrates what didn't appreciate decent cooking."

"Ye didn't mind consorting with criminals?"

The prisoner shrugged again. "Ach, yer honour—if ye're going to fret about mixing with villains these days, ye'd best seek a monastery."

"But ye came to Barley Cross instead?"

"I had to go somewhere, didn't I? If ye come through the mountains, there's only Leenane before ye get to here."

"Less of yer lip," growled the general. "What happened at Leenane?"

The prisoner lowered his eyes. "They shot at me, yer honour."

Larry Desmond thumped the table to still the laughter. "The looks of you, I'm not surprised." He turned his head. "Where's the Volunteer who locked this felly up?"

" 'Twas Seamus Gallagher," said a voice. "He's still on duty."

The general's eyes pinpointed Jemmy Boyle. "Off ye go, Jemmy. Take over from Seamus. Tell him I want him in here."

Volunteer Boyle departed at a run.

The general returned to the prisoner. "Let me see yer soles!"

"Me soul?" queried the prisoner.

"Of yer shoes, ye fool!" snapped the general. "I want to see their underneaths."

The prisoner turned his back on the general, and raised first one foot, then the other. Holes in each shoe revealed dirty flesh. "I've holes in me pockets, too," he volunteered.

"With shoes in that state, ye could have walked from Westport," conceded his interrogator, ignoring the prisoner's red herring. "Ah, Seamus!"

The door opened, and Volunteer Gallagher entered.

"Why did ye lock this felly up?"

Seamus Gallagher scowled at the prisoner. "Didn't I catch him hanging around the Gleasons' chickens in a suspicious manner?"

"Ah!" said the general.

"I was hungry," whined the suspect. "I'd had nothing to eat since I left Westport."

"That's a good thirty miles," whispered Claire Dooley to Molly Larkin.

"And ye proposed to steal a chicken?"

"Or an egg or two. I'd have paid for them if I'd had the money."

"And have ye no money?"

Unprompted, the prisoner turned out his empty pockets.

Larry Desmond rubbed his jaw. He was not a hard man, and found it difficult to ignore the pricks of his conscience. But vagrants were bums. And Barley Cross was no Tom Tiddler's ground. He said, "I'll tell ye what, man—I haven't a deal of time for vagrants. Especially them as consort with criminals. But"—the Desmond eyes grew imperceptibly less like pebbles—"I'm also the Receiver of Wrecks for Barley Cross. And

46

if ever I saw a wreck, I'm looking at one right now. So I propose to find you a dacent pair of boots from somewhere, give you a couple of punt out of Mooney's swear box—which is collected for charity as we all know"—the general glared defiantly round the room as he spoke—"so ye can buy yerself a bite to eat at Ryan's, and then get on yer way."

"Hold it, Larry!" The Lord of Barley Cross had stood unnoticed in the doorway for some minutes. Hearing his voice, several members of the audience made as if to rise, but Patrick O'Meara stayed them with a gesture. Waving a list of his castle's defects at the prisoner, he demanded, "Did you pass any empty houses on your way here?"

The prisoner's lips twitched. "Sure, I did no harm, sor. I had to sleep somewhere."

Patrick O'Meara sensed pay dirt. "Where did you sleep?"

The prisoner pondered, fingering his lips. "I stayed one night at a house near Mambridge—but there wasn't a scrap of food in the place, nor a pair of shoes to fit me."

Mambridge was no more than five miles from Barley Cross. "Were you hoping to steal a pair of shoes?"

The prisoner lowered his head. "Can ye steal from the dead, sor? They surely have no use for footwear."

The audience grew silent, considering the question.

"How do you know anybody was dead?"

"There was only an old man there, sor. He looked as though mebbe he'd starved to death. His ribs stood out like a picket fence."

"That'd be old Pete Carley," whispered an awed voice.

"So what did you steal?" asked Patrick O'Meara. There must have been unlimited opportunities for theft in an empty house.

"Not a thing, sor." The prisoner looked hurt. "I said a prayer for the old felly's immortal soul, then dug a grave for his corpse in the garden." The prisoner spread his palms in appeal. "Haven't we an obligation to bury the dead?"

Silence fell as those present reviewed the Corporal Works of Mercy remembered from childhood catechisms. Someone murmured, "There's an obligation to feed the hungry, I recall."

"And to clothe the naked," added another voice.

Larry Desmond's face turned red. He peeped guiltily at his lord. "I've promised him food and a pair of boots . . ."

Patrick O'Meara's eyes were on the prisoner. The fellow was

either a saint or a fool. "Have you anything else to commend yourself besides an ability to quote Christian obligations?"

The prisoner displayed crooked teeth. "Sure, I can turn me hand to most jobs, sor."

Patrick O'Meara scrutinised the man's palms. They were weathered and callused, no strangers to manual employment.

"Like plastering? And painting? Or a bit of joinery?"

The prisoner shrugged. "I once plastered for a builder, sor."

The Lord of Barley Cross considered. This vagrant might have picked up much useful intelligence on his travels. And news from outside was scarce in Barley Cross. The man's report on Pete Carley's demise could possibly solve the Fist furnishing problem. *Could* you steal from the dead? Patrick O'Meara made up his mind. "Put him on the strength, Larry. Find him somewhere to stay. He can start work at the Fist tomorrow."

Larry Desmond nodded, mind in a turmoil. Didn't they teach old lags trades like plastering and joinery in Dublin's Mountjoy Jail . . . ?

Taking the air at Mooney's front door the following morning, Patrick O'Meara heard the tramp of feet and the squeal of an unoiled axle. Down the road marched General Desmond and his Temporary Service Unit. Bringing up the rear in blue coveralls and new boots, the ex-prisoner pushed a cart laden with sacks of plaster and an assortment of buckets and tools.

The general waved a greeting to his lord.

The Lord of Barley Cross waved back. He wanted speech with the Volunteer marching beside the general. Andy McGrath had seen service in the Irish army, and knew one end of a rifle from the other—a rare trait in the Barley Cross Militia. He had also driven the tank back from the Tuam raid. Patrick O'Meara was in need of a tank driver.

"Could you spare Andy for half an hour?" he called.

General Desmond waved acknowledgment. "Fall out, Mc-Grath!" he roared.

Andy McGrath surrendered a shovel to his next in column, and fell out.

The Lord of Barley Cross watched his army march away before turning to the waiting soldier. "How about learning to drive a buttoned-up tank, Andy?"

48

Many of Patrick O'Meara's men were still unsure how to address him. Until a few days ago he had been their Military Adviser, fighting the village's enemies alongside them. Now he was their lord, and presumably above such dangerous diversions.

"If ye think I can manage it, sir . . . me lord," stumbled Andy McGrath.

Patrick O'Meara studied his man. "Would I ask you if I didn't?"

Andy McGrath looked pleased. Tank driving had panache. "Doesn't General Desmond want the job, sir?"

The O'Meara shook his head. "You couldn't persuade the general into that machine for a pension. I drove it because my gunner couldn't."

It was a private joke. Celia Larkin had been Patrick O'Meara's gunner. The schoolmistress had renounced military service when Patrick O'Meara was appointed Barley Cross's Military Adviser.

Andy McGrath had heard of their exploits. The combination of Larkin and O'Meara had been the first successful opposition to the local gangs of terrorists.

"Are ye giving up driving, sir?" he asked.

"Only so I can sit in the commander's seat, and fire the gun," grinned his lord.

Andy McGrath was not deceived. He came to attention. "I'll have a bash at it, sir."

The O'Meara gripped his arm. "Come on, then," he urged. "Let's see how you shape with the lid down."

The O'Meara's tank was kept in the village schoolyard. In the school, Celia Larkin pinned up wall charts, and tried to keep her mind on scholarly matters. There were no children in Barley Cross—perhaps not even in all Ireland—so she had no class to teach. Instead she prepared a lecture for the adults that evening. But her thoughts wandered. Just a week ago they had acclaimed Patrick O'Meara Lord of Barley Cross. The achievement, she believed, justified the plotting which had brought it about. If Patrick were the only man in Ireland capable of replacing the village's children, they had given him the chance to do it. And any private misery was a price she was happy to pay. Just the same, Celia Larkin hadn't been able to face Patrick O'Meara since his elevation.

She had grown used to seeing his tank parked in her schoolyard. Barley Cross was proud of its armoured fighting vehicle. But the monster filled the main street, leaving little room for traffic. And from the schoolyard its big gun still commanded the Clifden road.

Finding concentration difficult, the schoolmistress decided to go home. As she locked the schoolhouse door behind her, she noticed two men in conversation near the tank. She lowered her head, and hurried for the gap in the railings.

Patrick O'Meara heard the tap of heels on tarmac. He turned, and saw his ex-gunner. He clapped Andy McGrath on the shoulder. "Get in, and give her a run round the yard, Andy. Get the feel of her. I have to talk to someone."

He hurried after her. "Larkin!"

She halted, and waited, pulse pounding. She made her voice light. "Hi, my lord."

He drew near, head cocked to one side, brow furrowed. "Knock off the 'my lord' nonsense," he told her bluntly. "And tell me why you are avoiding me."

She flushed. She had forgotten his tank commander brusqueness. "Very well . . . sergeant," she said primly. "Who said I'm avoiding you? What are you doing here?"

His eyes narrowed. "I'm teaching Andy McGrath to drive our tank. Now, come on, Larkin—have I got the plague or something?"

She studied his open face, on which a smile alternated with a frown. He was still her O'Meara. And she was hurting him.

She sought for words. "You—you don't belong to me any more. You belong to Barley Cross now."

He said gently, "Come on, Larkin! I don't belong to anyone."

She shivered at the use of her surname. On his lips, it had become an endearment. She controlled a quaver in her voice. "But, Pat, if you're going to father the future children in Barley Cross, you have to stay unmarried. The women here won't accept a married adulterer. They won't cheat on another woman."

Unconvinced, he said, "How do you know that?"

She met his gaze. "Because I'm a woman. And I know. They'll tolerate your *droit du seigneur*. But this is not the twelfth century. They won't put up with it from someone's husband."

His face grew stern. "I've never asked you to marry me."

50

Her mouth opened, then closed. Colour flushed into her cheeks.

"But I'm ready to if you want me to," he added.

The colour went away. She stood, mute.

"You regretting any decisions, Larkin?" he asked. "Because I am." He scowled. "Why put a crummy village before our happiness?"

She shrugged. "What do you mean by happiness?"

He made a helpless gesture. "I mean . . . we could get married—start a family . . ."

She glared at him. "And the other folk here? Would you want your children to grow up alone? No playmates?"

"Look—" he began. He sought for the words. "It's not my fault that men aren't fertile any more. If you like, I could perform secretly . . . ?"

Her mouth set in a firm, uncompromising line. "Over my dead body, Mister O'Meara. No husband of mine gets to play around!"

He gazed at her, bewildered.

She said, "If you don't marry me, you can do as you please. I'll be content with what we've had. And with a bit of luck, we'll soon have a village full of children."

He shook his head, incredulous. "Don't you want kids of your own?"

She swallowed a pang. "I'll educate those you have by other women."

His face was incredulous. "And you'll settle for that?"

"I don't want to marry you," she lied firmly.

He gave up. "Then we'll have to manage without marriage."

"Oh?"

Somewhere in the distance a Chieftain tank clanked.

Had she talked him round? She said, hesitant, "What do you mean?"

He grasped her arms. "What I say. If I can't have you as my wife, then I'll have you as my mistress."

"Pat"—she pushed him away—"you're the lord of the village and I'm the schoolteacher. We should be setting an example."

He pulled her towards him. "We will—a good example!"

His jacket felt rough on her cheek. She mumbled faintly, "But,

51

Pat—only Doctor Denny knows about us. No one else must find out. We daren't—"

He rocked her gently in his arms. "Oh, but we do dare, Larkin!"

She lay limp against him. "How? People will see us!"

He stroked her hair. "We'll meet only when it's dark."

She hesitated. There was no way she could refuse him. "But where? I couldn't come to Mooney's."

He put a finger under her chin, and lifted her head. "Your place then?"

"With my brother and my niece on watch?"

He laughed. "Okay, then. Until my place is ready—what about the Chieftain? We could manage."

She smiled at the thought. They both knew what could be managed in a Chieftain. "After my evening class," she agreed. "When it's dark."

He hugged her. "Tonight, Larkin?"

She squeezed him back. "Tonight, sergeant."

She began to giggle.

"What's so funny?" he demanded.

She said, "It occurred to me—you'll be the only man in Ireland taking precautions tonight!"

Patrick O'Meara called on Doctor Denny Mallon the following morning. The doctor was packing a lunchbox.

"Come with us, Pat," he urged. "I've closed the surgery till tonight. Tessie will cut more sandwiches. A day's fishing will do you good."

"Us?"

"Kevin is coming. We're putting a boat out on Corrib." The doctor rubbed his hands. "Brown trout for supper!"

Patrick O'Meara grimaced. Kevin Murphy was not a man he'd want to gaze at all day.

"Sorry," he apologised. "I have to check the cupola MG. The feed is sticking."

Denny Mallon blinked, mystified.

Patrick O'Meara didn't enlighten him. Celia Larkin could have told him what a cupola MG was—she had fired one.

"I'm thinking of running out to Mambridge for a recce on Pete Carley's house," he continued. "There might be a chair or

52

two there worth liberating." He looked warily at the doctor, seeking approval. *Liberating* ownerless property was an old military custom. Doctor Denny Mallon might have civilian principles.

The doctor had not been present at Larry Desmond's interrogation of the vagrant, but he had received a full report. He refrained from any comment on the morality of robbing the dead. "I don't think you should go," he grunted. "You've upset the local villains. They all know about you and your tank. Some of them would love to trap you in an ambush." He wedged a thermos flask beside a plastic box. "Who knows you'll be looking for furniture?"

The O'Meara shrugged. Larry Desmond had claimed ignorance about the unfurnished state of the castle, but that was probably eyewash. He was willing to bet that the villagers had helped themselves to the missing furniture. So they would know he was looking for substitutes. Some of them still made trips to Oughterard. Outsiders occasionally visited the Cross. There would be gossip. Who knows what would be retailed about the Master's activities?

"Anyone wanting to knock me off could do it on Corrib as easy as at Mambridge," he objected.

"You wouldn't *clank* on Corrib," snapped the doctor. "Boats don't advertise their presence so plainly."

"Look—" said the Lord of Barley Cross patiently, "I only came to ask you if it's safe to sleep in Pete Carley's bed. I don't know what the old fellow died of—"

"Ha!" Denny Mallon emitted a harsh laugh. "Starvation's not catching. But if you're worried, I'll disinfect anything you bring back. You fetched enough prophylactics from Tuam to sanitise all Iar Connaught." He raised his eyebrows. "Or, alternatively, I can inject you for everything from measles to morning sickness?"

Patrick O'Meara gave the doctor a jaundiced look. "That shouldn't be necessary. As long as you assure me I'll not be bringing anything malignant back to the village."

Denny Mallon slammed the lid down on his lunch. "Dammit, Pat, I'm not clairvoyant. Old Carley probably died of old age compounded by insufficient food. If you're worried, get yourself a wife who'll cook you regular meals and maybe give you children to keep you young—"

The doctor paused, suddenly aware of what he had said.

Patrick O'Meara's face whitened. He said stiffly, "I thought we'd agreed that I should stay single."

The doctor's eyes were pleading. "I'm sorry, Pat. My tongue ran off with me."

The O'Meara drew a deep breath. Sometimes he wondered if these people knew what they had demanded of him. "Forget it, Denny," he said. "Though I'll bear in mind your advice about regular meals."

Denny Mallon was crestfallen. "I should watch my big mouth. After what you've done for us—"

Patrick O'Meara smiled. You couldn't upset a Grenadier Guards sergeant with mere words. Denny Mallon was probably sweating now in case his new lord took umbrage, and maybe changed his mind about being their stud. Denny Mallon didn't realise that Pat O'Meara valued the crazy sanity of Barley Cross just as highly as Barley Cross valued his genes. He took the doctor by the shoulders, and shook him gently. "I said 'forget it,' Denny."

Denny Mallon swallowed a lump of anxiety. "Thanks, Pat. You sure you won't come with us?"

The O'Meara shook his head. "I told you. I've got to look at a machine gun. Then I'm going fishing—for information."

When he had cleared the ammunition feed of the Chieftain's ranging machine gun, the Lord of Barley Cross climbed Barra Hill. The temporary service unit was busy at his future residence. Tom O'Connor knelt by the front door, replacing the lock broken by Larry Desmond. Patrick O'Meara caught the reek of varnish from within.

"They're doing your stairs, me lord," the carpenter explained. "I fitted a couple of new rails in the banister. The wood don't quite match, but the ones I took out were too rotten to leave in."

"Good man," approved his master. "Don't want to risk falling downstairs. How's the new man doing?"

Tom O'Connor paused, mallet hovering over chisel. "I think Dooley is upstairs, plastering a bedroom."

"I'll pop up and speak to him," said the O'Meara.

54

Pallet in one hand, float in the other, the new man was smoothing plaster below a window. When the O'Meara entered the room, he stopped work. "Good day, me lord."

So the fellow had learned how to address him!

"God bless the work," responded the O'Meara. "Are they treating you well?"

"Everything's fine, me lord. I'm pleased I got meself arrested in your village."

"Don't make a habit of it," cautioned the O'Meara. "We're not always so charitable with strangers."

The visitor looked sheepish. "I'd like to stay on, if I might. General Desmond says as how it's up to you."

Patrick O'Meara nodded. "The general is right. Barley Cross is a free and independent community, and what I say goes."

Dooley nodded, seeing an application for citizenship congealing in the air.

"Tell me more about the Clancy house you slept in," invited the O'Meara. "Is there any decent furniture there?"

Dooley patted the plaster on his pallet. " 'Tis a bit old-fashioned, me lord. Well-worn. But decent enough. There's a whole houseful."

"I was thinking of running up there and picking out a few bits for this place," mused his lord.

"In yer tank, me lord?"

"So you know I have a tank?"

"Sure, the lads have told me about you."

"Why did they shoot at you in Leenane?"

Patrick O'Meara's victim blinked. The change of subject seemed to unsettle him. He hesitated a moment, mouth twitching. "There's another gang at Leenane, me lord. They don't get on with Garvey's men. There's been fighting between them."

"And you're a Garvey man?"

Dooley flushed. "Sor! I *was*. I have admitted that."

"And whose man are you now?" pursued the O'Meara. "Or have you not yet made up your mind?"

Eyes squeezed shut, the plasterer hesitated, thinking hard. He made a decision. Face twisted with anguish, he blurted, "Don't go up to Mambridge for that furniture, me lord. 'Tis a trap. That Garvey felly is after you. He's not been able to loot in Barley Cross since ye took over. He wants ye dead!"

55

The last bit wasn't news, anyway. Garvey probably didn't enjoy being barred from Barley Cross any more than Moran Healey and his gang. "And how does he know I'm looking for furniture?"

"One of his men was in grocer Gleason's in Oughterard. He heard them talking about yer move into this place. Garvey sent me here to lay the bait."

"And now you've laid it?"

Dooley studied his boots. "I'm terrible ashamed of meself."

The Lord of Barley Cross hid a smile. "That's something, anyway. How did you know I would ask you about the Carley house?"

The penitent looked up. "I didn't, me lord."

"We might have sent you on your way without a question."

"I expected ye to do that." Dooley's mouth twisted in a smile. "I'd have told someone about the place before I left."

"So? You're a thoroughly accomplished villain—"

The penitent lowered his head. "Beggin' yer pardon, no, me lord. I was butler to a rich Westport family before Garvey and his gang took over."

Patrick O'Meara blinked. If all the little plasterer claimed was true, it would be a pity to waste him on a gang of villains. He said, "And what did Garvey expect you to do after you'd laid the bait?"

"I was to get back to Westport as fast as I could to let him know."

"And then?"

"They intend to lie in wait for you near the Carley house."

The Lord of Barley Cross smiled. "It would be a pity to disappoint them. Let's say you obey orders, and get off to Westport right away?"

Aghast, Dooley almost dropped his pallet. "I couldn't do that, me lord!"

"Why not?"

"If ye go after that furniture, ye'll be kilt."

Patrick O'Meara shook his head. "In my tank? I don't think so."

"Me lord"—the plasterer waved his float helplessly—"there's some clever fellers from Belfast has hitched up with Garvey.

They know tricks with weedkiller and sugar that could upset yer tank."

Patrick O'Meara was not unacquainted with homemade bombs. Perhaps this one-time butler had a point. "I'll bear that in mind," he promised. He grew brisk. "Tomorrow morning then I want to see the back of you."

The man's features drooped. "Are ye throwing me out?"

The Lord of Barley Cross nodded. "I'm sending you back to your old boss to tell him the bait is laid. He can get his ambush ready. I'll be going up to Mambridge in a couple of days."

"But, me lord—"

"And then you can come back to Barley Cross. I think I can find another job for you."

Ex-Grenadier guardsman Patrick O'Meara stood in the commander's cupola of his Chieftain tank, senses alert. Inside the turret, his gunner, newly-promoted Lance-corporal O'Malley, peered through the optical sight, glad that the commander could override his control of the big gun if the need arose. Behind him loader Flinty Hagan waited, hand resting on the shell rack. Outside, an open hatch in the glacis revealed the black locks of Sergeant-driver McGrath.

Over the intercom, the commander said, "Let's stop a minute, Andy."

The tank came to a halt.

Behind them, Brendan McCarthy's largest van, driven by Tom Burke, also came to a halt.

The silence was almost palpable, apart from the low rumble of the Chieftain's engine, and the panting of the van motor. Patrick O'Meara heard a lark trilling. He became aware of a gurgling river ahead.

He rotated the cupola, field glasses to his eyes. To the right lay the western reach of Corrib, dotted with islands. On the left, barren slopes climbed towards the Maamturk Mountains. Ahead, the road narrowed approaching a bridge. Across the bridge rose other mountains. No sign of lurking villains. Scant cover for an ambush.

Pete O'Malley's head emerged from the hatch beside the cupola, leads dangling from the padded phones over his ears. He raised one doughnut. "This is Mambridge, sir." He pointed lakewards. "There's the ruins of Hen's Castle on that island."

"They say it was built by a witch for the O'Flahertie," volunteered Flinty Hagan, eavesdropping.

"Rubbish!" interpolated Sergeant McGrath. " 'Twas built by the sons of Rory O'Connor, the last king of Ireland."

"Cut the chat, lads," ordered their commander. "There are bandits about, somewhere . . ."

Where were Garvey's villains? Had his little messenger let him down? Patrick O'Meara was almost sure the plasterer's penitence had been genuine. The Carley house was just beyond the bridge. Would they try an ambush there?

Patrick O'Meara felt uneasy. Instinct warned him off the bridge. Bridges were always a risk. And the tank was his only trump card. Bridges restricted manoeuvrability. Bridges could be blown when you were halfway over. He recalled the plasterer's warning about compounds of weedkiller and sugar. He swore. "That bloody bridge is mined!"

He heard McGrath's sceptical sniff. "I doubt it, sir. The villains need it for raiding the Cross."

Pete O'Malley and Flinty Hagan stayed quiet out of respect for professional opinion.

Patrick O'Meara tucked away his binoculars. "Something's fishy. Cover me, Pete," he ordered. "I'm going to recce the bridge."

He braced his arms on the rim of the cupola, preparing to heave himself out.

He heard a shout. "Go back, sor! The road is mined!"

He recognised the voice. Then a gun cracked.

He dropped back into the turret. "Button up! Get us off the road, Andy!"

The motor whined. The Chieftain swivelled on one track, and lumbered into the scrub on their left. Corporal O'Malley rotated the turret, holding the bridge in his gunsight. Behind them, the van began to advance. Flinty Hagan grabbed his commander's leg. "Tom Burke is moving, sir!"

"Jasus!" Patrick O'Meara pushed open the cupola hatch. He stood erect to wave back the van. A figure rose from concealment near the bridge. A burst of machine gun fire tracked up the front of the van. A headlight sprayed glass. The windshield shattered. Tom Burke slumped. The van halted.

Patrick O'Meara swung the cupola gun. He sprayed bullets around the bridge. "Forward slow, Andy," he ordered. "Keep off the road. We'll try to enfilade them."

Why had they stopped the van? Angrily, Patrick O'Meara loosed off another burst at the bridge. He knew why. They weren't after the van. Even *he* wasn't the target. The tank was the prize! A tankless O'Meara would be a nobody. And, tank gone, Barley Cross's clodhopping militia would revert to being easy meat for Connemara's bandits.

He sent another hail of steel bridgewards.

Pitching and sliding along the verge, the tank approached the bridge. The Failmore River came into sight. Figures sprouted from concealment. Handguns spitting, they scrambled up the bank. Heads down, they scuttled across the bridge. Patrick O'Meara chased them with the cupola machine gun, chipping flints from the parapet.

"Only three of them," commented Corporal O'Malley, disgust in his voice.

"Enough to cope with a disabled tank," pointed out Andy McGrath.

The villains had taken cover behind the parapet at the far end of the bridge. Sporadic sparkles revealed their positions. Patrick O'Meara ducked into the turret. "See if you can dislodge them, corporal," he ordered his gunner. "Try to leave the bridge standing."

Pete O'Malley had a round of AP ready up the spout. The range was point blank. With the far end of the parapet in his sights, he squeezed the trigger.

The turret bucked. The end of the parapet bloomed like an opening flower. Something struck the distant hillside, sending up a spout of dirt and splintered rock. Three figures scuttled from cover.

Pete O'Malley knocked them over with a burst from the ranging MG. "That's for Tom Burke," he muttered, forgetting his microphone.

The O'Meara concealed his surprise. Clodhoppers apparently learned fast. "Keep an eye peeled while I check the road," he ordered.

Heaving himself out of the turret, he dropped down to the verge. There was a mine concealed under the road somewhere. Ten yards away, beneath scattered gravel, the tarmac had been disturbed. He crossed, keeping well clear of the broken surface. On the other side of the road, a pair of wires emerged from the dirt. He followed the leads to a quarryman's detonator on the ground beneath the bridge. He heard a groan as he unscrewed the wires from the box. Further down the slope, a body lay with both legs in the river. Patrick O'Meara recognised the old police jacket which had no longer fitted Larry Desmond.

Gently he turned his little plasterer over.

The wounded man opened his eyes, and grimaced. "They didn't like me shouting that warning, sor."

"Lie still," said the O'Meara unnecessarily. "I'll get something to carry you on."

An army greatcoat and two long-handled spades from in the van made a serviceable stretcher. They carried the wounded man up to the road.

Tom Burke, his face bloody with glass cuts but far from dead, said, "We could certainly use a bed now, me lord."

Andy McGrath manoeuvred the tank back onto the road. They fastened a tow rope to the van's front axle, and standing well back, watched Andy drive the Chieftain across the bridge, dragging the unmanned van after him.

The vehicle passed over the disturbed patch in the road without incident to reach the bridge unharmed. Patrick O'Meara exhaled. "We haven't time to be digging up mines," he told his men. "Maybe another day . . ."

The rest of the operation was a cakewalk. No one interfered as they ransacked the Carley residence. They stacked the loot in MacCarthy's van. Flinty Hagan, despite his nickname, had a soft heart. He jerked a thumb at a wooden cross in the garden. "What about them fellers on the road, me lord?"

Patrick O'Meara concealed his feelings. "I have a policy for dead dogs," he said. "I leave 'em for the crows."

Flinty Hagan flinched. When he told the young widow he was courting about the day's events, he would have to skip some bits.

At Barley Cross, Patrick O'Meara sent his furniture up the hill, and took his casualties to Doctor Mallon.

60

The doctor stretched out the worst casualty on his kitchen table, and prepared for butchery. The wounded man took no notice. He had conveniently lost consciousness.

The O'Meara watched in silence as Tessie Mallon snipped away bloody cloth, carried in steaming basins, and held dripping instruments. The Mallons had evidently done this sort of thing before.

Twenty minutes later, he heard the clink of a bullet in a bowl.

"He'll live," said Denny Mallon, brow dripping perspiration, "even if I says it as shouldn't. Bind him up, woman. I'll take a look at Tom."

Patrick O'Meara breathed easier.

Magnifying glass and forceps in hand, Denny Mallon bent over Tom Burke's face. He nodded at the unconscious Dooley. "Can you put him somewhere else? We eat off that table."

The O'Meara grinned. "He can go back to Ryan's for a week or so. He had a room there while he was working at the Fist."

"Tell them to give him plenty of steak," advised the doctor. "The littler bugger's undernourished."

"Strange," mused Tessie Mallon. "I heard he was a cook for some villains at Westport."

The O'Meara shook his head in regret. "So he was. But he wasn't a very good villain."

The wounded man's convalescence lasted two weeks. Patrick O'Meara's preparations took the same length of time. Two floors of the Fist were furnished with Clancy loot. Celia Larkin had provided, and hung, drapes at the unarmoured windows. A carpet loaned by Father Con covered most of the parlour floor. A battered settee donated by Brendan MacCarthy helped ameliorate the seating shortage. Patrick O'Meara was grateful for all the help. Nothing like a housewarming to break the ice, he enthused. He smiled at his guests, trying to fit names to faces. He would get to know them all in time.

General Desmond shared Brendan MacCarthy's settee with the MacCarthy himself, Kevin Murphy, and a bottle of poteen. Celia Larkin had brought a stool from school. She perched on it primly, sipping tay to which had been added a drop of the craythur. In the depths of an armchair on the other side of the fire, Denny Mallon nursed a half-filled glass, his wizened face

61

thoughtful. Flourishing a sandwich, Tessie Mallon chatted with the young widow Neary, who had arrived on Flinty Hagan's arm. Sausage roll forgotten, Andy McGrath was making heavy weather over a theological point with Father Con—who, somewhat surprisingly, clutched a tumbler of poteen. Over plates of ham, Tom Burke and Peggy, his sister, had their heads together with the McGlones who ran the creamery next door to their butcher's shop. The plump girl sitting next to Pete O'Malley must be Nelly Dolan, his current passion. Tom O'Connor's fiancée Brigit Cullen swung dainty feet from a Clancy chair, and lectured Willie Flanagan, whose wife farmed while he poached. Willie was almost unrecognisable in a suit.

Patrick O'Meara gave it up trying to put names to them all. So many of them. And so many single girls he had heard spoken of by the Volunteers. Would that be coincidence? Tessie Mallon had made out the guest list. Was she privy to the plot to regenerate the population of Barley Cross? Letting all the marriageable girls take a squint at their new lord before the reality of his *droits du seigneur* had to be faced? Patrick O'Meara grimaced. That was a problem he had yet to tackle. He hoped Tessie had left off nobody who should have been invited—like McGuire the miller, who also distilled hooch, and Mooney the publican, who sold it, and poor Eamon Toomey, who couldn't hold it! None of them had arrived yet.

The Lord of Barley Cross dabbed his brow. Thank goodness the furniture was salvage. When they started jiving to Franky Finnegan's fiddle, the place would be a shambles! Still, they had all accepted his hospitality. That was a good start to his stewardship. Would they expect him to make a speech?

Larry Desmond caught his eye. The general waved an empty bottle. " 'Tis a dry time we're having, me lord!''

That man and his thirst! Patrick O'Meara tugged at the bell rope behind him. A smallish man opened the door. He carried a tray in one hand, a folded napkin in the other. His green baize apron failed to hide the burn holes in his waistcoat, nor the shine on well-worn pin-stripe trousers.

The O'Meara eyed him critically. Despite Denny Mallon's old clothes the fellow might just be mistaken for a butler. No sign that two weeks previous, bleeding from a bullet wound, he had lain, executed and abandoned, half in and half out of the Fail-more River.

Patrick O'Meara addressed the man who claimed to have but-tled for the cream of Westport society. "Would ye bring us another bottle, Michael?"

Michael Terence Dooley permitted himself a glimmer of a smile. It might be a bit of a comedown from the old days—but he fancied he had at last got himself a job with a future.

He bowed to the man who styled himself Lord of Barley Cross. Voice betraying no whit of condescension, he murmured, "Very good, me lord."

HALF THE BATTLE
Harry Turtledove

EDITOR'S INTRODUCTION

For over a thousand years the glory that was Rome towered over the Middle Ages: even the fabled Renaissance was but one more attempt to recreate the classical culture of Greece and Rome. It was only after the Age of Enlightenment that mankind began to conceive of what we know as "progress" and the startling new idea that the future could actually be better than the past.

Throughout most of history men have lived beneath the shadows cast by the ruins of past glory; the future was seen only as a continuation of the present, different only in details and personages. The idea that man could improve his lot in life, that of his children, and even the world around him is a very modern concept: a primary reason why most medieval and Renaissance paintings of Biblical scenes were done in then-current fashions—incidentally, now the major source of most of our present knowledge on medieval dress and fashion.

If the fortresses and buildings of ancient Rome cast a thousand-year shade over the future, what shadow might the towers of our great civilization cast over the future After Armageddon . . .

"A GUN THAT SPITS BULLETS ONE AFTER ANOTHER? I DON'T believe such a thing is possible." King Bryon of Canoga frowned on his throne. The guards who flanked it carried matchlocks.

Pedro the scribe bowed to his overlord. "Truly, sir, I believe it is. In searching through the fragments of the ancient books, I've found many references to what they call a Gatling."

"All kinds of wild things are in the ancient books," King Bryon said, rolling his eyes. He kept blinking at Pedro—the sun was in his face. His palace had been a church two centuries ago, before the Burning. Even in Ellay's mild climate, though, only bits of stained glass remained in the windows.

"One of my assistants has found what he thinks is a picture, my lord."

"A picture? Hmm." Bryon rubbed his chin. That put a different light on things. Everyone knew the strangest imaginings in the pre-Burning books came from the ones without illustrations. Words were more seductive by themselves.

Pedro pressed his advantage. "The master armorer thinks he can build the thing, my lord. The ancients had them. We know that, truly we do, and knowing something can be done is half the battle. Remember the lathe? That was new in your father's time, recovered from the old records."

"So it was," Bryon admitted. "Aye, we bring in many dols with our fine woodwork. And Duke Rico of Pacoim has more soldiers than we do, and more muskets. If your gun works, it may give us the edge we need to hold the old freeway line. Go ahead, Pedro, see what you and the armorer can do."

"Demons curse it, how did they make their damned engine so light and so powerful at the same time?" Jenk the engineer glowered at the torn, yellowed sheet in front of him. "I think your equivalents for these dimensions are wrong."

"They are not," Dorland the librarian said positively. "Of course the ancients knew more tricks than we do. But the numbers, those few we've recovered for this engine, are accurate. The powers-of-ten batch and the other crazy system they used both give the same results."

"But those are impossible!" Jenk said. "This thing weighs

no more than a ground-wagon engine, but puts out four times the power.''

"It has to, to propel a flying machine of useful size. We have no petrol to fuel it with, of course, but alcohol will serve.''

"Not as much energy,'' Jenk reminded him.

"Close, though: enough to carry a pilot and mount Gatlings on the wings. I don't suppose I have to tell you his majesty's father thought Gatlings couldn't exist.''

"His majesty's father was a robber chieflet, no matter that he called himself king.'' Jenk and Dorland were old friends and alone, or the engineer would never have dared say that out loud. "King Burger rules all of SoCal. If anyone can reunite us, he's the one.''

"I agree with you, but he needs the arms to do it. Vegas wants revenge for the last war, and we have to have airpower to stop them. Come on, Jenk, give it your best try. They knew how to make this engine work before the Burning; surely you can match them.''

"I'll keep at it,'' Jenk sighed. "I don't think I'll end up with a''—he looked down at the paper again—''*Messerschmitt*, though, whatever a *Messerschmitt* was.''

The sonic boom from the descending shuttle came down on the desert landing strip like a god's fist. King Burger's eyes glowed as he spotted the spacecraft gliding toward touchdown. He was an old man now, but the head archivist's shoulder ached from the strength of his grasp.

"I never thought I'd live to see it, Jorj,'' he said softly, "but we're approaching the pre-Burning days at last! We couldn't have done it without your team.''

"That book we found in the Zona ruins was the key, sir,'' the archivist said. "Once we knew just what the parameters of the thing were, the hardware was a lot easier to design.''

The Space Minister slammed his fist down on the desk. "It can't be done, I tell you!''

"Oh, but it can, Billi.'' Grinning like a man with an ace up his sleeve, the Commandant of the Technology Recovery Section dropped the photocopies of his unit's latest find on the minister's blotter.

Billi went through them a page at a time, quite slowly. "Where on earth did you come up with these, Claud?" he asked at last.

"Not on it—under it," the commandant replied. "You know the biggest problem we have with pre-Burning texts, especially the late ones that are of most interest to us, is the bad paper the ancients used. Exposed to air, it oxidizes fast. This book was buried so deep, it was sealed away from all that. I'd be surprised if another copy exists anywhere anymore."

"I should say not!" the Space Minister exclaimed. "All the previous ancient claims of FTL travel have been shown to be fiction. But this—"

"Yes. Here we have detailed engineering drawings of a starship. Of several classes of starship, in fact."

"Not as detailed as I'd like. They don't show a great deal about the engines."

"You're nitpicking, Billi." The Space Minister flushed; he knew Claud was right. The commandant sank the barb deeper by pointing out the obvious: "They didn't have much more to go on in my grandfather's time, when they built the first shuttle. Oh, sure, it'll take time to find the tough spots and work them all out, but remember, knowing it's possible—"

"—Is half the battle," Billi finished sourly. Really, the commandant was going too far. Everyone in the Namerican Empire knew the Technology Recovery Section's motto.

The captain of the starship *Claud* pressed a button on the communications panel at his station. "Engineering here," came a tiny voice.

"Are we ready to travel, Gomery?"

"That we are, sir. I only wish Claud himself could have lived to see the day."

"And I. He's in the lap of the gods now, though, cheering us on. Give me warp factor three, Gomery—we won't go too boldly at first."

"Aye, sir. Warp factor three it is."

ONLY THE STRONG SURVIVE
F. G. Wyllis

EDITOR'S INTRODUCTION

Despite the allure of new beginnings, life After Armageddon is not going to be the romantic picture painted by most writers and survivalists: first, few survivors will be properly prepared, including many who believe otherwise; secondly, the conditions of everyday life are going to be far more nasty, brutish, and short than most of us can imagine; finally, not many of us are psychologically prepared for the breakdown of everything which we accept as normal living—from the mundane aspects of cleaning our own kills to the changes in the nature of friendship and family.

In "Only the Strong Survive" we get a frightening glimpse at the price some might pay in the years following the aftermath; once again proving that the best way to survive After Armageddon is not to have one in the first place.

━━━━━━━━━━━━━━━━ ▪▫▪ ━━━━━━━━━━━━━━━━

TOD BRACED HIS FEET AND PULLED ON A BOARD USING ALL OF his weight and straining every muscle until the nails came out and the board popped free from the twisted pile of lumber that had once been a home. The Johnsons had lived here, an old couple, both of them short and fat with pure white hair. They had been real friendly to the Littles, always giving them homemade jam and stuff. That was in the good old days before the war. They were gone now.

His hands were numb with cold as he stacked the board on the old milk cart. He faced away from the wind that seemed to be constantly scouring the earth and that felt like sandpaper when it cut across his face. He cupped his hands over his mouth, blew into them, rubbed them together for a minute and stuffed them into his coat pockets. His little brother, Danny, still struggled with a piece of wood too big for him.

"That's enough," Tod shouted. "We'll never get this cart home the way it is."

The boys began pushing the milk cart down the hill to the public road. The cart rolled easily on large metal-rimmed wheels, but it was so big and heavy it took all their strength to control it. They turned onto the public road and started toward their house a half a mile away. There was ice and snow mixed with the gravel of the road and the steel-rimmed wheels of the cart would slip and slide in the old ruts worn in the road surface by cars long ago.

Tod pushed the cart from behind so he could watch for boards falling off. Danny pulled the cart with the draw bar, pretending to be a draft animal. They had to go over a small hill that lay between them and home. It didn't seem like much of a hill when they were riding their bikes, but hauling wood was different. The cart got heavier with every step they took.

Near the top of the hill Danny's worn leather shoes slipped on the snow and he went to his knees. The draw bar fell, spearing the ground. The cart stoped with a jerk, piling Tod into the load of wood. He fell and another button came off his coat. He screamed at Danny to be more careful as he felt around in the cold, icy gravel with numb fingers for the button. His mother might be able to sew it back on, though he really needed a new coat. He had outgrown all of his clothes in the past year and he didn't dare hope for new ones.

The sky kept getting darker as they neared home: light and dark gray, swirling clouds forever trying to get mixed smooth, but never making it. There was something about the clouds and their constant turbulence that was really scary. Tod's mother had told him that all living things needed light to grow and they weren't getting it, so everything was dying. They hadn't seen the sunshine since they came out of their house after the all-day war, and that was over a year ago.

By the time they got home, it was almost dark enough for a fire. Their dad didn't want chimney smoke attracting prowlers in the daytime, but a fire at night was OK. Even though you could smell the wood smoke for a mile, it was too dark at night to find your hand in front of your face, let alone a house half buried in the earth.

They turned off the public road into their yard and followed a long driveway right into the garage. They unloaded the cart and broke up the wood with an axe into smaller pieces that would fit in their stove. They piled the scrap wood on a piece of canvas and dragged it to the house.

Their father had built his house in the side of a hill so the earth would insulate it from the elements. Only the upstairs windows looked out over the earthen bank, and earth had been cut away to expose the front door.

Tod knocked on the door with his special knock and watched the peephole. He couldn't see through it, but it sort of clouded over when someone looked out from the inside. Then there was a rattling of chains and the door opened. Heather Little, his mother, stood in the doorway, a smile filling her hollow cheeks and her blond hair poking out from under a black stocking cap. She wore a big bulky sweater with a coat over it to ward off the perpetual cold that seemed to seep into your body until you ached all over. Hanging down below the coat was the holster that held a .44 magnum she carried for protection.

The boys brought the wood in and piled it by the stove. It took them six trips.

"Oh good," she said. "You've got enough wood there to last all night. I'm really proud of my little men."

The boys went with their mother to the basement and helped her pick mushrooms. Tod hated mushrooms. He looked longingly at the boxes of dried food stacked against one wall. He knew they were rationing it. They had to make it last till they could grow crops again, and they didn't know how long that would be. It might be "years and years," his mom had told him, before the sun came out.

"Are we going to have to eat these plain?" Danny whined.

70

"I suppose we could have something with them. Which would you like: onions or garlic?"

"Onions!"

She picked out a plastic bag of dried onions, then added a bag of dried beans and even a bag of dried apricots and a tin of flour. Tod's eyes got big with excitement.

"We're having a special dinner tomorrow," she explained. "A banquet. We'll have beans and apricot bread to celebrate the lights. Your father and Mr. Bradford got the generator working. It won't be long before we have a garden. Then we can eat *fresh* vegetables every day."

They came back upstairs, the boys bounding ahead of their mother. They had found new energy in the expectation of beans and apricot bread. She let Tod start the fire in the stove and light the lamps. The lamps were old jars filled with tallow, with strings for wicks. They had a sickening smell when they burned. By the time the fire got going good, there was a knock on the door. Danny raced to the door and opened it without taking the chains off. He looked out through the gap.

"It's Fred and Teach," he announced.

"You mean it's your father and Mr. Bradford," Heather corrected.

Danny closed the door and unhooked the chains, then opened the door again and the men came in.

Fred was a big man in his mid-thirties with long black hair and a full beard to match. He looked like an old-fashioned farmer dressed in a plaid shirt and bib overalls, laced boots that came halfway to his knees, and a heavy, fur-trimmed parka.

Mr. Bradford, or "Teach," as the boys liked to call him, was not as big and much older. His hair was almost all gray. He didn't have big muscles like their father, but the muscles he did have had grown hard. He had lost a lot of weight in the past year, so that skin hung in folds on his face. He had been a high school physics teacher and he tutored the boys in math, but his real reason for being there was to help Fred build a wind generator and hook up lights in the old barn. That's why Fred had taken him in a month ago.

The men were excited because they had the lights working and all they had to do now was start planting vegetables. All through supper they talked about how the manure decomposing in the barn and heat from the lights would keep the plants from freezing unless it got real cold, and how if the wind died down and the lights went off, the plants would think it was night and just go to sleep till the lights came back on again. All they had to worry about was that their seeds were all a year or more old. They weren't sure how many would germinate.

After supper Fred paced restlessly. "Well, I can't sit still. I think I'll go out and start preparing the seed bed."

"Want some help?" Mr. Bradford asked.

"No thanks. You stay here and give the kids their lesson. I can handle it."

Heather cleared the dishes from the table so the boys could do their lessons in a warm room. Tod got the box with the paper and pencils in it. He picked the biggest pencil in the box and a piece of paper with writing on only one side, then handed the box to Danny. In the beginning they had burned scrap paper in the stove to start fires. Now that they didn't have much left, he wished he had saved it.

Teach made up some math problems for the boys to work on—fractions. The boys hated them.

"Why do we have to learn all this stuff?" Danny whined.

"If you're going to be a survivor, you have to learn all you can about everything," Teach explained.

"What's a survivor?" Danny asked.

"That's someone who doesn't give up when the going gets tough," Teach said. "It's a person who's prepared for a catastrophe and looks at it as a challenge rather than the end of the world."

"Why doesn't everyone think like that?"

"It's a long story, son."

"Aw c'mon, tell us."

"Well, to begin with, all animals adapt to their environments. The giraffe has a long neck so it can eat leaves from high in the trees where other animals can't reach. The anteater has a long sticky tongue so it can lick up ants. Can either of you boys tell me how man adapts to his environment?"

The boys shook their heads.

Teach tapped his forehead with a finger. "His brain," he said. "How does your brain help you?"

"Let's take an example. Back before the war, everything was

sunshiny and warm. No one had a care in the world. If you had asked people how they felt about the world they lived in, you would have gotten a lot of different answers. Some people thought that there would never be a war. Others thought there would be a war, but no one would survive. Still, a few thought there would be a war and if they were prepared, they could survive, so they prepared themselves. They built houses, like this one, that would retain their heat. They put in wood stoves that could burn trash. They stored food. They pretty much made themselves independent of the outside world."

"My dad did that," Tod said wistfully.

"Yes, I know. The bombs only killed about ten percent of the people. Most died from starvation caused by the forever winter. Then, there was a breakdown of social organization when people turned against one another and tried to steal what they couldn't grow."

"You mean like the prowlers?"

"Yes."

Mr. Bradford's eyes kept following Heather. The room was warm from the fire and she had taken off her coat and pushed up her sleeves as she worked, punching and poking at her bread dough. The smell of onions that lingered from supper was joined by the smell of yeast and apricots.

His eyes studied her faded jeans, which had been washed so many times they were almost white and had shrunk a little bit more with each washing until she could hardly squeeze into them. The holster with its gun covered her abdomen, the barrel pointing to the gap between her legs and slapping lightly with her movements.

"But," he added, "people have used their brains to adapt to living in every part of the world in a thousand different lifestyles, so it was impossible to wipe them all out in any one catastrophe. The ones who survive today have three things in common: like us, they're tough, self-reliant and they don't trust people."

"Anybody?"

"Nobody! Not if you want to grow up, not if you want to be part of the new race of man." The old man's blue eyes twinkled.

"What will the new men look like?"

"Go look in the mirror," Teach laughed. "I mean the people who survive the forever winter will be different than the people

73

who lived before. They will have evolved just like the giraffe and the anteater. All the soft trusting souls will be gone. The survivors will be solitary animals. They won't trust people, so they won't work together and form societies, not for a thousand years."

The laughter slowly dissolved from Mr. Bradford's face until it became a sardonic grin. He stared at the flame of the lamp. His face clouded over and Tod sensed dark thoughts forming behind those powerful—knowing—gray eyes. Tod couldn't concentrate on his made-up problem. He sat transfixed watching Mr. Bradford's face growing meaner and meaner.

Suddenly Teach sprang from his chair and grabbed Heather around the neck with one hand and her gun with the other. A bread pan went flying from her hands and landed in a pile of dishes in the sink. There was the sound of broken glass and then dead silence. He held her in a choke hold and pointed the gun at her face, the barrel almost touching her eye.

"As long as we're on the subject, I wonder what kind of a surprise your old man is cooking up for me out in the barn."

Heather didn't say anything, but her face turned as white as her flour-covered hands.

Tod saw his mother was frightened and he wanted to help her, but he was petrified, afraid even to breathe.

"I've been doing a little math of my own and I don't like the way it adds up," Mr. Bradford said. "The project's over, the generator's working, and Fred isn't the kind to keep someone around his table if he doesn't have to. And he isn't dumb enough to send me packing now that I know the layout of this place. So we're going to walk out to the barn and surprise him before he surprises me."

They left the house, Heather obediently leading the way. Tod and Danny ran to the window and looked out, but it was too dark to see anything except the strange iridescent glow that filtered through thin spots in the clouds. What his mom called a nuclear rainbow.

The barn door opened and he could see his mother and Mr. Bradford silhouetted in a square of light. Then they disappeared inside. The door swung shut for a minute and he thought he heard a shot. Long painful moments later the door opened again and he recognized his mother's figure framed in light as she came out. Tod ran to the door and threw it open. Heather crossed the yard, walking rapidly towards him. He started towards her. Danny raced past him and threw his arms around her, crying unashamedly.

"What happened?" Tod stammered.

"Don't worry. Your father's all right. Let's go inside and close the door before we lose all of our heat."

"What happened to Teach?" Tod asked.

"Mr. Bradford isn't with us anymore."

"Where did he go? What happened to him?"

"He's dead."

They went inside and closed and chained the door. Heather sat down quickly in a chair as if she was dizzy.

"What's dad doing? Is he going to bury him?"

"No. Your father's cutting him up so his body will freeze easier. That way the meat won't spoil." She spoke softly as if she were tired and covered her mouth with her hands. She looked like she might be sick and then her eyes clouded like she was getting ready to cry real loud, but nothing came out.

"We're not going to have to eat him, are we?" Danny pleaded.

"No! Of course not." She put her arm around Danny and squeezed him tight. "We're going to have a garden, remember." Heather had regained her composure. She hated to tell the boys certain things, they were so young, but she couldn't lie to them. She had to tell them the truth. They would be growing up in this world and they would have to be prepared for the reality of it. "We'll need oil for our lamps, though."

That night Tod lay in bed waiting for sleep to come. It seemed every time he was ready to fall asleep, he would think of something that would make him wide awake again. He was glad Fred hadn't been killed. Fred was the third father he'd had in the past year. He didn't like getting new fathers all the time. The other two had died just the way Teach said. They trusted people. When he got big, he wouldn't make the mistake of trusting *anyone*.

There was something else Teach had said that bothered him. How long would Fred keep *him* around if he didn't need him?

THE LAST CRUISE OF
THE ZEPPELIN *TEMPEST*
J.P. Boyd

EDITOR'S INTRODUCTION

An all-out nuclear war is not the only way to Armageddon. Sometimes a conventional war that drags on too long can be as decisive in its effects as a shorter, more devastating war. Athens and Sparta learned this during the Peloponnesian war, which Athens officially won but never recovered from, both in its economic effects and its erosion of Athenian democratic principles. For a while afterwards Athens still wore the mantle of empire, but really it was just holding it for an upstart Macedonian named Alexander.

On the planet Eahonua, a former Earth colony, the two major powers are engaged in a prolonged conflict that threatens to grind both nations down to dust. A few can see this and have the courage to speak out.

In any society it is the soldier's job to uphold the principles of his country—be they just or unjust. In free societies many intellectuals believe it is their job to uphold civilized values—be it peacetime or war. When these two forces collide in the arena of war, there can be only one winner.

———————————————•|•———————————————

JOHN MARKHAM, THE FLOTILLA COMMODORE, WALKED ALONG the beach between the bay and the zeppelin hangars. He was a very tall man, and even though he leaned on his cane, the elderly gray-haired intelligence officer beside him had trouble matching his stride.

Over most of the planet Eahonua, the Archipelagan War had staggered into its sixth year. Ground armies contested the Isle du Haut while fleets of zeppelins took turns hurling bombs across the ocean. And yet here, on the northern coast of the demi-continent of Grasse, none of them had so much as seen a Karlan in over a year. The ocean waves broke as softly, as gently, as they had for all the thousands of years since the starship from that now-mythical world, the Earth, had fallen like a meteor and broken its back. And the blue-green sky, two dozen times denser than that of man's now-forgotten home, was empty and peaceful except for a handful of fluffy clouds.

" 'A pocket carrier raid within three months. Perhaps the Karlan has weighed off already.' That was my message, Commodore. But what do I tell the Admiral?"

Instead of answering, the tall man, who was not yet thirty, stopped and looked sadly at his aching, shattered leg.

"Pain, Commodore?"

Markham looked down at the intelligence officer, an ex-professor old enough to be his father or his teacher, and nodded. "Use it or lose it, the medics said." It hurt damnably, but his three-times-a-day walks had made it stronger.

"But I do owe you an answer, Lieutenant. While you were still sleeping, I had a brief staff meeting and gave my orders. If the Karlan swings north to the ice line to escape the patrols from Vzygny Island, as I-Branch thinks, then we'll have to stand out far to sea, and make much longer patrols than my ships were designed for."

The old scholar nodded. In the five years since he was drafted, he had only worked his way up to the two rings of a lieutenant, but he could read performance specs as well as any admiral.

"Yes. They know about the coastal watch. The decoded radio traffic and the reports from our laborer in the shipyard indicate—"

"—the carrier zeppelin will stay far at sea, and launch its Heavier-Than-Airs from maximum range. Yes, Lieutenant."

The commodore continued, "*Tempest* is the only one of the four zeppelins under my command with sufficient endurance to take the first watch. The other three—"

77

"That old woolback?" said the lieutenant incredulously, using the service slang for a canvas-hulled airship.

Markham shifted his cane and resumed walking. "She's all I have. And I'm going to go cloud-walking myself. No one has regularly flown airships on such long missions. *Tempest*'s captain is a pimple-faced young man who would still be in college, perhaps hearing you lecture, if it hadn't been for the war. He's good, but I have to see for myself."

"And the rest?"

"The Flag Wheel-King—" He stopped, embarrassed at the slang, and went on. "The Flotilla Engineer, to give him his proper title, will supervise the modifications. One ship on patrol, one on ten-minute standby, one in the hangar under the welding torches. He'll add additional fuel tanks and storage."

"But how will you weigh-off?"

"We won't. We'll have to use the runway." Markham saw the older man's face blanch and smiled. "I know. But we don't have any choice."

"And *Tempest*?"

"He'll stay as he is. There are rumors he'll be recalled to training branch soon, if he lasts. He's one of the five oldest zeppelins in Fleet Aero."

"Commodore, this coast has been stripped of flack guns to supply the embattled cities in the south. If a raid comes, a handful of incendiaries could put Old Town to the torch and roast thousands of civilians, and H.E. on the ball-bearing factory on the Inland Waterway could halve our aircraft production for months. But if the carrier planes turn on one of your reccos—"

"I know, Lieutenant. My four zeppelins will become three."

On that gloomy note, their conversation ceased. They walked on in silence for a few more minutes and had turned back from the fern that was Markham's current limit of endurance, when the serenity of the waves and sea-breeze was broken by a shout.

"John!" A voice hailed them from behind the sand dunes. The lined face of the I-Branch officer wrinkled with anger. It was galling to salute men thirty years his junior, but to hear a subordinate call the commodore by his first name—

A short, stocky figure appeared at the top of the sand. His uniform was half-buttoned, his hair wild and uncombed, and he staggered down the slope unsteadily.

Markham leaned on his cane and said, "Korvette-Captain Talin, Deputy Commodore. Lieutenant—"

"Why the hell wasn't I awakened? You had a staff meeting before breakfast?"

Talin's alcohol-sodden breath almost made the old man retch.

Commodore Markham ignored the interruption and the powerful, muscular arms waving in his face and said mildly, "Yes, Bram. And training is more important than ever. I didn't need to wake you up to tell you your job. Loading *Tempest* is taking longer than I hoped. You have time to go flying."

The deputy commodore nodded, blinked, and looked at the ground as if dazed. Then he murmured some indecipherable pleasantry toward the I-Branch lieutenant and staggered back over the dune.

"Sir, that man is drunk! He was insubordinate and intoxicated and—"

Markham waved one arm while balancing on his cane with the other. "Patience, patience, Lieutenant! He's a good man when he's on wing. He's coming cloudwalking, too."

"The two senior officers both on a single ship?"

Markham nodded. "Something's been eating him up from within like a cancer. Over a year. I haven't been able to find it, but maybe if we're both on the zep— I don't know what else to do. Unfortunately, he's a Heavier-Than-Air pilot like me. We both need to see firsthand what it takes to push an airship—and its crew—beyond their normal limits. There's nothing in the ops manual about a two-week patrol."

The lieutenant shut up, but as they walked back towards the administration hut, Markham began moving slower and slower. When he finally could go no farther, the I-Branch officer helped him to sit on the sand and then knelt in front of him.

"You mustn't push yourself so hard. If you'll forgive me for saying so, sir, I think the reason that both you and the Deputy Commodore were transferred here, where it's as quiet as a training base, is because General Staff thought you were both finished."

Markham rubbed his aching leg. "General Staff is probably right. But the war isn't finished, Lieutenant, and until it is, the two of us are going 'walking."

* * *

Korvette-Captain Bram Talin banked his obsolete Piradot fighter and tried to ignore the dull ache of his hangover. Five hundred meters beneath him, a flight of clumsy, two-seat Pelican scouts dove towards the clear waters of the bay. Ahead on the narrow peninsula that housed the airship base, the target crew flashed a green signal lamp. Talin dove after his charges, carefully watching their technique as they leveled off just above the waves and made their firing passes, one by one.

In the dense air, infantry rifles had a useful range of less than one hundred meters, so aerodynes and zeppelins dueled with rockets. The Pelicans' wing-root cannon flung little rounds only twice the thickness of a man's thumb, but the shells could wreck a truck or a half-track. Aurelle, the senior pilot of *Tempest*'s reconnaissance flight, opened fire, and thin plumes of smoke, stained with bright red dye as a tracer, reached out towards the huge paper squares.

When the four planes had rolled up and away towards the zeppelin hangars, Talin's radio crackled, "I have the scores, Deputy Commodore." He listened intently for a moment, then slammed his fist against the side of the cockpit in frustration.

The throbbing in his head flared up, and he waited a moment to calm himself, then touched his chin mike. "Take your flock to the barn, Piotr. We don't want to miss our ride."

As he turned back over the airship hangars, he saw that the woolback *Tempest* was already out on the field, loading extra food, avgas, and oil. Two of her four planes would be left behind; the other pair would hook on only after the zeppelin was airborne. And John Markham, who was to blame for all this, including the hangover, was watching from the grass, braced on his cane.

"To shield the coast, our zeppelins are going to have to break the patrol duration record," the flotilla commodore had told him after the I-Branch lieutenant had delivered his bad news. "One ship on long patrol while the new ships are modified, then two ships thereafter. I-Branch is being cautious, but their best guess is that the raid won't come until the southern rainy season begins."

Talin had been against making *Tempest* the guinea pig right from the beginning. "His two senior officers are barely out of their teens, John. Seth Arden should be stringing for a newspaper, not commanding an airship. And Cal Corliss would still be in college if it weren't for the war.'' But instead he was the Wheel-King, the chief engineer, for an airship so old its diesels were no longer made.

"Nevertheless, I have four zeppelin crews who are torn up with guilt because men are dying by the thousands in the south, and they haven't even *seen* a Karlan on this coast since before either of us was assigned here. We not only need to protect Old Town and the factories scattered along the coast, but we also need something to give this base some pride. To help them live with the guilt.''

And then Markham had told him that both of them were going along, not as pilots but as supercargo, and Talin had flown drunk for the first time since that disastrous wheels-up prang at Kirin. He had been drinking long before that crash, of course, but only when the field was socked in or he couldn't fly. Then, after he had been put out to pasture, he had been in a haze for weeks until his old friend Markham, too badly wounded to fly again, had been sent here as commodore.

"Ah, John!'' Talin muttered as he banked in a lazy spiral over the field, remembering. They had first met while teenagers, working odd jobs around the aerodrome in exchange for lessons. Markham, who had been a training instructor during the height of the Firsten campaign, knew how much he loved to fly and encouraged him.

"They're all so *green*, Bram. You know how risky the first five missions are. If a rookie survives those, his odds rise faster than sunlight. We have to give them our experience. I can only teach down here, but you can take them up in groups, fly four or five times a day if you have to, and teach them to survive. Dogfighting, ground attack—then we'll weigh-off the zeps and have the planes and airships duel each other.''

And so it was. When he was flying, Talin was happy, and mostly sober. It astounded him how much he enjoyed training the pilots, the shop talk with them and Markham in the officers' mess. But when the rains came, or avgas was low, his drinking became uncontrollable again. And so Markham was going to dry him out in a great raddled hulk of an airship, and Talin had drunk himself to sleep last night because he could not bear it.

After he had landed and collected his duffel bag, he found

Markham still watching the old woolback swell with gas from the hydrogen vans. But his leg must have pained him, for an airman had brought a stool.

Markham looked somberly at the elderly airship. "If we're ready when the carrier comes, the kids will stop feeling so guilty. If they survive."

Talin swung the bag down from his shoulder and squatted on his haunches. "Sometimes, John, survivors feel even more—" But the freckle-faced Wheel-King had climbed down from the keelway to interrupt, motioning them to come, and Talin never finished his sentence.

Seth Arden was nervous, unconsciously stroking the white cap that he alone wore as the traditional emblem of zeppelin command. Farther back in the control gondola, Commodore Markham had awkwardly folded his very long legs under the chart table and parked his own cap, blue but gold-trimmed, on top of a map. He understood the young captain's tension. In the first place, Arden's flag officer was aboard, and in the second, the youth knew only too well that his boss was inexperienced in airship operations.

Markham had heard the grumbling. "You're a wingfoot, John, a Heavier-Than-Air pilot just like me," Talin had told him. "The cloudwalkers expected that another line officer would be assigned, not a semi-invalid." Markham, who had been badly wounded—and lost his mothership—during that debacle now known as the Second Battle of Corlino, had in fact spent a major part of the war aloft in zeppelins, but the wingfoots were only passengers, and the cloudwalkers did the driving. Now Markham would have to become a cloudwalker, too.

Lt. Arden's other worry was that this flight would be *Tempest*'s first dynamic takeoff in a decade. Even with the planes and pilots, one mechanic, and the cook left behind, the extra supplies made the zeppelin too heavy to simply drop ballast and weigh-off. Instead, the airship would have to run up to speed like an aerodyne and then raise the nose to generate enough lift to unstick.

Kallen, the wizened coxswain, stood with his hands on his wheel and grinned at his captain. "The tinhulls take off dynamically all the time," he said, as if it were a treat.

Lt. Arden, who would never reprimand a good man, made a rumbling noise in his throat and scowled at the keelway overhead. Markham could barely suppress his mirth as Arden yelled up the ladder. "Hurry up! Get it lashed down. Takeoff in three minutes!"

Moments later, he looked down at the weight list and shook his head. "A zeppelin hull is not a very efficient airfoil." He glanced at the commodore. "But it's the only wing we have."

Markham merely nodded. On a large ship, the executive officer would oversee the ship's trim, but on a small vessel like this with only three officers and two dozen crew, excluding the HTA's, Arden served as his own ballast-master.

Cal Corliss, the freckled chief engineer, climbed down the ladder from the keelway, bareheaded. Like the ship's captain, the chief engineer by long tradition wore a cap of unique color—black—to symbolize his special authority, but by equally long tradition, the cap was parked on a nail as long as the zeppelin was in the air.

Smoothing his unruly, windblown mop, the redhead grinned. "The engines are as good as the day they came from the factory, Captain. We stripped each one and reground the cylinders, and they're all humming like fine watches. Ready to weigh-off, sir."

Markham hid a smile. Lt. Arden had watched the engine rehabs from afar during the weeks when Corliss and his black gang were rejuvenating the elderly diesels. Nonetheless, tradition demanded that line officers should feign ignorance of life in the motor gondolas, and that the engineers and mechanics in turn socialize only among themselves.

Divided like cloudwalkers and wingfoots, he thought. The Navy has too damn many cliques.

While he was finishing his reflections, Arden reached for the logbook and made the mandatory entry as ballast officer, then had the redhead sign. He nodded at the coxswain. "Engines to full power. Signal ground crew to prepare to release chocks."

The Wheel-King sprinted up the ladder as the ensign called out the readings from the engine repeaters. "Revolutions increasing, sir. Passing eighty percent. Ninety percent. A hundred percent. Full war emergency, sir."

"Release chocks!" Arden dropped into his chair. "Hold him

down as long as you can—'' But by then the airship was already moving.

Tempest's bulky, sixty-meter length accelerated slowly. When he reached sixty kilometers an hour, as fast as he had ever traveled even in the air, Arden shouted, ''Elevators hard up! Hold him at six degrees—maximum dynamic lift!''

They were rapidly running out of macadam, but as the sea came closer and closer, the nose lifted, sluggishly. Arden cursed under his breath and said out loud, ''He's so damned heavy!'' Then the inclinometer showed that the up angle had increased to maximum lift and Arden shouted, ''Release the trollies!''

As the heavy undercarriage frames dropped away, the nose pitched up. For one awful moment, it appeared that the nose-up would continue until the hull would stall like an airplane wing. Then the elevator man corrected, and slowly, ponderously, the bow came down a handful of meters. As one trolley jackknifed over the restraining barrier and came to rest upside down, half awash in the sea, the airship cleared the wooden fence by a couple of meters.

Markham watched the waves skipping by underneath him, astonishingly close, and shook his head in wonder. He had never watched a takeoff from the control gondola in half a thousand zeppelin flights.

The young lieutenant waited until the tail was fifty meters up and then let out a deep breath. ''We made it, Commodore.''

''We did indeed.'' And then Markham sighed, for he had suddenly realized how very boring the next two weeks were going to be.

Kvt.-Capt. Talin became morose and withdrawn. He spent most of his spare time reading the trashy, escapist novels he had brought with him or obtained by trades with other airmen. When reading bored him, he stood on the top of the hull with the bow lookout, feeling the wind on his face as the airship slowly pushed through the thick, blue-green sky under the power of just one of its four wheels.

Lt. Arden was disturbed by this alteration in the usual routine of his ship. ''My man can't be too comfortable with a three-stripe Korvette-Captain looking over his shoulder.''

Markham merely smiled. ''The Deputy Commodore is farsighted, the best pair of eyes I ever knew. That's why he was the best.'' And so Talin was left alone.

The real incidents of the first ten days of the patrol were the predictable crises of a long airship flight. Number 3 wheel lost a main bearing, and the mechanics had to strip the whole engine. A modern, duraluminum-clad zeppelin wore an insulating layer of helium just inside the hull to reduce the risk of fire from the hydrogen in the inner cells. *Tempest* had been one of the first ships with the double lining, but her engines were still slung in gondolas beneath the hull in the old style instead of in fire-walled capsules within it. The mechanics had to haul parts up and down the open ladders, cursing like dock laborers. Arden let his command drift with the wind until the job was done, and then restarted but a single engine.

The scout planes had hooked onto the airship's trapezes almost as soon as *Tempest* had reached its cruising altitude of a thousand meters. Dropped from the overhead monorail that ran the length of the hangar, retrieved by pulling the nose up sharply until the plane's hook struck and locked onto the metal bar of the trapeze, the aerodynes flew alternating missions, one in the morning and one in the evening, until they had burned off enough fuel to lighten the badly overloaded zeppelin. When the avgas ran low, however, Arden ordered the flights suspended until two days before mission end when the airship would again be close to land.

Piotr Aurelle was decidedly unhappy. The senior HTA pilot wore two stripes like Arden himself. ''The airplanes are the eyes of the airship! We can search great swaths of territory to either side of the ship's path, covering as much ground as *Tempest* himself could watch in a whole day. What is the point—?''

Arden, who was sitting at the chart table in the control gondola, shrugged helplessly. ''We can only carry so much fuel.''

Up in the keelway, which was a triangular passage framed by three large beams that ran the length of the ship, Talin whispered to Markham, ''No wonder we wingfoots are so unpopular!''

It was the first time the deputy commodore had smiled in a month. At dinner that evening, Ensign Ishikawa was officer-of-the-watch, so Arden and Corliss were crowded around the small table with their superiors.

For several days, they had eaten in almost complete silence.

Markham would ask a few routine questions about the families and background of the two young officers, and then run out of small talk. Lt. Arden and his redheaded, freckled lord of the engines were too intimidated to initiate conversation on their own. Tonight, the commodore tried a different tack.

"You two remind me very much of Bram and I when we were younger. You, Captain, are like me. Very responsible. When I was given my first flight, I was so damn serious about looking after the young ones that I flew more than a hundred missions before I scored my first air-to-air victory. I had been pulled back from the front in disgrace and given a training squadron."

Talin looked up from his corned beef and said, "A Wyndan, wasn't it? A four-engined flying boat?"

Markham nodded. "Yes. It was scouting for a zeppelin raid. I took a big torpedo-plane out, alone, to look for it in fog and rain. I had already turned for home when I found it."

A half-smile crossed Talin's face. "Yes. It always amused me that after such a long famine, you broke your maiden in such a big way. Four engines!"

Markham looked at the awe in the eyes of the two youngsters and almost laughed. "Actually, the sheer size of the Wyndan made it simpler. I didn't have to dogfight. Just line up and shoot. And I was always a good shot."

Arden found his voice. "Captain Talin, how did you break your maiden?"

Talin stirred his potatoes with his fork and smiled. "I was still flying ground attack. Four hundred sorties before I was transferred to fighters. Our escort was up topside, tangling with a flock of Karlans, and as the swarm broke up, this bandit dove down out of the melee and leveled off a few hundred meters below me. Afterwards, my squadron leader chewed my tail off. 'A Stormdragon is not a fighter, Sublieutenant Talin. Your mission is to attack tanks and strafe ground troops, Sublieutenant Talin.' But it was the best bounce I ever had."

He held his hand high, palm down, and then brought it down in a parody of a dive. As he flattened his hand parallel to the table, he imitated the sounds of rocket shells whooshing from their launchers. "Right on his tail. Later, I bagged two more, the worthy and late Lieutenant-Captain Pines notwithstanding. Then it was decided my true talents lay in other directions than ground attack.''

He suddenly laid down his fork. "It's queer how little I remember them, my first squadron-mates. Bombing 14, attached to the mothballed-but-technically-still-active zeppelin *Hurlant*." Then he began eating vigorously, with his head almost on his chest.

Markham said softly, "Why not?"

Talin put his fork down again and looked at the commodore. "Because they're all dead, John. Twenty-three of us when the war broke out. You were a college boy in the reserves, flying for fun on weekends, but we were all regulars. Professionals. And I'm the only one who's left. There might be a gunner in a nursing hospice, one or two. But all the pilots are dead except one. And he would have joined them if he weren't such a yellowbelly.''

Abruptly, Talin pushed away from the table and bolted. For a few seconds, there was shocked silence, and then Markham picked up his knife and fork and resumed eating. Eventually, the two youngsters followed suit. The redheaded engineer said timidly, "He was very heavily decorated, wasn't he?"

Markham sighed. "Yes. The Golden Star with three bars. The Black Cross with Oak Leaves. He shot down 27 aerodynes, burned a small aerostat, and destroyed heaven-knows-how-many tanks. He flew more than six hundred sorties.''

Arden paused, as if screwing up his courage, and asked, "Why was he assigned to a non-flying post?"

"He pranged a plane by landing with the wheels up. Ground-looped another. Although he was usually more or less sober for missions, he was soused whenever the field was socked in, or there was a lull. After his leave, he just wasn't effective anymore. And he had become a danger to his squadron-mates.''

The two young officers suddenly were very quiet. Markham waited until they were almost finished, and then said softly, "War's not a very romantic business, and sometimes even the survivors, the bravest of the brave, are casualties. But you'll do fine when your time comes. And Bram will someday be himself again. I'm sure of it.''

But that night, Talin awakened half the ship when he began

howling in the middle of a nightmare. Markham closed his eyes, turned on his side, and tried to forget.

The following afternoon, Kvt.-Capt. Talin was back at his usual spot in the lookout cockpit on the top of the bow. When the zeppelin was moving at full speed, the slipstream was as powerful as a fast-moving river, and the lookout hid within a glass-sided canopy faired smoothly into the hull. At low speed, however, one could open the canopy and stand up for a better view.

Talin wasn't pleased with his nocturnal moaning, but after half a dozen years of war and a few months of heavy drinking, he seemed to have lost his capacity for being embarrassed. As he scanned the horizon with his binoculars, the emotional numbness he felt was what he had once sought in liquor. Now, he had not taken a drink in almost two weeks, and he felt—himself.

When his legs tired, he sat down, but the lookouts stood throughout their whole watch. "Your legs are younger than mine, Nieland."

"Yessir." But there was doubt in the boy's eyes, and Talin realized why: for all his rank and experience, the deputy commodore was only twenty-five.

When Talin rose into the slipstream again, he slowly panned the horizon—and stopped. "Aircraft. Bearing two points to port."

The teenage lookout strained his eyes, but saw nothing. "Sorry, sir. I don't—"

"Control room." Cupping his ear to the intercom, Talin waited for a reply. "Multiple aircraft. Friendlies in the area?"

Down below, he knew Lt. Arden was poring through flimsies of routine traffic in the radio room while Markham consulted the advisories from C-in-C, North Grasse.

A sputter and then a backfire told him that the three idle engines were starting up. Talin sat down and tugged at the airman until he had done the same, then pulled the canopy over them. After a minute of cursing the sunlight glinting off the curved glass, he made the boy raise the canopy a few centimeters so that he could poke his binoculars through the crack.

The zeppelin turned to run away from the Karlans, but after a couple of minutes, it was clear that the airship had been seen, and was slowly being overtaken. In the dense air, the economical cruising speed of an aircraft was only moderately greater than that of a modern, metal-hulled zeppelin. The airship had the advantage of a higher ratio of volume (and horsepower) to skin area. "A battleship is as squat as a tramp coal-barge, but it sails as fast as a destroyer," a lieutenant-captain in the sea navy had once told him. But *Tempest*'s tired engines and oft-patched linen hull, which sometimes showed little sand ripples at high speed, were even bigger handicaps.

Six Kutara dive bombers and six Starspray fighters. He was close enough to see them clearly now. No doubt the original target had been land installations, but *Tempest* had already radioed a warning to the mainland. With surprise lost, a zeppelin would be a much worthier and safer prize.

Talin rested the binoculars in his lap for a moment, and thought of the irony. So many hours in planes, and now he, the last of Bombing 14, would die in the final, fiery fall of a burning zeppelin. So helpless, and yet what a spectacular finish to all their dreams!

Beneath him, he felt the slight rumble as the airship's two remaining aerodynes, two-seat Pelican reccos poorly suited to dogfighting, were towed to the end of the monorail and dropped off. A little lighter, the zeppelin gained a couple more kilometers per hour. His escorts flew the same course, but rising, trading speed for height.

The Karlans were gaining altitude, too, albeit more sluggishly.

"Why are they climbing?" the boy demanded, eyes glued to his lenses.

Talin put a reassuring hand on his shoulder. "The bandits have a little problem. The Kutaras are dive bombers. Instead of carrying armor-piercing rockets like a zep-destroyer, they're armed with free-fall bombs."

"Bombs?"

"Why waste a rocket motor on a bridge?"

The youth smiled, and Talin decided it was time he stopped feeling sorry for himself and went to war.

Down in the control room, the mood was very somber. Markham nodded as Talin jumped the last three rungs of the ladder and turned around.

"We've flashed the mainland, Bram, and the standby ship is already in the air. *Wrathful* is offloading reccos in favor of fighters, and fueling. She'll weigh-off in half an hour. The coastal aerodrome has sent two flights of fighters, but they're at least an hour and a half away."

Talin nodded. The commodore was a cautious and systematic man, and one zeppelin was always kept on ten-minute notice, even in the quiet theater of Grasse, but *Tempest* was too far at sea.

"In short, it's up to Piotr and Harry."

Markham nodded.

The junior officer, Ishikawa, called out, "Our planes have turned back! They're getting in position!"

So they were, but many minutes passed before the Pelicans made their pass. Then, far above the Karlans, the two scouts fell like thunderbolts.

Staring through his binoculars, Talin muttered, "Get close, Piotr, get close!" Only a split second before the two tiny dark dots collided with the higher of the two flocks, flashes of flame erupted from the wingroots.

A Karlan Starspray rolled over and shed a wing as the two Sylvans shot through the flight of fighters. "My God, Harry almost hit him," said Arden, as the more distant recco zoomed over a banking fighter, and just missed the rising wingtip. Then the heavy reconnaissance planes, still diving, bore down on the bombers. When the Pelicans leveled off, above and behind so as to have overlapping targets, big flashes of flame appeared under their wings.

"The 'Bolts!" muttered Lt. Arden, using the service slang for the ten-kilogram rockets that the reccos carried on quadruple racks under each wing.

A split second later, huge flashes appeared against the blue-green sky. One Kutara was hit in the tail and port wing, and disintegrated. Another rocket took a second bomber in the engine, and the aircraft fell seaward as a giant ball of flame. Then—

One scout dove cleanly through the wreckage, but the other Pelican flew into a storm of debris, and fell tumbling towards the sea.

Even now, as Lt. Aurelle made a broad, sweeping turn to get the sun behind him, the fighters were re-forming.

Talin brought his binoculars to his chest. "Piotr won't last long now."

Markham nodded. "But it was magnificent for their first fight. You were a very good teacher, Bram."

"The interesting question is, what will the bombers do?"

Seth Arden, who had commanded his ship calmly in spite of his youth, suddenly lost his temper. It was one thing to die, his feelings told him, but another to listen to a fool. "Climb above and let go! What do you think they'll do? Sir."

The coxswain said, "Not all of them, sir."

In a moment, the others understood what he meant. One bomber was not climbing, but had turned away towards the horizon and its distant mothership.

"Shrapnel from a 'Bolt or a shell from their wing cannon. Maybe even friendly fire. The bomber gunners must have cut loose when the rockets ripped through." Talin paused. "Only three left. This is beginning to have possibilities."

Markham spoke sharply. "What do you mean?"

"Look, we have half a dozen turrets of anti-aerodyne cannon plus our main armament. The bombers can't simply match course and speed and drift in close. Our shells would cut them to pieces. They'll start their runs a couple of kilometers up, tip over, and dive on us. That's what they're trained to do!"

"But we're not a stationary target."

"No. Seaships zigzag like crazy when they're being bombed, and sometimes a whole stick will miss. We're faster and more maneuverable than anything in the wetbottoms."

Also wider, but Markham forbore to say so.

"The critical moment is when they've committed to the dive. It's very difficult for even a veteran pilot to change the angle once they've pushed over."

Markham put his lenses to his eyes for a few moments, thinking.

"Bram, you have the best eyes, and the experience as an attack pilot. At the right moment—"

Talin nodded.

. Lt. Arden added, "I'll order the men to act directly on your command, sir. One word. Motor crews, too."

The four propellers were mounted on gimbaled outriggers so

that they could be rotated forwards, backwards, or down to give fine control for landing. In a pinch, however, the wheels could also be spun to turn *Tempest* in his own length.

As Talin sprinted up the ladder into the hull, the commodore turned to his young captain and said, "Before they dive, let's see what we can do to spoil their aim, Seth." And the airship began to twist and turn at random, climbing and diving, using his full three-dimensional freedom to confuse the bombers.

Tempest's hull was built on three triangular keelways, themselves forming a triangle, and the upper port and starboard keelways anchored two turrets of 12cm rocket guns and four smaller mounts of paired 30mm cannon. At the bow and stern, the keelways shrank into single beams that curved together and merged, and provided the foundation for two more light cannon pairs. A moment after the zeppelin began to dodge, her main armament began to fling heavy rockets skyward.

Talin was banked and buffeted by the zigzags as he climbed up to the lookout station, but the gunners had it worse.

The lookout cursed and said, "Our shells are way off, sir." The time-fused rockets seemed to be bursting at the right altitude, but the ship was jinking so erratically that the smoke puffs were as much as three hundred meters wide.

The Karlan dive bombers were at least a kilometer above them, but still climbing in a broad, lazy spiral. "We're not a bloody bridge," Talin muttered to himself. One shouldn't attack a moving target from the same great height that was appropriate for a foundry or a roundhouse, and in some perverse way, the Karlans' stupidity bothered him.

He had little hope for the big rockets. In the heavy atmosphere, projectile weapons were useless beyond a hundred meters, and only ground troops carried them. All longer-range shells had to be pushed along through the dense air by rocket exhaust. But even the heavy 12cm rounds traveled so slowly that they could be easily dodged at long range.

For what seemed an eternity, the planes and zeppelin continued their mad dance. Climbing, always climbing, the bombers mimicked the airship's course changes with disdainful nimbleness. When they broke the spiral, Talin gripped his binoculars harder. Simultaneously, each plane reversed in a split-S, snapped out of the half-roll, and pushed over.

92

He had only a moment to decide. "Port!" The zeppelin slewed violently under the combined push of full rudder and the four pivoted wheels, but the bombers were falling like stones.

The light guns opened up as the planes fell within a kilometer, and thin plumes of red-dyed smoke crisscrossed his field of view. The bombers sideslipped, adjusting, and kept coming. The ack-ack plumes slewed as the airship turned, and then swung—too slowly—back towards the planes.

"Up! Stand him on his tail!"

Tempest's nose pitched up under full elevator, and the propellers were pivoted again. The bombers had been forced to flatten their dives as the zeppelin turned away from them. Now, suddenly, it rose before them like a whale sounding from the sea.

The planes abruptly rolled away. Fingers of smoke erupted as they turned—the tail gunners trying their luck—and a few shells ripped through *Tempest*'s outer cover.

Talin grinned at the white-faced lookout, who was clinging to an exposed corrugated beam as the airship stood on its nose. "An aerodyne would have stalled at a steep angle like this, but a zep is buoyant. We can climb vertically if we must!"

The intercom crackled. "Commodore to Deputy. We'll make a cloudwalker of you yet."

"Sir. They're coming back!" *Tempest* was already pitching down, but nose-up, it was a stationary target, and the bombers had reversed quickly even at the price of diving at a much shallower angle than in a conventional attack. Talin mentally compared the rate of pitch and the speed of the oncoming Karlans and muttered, "Not quite yet, you bastards!"

And then *Tempest* leveled off and turned, spoiling the aim of the shallow-diving aircraft. Again they rolled away to the left and right without releasing their bombs. And the dance continued.

For ten minutes, twenty minutes, half an hour, the three bombers and the zeppelin traced a three-dimensional minuet in the blue-green sky. Four times, the Karlans bluffed a run; three times, they closed near enough for their gunners to rip more holes in *Tempest*'s rubberized linen. The airship was leaking helium, but unlike a blimp where the lifting gas was pressurized to stiffen the limp outer cover and maintain its teardrop shape, the cells in a rigid were paper-thin, and connected to spring-loaded valves.

Nieland knew this, but was still worried about loss of lift.

Talin sighed, still peering through his binoculars. The Karlans were circling, as if their baffled flight leader was hoping for inspiration. "The valves pop open if the over-pressure is even a single millimeter of mercury. The helium isn't hissing out; it's *diffusing*. Don't worry."

The intercom crackled. "Bram, their mothership is coming, and this dance has brought us no closer to land. We have to end it."

Talin listened carefully and acknowledged the message.

The whole ship had heard, but Nieland was puzzled. "Sir, are we really—?" The ship lurched into a tight turn and held it, spinning round and round in its own length as if its helm had jammed hard over. After ten dizzying revolutions, the zeppelin straightened out and ran for the coast.

For perhaps half a minute, the baffled Karlans hung in the sky, waiting, and then they dove.

Talin watched the heavy rockets of *Tempest*'s main turrets etch the blue-green air with thin lines of red-and-black smoke and the great black time-bursts. In the background, he saw that three fighters had returned to fly top cover. Pity. He had liked Piotr Aurelle, even with his rages.

In the dense atmosphere, the air bursts were rattling the Karlans like depth charges shaking a submarine, but the gunnery ensign had fired more live rounds today than in all his previous service. So late in the war, ammunition was too precious to waste on training. The dive bombers continued on a steady course.

Talin waited, willing his eyes to concentrate on the bomb bay doors of the lead plane. When he saw a sudden flash of black, he shouted, "Starboard!" Yet he was still surprised by the abrupt sideways acceleration.

Six black bombs hurling downward like winged raindrops. Slender as pencils to cut through the thick mixture of argon, nitrogen, and oxygen. Live by the bomb, die by the bomb, even if he had flown twenty dozens of sorties in a fighter.

The iron darts flashed past. For one heart-stopping moment, Talin waited for an explosion, and then relaxed. He was puzzled by the ugly plumes of smoke trailing sideways from the bow, but— He froze. On the port side, almost hidden by the curvature of the hull, was a crater a meter in diameter.

"John, we've been hit! Portside! How bad—?"

Astonishingly, he heard laughter. When it subsided, Markham explained, "The bomb ripped right through the wool and the bags, missing the framework. The time fuse detonated it a few meters below us and it blew in a couple of windows in the stern motor car."

Talin laughed, turned around in his seat, and let his head slump back against the glass.

"Thank God for woolbacks." And then he laughed again, clapped a very confused Nieland on the back, and climbed down to the control car.

Talin looked at Markham and smiled. "They were very green, John. Real pros wouldn't have been bounced by a couple of clumsy Pelicans, or made so many dummy passes, or—"

"Or been fooled by our wholly imaginary rudder problem. Too true. A virgin air group, sent to get experience on a milk run. That's my guess."

Talin nodded. "How the hell did we turn so fast?"

"I had Ishikawa unscrew the warheads on a couple of rounds and brace them against the bow frame with a firing line running down to the control car. It was tough while we were zigzagging, but the riggers did it."

Talin shook his head and mentally amended his earlier prayer: And thank God for Markham's two years at the university before he was called up.

"It's good to see you smiling, Bram."

"It'll be even better to have solid ground under my feet again."

"Well, you'll have to wait a little longer. With most of our fuel and supplies gone and no more aircraft, we're still buoyant even with the gas we lost. We're going to continue the patrol until we've set the record."

Wrathful's scout planes spotted the pocket carrier just as it launched a second strike. A land-based squadron was vectored to intercept while the strike was still far from land, and half a dozen Karlans tumbled flaming into the ocean. The carrier itself, however, stayed well at sea and escaped.

The evening after the battle, Markham's aching leg and the excitement kept him from sleep. He found Talin in the auxiliary control post built into the lower tail fin, weeping.

When he bumped into Talin, the tears had stopped, but the big streaks still wet his cheeks.

"I'm sorry, Bram. I was on my feet too much today, and my leg—"

"Don't apologize. I couldn't sleep either."

"I'm glad you were with us. You saved us, Bram. But I'm sorry I put you through all this."

Talin looked down at the moonlight glinting off the waves. The control position was cramped, just a window with a rudder wheel directly under the glass and the elevator wheel to the left. He had wedged himself awkwardly between a couple of beams. Then he shook his head.

"No, no. You don't understand. It's not the drinking. It's the dead."

He got to his feet and rubbed his head, almost hitting Markham in the process. The little station was too cramped to pace, so he looked up at Markham and went on, "This was the first time I ever cried. In the whole war. The first. Maybe that was what I needed."

He fingered the inclinometer. "The others in Bombing 14. They had wives and girlfriends and mothers who cried for them. Maybe even over them if the bodies were recovered. But they weren't *there*. They could never understand what it was like. Civilians can't understand us, John. What we dream about. The camaraderie in a squadron or a zep."

He looked up at his friend. "Maybe what was missing was someone to mourn for them. Maybe that's what the last survivor was supposed to do for his wing-mates."

Markham leaned back against a beam and let his hands and his good leg take his weight. It was difficult to concentrate while his leg ached, but he thought he understood.

" 'Why me?' Is that what you couldn't answer?"

"I think so, John. Why I alone survived. I'm not more virtuous. I don't have more children. There were a dozen pilots

96

with more reason to live than I had. I couldn't live with the unfairness."

Markham let out a deep breath. Survivor guilt, a medical officer had once told him, was pinned over the heart with every non-posthumous medal.

"We all have to handle it, Bram. I suppose my way was to become the good shepherd. The flight leader who never lost a rookie. Who worked his training squadron to death. You got into that same mode when you were in the air, but on the ground—"

"I'm a dumb fighter jock, John. I— In the air, I was always happy, but when I was on the ground, nothing in this bloody world made sense."

They talked a few more minutes until Talin seemed himself again. He was still in the auxiliary control station, asleep, when an airman on rounds found him the following morning. But his last question troubled Markham, and left him wondering if Talin would relapse.

"Why me? What am I still here for?"

But near nightfall, as if in answer to a prayer, Talin saw Aurelle and his gunner drifting on the sea, even as he had been drifting.

For all of them, it was time for deliverance. He opened the intercom and set the rescue in motion.

THE FUTURE OF THE GREAT POWERS
Alan Brown

EDITOR'S INTRODUCTION

We live in an age of specialists, particularly in the academic disciplines of history and political science. Most scholars today are better at cataloging details than at charting the grand sweep of history. Yet occasionally a book comes along that blows the cobwebs right out of the dusty halls of academia; *The Rise and Fall of the Great Powers* is one such book. I do not agree with all of Mr. Kennedy's conclusions, but his book is thought-provoking and raises a number of important questions, much as Edward Luttwak's book *The Grand Strategy of the Roman Empire* did. A fitting companion to both is Paul Johnson's *Modern Times*. The three taken together give one much to think on.

Here Alan Brown provides us with a welcome introduction to *The Rise and Fall of the Great Powers*.

———————————— • ¦ • ————————————

OCCASIONALLY, A BOOK COMES ALONG WHICH OFFERS A REVOlutionary view of the world and its future, yet also is immediately and widely recognized as valid and authoritative. *The Rise and Fall of the Great Powers*, by Professor Paul Kennedy, is such a book. At a time when most historians seem obsessed with minutiae, and political scientists limit themselves with deterministic mathematical formulas, Kennedy has delivered a work which looks at the broad sweep of history and makes a number of insightful observations based on this analysis. As with any book which stands out from the crowd, however, Kennedy's has generated a storm of controversy that has spread far beyond the cloistered world of academics. In this article I will show how Kennedy has addressed the past, present, and near future. I will also attempt to put some of his ideas in context with those of his critics. I will then look at what impact Kennedy's book could have on the field of science fiction, and what guesses we can make about the future using the principles he identifies. First, as an introduction for those who haven't read it, and as a recap for those who have, I will review the main points of Kennedy's book.

The Rise and Fall of the Great Powers

Despite the fact that most of the attention given to the book concerns its analysis of present events and speculation on future ones, Professor Kennedy's work is first and foremost a study of history. It is framed within the "Great Power" system that emerged during the Renaissance, where individual nation-states have vied for power within an ever more limited world. It is a dual history, looking at both the economic and military histories of these Great Powers. By doing so, it reveals the interdependence of these two areas, and points out the huge impact that economic conditions have had on military conflict.

Kennedy's book presents a view of history from a different perspective than most history books. Most historians, especially military historians, concentrate on rulers, treaties and battles, and follow in the tradition of the venerable English historian Sir Edward Creasy, considering battles to be the turning points of both wars and history. Kennedy, on the other hand, concentrates on strength and composition of forces, logistics, and fiscal policies, and sees the outcome of individual

The views expressed in this article are solely those of the author, and do not reflect the official policies or positions of the U.S. Navy, Department of Defense, U.S. Coast Guard, or Department of Transportation.

clashes being less important than the broader forces of economic strength. This focus on lesser-known facts can make Kennedy's book a difficult read in places, especially when the reader is unfamiliar with the portion of history being covered. Yet when the reader reaches sections of the book discussing a period of history that is more familiar, the different perspective gives a new appreciation for the factors which other history books overlook. The Napoleonic Wars, with their attendant economic clashes, their blockades and embargos, appear quite different when the economic underpinnings of military strength are examined along with the military history itself. The Battle of Waterloo, often seen as the decisive end of those wars, is seen as a less important coda to a war that had been decided long before. The rapid expansion of Hitler's Third Reich, long seen as a reflection of his insane ambitions, instead is seen as a desperate race to fuel the artificially imposed economic recovery of Germany with the raw materials and wealth the nation lacked.

Kennedy's conclusions from his analysis seem rather obvious when presented at the end of the massive discourse that supports them. His first conclusion is that the relative strength of Great Powers is not static, and rises and falls due to changes in economics, technology, and political and other factors. The second is that these changes in strength, and the economic competition before Great Power wars begin, are the deciding factor in the outcome of those wars. The normally cautious Kennedy goes so far as to state that in the major Great Power wars ". . . victory has always gone to the side with the greatest material resources." Whether you agree with this position or not, Kennedy's analysis makes it clear that economic factors have played a huge role in the history of warfare, a fact many military historians tend to downplay or overlook. A last point is the identification of what Kennedy calls "imperial overstretch." This is the almost-human tendency of Great Powers to ignore the erosion of their strength, rather like the aging prizefighter who continues to fight long after he should have retired. As Kennedy has pointed out, however, since the erosion is often relative to other powers rather than in real terms, it is difficult to perceive without the benefit of hindsight. Kennedy implies that it is the cost of maintaining empires or hegemonic dominance that is the force which eventually brings the dominant Great Powers down.

As I have said before, the attention to Kennedy's book has been focused not on his historic research, or even on the conclusions he draws from it. Instead, the controversy has centered mostly on what he says about the present and near future in the book's final chapter. When he speaks about the inevitable rise and fall of Great Powers in the past, the reader tends to nod along in complacent agreement. But then he applies those same lessons of history to the current world, and that same reader begins to feel uncomfortable. What we are willing to accept in conjunction with others becomes chilling when Kennedy shows how it relates to us, how the United States has seen its peak and is now following the path of relative decline, like the other dominant Great Powers before it. Kennedy goes to great lengths to show the decline of America's economic and strategic position since its height in World War II. While he takes pains to point out that this decline is only relative at this point, the analysis still stings. The other preeminent power in the current "bipolar" world, the Soviet Union, fares no better; in fact, Kennedy's prognosis for them is even bleaker. Instead of the current balance of power where two states dominate the world strategically, Kennedy sees a return to a world where a larger number of Great Powers jockey for position. He shies away from specific predictions, but does point out that for a number of reasons it appears that Asian powers, notably Japan, appear poised to take a much greater role in the world, due to their increasing economic strength. One other potential power he points out is the European Community. Due to its diversity of governments, languages, and cultures, however, he does not see its coalescing into a single power bloc as being too likely.

Kennedy sees the challenge to modern politicians being a threefold one involving the provisions of military security, the satisfaction of socio-economic needs of their peoples, and the encouragement of sustained growth. Without the first two the nation will suffer in the short term. Without the third, however, he points out that there is no long-term strength or security.

Kennedy's work, in addition to being extremely popular, also triggered widespread debate. He became typecast as the leading proponent of what was branded as "declinist" literature, and his work was widely quoted by persons of all political persuasions. With the 1988 presidential election race at its peak, the book and its ideas had become the focus of much of the introspection and reexamination that invariably accompanies an election year.

Kennedy's points cut counter to the campaign rhetoric of Republicans, eager to convince the electorate that the course steered during the Reagan era was the right one. When viewed from Kennedy's viewpoint, the huge Reagan buildup in military strength, bought as it was through a huge surge in the national debt, could be seen as an attempt to regain past glories at the expense of future strength. It is not so much the military expenditures themselves that hurt, it is the way they were purchased.

Yet the Democrats, who embraced Kennedy's seeming condemnation of defense spending with open arms, also fell short. Their answer was not to spend less, but to transfer monies cut from defense into social programs. It is clear that in campaign promises, the true crisis went unaddressed or glossed over by both sides. This is the need to encourage the long-term strength and growth of the U.S. economy. No one said that it was time to tighten our belts, to cease the deficit spending that both parties share the blame for, to cease covering up reverses in the economy by mortgaging the future. It may be that this is one of the signs of "overstretch," this unwillingness to pay the price of continuing to build our strength as a nation.

As I have said before, Kennedy's application of his "lessons of history" to the present Great Powers has generated much discussion and debate. While the general press, publications like *Time*, *Newsweek*, *The New York Times*, and *The New Republic*, generally praised the book, the reaction from Kennedy's peers, especially more conservative ones, was not as positive. One of the most persuasive (and scathing) rebuttals to Kennedy came from historian W.W. Rostow in an essay printed in the Spring 1988 issue of the journal *Foreign Affairs*. Rostow points out that unlike the hegemonic powers before it, the U.S. has not attempted to conquer the world, only to lead it. Since Rostow believes that the sapping of strength of past powers came from attempts to maintain empires created at others' expense, he does not see the U.S. following them in a similar decline. He also feels that Kennedy is much too deterministic in his analysis, and that we have much more control over our destiny than Kennedy would lead us to believe. In this point I think he has uncovered one flaw in Kennedy's analysis. I think Kennedy is right in his assertion that the U.S. is not blessed with a permanent dominance of world affairs. But I think it is too soon to tell whether the trends of the relatively short period since World War II are indications of a permanent decline, or merely a temporary reversal of fortunes. While I think we must heed Kennedy's warnings on the perils of taking long-term strength for granted, I would prefer to see leaders making decisions based on optimism rather than pessimism.

A more balanced rebuttal to Kennedy's work, which also appeared in *Foreign Affairs*, came from Professor Samuel P. Huntington, director of the Center for International Affairs at Harvard University. As with other critics, Huntington focuses on Kennedy's assertion that the U.S. is in decline. He points out that, contrary to Kennedy's views, the current problems which the U.S. faces are not systemic or inevitable, and thus will be easier to contend with. Huntington claims that it is not so much excessive military spending as it is consumerism and overindulgence that threaten long-term U.S. economic strength. This is a common counterargument to Kennedy, which I believe is more a byproduct of his intent to focus on the interplay between economic and military matters, than it is an indication of academic oversight. But in the end, Huntington has a compliment for Kennedy and those of his ilk. Huntington sees Kennedy as providing a valuable service: "The more Americans worry about the health of their society, the healthier they are." He sees the introspection and critical self-examination Kennedy has inspired as being a valuable force against the very decline Kennedy predicted.

I was fortunate enough to have the opportunity to interview Professor Kennedy in October of 1988. Kennedy is a Dilworth Professor of History at Yale University in New Haven, Connecticut. The campus there is beautiful, but with the shabby, rundown elegance of old money. Somehow the surroundings seem appropriate for meeting a man whose name, for better or for worse, has become associated with the idea of a declining America. The door of his small office off a quiet courtyard is decorated with cartoons and notes to students. He came to the interview in the de rigueur blazer and sweater of academia; a slight, gracious man with a neatly trimmed beard. His voice has a definite accent that instantly betrays his British origin.

At the time of the interview, *The Rise and Fall of the Great Powers* had been out for almost a year. The book, which had received an initial printing of 9,000 copies, was approaching sales of over 200,000 copies. Kennedy had been interviewed extensively, had lectured on his work, debated it, and even testified on his ideas before Congress. He was not, however, prepared for all this, and seemed rather bemused, and even a little intimidated, by all the attention. He was most amused by those who called his book, and its release in the election year, "well timed." The book had been in the works for years, and had actually been planned for completion much sooner. Kennedy had not expected his work to receive general attention, but instead thought it would be of interest primarily to social scientists and his fellow historians, who he felt might comment on his "rashness."

A student of noted British strategist Sir Basil Liddell Hart, Kennedy is no stranger to military and diplomatic history. He has a number of quite excellent history books to his credit. In fact, one of his previous works, *The Rise and Fall of British Naval Mastery*, a study of the fortunes of the British Empire and the naval power that built it, foreshadowed his most recent book, albeit on a smaller scale. He is an extremely intelligent man, and has a broad grasp of many subjects. During the interview, he displayed an ability to give insightful and extended answers that would put many people's prepared speeches to shame.

After speaking about his surprise at the book's reception, we spoke about the controversial contents of his final chapter. Kennedy pointed out that the final chapter was, in his mind, rather tentative. He pointed out that his conclusions were what the relative positions of the Great Powers of today *could* be, *if* present trends continued over the next twenty years or so. He felt that those who attempted to apply these conclusions to today's situation, and to say, for example, that the U.S. is currently in a state of "imperial overstretch," had not appreciated this point. He pointed out the danger of simply extrapolating trends, and expecting the future to cooperate with your predictions.

With that in mind, we went over his views on each of the Great Powers of today. At my request, we focused on Japan, a nation many feel has the potential to significantly change its present status, due to its burgeoning economic power. Kennedy again stressed that while present trends seem to point to the upswing of Japan, there are also many factors that could stifle that trend. He also pointed out that while economic power is an important factor in national strength, it does not necessarily translate into military and political power.

He sees three major challenges from Japan which the U.S. must consider. The first is our increasing financial dependence on Japan, a fact brought about by our fiscal and trade deficits. The second challenge is in high-tech manufacturing and research. The U.S. owes much of its current leadership in the world economy to our expertise in these areas, so the improvement of Japan's position does not help ours. The third challenge is in the area of political and military power. Even with their current military spending capped at one percent of GNP, Japan still has huge funds to spend on military power. And their status as a leading creditor nation gives them huge power, which they have so far been hesitant to use. So while Kennedy shies away from firm projections, he sees Japan as a power to reckon with in the future.

Despite the claims of his critics, Kennedy does not think that the U.S. is going downhill to the point where it will lose its current Great Power status. His concern is more what might happen if the wrong political and economic decisions are made in the coming years. He is concerned especially with the erosion of our financial position, our manufacturing base, and our

105

educational system. By no means, though, does he believe that the U.S. is likely to fall into the second rank of lesser powers.

For those who feel threatened by our archrival since World War II, the Soviet Union, Kennedy offers some hope. For although the position of the U.S. is eroding on a relative basis, the Soviet position is slipping even more swiftly. While Kennedy sees some hope that Gorbachev's reforms will lead to a healthier and less militaristic Soviet state, he does not seem too optimistic about Gorbachev's chances of success.

The other major power blocs, China and the European Community, Kennedy sees as question marks. While both have huge potentials, they both must contend with factors that would limit this potential. Europe must first answer the question of unity and cohesiveness, while China must reconcile its capitalist potential with its Marxist ideology.

After covering the current Great Powers, we spoke of military and naval history. Kennedy is one of the foremost historians in this field in America today and has a wealth of anecdotes to reinforce his points. It became clear that what Kennedy feels most strongly about is the neglect of economic power as a component of military strength, or of what Kennedy referred to in a more recent lecture at the Naval War College as the "Sinews of War." He has serious concerns that attempts to amass too much military power in peacetime at the expense of growth and financial stability may actually result in a sapping of strength in the long run. In my opinion, his feelings on this topic are what motivated him to write *The Rise and Fall of the Great Powers*.

One area Kennedy also feels quite strongly on is academic freedom. He has come under criticism for stating opinions many conservatives feel are dangerous or damaging to our national strength. Yet as he pointed out in a letter to me, "nothing is *more* conservative than buttressing a nation's long-term strength." And in the interview he pointed out (quite correctly, I think) that nations can handle the "fog of war" better when it comes, if critics and other "awkward people" are allowed to speak in disagreement with current policies, and if defensive strategies are challenged and debated.

To look at Kennedy's views and what they say about the future, we must look beyond what he says and instead look at what the conclusions he stated imply. While not going as far as constructing models and using them for forecasting, Kennedy has come closer to a more rigorous mathematical approach than one would expect from a historian. Kennedy extended his view to the opening decades of the 21st Century—again, unusual coming from a man who is first and foremost a historian. It is the long-term implication of what Kennedy says, and the applicability of his principles to the period beyond that he describes, that have attracted me not only as a student of strategy, but as a reader and writer of science fiction.

Science fiction authors have always been influenced by works of social science. Utopian authors like Huxley and Orwell owe inspiration to Plato's *Republic*. Isaac Asimov has credited Edward Gibbon's *The Decline and Fall of the Roman Empire* as being an inspiration for his *Foundation Trilogy*. British historian Arnold Toynbee has gained many adherents in the field of science fiction since his *Study of History* was finished in the '50s. Poul Anderson, H. Beam Piper and Jerry Pournelle, in the design of their respective "future histories," all show Toynbee's influence to some degree.

Kennedy's work has been compared many times since it came out with the work of Toynbee. This is an accurate comparison, since both have looked at the changing fortunes of nations and empires over the sweep of centuries. Yet where Toynbee looked at the classical or ancient world, Kennedy focuses on the modern system of competing nation-states that arose from the Middle Ages. Some, who think that Toynbee's theories of rising and falling empires will continue to apply in the long run, will see Kennedy's theories as a corollary of the other man's. Others, who see these nation-states as establishing a new pattern of development, may see Kennedy as supplanting Toynbee and being more applicable to the future. Still others may feel that both are outmoded, and that new forces in our societies will shape the future.

Another way of putting Toynbee and Kennedy in context is to consider them in the framework outlined by Alvin Toffler in his book *The Third Wave*. In that book Toffler outlines three phases, or waves, of human civilization. The first of these waves is agricultural society. The second is industrial society. The third, which Toffler says is behind most of the changes our society is experiencing now, is the information society. In this context, Toynbee would be seen as a historian of the first wave, and Kennedy of the second. The question is then, what elements of the first two waves will we see repeated in the third? If we look at what is common to the first two waves, we see a continuing cycle of nations overreaching themselves in pursuit of hegemony, only to meet with eventual failure. While we can hope that the information society, by drawing the world closer together, will arrest, or at least slow, this vicious cycle, it appears unlikely that this will occur. It seems more likely that the struggle to dominate human society will continue, despite the indications that society is actively resistant to attempts to unify it.

And what does Kennedy's work imply in particular about the far future and the world of science fiction? First, he believes that even if Great Power wars should come again, a world-ending nuclear war will be avoided. He sees the Great Power system as being stable for a long time to come, even though the balance of power between individual nations may shift. Since he sees a weakening of the Soviet Union and the United States relative to other powers, a situation neither one wants to face, perhaps in a more cynical moment he would not be surprised to see an alliance between the two, or "CoDominium," come into being, like that predicted by Jerry Pournelle.

One extension of Kennedy's work, which I am not even sure he has thought of himself, is the potential impact the development of space could have on the world's balance of power in the future. Those who want an accurate and clear description of the impact of the opening of the New World on the European powers need look no further than Kennedy's book. The power this expansion gave to those nations who exploited it properly was immense. With the Soviet tortoise now pulling ahead of the American hare, and other nations, notably the European Community, entering the race for space, this is a factor which could have a tremendous impact on the future balance of power.

It may be, however, as Isaac Asimov now believes, that the exploration of space is too large an undertaking to be the effort of single, uncooperative nations. In that case the model for the exploration of space would not be that of the opening of the New World, but would follow some other course. This type of speculation is an example of the power of Kennedy's work. Once the reader finishes, it is virtually impossible not to feel the pulse of the forces of history, and wonder about the shape of human society as we move into the future.

Science fiction takes a long view. The "future histories" writers map out often cover centuries. Thus, to really offer the kind of analysis that is helpful in determining these long-term views, a scholar needs to take a broad, sweeping approach that cuts across many disciplines. As a result, a long time passes between works that have an impact on what we see as the shape of societies in the future. Contemporary works, like Toynbee's *Study of History*, are few and far between. Other contemporary nonfiction writers who have had an impact on the field of science fiction include Alvin Toffler, whose *Future Shock* and *The Third Wave* inspired a spate of stories dealing with the ever-increasing pace of technological change, and The Club of Rome, whose *Limits to Growth* study inspired numerous stories of an earth reaching the end of its available resources. With the success and strength of Kennedy's work, it seems likely that he will do the same. It may be a while before we see it—after all, future histories are not written in a few days—but it looks like Professor Kennedy will leave an impact on the field of science fiction for years to come.

Bibliography

Asimov, Isaac. "The Tail Wags the Dog." Introduction to *The Man Who Pulled Down the Sky* by John Barnes. New York: Worldwide Books, 1988.

Creasy, Sir Edward S. *Fifteen Decisive Battles of the World*. Harrisburg: The Telegraph Press, 1957.

Gibbon, Edward. *The History of the Decline and Fall of the Roman Empire*. New York: Bigelow & Co., Inc. (date not shown).

Huntington, Samuel P. "The U.S.—Decline or Renewal?" *Foreign Affairs*, Winter 1988, pp. 76–96.

Kennedy, Paul. *The Rise and Fall of British Naval Mastery*. London: The Ashfield Press, 1986.

Kennedy, Paul. *The Rise and Fall of the Great Powers*. New York: Random House, 1987.

Letter from Paul M. Kennedy to Alan L. Brown, August 31, 1988.

Interview with Paul Kennedy, Dilworth Professor of History, Yale University, New Haven, CT: October 21, 1988.

Kennedy, Paul. "The Sinews of War." Lecture given at the Naval War College, Newport, RI, on February 16, 1989.

Meadows, Donella H., et al. *The Limits to Growth*. New York: Signet, 1972.

Rostow, W.W. "Beware of Historians Bearing False Analogies." *Foreign Affairs*, Spring 1988, pp. 863–868.

Toffler, Alvin. *Future Shock*. New York: Bantam Books, 1971.

Toffler, Alvin. *The Third Wave*. New York: Bantam Books, 1982.

Toynbee, Arnold J. *A Study of History*. As abridged by Somervell, D.C. London: Oxford University Press, 1956 (Vol. I) and 1957 (Vol. II).

THE VOICE OF THE COCKROACH
Leslie Fish

EDITOR'S INTRODUCTION

I was once an editor of *Survive* Magazine. This was in the '70s, when things looked considerably more bleak than they do now: in those days you could hardly open a book or magazine, or turn on the TV, without being told that Western civilization was doomed. Those were the days of President Jimmy Carter's "national malaise"; when the President of the United States wasn't sure that the people who had elected him were moral enough to warrant the favor of heaven; when much of the intellectual class was sure we weren't.

Not only was Armageddon coming, but it served us right.

I wrote this back in those days to show that a few of us thought differently:

Rogue River is a fine place, as are many of the small towns recommended by and for serious survivalists: but what, if anything, can we big-city dwellers do? How will we get past that day?

First: As I have said before, the best way to survive a nuclear war is not to have one. Once they start throwing atom bombs around, there's no telling *where* the destruction will stop. You can have a deep shelter with lots of food, everything thought out in advance, and still find yourself in the wrong place at the wrong time. The wind shifts, or an ICBM goes off course (probably assisted by an anti-missile)—and there you are.

There are several ways not to have a war. One is bribery: Pay the other guy off, and maybe he'll leave you alone. Kipling knew the difficulty with that one:

It is always a temptation to a rich and lazy nation
To puff and look important and to say:—
"Though we know we should defeat you, we have not the time to meet you.
We will therefore pay you cash to go away."

And that is called paying the Danegeld:
But we've proved it again and again,
That if once you have paid him the Danegeld,
You never get rid of the Dane.

Paying the Danegeld is not likely to appeal to readers of this anthology, so I won't belabor the point.

The other way to avoid war is as old as time, and was perhaps best put by Appius Claudius the Blind in a speech to the Senate of Rome in 280 B.C.: "If you would have peace, be thou then prepared for war."

The problem is that the United States is not prepared for war. To be precise: There is no war that the United States could win against the Soviet Union. None. To make it worse, there are many U.S. "leaders"—some of them highly placed military officers—who would understand that sentence to mean something as inane as "there are no winners in a nuclear war."

That is not what I mean. It is not what the Soviet marshals mean. They think there will be future wars, and that they will win them; while we not only have not prepared for war, until recently we very deliberately told everyone that we were not prepared and would never be prepared.

We dismantled what little civil defense system we once had. We signed a treaty that allowed us to defend missiles, but explicitly said that we would not defend our people. Then we adopted a doctrine of "wait it out." Now tell me: If we really do allow

112

the Soviet Union a free ride, a full first strike, what do you think the remaining U.S. forces can do? The remnant force won't have much coordination—if any. Our Command, Control, Communications, and Intelligence (C3-I) system will be crippled. We won't even be able to choose the targets.

What targets will we shoot at? Soviet cities? Which ones? Kharkov and Kiev? Warsaw? East Berlin? Well, no. Moscow? Why? It wasn't the people of Moscow who declared war on us. Or don't we believe our own propaganda?

How, then, should we prepare for war?

Well, first we have to recognize who the enemy is; and it is not Russia, or even the Union of Soviet Socialist Republics; it is the Communist Party of the Soviet Union (CPSU). Specifically it is the leadership of the party: a few tens of thousands of people known as the *Nomenklatura*, the top bosses and the up-and-coming party members. It is the group that controls the Soviet Union; it is this group that has declared war on Western civilization; and it is this group that must be made afraid of what war can do.

Killing a lot of Poles and Czechs and East Germans won't faze them a bit. Killing Ukrainians won't do it. And although most of the *Nomenklatura* are ethnic Great Russians, killing random Russians won't do it either. Hannah Arendt (author of *Origins of Totalitarianism* and one of the foremost authorities on 20th century politics) put it best: "The totalitarian rules as a foreign prince in his own country." The *Nomenklatura* doesn't much care what happens to its subjects as long as the Party stays in power; after all, in a war with the United States, the prize is literally mastery of the world.

Next a bit of data: When the space shuttle *Columbia* was first in orbit, there was some concern about whether she had lost heat-absorbing tiles in crucial places. Those tiles are small, no more than a few inches long. And miracle of miracles, the Air Force was able to see that none were critically damaged. Mind you, they didn't admit that we have optics capable of looking at Columbia tiles from Earth, but it's safe to assume we have. It's also safe to assume that we have similar optics in orbit looking down.

And wouldn't it be nice to publish a target list that included the *dachas* of the major Party figures, with high-resolution satellite photographs . . .

If Party leaders believe truly that they won't survive a war; if they know that *we* consider *them*—and not their populations—our enemies; if they know that we will target their communications systems, fallout shelters, homes and resorts; if the one certain fact about nuclear war is that *they* won't survive it—well, you can draw your own conclusions. But can we accomplish this?

To some extent, but not very well right now, because we haven't been thinking in terms of war-fighting capability. Our whole doctrine has been deterrence through Mutual Assured Destruction, MAD if you like, which deliberately puts our population hostage and threatens the Soviet population but not its leaders. Indeed, there has been strong sentiment for deliberately sparing Soviet leaders so there will be someone to negotiate with. The rigid logic of MAD knows no limits.

Let us suppose, then, a new kind of strategic doctrine; one that emphasizes war-fighting capability, and makes it clear that we intend to destroy the other side's leadership class, the *Nomenklatura*, the instant that war begins. Suppose that we buy our weapons accordingly—which means that we must retain our C3-I capabilities even in the face of nuclear attack; that we have a presence in space, and work on making it survivable; and that we develop credible warning systems that can't be knocked out without operations that are themselves a war warning. Suppose all that, and it's very unlikely that we'll have a war. There might be some other crisis to get through, but fallout won't be among the hazards of survival. . . .

That was then. In 1980, the country had had enough of Carter's national malaise, and elected Ronald Reagan; and an hour after the Old Cowboy took office, the Iranians released our hostages. There was probably a connection.

One of Reagan's innovations was "The Transition Team": people who would *not* be taking public office, but who assisted in the transition between Carter's administration and Reagan's. One of those teams was headed by General Bernard Schriever, USAF (Ret.); it analyzed national space policy, both civil and military. A group of experts convened in Southern California to write reports for General Schriever, and through an odd chain of circumstances I ended up as its chairman. Thus was born the Citizens'

Advisory Council on National Space Policy, a group which continues to this day.

One policy we recommended was that the U.S. abandon the goal of Mutual Assured Destruction and adopt a doctrine of Assured Survival: to structure our military force to ensure the survival of the United States and its citizens. We thought we had the technical means to do that; and as the Council pointed out, it was certainly more in line with the Constitutional requirement to "uphold and defend the Constitution" than was Assured Destruction.

On March 23, 1983, President Reagan challenged the science and technology community to do just that: to provide a defense that defends.

The result was intolerable pressure on the Soviet Union. Whether or not they could build weapons to penetrate strategic defenses, it was certain that they didn't have such weapons; whether or not the U.S. could make all ICBMs "impotent and obsolete," it was certain that we could make nugatory the weapons the Soviet Union already had. The U.S.S.R. was nearly broke from the cost of building the force they had; they'd never be able to afford a whole new missile establishment.

That, at least, was the strategy; and it appears to be working. There appears to be a new regime in the Soviet Union, new leaders more concerned with economic stability than accumulating weapons.

How long that will last we can't say. Certainly it won't last past the day when the United States takes the pressure off. Events in China have shown that the Old Guard doesn't give up easily; and the peace of the grave that has descended over Tiananmen Square could as easily fall onto Red Square. The *Nomenklatura* are not finished yet.

Suppose, then, we haven't learned; that we return to MAD as our primary defense, and the unthinkable happens. Leslie Fish, onetime member of the IWW, shows us one possible outcome . . .

———————————————— • **I** • ————————————————

THERE HAD BEEN A BATTLE HERE, AND NO MORE THAN A DAY ago, to judge from the squabbling eagerness of the coyotes and the buzzards.

Welcome to the Hardware Store, said The Voice.

Ryder low-geared his ancient Jeep Apache and rolled slowly down the slope, eyes tracking rapidly over the narrow desert valley, trying to take in the whole scene at once, checking for any movement besides the busy scavengers. A few rags flapped here and there, a small mirage shimmered on the cracked white road, a cloud of flies rose as another buzzard landed on a tangled wreck . . .

And was that a pool of spilled oil or gasoline gleaming on the asphalt?

Jesus, fuel!

Ryder reined back the spurt of hope and crept forward carefully.

Joy juice. Oh, hallelujah! The Voice snickered.

He ignored it.

There were the remains of three cars, one pickup, maybe half a dozen cycles: pieces and scraps strewn all over the baked road, some of them ragged plates of jerry-built armor. Rusty smears showed where pieces of bodies had been, too, before the coyotes had carried them off. Guessing from the scraps, smears and tire-marks, the battle had centered around a low concrete drum-shape to the left of the road. Why there? What was it? Ryder steered toward the oddity, buzzards flapping resentfully out of his way.

It was a well. The cover had been wrenched off its hinges, then carefully replaced. He guessed that the water-level would be within reach of the nearby bucket on a rusty chain. Behind the far well-curb lay a fallen skeletal tower with its windmill still attached. So, the pump was down, but there was still enough water to fight over. Ryder almost smiled as he pulled up beside the well. Of course road-gangs would fight for water, out here in the Mojave: on this stretch of the asphalt, it was probably worth more than fuel.

So drink, then get the gas, The Voice in his head nagged.

Patience! Ryder snapped back without thinking.

Nice to hear you answer for a change. Jiminy Cricket got more attention.

Ryder ground his teeth. Shouldn't have answered, shouldn't answer now. *You're Jiminy Cockroach, the X-rated version,* he couldn't resist saying. *More a plague than a conscience, probably the result of radiation damage. Get out of my head!*

116

After World War Three, you expect the Disney version? The Voice stopped sneering, turned flatly serious. *Cockroaches survive anything, remember? You're stuck with me.*

Ryder took a deep breath, mentally turned his back on The Voice and concentrated on the simple steps: look around, cut the engine, check pistol, open door, slide out, swing radiation-counter for background check.

You can't lose me, Ryder, The Voice whispered, dwindling away.

He waited until it was safely gone before taking another step. No distractions now; even the animals could be dangerous. No more of this craziness, this thinking at himself, or soon enough he'd be talking out loud to himself, then hallucinating full-out, and then dead.

Despite everything, he didn't really want to be dead.

Therefore: proper steps, proper caution, walk slowly to the well.

The coyotes, losing their fear of man these days, snarled and held their ground until they saw that he wasn't interested in the meat.

Indeed, he wasn't; the pickup had rolled a few times before settling on its side, the cab was thoroughly crushed, and nothing left therein could be of any use to him. After a day or so in this heat the bodies stank loud; luckily the air was still and the smell faded after a few yards. Ryder kept as far as he could from the cab and its scavengers, went to check the gas tank. It held a good two gallons, reachable with a siphon. He loaded a jerrican and moved on to the next wreck.

This one—a former mid-sized two-door car—was still on its wheels. There were no coyotes poking about, and that was odd enough for caution. Ryder circled the wreck carefully, taking advantage of what little cover there was amid the scattered scrap, finally spotted a buzzard-picked coyote carcass lying near the barely-open offside door. He scratched a sweat-itch caught under his patched body-armor, and inched closer for a better look.

Some kind of fairly heavy bullet had caught the coyote just under the jaw, taking out the throat and ripping the head halfway off. Judging from the position of the carcass, the shot had come from low inside that door. Maybe a booby-trap: maybe someone still alive and shooting.

117

Ryder crouched lower, crawled around to the front of the car and ducked below the rough-armored radiator grille. He checked his .45 auto one more time, took a deep breath, sprang to his feet and fired three shots fast through the windshield, then ducked down again.

Some nearby buzzards flapped for the safety of the air, circled awhile, then settled again. The other coyotes darted for cover, paused, then poked their noses out to watch. Nothing else happened: no other motion or sound.

Ryder stood up carefully, peered at the shattered windshield, noted the pattern and shrugged. Nobody alive in there now, anyway. Booby-traps were still possible. He climbed onto the wreck's scarred hood, beat out the rest of the windshield with his gun-butt, and crawled through the resulting gap.

It had been a booby-trap, all right: set by the last driver or his departed friends. It hadn't helped the driver any; he'd been dead for several hours, and the ants were already busy at his badly-bandaged and noticeably-swollen leg. That explained why he'd stayed when the rest left. A worn-looking Mossberg carbine was tied across the steering wheel, aimed toward the door. Its trigger was gone, replaced by a string that looped back around the steering wheel before stretching out to the door's handle. Very neat, very nasty.

Ryder brushed ants away, cut the string and poked through the tattered interior of the car for anything worth taking. The carbine first: useless in itself, half rusted out, lucky it had even worked on the coyote—but the ammo was .357 Magnum and would fit his other gun. Further hunting through the corpse's patched denim-and-leather rags harvested two boxes of reloaded .357 shells, maybe three-fourths of them reliable, an old K-Bar knife desperately in need of sharpening, and several ant-bites. The glove compartment yielded part of a torn road map, some rad-counter batteries, a couple wrenches and a few other small items. He took them all, stuffed the loot into his Jeep and returned to the wreck's gas tank. Exquisitely thorough siphoning yielded only a quart of gas. The oil and spark plugs were possibly worth taking. There was nothing else: absolutely no food. Damn.

Ryder was coming back to his Jeep with the second load when he saw the newcomer. It was a lone car, apparently idling on the road at the far end of the valley, watching him. He could make out none of its details through the shimmering heat-waves, but its rough-squared outline suggested armor.

Ryder hurried to his Jeep, thrust the salvage inside, crouched behind the open door and waited to see what that watcher would do.

The distant car rolled slowly into the valley and stopped midway to the nearest wreck—idling, wasting fuel—plainly looking to see where he'd gone and what he was doing. Ryder could see now that it was a big car—the lines suggested a Thunderbird—armored with neatly welded or bolted metal plates. Even the windows and windshield were covered with what looked like thick metal venetian blinds, and the wheels sported armored hubcaps that extended out over most of the tires. There was something odd, shiny and box-like on the roof. He couldn't see any gun-ports, and no weapons were visible, but Ryder didn't doubt that the car's occupants were armed. Everybody was, out here.

For long, hot, crawling minutes, nobody moved. Even the buzzards waited.

Ryder rubbed sweat off his neck, considered the odds of heatstroke, and guessed that the stranger wasn't about to attack—at least, not right away. He slid into the Jeep's driver's seat, still watching the other car, which still didn't move. He turned on the engine. The stranger did nothing.

Well, are you going to dance around all day? Jiminy Cockroach needled.

Ryder ignored him, judging the odds good that if he simply turned around and drove away, the other car would let him go without trouble. Very likely, the stranger only wanted the water.

And the gas. And the salvage, Cockroach added. *Let's have a salvage party.*

No, he couldn't leave. That other car might have plenty of fuel, considering how it could afford to wait with its engine running, but he didn't. He was almost out of food, and matches, and very low on ammo for his Colt. He couldn't abandon the salvage, not until he'd gone through the lot.

I'll fight you for it, he decided, steering toward the next wreck. Sweat crawled down his back under the armor, making him squirm. A fight with a well-armored car, unknown number of people, unknown weapons: bad odds. Maybe it wouldn't come to that. Maybe he could bluff them off.

Maybe you could negotiate, Jiminy Cockroach suggested.

Ryder ignored him, watching the watcher.

But the waiting car did nothing whatever while Ryder drove to the wreck, braked beside it, opened his near door and cautiously slid out behind its cover. Perhaps the other driver was alone, timid, didn't want to take any risks. Fine. To hell with him. Ryder turned deliberately away from the waiting car and poked into the wreck.

The gas tank was ruptured, and had spilled empty hours ago. The oil pan looked much the same. The rest of the vehicle's guts were shot to pieces and strewn over several square yards of sand. The driver's corpse was likewise in pieces, most of which had been dragged away by the coyotes, the rest buzzard-picked and shimmering with a cloud of bluebottle flies. There was nothing to salvage here but a tire or two, a few plugs, another wrench and a screwdriver. Ryder hauled out what he could, and turned another glance on the waiting car.

It had sneaked closer while he was busy. Now it stood only a dozen yards away, engine still running. Through the louvered window-armor he could make out two—no, three—silhouettes, none of them showing hands or weapons. Sunlight glinted off the curious glassy tent-shape on the roof. There were no outside weapons visible. And still the car idled, wasting fuel. What the hell did these people want?

In any case, they were within shooting range. Ryder pulled out his Colt .45 auto and dropped to a menacing crouch behind the door. He didn't know if his slugs could get through those screened windows. He didn't know if the car's inhabitants knew that.

The car stayed put, engine purring quietly. Nobody got out. Nobody moved.

They're peaceful, you fool, The Voice volunteered. *Can't you read the signs? An attacker wouldn't act like that.*

Sneaky maybe . . . Ryder countered, but the argument sounded thin even to himself. It occurred to him that there weren't many ways to signal peaceful intentions without actually stepping out of a vehicle, and thereby being dangerously exposed.

120

And you've done your best to look dangerous, haven't you?
Jiminy Cockroach reminded him.

Hell, Ryder grudgingly admitted, hating to do it, *they probably just want the water.*

He backed away slowly, holstered his gun and climbed into his jeep. The people in the other car still did nothing. He shrugged, started the jeep and steered off to the right in a wide circle—toward the farthest wreck and away from the well. If the mysterious visitors wanted only the water, they had a clear road to it now.

Sure enough, the thick-armored car rolled down the littered road and turned toward the concrete well-head. Ryder sighed in relief, braked beside the wreck—this one a mangled heavy cycle—and let himself concentrate on business.

Damn, this was a total ruin: smashed, drained, burned out, even the tires shredded and burned. There was nothing to take but the metal itself, and he couldn't make any use of that.

At least there was a reasonably-intact corpse not too far away, still wearing a loaded tool/weapons belt that might contain some usable goodies. Ryder went to it, wrinkling his nose at the growing stink, kicked sand at a buzzard that didn't give way fast enough, and knelt down to examine that tool belt. Yes, there was a good hatchet, a not-bad small crossbow and several belt-loops full of homemade but serviceable bolts for it. Not a bad haul. What else was there? He rolled the corpse over.

The face was gone. So was the throat and much of the belly, leaving the whole front of the body soaked with rotting blood and covered with ants. The chest was intact only because of two hammered-metal armor plates—no, cups—bound on with chains, forming a sort of exotic brassiere. The biker had been a woman.

Ryder flinched away and kicked the corpse back over on its belly. No, nothing more here. Let the buzzards and coyotes take the rest. He tucked the hatchet in his belt, stuffed most of the bolts in his jacket pockets and loaded one of them into the crossbow. Then he remembered the other car, and turned to check on what its crew were doing.

The car was pulled up between the well and the wrecked pickup, and all three occupants were outside. There was a tall muscular-looking man in mixed body-armor, holstered pistol on his right hip, probing the wreck with wrench and hacksaw: at

121

his feet lay a collection of metal tubing, wires, assorted odd bits, all made of copper or brass. Around the corner of the wreck came a tall, rangy woman in a cycle-helmet and homemade chain-and-plate armor, two revolvers on her gunbelt: she had a rad-detector in one hand and a sack of similar copper and brass pieces in the other. At the well stood a young boy—no, girl (blond hair cut punker-short, almost no shape, wearing thick studded-leather armor, sex hard to tell)—pouring water into a clutch of plastic gallon jugs. A small shaggy dog darted back and forth among the three, sniffing at wrecks, barking bravely at coyote-tracks.

Despite their weapons, armor and tasks, they looked jarringly like a normal family.

Ryder shivered and looked away. Sure, an ordinary family on an ordinary Sunday outing: Mom, Dad, kid and dog, out for a drive and a picnic. They just happened to stop and loot the wreckage of a battlefield. Normal. Sure.

As normal as you're ever likely to see, Jiminy Cockroach nattered in his head. *Enjoy the sight while you can.*

Ryder carefully ignored The Voice, and went back to his Jeep. Load and loot, climb into the seat, and where next?

Damn. The next untouched wreck was back toward the well, and the busy family. Best to move slowly, not scare them. He clutched into first gear and rolled toward the wreck in a wide, slow, nonthreatening circle.

The others paused to watch where he went, then turned back to their respective tasks. No, they weren't afraid of him.

Ryder pondered that as he picked over the remains of another cycle. Not threatening, not afraid, not after food or fuel. Puzzling.

Look closer, The Voice prodded. *They may be good people, and useful.*

Shut up! Ryder snapped back. Closer, like hell. Nonetheless, it was a good idea to keep a more watchful eye, and ear, on the strangers . . .

"Just take the copper," the woman was saying. "Leave the rest until the Fleet comes in."

Copper? Ryder wondered. *Fleet?*

"And the brass," the man added. "There's plenty here. Quite a haul."

The punk-styled girl came hurrying back to the car with her water-cartons, glancing nervously around at the scenery. Ryder could see now that she wore a revolver in a heavy gunbelt, and was dripping with assorted knives.

"Figure two hours or so," the woman said, loading the collected pieces in her sack. "Not much risk."

She looked up at Ryder, smiled pleasantly, nodded hello, and went back to her task.

Downright friendly, Jiminy Cockroach noted.

Ryder only gulped, trying to understand that. Nobody was friendly out here, not in the Mojave, not in these burning days. Everyone was an enemy now: weaker, and they ran from you; stronger, and you ran from them; equal, and you fought or both backed off. Neutral was the rare best one could hope for. Friendly? No, impossible.

Try it, or have you forgotten how? The Voice jeered. *Just keep your hands in plain sight, stroll up and say howdy. Remember?*

Too risky! Got to be a trap, Ryder insisted, knowing it wasn't. He rubbed a boot-toe in the sand, disturbed a scorpion, stepped on it.

Trap? With their kid right there, and everybody busy working? Sure!

Hell, that made sense. It wouldn't hurt to go and look, maybe even say hello, negotiate for food. Maybe try to find out why these people were so . . . damn laid-back and confident and actually friendly right here in the middle of hell.

Ryder placed his hands carefully on his belt—near the buckle, not the holsters—and edged closer.

He noted now that the plate-armored car was carrying what looked like a plastic greenhouse on its roof, fogged with steam and trickles of clear liquid, with a shallow square tank beneath it and a tube running down into the car's trunk. A solar still, maybe? For water? Never mind. Another few steps closer. Try to look peaceable. Try to remember how to smile without looking crazed. Careful, careful . . .

The man was closest now, busy detaching the pickup's battery. He glanced up, smiled, hauled the battery free and set it down. "Hello," he said, rubbing grease off his hands, making no move toward a weapon.

123

Answer, you fool! Jiminy Cockroach snapped. *Forgotten how to talk, too?*

"Uh . . ." Ryder hunted frantically for something to say. "The fuel. You don't mind?" God, how weird his voice sounded! How long had it been since he'd used it?

"Huh?" The man blinked at him.

"Gas. You don't want it?"

"Oh, right." The man laughed, understanding. "No, you can take it. We've no use for it. We make our own."

"Make . . . ?" Ryder repeated, feeling like an idiot. He could hear the Cockroach chuckling.

"Fuel alcohol." The man pointed to the greenhouse on top of his car. "That's a solar still—very useful around here. There's a small cook-still in the trunk if we need it, and a brewing-tank too. We've got a yeast that makes good fuel-grade alcohol out of any kind of cellulose: grass, sawdust, sagebrush choppings, whatever. All our cars're adapted for it. No, we don't need gasoline. Take it all."

"Fuel-grade alcohol. Right." Ryder looked at the still, impressed by the elegant simplicity of the whole idea. Homemade fuel: total independence, go anywhere, not just hunt from one dwindling supply to another. And "all our cars," he'd said, which implied more of them out there—that "fleet," no doubt. An alkie-powered community. Damn!

Stick around, The Voice nagged. *Be friendly. Be helpful. Make yourself useful, and maybe they'll share the tech with you.*

Ryder only shook his head. He'd forgotten how to deal with people—not that he'd ever really been that good at it—and now he didn't know how to begin, or what to say.

"Name's Jack Lomax," said the big man, sticking out his hand. "Yours?"

"Uh, Ryder." He hadn't quite forgotten how to shake hands. "You from around here?"

"No, we're scouts for the Merchant Fleet, heading back from Boulder City. They're a couple hours behind us, maybe less. Where're you from?"

Merchant Fleet? "Uh, from around here. What's Boulder City like?" He'd thought of going there, more than once. His sister's family might still be there. If the dam still held they'd have electricity, good farming along the lower Colorado: not a bad

124

place to live, probably. Somehow he'd never got around to going there . . .

"Forget it." Lomax made a face. "All the refugees from Las Vegas headed for the river, right after Black Thanksgiving—"

Ryder flinched automatically at the name.

"—And I mean *all* the refugees: the government, the cops, what was left of the local troops—and of course the Mafia boys. They took over everything from Lake Mead down to Bullhead City, at least on the Nevada side, and they run it like a goddam feudal estate. It was pure hell trying to trade with them; they give a whole new meaning to the name Robber Baron. No, you don't want to go there."

Ryder shrugged. It had only been an idle dream, anyway. "What about the Arizona side?"

Lomax chuckled. "The Sunbirds're doing well enough, but they won't let anyone cross the river from Nevada-side, and they don't want much to do with anyone from Southern California, either. They've got long memories about the old water-wars."

So much for that. "Anything left to the north?"

"Oh hell, yes!" Lomax laughed. "Lots of trade, inland—as long as you know the territory."

"Which, I take it, you don't," a new voice cut in.

Ryder turned to see that the woman had come up on them. So, she could move silently if she wanted to. How long had she been standing there, anyway? There was something vaguely familiar about her face . . . He wondered what her hair looked like, under that mail-draped helmet.

"Have you always lived around here?" she asked. There was something naggingly familiar about her voice, too.

"Pretty much." Ryder looked away, squelching the silent questions from Jiminy Cockroach. No, he didn't want to meet anyone from the old days. That whole age of the world was gone, and best forgotten.

"Not much to live on in the Mojave." She sounded sympathetic, maybe curious. "I'll bet you're hungry. Want some lunch?"

Right on cue, Ryder's stomach growled.

The other two laughed. Ryder's internal Voice sniggered. He blushed in the heat. "Come on," said Lomax, slapping a good-natured hand to Ryder's shoulder. "We've plenty to spare."

125

Ryder followed them without questions. The offer of free food was almost too good to believe.

Not exactly "Dejeuner sur l'herbe," Jiminy Cockroach commented on the dining arrangements. *Not precisely "alfresco," either. Luncheon à la Tarpaulin? Picnic in the Wreckage? Mind your manners; we're suppering with an elegant crowd.*

Shut up, Ryder replied, vividly picturing his booted foot stomping on a Disney-cartoon-style cockroach in a ragged tuxedo and top hat. The Voice gave an indignant snort and shut up, leaving him free to study the bizarre scene.

He had to admit this was the best meal he'd had in all these nightmare months (how many of them now? A year? More?), even if the setting was weird and left him distinctly off-balance. The others had pulled up their car close beside the pickup, spread a tarpaulin on the ground between the two cars, stretched and quick-tied another overhead to form an open tent. Outside the shaded cloth and metal tunnel blazed the desert full of wreckage, where coyotes and buzzards pecked at rotting corpses—and in here was a little oasis of polite kindness and plenty.

To Ryder's right sat Lomax, calmly shoveling down an oversized sandwich of smoked ham slabs on thick homemade bread. To his left the woman, introduced as Lena, shake-stirred a thermos full of lemonade. The shy punker-girl—Spooky, they called her—kept her distance, gnawing on a cold chicken leg while she stalked in ragged sentry-circles around the encamped picnic. The dog, Yappy, alternately chased after her and raced back to the luncheon-spread to beg food. In the center of the spread tarpaulin perched a now-empty freezer-chest surrounded by plastic bowls of ham, bread, chicken, dried fruit and even a bottle of homemade berry wine. The drinks were served in aluminum camper's-cups, and the plates came out of good quality backpacker's messkits. There were even clean bandannas for napkins.

Goddammit, I don't belong here, Ryder thought, squirming. *They're too . . . normal.* Or maybe "decent" was the better word, given what "normal" meant nowadays. He felt like a tramp who'd stumbled into a church picnic, and cringed at how dirty he looked. Grease and road-dust covered his boots, worn breeches and scarred leather jacket—at least covering the holes where his badge and patches had once been. Under the leather, metal-patched kevlar and sweat-soaked cloth, his skin stank strongly enough that he could smell it himself. Why had he so rarely thought of washing, even when he had enough water? He wished he could sit downwind from the others, but there was no wind anywhere.

And they treated him like a proper guest, an equal.

Ryder shook the confusion out of his head and concentrated on the food, which tasted good enough to make his bones ache. He nibbled his way from dish to dish, trying not to grab, not to look as hungry as he really was, wondering where these people came by such wealth, such confidence, such troubling generosity for a stranger.

"What's the Merchant Fleet?" he asked.

"A whole bunch of us . . ." Lomax finished off the last of his sandwich and took a gulp of lemonade. "Assorted weirdos, survivors from the cities, folks who lived further out in the country—basically, a lot of people who were halfway prepared for the One-Day War or something like it, and got out alive."

"Not to mention, set up the Settlement," Lena added over a cup of wine.

"I'm getting to that." Lomax tossed his food-scraps out onto the burning sand, where Yappy pounced on them, and set his plate by the freezer-chest. "You know there were always dozens, maybe hundreds, of odd little experimental communities up in the hills . . ."

Only a Californian would call them hills, Jiminy Cockroach noted. *And only where the Coastals, the Sierras and the Rockies are close enough for comparison.*

Shut up, thought Ryder again. He hated it when that damned Voice showed off its damned education, dredging up details from dull old schooldays that he'd mercifully forgotten. It had been more important to be street-smart then . . .

"Well, ours at least had enough people—with wide enough knowledge—to be in pretty good shape afterwards. When the first wave of refugees passed, we had a secure enough base to send out some explorers. Naturally, we used alkie-fueled cars, armed and armored 'em, got working CBs for everybody, supplies, all that. The first fleet only went out to explore, expecting marauders and road-rats and trouble. They found that, all right,

127

but they also found plenty of other survivors who wanted communications and trade.''

"Ready-made market." Lena shrugged, casting an eye out across the desert. "The rest came naturally."

"So, now there's the Merchant Fleet: a big armored caravan that makes regular rounds among the towns we know, and goes looking for others. Most people are glad to see us. The ones that aren't, well, we can deal with them.''

"This is only our second circuit through the Mojave," said Lena, giving Ryder a puzzled look. "Have we met before? Where's your settlement?''

"Don't have one." Ryder looked away, hunting something else, anything else, to fix his eyes and attention on.

"You're nomad, then?" Lomax asked, giving him an odd look. "Solitary?"

"Uh, yeah." Solitary. Right. The damned Voice didn't count. His eye fell on the girl, Spooky, roaming several yards out among the wrecks. "Hey, your daughter's wandering pretty far afield. Better call her back.''

"Hmm, she's not too far," said Lomax, peering out into the blazing daylight. "Anyway, Yappy's with her.''

Lena was looking thoughtfully at Ryder. "Spooky's not our daughter," she said. "She's a road-orphan. We found her off Route 40, in the Clipper Mountains.''

Ryder knew that territory. "What was she doing there?" he asked, trying to imagine a lone girl, maybe twelve or thirteen years old, surviving in those howling barrens.

"We fought and beat a gang of road-pirates." Lomax sighed, flicking a glance at Lena. "We found their camp afterward, and she was in it.''

"How'd she survive—" Ryder stopped right there, wishing he could call the half-formed question back. He could guess what the answer was.

"How do you think?" Lomax growled, squinting out at the wrecks. "She had scars and VD in damn-near every orifice. So did the other kids.''

Ryder lowered his head and shuddered. Oh yes, he could see it, and it *hurt*. And there, his defenses were down for once: actually sympathizing with someone else, a wide-open target for

128

Jiminy Cockroach to snipe at, and why didn't the damned Voice come and say it, tell him what he already knew?

"The Fleet took them in, of course." Lomax was still talking, apparently not noticing Ryder's reaction. "Spooky wanted to come with the scouts, so we let her. She does know the land around here, and if she wants to look for some revenge along the way, well, hell, she deserves it."

"Yeah," Ryder whispered, knowing that he hadn't done any fraction as much good, nothing really to help anyone, he who'd once taken oath . . .

"So, we went out by Route 40, and now we're coming back by the side-roads," Lena took up, unfastening her helmet. "You've been around here? Do you know where the next water is? Or any halfway-decent settlements?"

She pulled the helmet completely off, and scratched vigorously at the back of her head. Thick mahogany-red hair cascaded down to her shoulders.

Ryder stared at her, his cup falling out of his numb fingers. Dark red hair: mahogany-red, manzanita-bark-red, almost wine-red in the twilight. He remembered her now.

The redhead in the Jaguar. On Route 14. On the curve beyond the Soledad Pass. Sundown, on Black Thanksgiving.

He closed his eyes, felt the darkness reaching for him, braced himself fast on his arms and pulled a deep breath.

"You all right?" Lomax asked, gripping his shoulder. "Heat getting to you?"

Ryder shook his head, scrambling for a fast excuse and escape. "N-no. 'M alright." He struggled to his feet. "Medicine," he said, pointing jerkily. "My car . . ."

Now out and away, back to the Jeep, fast, oh fast.

He could feel their eyes on him all the way.

And he almost forgot the booby-trap on his own door-latch. Age-long seconds passed before he got the damned thing disarmed, opened the door and stumbled in. He pulled the door shut, lay down and curled up on the seat, shivering in long and heavy spasms.

Out of all this burned-up world, after all these months and miles, why her?

The heat was like an oven, like hellfire.

"Be sure your sin will find you out."

129

He didn't know or care if that was the Cockroach's thought or his own. The pain beat on him like the hammering sunlight, and all he could do was shut off the memory and endure.

After measureless time, he heard the dog yapping. At buzzards probably. He pulled his eyes open and sat up. Yes, breathing steady, eyes clear. Time to go.

Buzzard-man, Jiminy Cockroach jeered. *Running again? Scavenged enough? Take the hospitality and run?*

Ryder didn't answer, only started the engine, clutched, geared and rolled out.

Idiot! The Voice raged at him. *They're the best chance you've seen in more than a year, better than you're ever likely to see again. You're ruining yourself!*

I'm already ruined, long since, Ryder snapped back, aiming for the road. *Lucky she didn't recognize me. Would have, if I'd stayed longer.*

That's worse than what you're going to?

The Jeep's wheels grabbed the pavement. Ryder steered onto the solid center of the road and geared up for long running, setting his eyes on the horizon, tightening his concentration.

Consider the fuel, Jiminy Cockroach nagged, voice growing fainter in the rising wind of passage. *Consider the food. How often have you eaten coyote, or rattlesnake? Think of what they have. Consider safety. Who guards your back when you sleep? Consider . . .*

Ryder watched the distant rise of the far pass flowing toward him, gleaming chalk-yellow in the hard sunlight, hearing—at last—no sound but the rushing air and his wheels singing on the road. He breathed easier and leaned back in the seat. He'd forget now, safely forget the whole incident, go on to the next water, the next food, next fuel, next campsite and next scavenging. Tomorrow would be no different from yesterday, and he could deal with that.

The pass rolled under his wheels, bare rock-cuts whipping past to either side, and the next valley opened before him: empty yellow desert with the white road running through it.

Except that the road wasn't empty.

Cycles, big ones, maybe six or seven, glittered and roared in the hot, still air, filling the two lanes of cracked pavement in a

130

rough chevron formation. They were almost halfway across the valley, and coming this way.

Ryder slammed on his brakes, geared down, scrabbled on the seat for his cracked binoculars. He peered through the one workable eyepiece at the oncoming crowd, wondering if they'd already seen him topping the pass.

"Shit!" he whispered aloud, hearing Jiminy Cockroach echo him.

No harmless bikers.

They wore mixed armor—leather, chain-mail, odd plate—but all of it decorated with bones and teeth. They were half covered with hand-weapons—mostly clubs, axes, chain-maces, a few crossbows. Their cycles carried more than a few long guns—some shotguns, the rest homemade, maybe bangalore-torps—wired to the handlebars. The fork of every bike was decorated with a skull, all of them human, not all of them completely fleshless.

Ryder dropped the binocs on the seat, swung the Jeep around in a fast, tight U-turn, and raced back into the valley with the well.

Which way now? Back down the road or off into the desert? If he could get to one of the near hills fast enough, pull behind it or into a gully before the bikers topped the rise and saw him, they wouldn't bother hunting for him. They probably wouldn't even look for his tire-tracks turning off into the dirt once they caught sight of the wrecks, the loot . . .

And those people. The Voice was totally cold and grim. *You have to warn them. A coyote would do as much.*

Ryder chewed his lip, sweated, and kept his Jeep on the road.

The three scouts had finished their picnic and were back at scavenging when Ryder pulled up by their car. The red-haired woman was closest, and Ryder winced as he shoved the door open and leaned out to yell at her: "Pack up and run! Road-pirates coming, maybe five minutes away. They'll stop for the water and the wrecks. Run for it!"

"How many?" she shot back. "How well armed?"

"Half-dozen, maybe more. Shotguns, axes—nothing really long-range. Go fast, get away clean." In the outside mirror he could see Spooky and the dog running toward their car, Lomax hurrying close. "Move now, dammit!"

131

"But that'll put them between us and the Fleet!" Lomax panted. "Besides, we can't just leave all this to them."

"Die, then!" Ryder slammed the door shut, geared into reverse and backed out fast. As he turned toward the road he saw the girl jump into the armored car, Yappy right behind her, and slam the door. He hoped she'd have the sense to start the car and get out of there. The other two (fools! damned fools!) were scrambling, guns drawn, to take up positions between the car and the wrecked pickup.

Hell, they might survive anyway. Ryder double-clutched and fled away down the open road. Not his problem anymore. The pavement began to sing under his speeding wheels, and the far rise beckoned. With any luck, the bikers wouldn't come after him.

He was almost to the rise when the sound of unmuffled cycle engines clattered out of the pass behind him and echoed through the valley. Ryder automatically stepped harder on the gas, feeling sweat crawl down his neck. The bikers might see him, might prefer live prey to the motionless wrecks after all. They could always come back for the scrap at their leisure. He fixed his eyes on the rising slope ahead, wondering how much lead he'd have when he crested it, how long he'd be out of the bikers' sight afterward, whether he could get far enough off-road to hide the Jeep before they came into view again.

The crack of gunfire rattled off the road behind him.

Startled, Ryder spared a glance for the rearview mirror. In it he saw a cycle and body go tumbling, knocking a second bike into a skidding fall before the others could steer around it.

The scouts. Nice shot, Jiminy Cockroach commented, *especially at that distance.*

Ryder turned his eyes back to the road, corrected a brief drift, then couldn't resist another look in the mirror.

The bike-mob was turning, spreading out, wheeling toward the well and its defenders that they couldn't yet see, already firing a few of their cycle-mounted guns. Others, smarter, were reaching for hand-weapons. The skid-victim had stumbled to his feet and was limping toward a tail-end bike that slowed to pick him up.

The cycle-marauders had definitely lost interest in the rest of the road and anyone on it.

132

I'm free! Ryder eased his foot off the gas. He could save fuel from here on out.

The scouts got the road-scum off your ass, the Cockroach noted. *Nice of them. They could have just sat tight and let the bikers come after you.*

Shut up! Ryder pounded his fist on the steering wheel. The road was rising ahead of him, the hillcrest only a hundred yards away. *Just shut up, JC!*

Not this time, and not hereafter, Jiminy Cockroach promised, as cold as Ryder had ever heard him. *Not by waking and not in your dreams. Not if you run or hide or cut your own throat. You'll never be free of me if you run away now.*

Ryder slid on the brake, eased on the clutch, with feet gone cold, hands cold, grave-deep chill crawling over his skin. The open road swam in the heat before his wide eyes. "What do you want?" he whispered. "What the hell do you always want from me?"

Remember your oath, and turn back.

Ryder pulled a long, shaky breath. Yes, he knew which oath The Voice meant, could remember repeating the words at his swearing-in: a dusty formality, a dull starched-shirt ceremony, threadbare, unbelievable, and he'd been insulted at how hard he'd had to work to take it seriously, even then. And now? Now there was no law to uphold, and he was one of the guilty himself, and where in this world of ashes was there anyone innocent?

Back there at the well. You saw them. You heard them. You know what they are, and what they're worth.

"What's my life worth, if I turn back and take on those bikers?"

What's it worth if you run?

Another biker was down in the dirt, tangled with his cycle, blood and oil pooling together. The rest were circling roughly, trying to find paths through the assorted wrecks to get a clear shot at the big car's defenders. That was no light task, for the wreckage provided more driving-hazard than cover.

The scouts had taken down the tarpaulin awning, leaving room to climb on top of the dead pickup—which Lomax had done. He crouched atop the wreck with a good clear shot at everything not blocked by his own car. Spooky hid in the car and shot from between the metal slats of the window-screens, not aiming very well, firing in blasts that tended to empty her gun quickly, followed by longer stretches of reloading. Lena darted back and forth through the corridor between vehicles and shot at any cycles passing; she took more time to aim, used much less ammunition, and hit close enough to keep the cycles moving fast and safely distant.

The mess of wreckage kept anyone from coming too close, at any combat speed, from the west or southwest. The well and its fallen tower blocked close approach from the east. The north and south approaches were cluttered with enough rubble to at least slow wheel-traffic. The cycle-pirates circled the whole tight little junk-fortress at a safe thirty to forty yards out, trying to find some fairly fast way in through the maze of wreckage and rubble, possibly hoping to use up the defenders' ammo—and so far having little luck at either.

Siege, stalemate for the moment, Ryder considered, as he came rolling down the road and into the fight, windows open, .45 auto in hand, speed as high as he could safely steer. *Time to change the odds.*

The cycles were wheeling clockwise, and Ryder swung to his right to turn widdershins and meet them head-on. Shooting right-handed out his left window wouldn't be easy, but he could manage if he braced his wrist on his steering-arm. He had some idea of catching the bike-bandits in a shrinking circle between himself and the junk-fort, maybe pushing them into the wrecks so they'd spill and skid out. If it came to that, his Jeep could ride over rubble and wreckage better than their bikes could.

The nearest cycle roared toward him. The driver, intent on picking his way between one small wreck and the rubble of a larger while searching for attack-lanes, didn't hear or see the oncoming Jeep until it was barely fifteen yards away. Then he looked up, a downright shocked look on his face, and tried to pull hard to his right. The necessity of steering around a deep pothole delayed him just long enough.

Ryder braced his right arm on his straight left, aimed out the window, and shot the man neatly off his bike.

Three down. How many to go? The rest won't be as easy.

Ryder steered into the passage the downed cycle had just rolled out of, jolting through an unavoidable pothole, looking for the next target.

It came, forewarned. The biker made a tight turn around the tower and well, firing his cycle-mounted shotgun at the Jeep's front and barely missing. Ryder took a shot at the man just as his wheel hit another rough spot in the road, and missed too. In an instant, they'd passed.

At about that time the little knot of defenders spotted Ryder's Jeep and cheered. Lomax took a shot at the passing biker as he wove between two wrecked cars and a mess of rubble, and managed to blow out the rear tire. The cycle caromed off one of the ruined cars, losing parts, but the biker jumped clear.

Watch for that one! He's on foot but got cover now . . . Ryder tried to keep the man's position in mind as he swung around the well and its fallen tower, looking for another moving cycle.

Ah, shit, there it was: turning tight between the fallen windmill's end and some patches of rubble, going straight for the armored car and its knot of defenders, straight toward where Lena crouched in the slot between the car and the pickup—and the driver was fiddling with the damned bangalore-torp on the front of his bike.

Swearing desperately, Ryder squeezed off wild shots at the biker—none of which hit.

The torp fired with an amazing flare and smoke-burst. Splinters of armor flew from the back of the scouts' car. Lomax, bellowing with fury, pumped four shots into the biker before he could peel out, and knocked him rolling into the sand.

Gone. But did he get Lena? Ryder crushed a brief guilty hope, and tried to peer between the car and the wreck as he came around them. No, there she was, pulling herself up off the ground, looking unhurt. She must have thrown herself flat just before the biker fired. Lomax paused to wave at Ryder's Jeep, then went back to reloading.

Six bikes . . . Is that it? Are they gone? Except for the one on foot . . . As Ryder pulled wide around the next mass of rubble he tried to tally up the attackers. No, there was one left unaccounted for; another cycle, carrying double. Maybe the two survivors would see, or had already seen, that the odds were hopeless, would take off, get away clean while they could. Maybe not, if they were desperate for the water. And there was still

135

that one on foot. Ryder slowed and peered through the maze of wrecks, looking for motion.

There! Coming up the alley between a wrecked car and cycle, carrying double, heading straight for the car-fort: the last cycle, firing its shotgun, rear rider firing too—enough to keep Lomax and Lena pinned down for the moment, and at the wrong angle for Spooky to hit.

Ryder tried to keep the bike in sight as he circled; there was no way he could follow it through that narrow alley between wrecks. Damn! He slowed further, looking for a target, saw Lena firing while lying flat and Lomax on top of the tumbled pickup doing the same.

And there: the cycle appeared again, going flat-out for the scout-car's front, apparently bent on suicidal ramming or one hell of a close shot, still firing that shotgun—it had to be an auto-loader, and how big a clip?

It carried only one rider now.

Where's the other one?!

Quick look down the cycle's track: only one answer. The second man had jumped off somewhere near that wrecked car to the left, and was working his way closer on foot. Cursing between his teeth, Ryder pulled the Jeep into a tire-screeching hairpin turn and slowed beside the wreck. Where *was* the bastard? He could be hiding anywhere in that tangle of twisted metal, crawling closer to the car-fort every second.

Get out? Search on foot?

Ahead, wheels screeched. Ryder looked there and saw that the shotgun-carrying bike was still rolling. It had peeled out to the left at the last second, the driver firing a long handgun or short crossbow over his shoulder. He was crossing dead ahead.

Ryder didn't dare take his hand off the wheel to switch his pistol to his left hand and fire out the window—not on ground this rough.

No choice, and no time left.

He floored the pedal, shot the Jeep forward, and rammed into the heavy cycle.

The impact slammed him into the steering wheel, hard enough to stun him half-blind despite his body-armor. The screaming crunch of metal warned him that the Jeep had taken damage—maybe just the radiator gone, maybe worse. He stamped his foot on the brake and dizzily remembered to hit the clutch as well. As the Jeep jolted to a stop, his vision cleared enough to show that the cycle he'd hit was still rolling, in several pieces. So was the rider.

Leaves two. On foot. So am I.

Ryder fumbled the gears down and the engine off, remembered to pick up his revolver too, and half-fell out of the Jeep. Now where was the other road-pirate? Still in the wreck off to his right and behind him? A quick look showed no movement, but that meant nothing. He crept around the left side of the Jeep, searching.

Rising engine-noise and shots ahead jerked his attention back to the junk-and-car fortress. Lomax, and presumably Lena, were firing at another cycle that was just swinging widdershins around the well and tower. The biker on it was shooting back, some kind of heavy handgun, keeping them busy. Where the hell had that one come from? Ryder remembered the man he'd left on foot, back in the southward tangle of rubble. He must have found one of the downed bikes still workable, got it up and running. The bastard would be around this side in another minute . . .

Then Ryder saw something move beside the armored scout-car, something out of Lomax and Lena's sight. The missing cycle-pirate had made it to the fort. He crouched beside the car's right door, trying to pry it open with a crowbar. Inside, Spooky was screeching and firing ineffectively through the window, at the wrong angle, missing.

Ryder got up and ran toward the car, hoping to get a clear shot.

The roar in his ears drew his attention back to the oncoming cycle—an instant too late.

He saw the muzzle-flash just as the impact caught him high and left, picked him up and threw him backwards. He had a split second to wonder if the slug had gone through his patched and ancient armor, and then the earth came up and slammed him into black silence.

You can't stay here!

Ryder couldn't breathe enough to groan, nor think enough to squelch the image of Jiminy Cockroach kicking him in the face.

Get up, buzzard-man! Still danger, still the one at the car. The girl—

137

And there was still the noise of shots, of a single unmuffled cycle-engine circling. The last two pirates were still in the game. Yes, get up.

Ryder pulled his eyes open, tried to feel out his body. He could see, at least: endless miles of burning blue sky. He could move: right arm, right leg, left leg, couldn't tell about the left arm, left side of his body one solid pounding ache, breathing not too good—ragged panting, not enough air. Lung-shot?

You'll live. Move!

Still the sounds of engine and gunfire. Yes, move. Roll over. God, but it hurt!

Where are your guns?

He turned his head, pain stabbing his neck, trying to see where he'd fallen, where he'd been when the shot hit him, and all the ground between. Damn, he'd flown a good ten feet. Where were the guns? Where, in all that rubble-strewn sand? He slid, crawled on his right side, toward the spot where he'd been standing, looking frantically to left and right, pawing torn earth with his good hand. At least he couldn't see any blood on the ground under him; maybe the shot hadn't gone through. But the pain was getting worse, shock numbness wearing off . . . Ignore it. Reach farther.

Raw bone-ends sandpapered together, pain squeezing his vision down almost to black. He fought it off, panting, knowing that through-shot or no, he had a couple broken ribs, maybe worse.

Where? Gun. Where?

There: a shiny lump ahead. He pawed at it, couldn't quite reach. Jesus, to move forward just those few inches . . .

High-screeched string of curses and a burst of shots, too many, too close together, from the fort ahead. Spooky, losing nerve and sense. Invader getting too close, maybe prying the door open right now.

Ryder burrowed his good arm under him, arched up on its support, lurched, fell the last few inches.

Pain and buzzing black.

Somewhere ahead, desperate screaming in a high, thin voice.

Get up!

One eyelid pulled up, slow and heavy as a rusted portcullis. The shiny lump gleamed in front of him. He reached for it, clumsy hand crawling forward like a dying tarantula, dragging the unwilling arm after it. Touched. There. Smooth, familiar metal. The revolver.

Heavy as a boulder, so damned hard to lift out of the sand. Pull it up, point it. Look toward the car, the screams.

The screams had stopped.

Ryder looked, saw, couldn't bear to believe it and couldn't look away.

The bike-pirate had opened the door, was dragging the girl out of it by her short yellow hair. She hadn't shot him: maybe gun jammed, maybe out of ammo and no time to reload—and something wrong with her right arm, maybe he'd broken it with a lucky shot or a blow with the iron—but she hadn't shot him and couldn't now, and he'd have her out in another few seconds.

But her left arm was bent and moving, close under her chin. A red seam opened there, widening, following her hand. As it reached her ear, her hand pulled free, something red glinting in it.

Just as the road-bandit got her free of the door, her hand fell limp. A knife dropped out of it, and a bright red flood spilled out on the sand.

Oh Jesus—

Ryder sank all his mind into raising the shaky revolver, trying to line up front sight, back sight, target. Arm too damned weak. Rest the butt on the ground, concentrate on the front sight . . .

The man got Spooky's body clear of the door, out on the ground. He stared for a moment, then slammed a furious fist into her leached face.

Hold the front sight steady!

The bandit shrugged, making the bone-decorations on his armor leap and shake, then kicked the corpse's sprawled legs apart and began unfastening his pants. Clearly he'd hoped for a live, wriggling and protesting body, but even a still-warm one would do.

What kind of lunatic stops for a cheap corpse-fuck in the middle of a battle?!

As if the question had cleared his head, Ryder's arm steadied for an instant. The front sight aligned with the man's head.

A target.

Ryder squeezed the trigger.

The recoil threw his arm back, tore the gun from his hand and dropped it out of reach.

The biker's head burst apart in a red-and-gray rain. He jerked, flopped, sprawled beside the girl's body.

Done. Ryder's eye fell closed. He scarcely felt his hand hit the ground. *But if only I'd been a few seconds sooner!*

From the distance came a wild screech of tires, sounds of tearing metal, the distinct crack of shattering bones. The last biker, gone.

Silence.

Hot darkness swallowed him up.

. . . not by waking and not in your dreams . . .

The curtain peeled away, and he was back on the road. Route 14, on the curve beyond Soledad Pass, just before sundown. His patrol car sat parked on the shoulder some ten yards back, its radio chattering like an ignored conscience. He was standing beside a little green Jaguar XKE, pulled up to his full height, feet apart, doing his best Smokey the Bear pose, trying to get the driver to step out of the car.

The woman wasn't buying his act, wasn't acting like a Properly Respectful Good Citizen. "This road is posted for sixty-five," she was saying. "That is exactly what I was doing. I was certainly not speeding, and I will argue that in court."

Damn, how he hated these legalistic types who Knew Their Rights and made a big point of it. And why did she have to be wearing that bulky sheepskin jacket (all right, it was dyed the same russet-red as her hair, very nice) that hid her tits?

"Lady, I clocked you at over the speed limit." He used his best Imposing Voice; it usually made civilians cringe and turn pale, but dammit, not her.

"Oh? Do you have a radar unit in your car?" she came back. "May I see its printout, please?"

"To do that, ma'am, you'll have to step out of the car." God-dammit, if she'd get out and stand up he could get a look at her legs, probably her ass too in those nice tight jeans. Maybe he could used the search-for-a-gun excuse to get her jacket open, get a good look at those tits, maybe a grope too.

And damn, she must have guessed. "Why are you so anxious to get me out of my car?"

Come up with a reason! "Because I'm going to give you a drunk-driving test, that's why. Now get out of the car."

He set both hands on the edge of the door, as if he'd pull it open himself in another minute, and leaned over her so she'd have to twist her neck at an odd angle to look up at him. That usually worked too. Instead, she looked straight at his badge, as if memorizing the numbers. All he could see was the top of her red-haired head.

And right then, the whole landscape lit up in an orange-white glare, as if struck by lightning. He could feel the heat on his back.

"What the hell?!" He jumped away from the car, spun to look, saw a flare of light—not directly behind him, no, but covering the mountain-edged horizon to the south, and already sinking back down the cloudless sky. The yattering of his car radio blurred out into a roar of static.

The woman screamed—a hard, short, shocked sound. Whatever was happening, she knew what it was.

Then came the thunder—too long, too loud, too deep to come from any natural storm. He could feel it shaking the pavement, rattling his bones. It shivered the earth, but it came from the sky—from that flare of light beyond the mountains. Not even an earthquake.

"What is it?" He could barely hear himself shouting, even as the sound slacked off. "What is it?!"

Behind him the redhead was wailing, keening, high and shrill enough to be heard past the ringing in his ears. The sound quavered and broke into understandable words.

"Oh my god, it's Los Angeles!"

For just one blessed second he didn't understand. Then a single connection of thought, like the tick of a clock-gear, and he knew what it had to be. All that crap on the last week's news, all the "Current Political Crisis" everyone was so used to by now, all the war-scare noise on TV about the Oil Ultimatum—no, it still couldn't be real. No, that was just the generations-old bogeyman, a knee-jerk fear that scared kids and peaceniks, not something that would really happen. Nobody would be that crazy, really go that far, really hit the button, really turn loose hell . . .

Then came the blast-wind. He could see it knocking boulders

loose up on the skyline's mountains, driving strips of cloud impossibly fast across the sky, bending the tall pines as if they were grass in a field, and he knew that even this was just what had made it over several ridges of mountains. He threw himself flat just before its leading edge reached him, and the wind dragged him skidding down the pavement anyway, snapped off the tops of trees, whipped leaves and dirt and pebbles into a sideways hailstorm, and its roar filled the world.

It's got to pass, it's got to pass sometime, it can't last forever— And it did pass, and worse followed.

The wind had just slacked enough that he dared to raise his head, look around him to see torn trees and part of the littered road in the headlights. Then he looked to the south, numbly expecting to see that classic mushroom-cloud. What he saw instead was another glow across the horizon—flame-orange this time, the color of a city on fire, outlining the mountains against a suddenly dark and starless sky. The slackening wind grew thick with ashes, with the taste of smoke, and through it he could hear himself screaming incoherent curses.

And then the final note: a faint shivering and a deep rumbling in the ground, like a heavy truck passing, except that there was no truck and the rumbling grew louder, the shaking heavier, and suddenly all the ground was quivering like the skin of a horse shaking off a fly, and the thunder climbed now from earth to sky, like a responsive reading in hell. Earthquake: the old California nightmare, abused nature striking back in blind rage. Ryder hugged the cracked pavement and cried, the sound lost, like everything else.

Even that passed. The next sound he heard was off behind him, the Jaguar's engine starting up. He looked dully over his shoulder, saw the woman scrabbling among the gears of her now-colorless car, shifting, rolling away. She was still alive, at least. So was he. Ryder struggled to his hands and knees, crawled to his own car, which was now partway across the littered road. There, the door: and there, the radio—blank now, silent and empty, no matter how he worked the knobs or cried questions to it. He was alone, and World War Three had come to Los Angeles.

. . . and Samantha and Jennifer and Vicky, gone to Mom's for Thanksgiving . . .

But the car worked. He pulled it around in a tire-howling U-turn and rolled back up toward the pass at the best speed he could manage. Over the pass and south. West at the bypass around Acton—all the lights down, but plenty of fire in the distance, plenty of wrecks on the road shoulders, various cars and trucks howling up the road toward him, past him, running north for the safety of the hills and the empty country. Then southwest through the arm of the Los Padres Forest—trees down, trees burning, the first pattering of rain on the windshield, rain black with ashes, sky and air black with smoke and ashes, headlights at full power barely cutting twenty feet ahead and he had to slow down just to keep on the road. Then west on the Saugus short-cut—fire visible above the mountain ridge-tops, the black rain falling in sheets and still the fire glowing, air smoke-thick, past crawling traffic on the slick dark road, and God help any who stalled and stopped, for the other traffic would push them out of the way, right up into the scorched and toppled pines or down into the gaping canyons, no mercy, just clear the road. And then south on the I-5—eight lanes of traffic heading north through the rain like black mud, every vehicle smoke-stained black, the shoulders thick with wrecks that had dared to halt the flow, pieces of shredded tires and car parts and nameless things all over the road, no sound of horns, only the steady rumble of grim engines and voices coughing through improvised smoke-masks and the occasional crack of gunfire, and he had to pick his way along the sharp slope above the shoulder, going against the tide. Finally to Valencia . . .

Smoke, ashes, and thick black rain.

Streets choked with fleeing cars, abandoned cars, wrecks, pedestrians stumbling under bundles or pushing or dragging wheelbarrows, lawn carts, shopping carts. Too many buildings down, and bodies like bags of dirty laundry scattered everywhere. Lights out and wires down, phone cables like dead black snakes in the street. Ryder drove across yards churned to black mud, across barely-visible sidewalks, going by memory, landmarks gone, all changed—back to his own block, his own house.

Half the house was down, windows blown out, broken front door lying on the steps. He pulled up in the yard, scrambled across the slick ground, crawled in through the shattered front window and stumbled through warped dark rooms littered with broken furniture, thick with smoke and silence, even the intact battery-powered radio silent and dead.

No one was there.

Of course there wouldn't be: not one chance in a hundred that Samantha had stopped, changed her mind, come back before sundown with the girls. She was still down there, with the kids, and Mom, and all the rest of the family, in the old house just off the Santa Monica Freeway, at Thanksgiving dinner . . .

He couldn't imagine it, couldn't shape a picture of the hopeless reality, couldn't see anything but the whole family sitting down to dinner at the big table with the white-on-white embroidered tablecloth and the old silver candlesticks and the huge brown-toasted turkey on the wide silver platter, just as it had always been.

Common sense didn't enter into it, nor even much of self-preservation. He took the guns, loaded plastic cartons with everything drinkable that he could salvage from the toppled refrigerator, siphoned the last gas out of his patrol car and put everything in the old Jeep Apache, knowing he'd be off-road much of the time. Common sense was a lost voice wailing ignored warnings as he drove out, parallel to the highway, south along I-5 through the slackening rain, into still-thick smoke and air that was almost solid ashes, nose and mouth covered with a wetted bandanna and still struggling for air, past more lines of refugees and dead cars and bodies, more and more of them along the road, many of them burned to skeletons, up the long pass through the edge of the Santa Susanna Range, up to the rise where he could look down and see for miles into the wide flat land that had once held Los Angeles and its hundred suburbs, look down through the charcoal-gray dawn and see what was left.

A plain of ashes, bordered by distant low cliffs that had never been there before, lit by slow-walking columns of fire. Firestorms, fire-tornadoes, the nearest maybe half a mile high, lighting the tangled black plain where nothing stood and nothing lived. The landscape of an alien world: barren, deadly, and dead.

He sat on the ridgetop and watched the fire-columns stroll across the black land, watched for measureless time, one corner of his mind noting that he was probably soaking himself in fallout, would die in a few hours or days if he stayed here, but not caring, not thinking of anything, noticing after awhile that he was mumbling the words to an old rock song over and over again.

" ' . . . Only the good die young . . .' "

Seen enough?

That was the first time he'd ever heard The Voice. It sounded so clear, so very different from himself, that he'd actually turned to see if there was a real person sitting on the seat beside him. Of course, there wasn't.

Get your ass in gear, fool! it went on. *Nothing you can do here. Turn around and go someplace where you can be useful.*

He ignored it, of course. Hearing invisible voices was bad enough; actually listening to them was total lunacy. Still, maybe it was best to get out of there. The Voice might fade if he drove away.

So he did drive away: back up the I-5, northeast on 14 where a stop at an empty, quake-toppled Red Cross center provided him with a rad-counter, food and water, medkit, batteries. Then the shortcut through Ravenna to loot some gas from an abandoned garage he knew of. Then east on 18, and into the first of the road-pirates, and he knew there'd be more of them, so best avoid I-15 and go north by 395. And then on into the Mojave, into all that nice, safe, empty desert . . .

Into the wilderness, with your sins upon your head.

Ryder whimpered with pain and crawled back into the silent dark.

A different pain slammed across the blackness and drove him up to blazing sunlight. Someone was rolling him over, then pulling him upright by his good arm. His broken rib-ends brushed together, ever so lightly, and he howled in agony.

"Easy, easy," murmured a half-familiar voice. "We'll fix you up soon. Just a few yards. Hang in there."

Ryder groaned and wrestled his eyes open. They wouldn't stay open; he could see only in blinks, like a series of still photos. Lomax was beside him, half-carrying, half-dragging him toward the armored car. The buzzards were coming back, dozens of them, in a flapping cloud. Coyotes were crawling out from under wrecks to pick over the new food. The air stank of blood, black powder, cordite, spilled oil and gasoline. The dog sat by the car-fender, whining and licking at a plainly-broken foreleg. The armored car's radio crackled with reports and questions.

Near the car's right side Lena stood up, holding Spooky's dripping corpse in her arms. She walked away slowly under the limp burden, her face frozen in a tragedy mask.

Memory snapped into place. "The girl . . ." Ryder whispered. "She cut . . . own throat . . . saw it."

"Yes," said Lomax, very quietly. "One of the few things she ever said was that she'd rather die than be caught by those bastards again."

Ryder shook his head, trying to clear it. His strength had run out like water, leaving him nothing to fight off the memories, the pain, the stark awareness of his sins. "If I'd fired . . . ten seconds . . . sooner . . . could've saved her."

"No," Lomax sighed. "I saw. The blood trail started inside the car. He must've hit her with the crowbar when she ran out of ammo, stopped to reload. He reached in to haul her out, and she started cutting right then. You couldn't have got him, and couldn't have stopped her. The miracle is that you stayed conscious to fire at all. Your bullet-proof vest is shot to hell, and you took enough damage under it."

Ryder didn't answer. No point trying to explain that this wasn't the first time he'd failed, other times with less excuse, too many times willingly. Bad cop. Dirty CHiP. Pig, plagued by a cockroach . . .

They reached the car and Lomax eased him down, left him sitting with his back braced against the front wheel. "Just a minute, while I report to the Fleet," he said, climbing into the car.

The radio crackled again and Ryder bit his lip, stabbed by memories. He looked to his right and saw the biker's headless corpse sprawled in its pool of drying blood, warty genitals sagging out of opened pants, a buzzard poking at them.

So I shot some road-rats. Ryder closed his eyes. *Big deal. Too little, too late. Story of my life.* He wondered why Jiminy Cockroach wasn't kicking him, now that he was down and defenseless, a perfect target.

Lomax slid back out of the car. "They'll be here in less than an hour," he said. "Now let's get you patched up." He took hold of Ryder's good arm and pulled him to his feet.

146

This time, Ryder couldn't drag in enough air to scream. Buzzing blackness danced teasingly across his vision, but the pain wouldn't let him sink mercifully into it. He could feel his feet dragging on the sand, ribs sandpapering in his broken side, the shift of pressure as Lomax set him down carefully on something soft, then hands pulling away his punctured jacket, unfastening the ruined kevlar armor. He wished to God he could faint.

When the careful hands began probing for the shot-broken ribs, making the pain soar to white blindness, his prayer was granted.

Coming back took long, slow time. Awareness moved in cautious stages: feel of something soft under his back, feel of only mild heat, smell of water on cloth, sound of brief and distant CB noise. There was no stink of rancid sweat and blood, and no pain. In fact, he was surprisingly comfortable, lying in quiet shadow, on softness, not even hot or hungry or thirsty.

Where . . . ?

His eyes opened easily this time, and he looked up at the tarpaulin ceiling stretched between the scouts' car and the wrecked pickup. Someone had wetted down the cloth, which accounted for the coolness under it. Ryder found himself lying on a foam-rubber camper's bed-pad, with a small bedroll tucked under his head. He felt slightly vague and dizzy, maybe from some sort of painkillers, maybe leftover wound-shock. He was stripped to the waist, and barefoot. He'd been washed, and his hair was still damp. A loose sling supported his left arm. His ribs were taped, but beyond the bandage he could see the edges of a huge purple bruise that stretched almost from his shoulder to his waist. It looked as if he'd been kicked by a mule.

But still, no pain. He felt indecently good, in fact. He hadn't slept in a real bed, nor on anything softer than desert ground, since Black Thanksgiving. This comfort was downright seductive, and surely more than he deserved.

A soft whine drew his attention to the other side of the tent. The dog lay there, curled up on a folded bedroll, its foreleg splinted and bandaged. The small beast regarded him with sad brown eyes, plainly grieving for the girl it hadn't been able to save. Ryder knew exactly how the dog felt.

He looked away, and saw Lena sitting at the front of the make-

147

shift tent. She was gazing off into the pale-orange desert, her mahogany hair tumbled down about her shoulders. From somewhere out in the glaring sunlight came the methodical sound of a shovel digging into the hard sand-clay soil. Digging Spooky's grave.

Ryder squeezed his eyes shut. So they'd taken him in—and how could he get out? Maybe crawl out the back of the tent?

He tried to roll over and get his good arm under him, but he hadn't the strength to sit up, and his bound ribs ached enough to drop him back, panting, on the foam-rubber pad. Out, out, how to get out before the woman came back here, got a good look, finally recognized him? He had no idea.

But Jiminy Cockroach might.

Ryder pulled as deep a breath as he could, and braced himself for whatever would follow. He'd never tried to summon The Voice before, always the opposite. What would happen if he called it willingly, let it walk into his waking mind and settle there unhindered? Maybe it would take over completely, take his body for itself and squeeze him out into forever-dark, blot him out as if he'd never existed.

And maybe that would be just as well. He'd done damned little good for the world, for himself, in this beat-up flesh. Maybe JC could do better with it.

Cockroach, he called to it. *JC, where are you?* Then held his breath, waiting.

Here. The Voice sounded very calm and somber. It wasn't coming from the back of his skull this time, but from lower down, down below the bandage.

With a jolt of horror, Ryder realized that the thing had burrowed its way into his heart. Now that he knew, he could feel it there: a deep, fist-sized ache. The Voice didn't want to eat his mind at all; it wanted something else.

And he still had to ask its advice. *Damn you, Cockroach, how do I get away from here?*

You don't, said the implacable Voice. *You stay here, and you deal with these people. They've taken you in, given you a place with them, and now you start earning your keep.*

No! No! Ryder rolled his head back and forth on the makeshift pillow. *Not with them! The redhead— Any time now, she'll take*

148

a good look at me, and remember, and start asking questions—and what then?

Then you answer, and you pay for your sins—in whatever coin they ask. Jiminy Cockroach paused to let him think that over, then chuckled—somehow without his former sneer. *Besides, she may have guessed already. Have you thought of that?*

Ryder bit his lip, choking back a sob of despair and cold fear. What if it was true? What if she did remember, knew what he was, meant to make him pay for it? How? Torture? Slavery? He could imagine a dozen horrors, knew he deserved any or all of them, and for far more than the woman knew about. The Cockroach knew it all. *Is this why you brought me here? To make me pay?*

No. The Voice sighed. *You never would understand, would you? I just want you to be a decent human being, so I can go home.*

Home? Ryder clawed vainly at the skin over his inhabited heart.

I'm part of you, you fool, Jiminy Cockroach explained tiredly. *I'm the part you shut up, shoved away, tried to cut out of yourself—since long before Black Thanksgiving. We're supposed to be a unity, one creature. It was you that made us separate, and I damn well resent it!*

Ryder tried to imagine that, picture whatever was inside the thing that had gnawed at him, hounded him, kicked him back and forth across this desert for a year and more. He couldn't do it. The thing was just too alien, too knowing, too farsighted, too concerned with the whole damned world to be any part of himself.

. . . No, no part of James Currin Ryder, the one smart kid in a family of dull, pious, good little victims who'd been so pleased when he got his badge, thinking he did it to protect nice little victims like themselves, never seeing that he hated the thought of being like them, that he'd done it because the Highway Patrol paid well and gave him considerable power in a world where good obedient civilians had none, gave him power to play with, enjoy, get caught with . . .

And so he'd lived when they'd all died, gone to heaven in a flash of light, right enough, charred to instant ashes while they sat around the Thanksgiving dinner table, no doubt thanking the ever-silent Lord for their blessings, the blessings of being bullied around by even bigger power-suckers than he was, and he was out on the road beyond the mountains conniving to get a look at the redhead's tits.

No, no, you bastard! You'll only get me killed like them! That's all you ever wanted. No!

And what's your life worth?

No answer to that. Not now, not an hour ago, not in a long, long time.

He could feel his ribs rise and fall as Jiminy Cockroach sighed in disgust. *Fool,* The Voice whispered. *You never would look beyond your next meal or screw, would you? Now, by all that's holy, I'll make you look.*

The thing bit him.

He could almost see it: the cartoon Cockroach in the tattered tuxedo, ragged antennae drooping like a shabby bandido moustache, grabbing a fold of the dark-red throbbing wall of his heart and taking a healthy bite of it.

Out of the sudden hole burst a flood, vast and fierce as the Colorado breaking Glen Canyon Dam, not his heart's blood but pain, years' and years' worth, varied in all the colors of a dark rainbow: outrage and betrayal, the horrors of a world gone mad, grief as deep and wide as the blackened Pacific, and shame. Oh, that above all, that worse than the rest: shame running beneath all his memories like an earthquake fault under the ground.

I didn't just break my oath; I never believed it in the first place.

Whom had he served or protected? He'd seen from childhood that the laws were made by the powerful, who made themselves rich, and the rich who bought power, made for their own usage, made to serve themselves first and last with maybe an occasional trickling down of the goodies to all the good, obedient, power-less civilians. He'd seen three divisions in the world: the official power-suckers—ranged from beat-cop to president—who made the laws; the unofficial power-grabbers—street-crook to crime/industry boss—who broke or bought the laws; and all the good little victims who paid and obeyed them both. Hounds, wolves and sheep—and all he'd cared about was not being a sheep. Of the three, he'd despised the sheep most.

And yet those sheep, victims, good little citizens—they included his own family: Mom and Papa and Samantha and the kids and his brothers and sister and more . . . Everyone he'd loved, everyone he'd ever cared about—they were all good little victims, and he'd despised them for it.

That was what had earned him this life in a world full of wolves. Seeing that was pain enough to leave him writhing like a half-crushed snake, weeping like a child. The bullet had hurt less.

"Hush. Lie still," said another voice. "The Fleet will be here soon. They'll have some decent painkillers. Try to lie still."

Through the blinding flood, Ryder felt hands pinning his shoulders down. He looked up, blinked his blurred eyes clear and saw Lena looking down at him. There was nothing in her face but concerned gentleness.

If she'd despised him, he could have endured it. Her kindness was enough to break him. It meant that she couldn't know the truth.

If he told her, she just might be angry enough to kill him— and anything was better than this.

"I remember . . . you," he squeezed out, past ragged gulps of air. "I was . . . the cop . . . stopped you . . . Black Thanksgiving."

"I know." She smiled. "I recognized you when you walked in this morning."

"You knew?" Ryder gaped at her, momentarily shocked clear of the pain.

"It'd be hard to forget that evening." Lena sat back on her heels. "You probably saved my life, you know."

Ryder shook his head, understanding nothing.

"What, don't you see it? You stopped me—and you were standing between me and the flash when the bombs hit Los Angeles." She rubbed her eyes thoughtfully. "If I'd been driving then, I would've been flash-blinded—at over sixty miles an hour, on a mountain highway, with the wind and impact and earthquake coming close after. What do you think my chances would have been?"

Ryder slowly rolled his head back and forth in numb denial. He'd done good by pure accident, while trying to do wrong. "I didn't . . . stop you . . . because you were speeding. I was bored . . . and you were pretty . . . and I wanted to look at your tits."

Lena burst out laughing.

Ryder bit back a sob of misery; she didn't understand, and he'd have to crawl on with his confession, on and on until she saw the whole pattern. "Afterward . . . I just ran home. Never mind duty. Never thought of it. Just looked for . . . my family . . ."

"Who didn't?" Lena cut in. "Radio down, phones gone, total chaos, how could you even find any other cops? What could you have done, anyway? All the so-called Emergency Services were straws in the wind by then."

"God, you don't understand." He could feel Jiminy Cockroach grinning with his mouth full, chewing on the raw chunk of his heart. *"I was a dirty cop—and that's what saved me!"*

Lena raised a mahogany eyebrow at him. "You didn't nudge me for my wallet," she said.

"No . . . not corrupt for money. Worse. Dirty for . . . power. Bullying. God, I liked making civilians crawl! Leaning on them, scaring them, making them cringe . . . knocking them around, even, when I thought I could get away with it."

Lena sat very still, hands flat on her thighs. "I noticed," she murmured, "when you came swaggering up to my car: you had the Cop Waddle down pat. It was almost funny. You could have done it on stage and made a bundle . . . That's what put my back up, made me argue with you."

For a jarring instant Ryder wondered if that wasn't one of the reasons he'd done it, looking for that one civilian in a hundred who wouldn't cringe, wouldn't back down, would break the pattern, be something more than a sheep. But no, he'd especially hated the ones who did that, argued with him, tried to prove him wrong, upset the natural order of the world.

"Christ, do you know . . . why I was out there . . . patrolling that damn-near empty highway . . . on Thanksgiving evening? Punishment detail!"

"Punishment? For what?"

"Roughing up civilians." Ryder closed his eyes, feeling a breath of wind on his damp face. "Maybe one in a hundred ever complained. I thought I was safe . . ." He made himself look at her again. "Before you . . . I caught a carful of Guardian Angels going on patrol . . . shook 'em down, gave 'em hell . . . said they could maybe . . . get away with playing vigilante in the LA gutters . . . but I'd personally grind their butts . . . if they

152

tried it in a decent neighborhood. Jesus, I had fun saying that! Hated civilians who got uppity. God . . .''

"Uppity niggers, uppity women," Lena murmured. "Old, old game."

Yes, she was beginning to see it. "But they did complain. Squawked to Internal Affairs, and the civilian review board, and the papers, and a couple of councilmen . . . Hell, they squawked, and it caught up with me. Chief gave me hell. Two weeks' suspension, no pay—then work on the holidays . . ." He would have worked Christmas too, and New Year's—but there had been no Christmas, and not a new year but a new dark age. The Age of the Wolf: no more hounds or sheep. But then, where did these people fit in? What manner of beast were they?

"You got off lightly. So?"

Pain, blinding shame again: couldn't she see just *how* lightly? "So I was safe in the mountains when millions died! My city, my whole family, everyone and everything I ever cared about— I was saved because of my sins! Not my . . . my virtues, if I ever had any. All those innocent people died, and I was dirty so I lived, and none of it makes any sense . . ."

And that was the core of the pain. That was why he'd run off to the empty desert, the simple and straightforward hell of nature—because nothing else made any sense. If the world was hell, where only power and killing-skill mattered, then why did Jiminy Cockroach exist? Why had JC nagged him off that fallout-drenched ridge, driven him away to safety, saved his worthless life? Why did people like Lena survive and succeed? A world of evil he could understand and live with, but not a world of madness.

JC, say something! Save me!

"Bullshit," Lena answered calmly. "You survived by pure, blind luck. Your boss could just have easily have sent you patrolling the freeways of Los Angeles on Black Thanksgiving. Did you ever think of that?"

No, he hadn't. Ryder turned the idea over and over, like a baffled ant with a cigarette butt, trying to understand it. Yes, of course plenty of wolves and hounds had died, too, in the One-Day War. He might have been among them. But then, why . . .

"Others survived by foresight," Lena went on. "I was heading for the Settlement, up in the hills, when you stopped me.

153

Some survived by paranoia; they'd cut out when the political trouble started heating up, weeks or even months earlier. Some survived by claustrophobia, moving out to empty country years before, just to get away from too many neighbors. There must be a million reasons for survival. Nature isn't choosy; she takes a scattergun approach."

Crazy, crazy . . . ". . . By luck and my sins?" Ryder struggled to keep up with the idea. It was an answer, and it did make a perverse kind of sense. Maybe there was, had always been, still another kind of people besides the three he knew. Remember the mammals who survived, small and quick and unnoticed, through the Age of Reptiles—then came out and flourished when the dinosaurs were dead. And what manner of beast was this?

He looked up at Lena, noting how her thick manzanita-red hair draped her face like folded wings. Wings: a new breed of bird. Eagle? Or perhaps the legendary phoenix, that was born in fire . . .

Imagine a world much wider and freer than he'd ever been taught, ever seen, ever believed: a world where almost anything could kill or save him. Not chaos, no: he could glimpse emerging patterns in it, much more complicated than he'd ever thought. There might even be a place in those half-seen webs for a ruined hound, a poor mangled son of a bitch like himself.

You're finally learning, Jiminy Cockroach smiled.

"Tell me something," Lena cut in on the silence. "Why did you turn around and come back to help us? Was it just to get another look at my tits?"

Ryder winced. "No, nothing like that. I . . . had no choice. You were good people. I hadn't known there were any left, any that could live. I . . ." *The Cockroach threatened—* "I would have gone crazy if I'd left you to die."

Yes, The Voice whispered. *You need something to believe in, or you can't live. That's why I'm here.*

Lena brushed hair out of her eyes and gazed out at the waiting desert. "You know, you do have a conscience," she said. "Times past, maybe you ignored it or overrode it or excused your way around it—but you've still got it."

Ryder bit his lip to hold back a spurt of crazed laughter. His fingers clawed briefly at the fading ache in his heart. Oh yes, he knew.

154

"Yes, you've done your share of sins—but you *know* they were sins, and it hurts you. That alone puts you in a different league from the road-rats, the bandidos, the dirty little feudal lordlings—all the garbage we've seen on our expeditions."

She turned and flashed a smile at him.

"You're in our league, Ryder. We need people like you, and you need people like us."

Ryder closed his eyes, terrified of where this was leading. A new age, a new people, a whole new order to the world—and he just might fit in if he could change enough, find something of value in himself to build on.

Cockroach, he called once more. *This is what you wanted, isn't it? Go back to my old job, but this time do it right. Right? Dust off that oath, maybe recast it, believe in it this time. Protect the innocent, apprehend the guilty, uphold the law . . . whatever law they have. Law of Nature, maybe. But I don't understand it. I understand so little, and the world's turned so vast and strange, and I so badly need to believe in something . . . I'm scared sick, Cockroach . . . Cockroach?*

No answer. No further orders. Nothing but a faint ripple of memory where the pain had been: memory of how good it once was, just to have someone to care about. Much better than the greasy taste of power, of having someone to look down on.

So simple.

That was where I chose wrong, years before the bombs fell. I chose pride before love. The sin of arrogance.

And now he had a chance to choose again.

"Yes," he said, sinking back onto the bedroll. "Take me in."

"All right." Lena patted his good shoulder, then turned to look out again at the desert. The radio chattered again, noticeably louder. "They'll be here soon," she said. "Just rest."

Ryder let his eyes wander up to the cloth tent-ceiling, imagining the infinite flame-blue sky beyond it. Rest, when he had so much to think about? He had a whole new age of the world to deal with, a new stage of evolution to fit himself into. How in hell could he do it? All he had, as Lena had told him, was that one little pro-survival mutation: a conscience. And maybe some common sense: he wasn't too stupid, or he couldn't have survived this long. Maybe those would be enough to live on, despite all the garbage he carried with him, left over from the

155

age of the dinosaurs. Could he keep those survival traits and shed the rest? Maybe, if he regretted his failings enough.

Oh, repent thine evil ways! As simple as that? Hardly, but a start . . .

"Lord, have mercy on me, a sinner," he whispered.

"Aren't we all," Lena murmured. "Thank whatever gods there be for second chances."

A god in a cartoon cockroach, Ryder thought, hearing the distant sound of approaching engines, probably just clearing the far pass. The future was rolling toward him on a rush of wheels, booze-powered vehicles, machines for the new age. What new gods rolled in with them? *Deus ex machina?*

You could do a lot worse, Jiminy Cockroach commented. *Hell, you could* be *a lot worse.*

Ryder smiled at the tarpaulin ceiling and waited for the Fleet to come in.

SONG OF THE RED WAR-BOAT
Rudyard Kipling

EDITOR'S INTRODUCTION

In addition to writing stories, Leslie Fish is a well-known performer. Her unique voice is known to nearly every attendee at science fiction conventions.

Two of her best-known works are collections of Kipling poems that she has set to music. The two volumes are called *The Undertaker's Horse* and *Cold Iron*. Kipling fans will recognize that these are titles of two Kipling poems; each of the tapes has a dozen songs. They're distributed by Off Centaur, the science fiction song publisher, and available at most SF conventions.

One of the songs included in *Cold Iron* is the "Song of the Red War-Boat"; a tale of loyalty that's appropriate at any time: A man must stand by his master, when once he has pledged his word.

━━━━━━━━━━━━━━━━━━━ ▪▪▪ ━━━━━━━━━━━━━━━━━━━

SONG OF THE RED WAR-BOAT
(A.D. 683)
"THE CONVERSION OF ST. WILFRID"—REWARDS AND FAIRIES

Shove off from the wharf-edge! Steady!
Watch for a smooth! Give way!

If she feels the lop already
She'll stand on her head in the bay.
It's ebb—it's dusk—it's blowing—
The shoals are a mile of white,
But (snatch her along!) we're going
To find our master to-night.

For we hold that in all disaster
Of shipwreck, storm, or sword,
A Man must stand by his Master
When once he has pledged his word.

Raging seas have we rowed in
But we seldom saw them thus,
Our master is angry with Odin—
Odin is angry with us!
Heavy odds we have taken,
But never before such odds.
The Gods know they are forsaken.
We must risk the wrath of the Gods!

Over the crest she flies from,
Into its hollow she drops,
Cringes and clears her eyes from
The wind-torn breaker-tops,
Ere out on the shrieking shoulder
Of a hill-high surge she drives.
Meet her! Meet her and hold her!
Pull for your scoundrel lives!

The thunders bellow and clamour
The harm that they mean to do!
There goes Thor's own Hammer
Cracking the dark in two!
Close! But the blow has missed her,
Here comes the wind of the blow!
Row or the squall'll twist her
Broadside on to it!—*Row!*

Heark'ee, Thor of the Thunder!
We are not here for a jest—
For wager, warfare, or plunder,
Or to put your power to test.
This work is none of our wishing—
We would house at home if we might—
But our master is wrecked out fishing.
We go to find him to-night.

For we hold that in all disaster—
As the Gods Themselves have said—
A Man must stand by his Master
Till one of the two is dead.

That is our way of thinking,
Now you can do as you will,
While we try to save her from sinking
And hold her head to it still.
Bale her and keep her moving,
Or she'll break her back in the trough. . . .
Who said the weather's improving,
Or the swells are taking off?

Sodden, and chafed and aching,
Gone in the loins and knees—
No matter—the day is breaking,
And there's far less weight to the seas!
Up mast, and finish baling—
In oars, and out with the mead—
The rest will be two-reef sailing. . . .
That was a night indeed!

But we hold that in all disaster
(And faith, we have found it true!)
If only you stand by your Master,
The Gods will stand by you!

PRIMUM NON NOCERE
Paul Edwards

EDITOR'S INTRODUCTION

"Mass poverty, malnutrition and deterioration of the planet's water and atmosphere resources—that's the bleak government prediction that says civilization has perhaps twenty years to head off such a world-wide disaster."

Thus began a typical story reporting *Global 2000*, a study commissioned by President Jimmy Carter. More than one million copies of *Global 2000: Report to the President* were distributed. Before the report was completed, President Carter used its conclusion as the basis for discussions with other world leaders. The disaster was rushing upon us; something had to be done.

There were even news stories with headlines like "We have to get poor quick."

We don't hear much about *Global 2000* anymore; but it's still out there, still used by government agencies as a basis for predictions. The AAAS meetings in 1984 featured a panel called "Knock Down Drag Out on the Global Future." The idea was to have optimists face pessimists; the pessimists in general accept the conclusions of *Global 2000*.

The Resourceful Earth (Basil Blackwell, 1984) was edited by Julian Simon and Herman Kahn just before Kahn's untimely death.

The book is a collection of essays whose central thesis is simple: *Global 2000* is dead wrong. Where *Global 2000* sees dead-end problems, *The Resourceful Earth* see challenges and opportunities. Julian Simon is an economist; and though economics is known as "the dismal science," there is nothing gloomy about his views of our potential future.

As an example: when England was denuded of forests, many predicted doom and poverty. Instead, England turned to coal, and entered a period of prosperity unequaled in human history. We now call that "the Industrial Revolution."

We stand at such a crossroads again. We have the resources, we have the science, we have the technology; do we have the will to solve global problems? Or must we despair and die?

From population to pollution, crops, water, energy, and minerals, *The Resourceful Earth* presents an alternative to doomsday. The era of limits and the time of national malaise are over. The only limit to man's vast future is nerve.

In the event the unthinkable happens and we do have a nuclear or biological war, the pessimists will fall to the ground, gnash their teeth, pull their hair out, and soon fall still. Meanwhile, men like Doctor Mallin will see the disaster as a new beginning; an opportunity to do it right this time . . .

━━━━━━━━━━━━━━━•¦•━━━━━━━━━━━━━━━

DOCTOR JEFFREY MALLIN DISMOUNTED AND KNELT BY THE white globe, pushing the rocky dirt away with his bare hands. There was no danger; none of the sand of black glass such as covered the Tucson and Phoenix regions, sharp little particles that worked their way into your skin and wiped out your marrow. It was a skull, probably a young adult. Most of the teeth were present . . . might be valuable to the Dental College someday, if it ever got started. There was even a gold filling, which gave him a tremor of avarice, quickly suppressed by thoughts of the Second World War, an ancient horror. He lifted the smooth white bone and turned back to the horse, thinking, "Alas, poor Yorick." Somebody somewhere had to have a copy of *Hamlet*.

There was plenty of room in his pack next to the treasure from Brownie Johnson's mill. The trip from Quartzite to Blythe, the capital of California, didn't take more than a few days, and he was almost there. With a heave and a grunt he swung his leg over the saddle and eased himself down, scanning a full circle for danger: a survival habit from days of the Dark. But there was no danger now, years after the war, except for radiation, and that was easy enough to avoid by staying away from the bomb sites. In the desert, no one could sneak up on a survivor. An intact skull probably belonged to someone who had starved to death during the miniature ice age that followed the bombs. Just as the Doc was about to thump his heels into the tired mare's flanks, his far-sighted eye caught the flapping of a tiny red flag in the distance to the north.

He sagged. It meant spending the night out here, but the Oath was the Oath and he couldn't ignore what he had seen. He had enough water. He pulled the reins and headed off.

It was always good to come calling; people were always pleased to have what help they could get. Small and medium-sized children came running down the road with the universal sound of merriment and took Doc's reins and led him in. Ray Smith, the paterfamilias, greeted him with a beefy handshake.

"Good to see you, Doc, good to see you! New horse?"

"It's Brownie Johnson's. You know he's the only one in Quartzite who could afford to loan anybody a mount."

"Let me get you a drink," Ray said, and before he could turn, a young woman handed Doc a plastic drinking glass with no chips in it, filled with pale green water.

"It's real mint," she said. "It grows real good up here." She smiled, and her teeth were perfect.

Mallin smiled back, thinking about the other set of good teeth in his bag. Maybe I should have been a dentist, he thought. He shrugged his musings off and turned to Ray. "Where's the patient?"

"My wife, Marylou. Jeannie's with her."

Ray led him into the back. It was very cozy: a combination of unmortared rock, mesquite beams, and automotive sheet metal. These people were doing well for themselves. In a small bedroom, a woman huddled on her pallet, clutching her stomach and moaning, while a ten-year-old girl next to her wiped her face with a damp rag.

"Marylou, I got the Doc. Doc Mallin's here."

She looked up and focused on Mallin with an effort. "My

162

belly's killin' me, Doc! Please give me somethin' for the pain! Please, Doc!'' Her head fell back on clean, neatly folded rags.

Mallin knew exactly what he would feel before he put his hands on her belly, but the rituals had to be done so that the onlookers would know that he was a Real Healer. Wearing the automatic expression of intense concern and cerebration, he mused on the old days, when he would have gotten X-ray, and CBC, and U/A, and a second opinion to protect him from malpractice claims. What I really need, he thought, is a drum and some rattles. And poppies.

Her belly was stiff as a board. "Marylou, you're going to be all right. I'm going to have to do a little work on you, but it'll be all right.'' He stood up and told the pretty girl, "Bring her to the largest room in the house, boil at least three gallons of water, and if there's anything fermented to drink, bring that, too.'' He squinted at her. "You're Cindy, aren't you?"

He'd fixed an intimate little problem which she might have gotten from her boyfriend. It was shortly after the sun had come out. There could be no such thing as "the benefit of the doubt" when the sparse, stunted food they grew barely sufficed for the people you could be certain of. Doc remembered her stony ambivalence at the hanging of Typhoid Casanova, but of course, that was a quick mercy next to turning him out to starve, and safer than risking his turning thief or killer for food. And here she was, pretty, almost mature, and carrying that confidence which all the survivors of the Dark had about them.

"Yes, Doc." She looked down, embarrassed. "Ray took me in when my folks died.'' She turned away and began hollering at the children to help her move Marylou.

The soap they had was strong, with too much lye left in it, but Mallin had scrubbed with worse. He looked straight at Ray.

"If it's her appendix, it's probably ruptured already. If so, she'll probably die. If it's an ovary, she'll do fine, and if it's something from the Dark, all bets are off. I'll do what I can, but you know . . .''

"Sure, Doc. We're all glad you're here. We know she'd be dead for sure if you didn't come.''

"Can you hit her?"

"You mean knock her out? God, I don't know . . .''

"I'll take care of it.''

163

The whole conversation depressed him because it reminded him of all the drugs he used to depend on: all gone, never to be replaced, while *he* was practicing at least. The herbalism of the Southwest was just beginning to be rediscovered; if there were any medicine men left, they could hardly be expected to share such knowledge with the race which had burned their lands beyond the capacity of any spirits to heal.

He always took all his tools with him wherever he went. His pride and joy was a prewar tissue forceps that worked perfectly, its little teeth matching exactly. It sat in a tray next to his delicately hand-made instruments in an inch of 'shine.

The cloth lay over Marylou's face.

"Okay, honey, now hold real still." He had measured the sand precisely into the little sack, and knew exactly where to strike: the result of the neurosurgeons' research. This grotesque parody of anesthesia frightened him almost to trembling, but nothing could budge the mask of confidence he wore for the family. There was a groan and Marylou sagged.

For an old man, Mallin could move when he wanted to. As he screamed at Ray to start blowing air into her mouth and to hold her jaw the way he'd explained over and over, he cut in one stroke to the muscle, through thin sprays of blood. In five seconds he had the gut exposed, and the stink of pus filled the room. It depressed Mallin to have his gloomy predictions verified, and it terrified and nauseated the family, but he kept yelling for this and that while pulling the bowel up into the wound, and finally he saw the source of all the trouble, and, sure enough, it was the appendix, black and ragged. In moments, he had tied the boiled threads around blood vessels and around the stump, and then Marylou began to wake up. Mallin, yearning for the succinyl choline he'd never use again, reached over and smacked the side of her head, and she stopped pushing her guts into the room. In a few minutes, he had the stitches in the fascia. The skin and the fat he left open and put a freshly boiled dressing on. Then he got the rubber tube.

"I'll be coming back to get this, and it better be in good shape! Now watch closely!" He lifted up one of Marylou's legs and shoved the thin tube into her rectum as far as it would go.

"You only use fresh meat, and boil it for at least three hours. Then let it cool to just a little warmer than room temperature.

Drip it in through the tube around the clock until she farts, then let her have sips and cut the drip to half a day per day, until her bowels start to work. Then you can take it out. And make sure she's taking deep breaths all the time. Understand?'' And that's modern surgery, Mallin thought. Someone's just got to learn how to make ether.

Dinner was rabbit and mint salad, and not bad.

"I hear ol' Brownie's really got his mill going," said Ray, passing the water jug. "Got four or five people working for him, doesn't he?"

Mallin forced politeness through his exhaustion. "Once he got the lathe working, he got some perfectly smooth rollers turned pretty quickly. His sheets are as smooth as silk."

He glanced around the table, feeling guilty for mentioning silk, an unreclaimable sweetness from Before. "This salad is really good."

"Will you be able to stay tomorrow?" Cindy asked.

"I'll have to be going in the morning. This is the first real medical conference since the Dark. After all the talk about the medical school, they're finally going to do it." She couldn't hide the sad look. "I have to be there." He looked down at his plate and selected a small bone to gnaw.

Ray made a signal to conclude the meal, which made Doc grateful that he wouldn't have to put out any more chitchat. The children led him to his room as Ray and Cindy began a whispered argument that wasn't quiet enough.

The bed was firm and comfortable, and the oldest child brought heated water to wash with. From the look on his face, he'd thought of this little touch himself. Mallin wasn't used to treating himself so decadently, but he could hardly refuse the youngster. He made some hopeful lies about Marylou, and sent him out. His next visitor was, of course, no surprise.

Cindy had washed, and brushed her hair. She entered after a knock but without waiting for an answer, and found Mallin under the thin blanket. She knelt beside him.

"I just . . . I just wanted to thank you," she began lamely. "You've always been a hero to me." It sounded ridiculous and she knew it.

"If you want to seduce someone, make them feel sexy and

165

make them feel you absolutely have to have them. Don't offer sex out of gratitude. It makes people feel like you're doing them a favor.''

She rocked back on her heels, tears filling her eyes. "I'm sorry,'' she stammered, "I didn't mean to—'' and she tried to go. Mallin's hand caught her.

"*I'm* sorry,'' he said. "I shouldn't have snapped at you. You know, it couldn't happen. You've been my patient. It's the Oath.''

"But that was so long ago! And everybody knows you live alone, and that isn't good, especially now—''

"I'm just used to being a widower, that's all.''

"Does that mean I can't do something nice for you? Roll over.''

What the hell. He let her put firm healing hands on his back, and didn't object as her massage became more extensive. Such decadence. Minutes passed and Mallin heard the silence of the household sleeping, and felt himself slipping away as his muscles finally gave up their tension and relaxed. He almost missed the hesitation in her voice.

"Doc?'' she said.

"Hmm?''

"Ray's got something you might want to see.''

"Let him show me in the morning.''

"Maybe I ought to get it now.''

"Whatever.'' Suddenly there were no hands on him and no presence near him, and then he was being rolled over out of a sound sleep and a book was put into his hands.

A book. He blinked his eyes at it. The front cover had been ripped off, and a dog had chewed one end, but there it was, all the line drawings and garish colors he remembered from his medical student days. He hadn't seen Grant's *Atlas of Anatomy* since before the Dark. Wiry fingers trembled as they gently turned the shiny pages.

"Where did you get this?''

"I don't know. Ray got it somewhere. It's worth a lot.''

Cindy, you have no idea. "Are there any other books hidden away out here?''

"I don't know.'' She looked down at it, touched it with her forefinger as though it were a relic of power. "He told me not to tell you about it.''

166

"Why not?"

"So he could sell it, I guess. He keeps talking about mining, you know, they used to do mining right around here Before. But just living is so hard, and you have to have people working for you to get anything going. He talks about Brownie Johnson all the time. Sometimes he gets . . . kind of scary. He'll be madder than hell about this, I know."

"So greed and envy get started again, before we've barely gotten back on our feet." He looked at her raised eyebrows. "Philosophy," he said. "Occupational hazard." He looked at the open book, and the dissected layers of the muscles of the shoulder looked back. "The medical school needs this. *Must* have it. Understand?"

She nodded. She was ready to steal it, had been ready for some time. Mallin looked closely at her and tried to see what was between her and Ray. Her face was a proud mask; she didn't want to discuss it, and the truth was, neither did he. Besides, it might lead toward talk about how she had survived the Dark. That was taboo: a topic not even a doctor would discuss.

But he didn't want to violate Ray's trust. Since the Dark, travel was possible only because the mutual obligations between host and guest were held sacred. A guest did not steal from his host.

And there was the Oath. "Into whatever house I enter, I enter to heal the sick, and will abstain from the seduction of man or woman, bond or free" and all other assorted vices.

But what about all the effort to get the country back on its feet? Wasn't every human being responsible for the rebuilding? Especially this little niche of it, the reclaiming of lost books, lost knowledge? What right had Ray Smith to hoard this priceless thing, of no value to him, save as it might give his cockamamie schemes a brief breath of life before going belly up? And especially a *medical* book, now that a real medical school was getting started?

A real medical school without medicines, whose main value would be to transmit the knowledge of the past into a future where it wouldn't have to be rediscovered when the technical end of the matter had gotten itself back together—

Books. He missed *Hamlet*, and especially *Lear*. But if there were a Europe to get them from . . . but there had been no word from Europe or Asia or Africa since the Dark. The stories of

167

horror from Mexico City when the sun went out, tens of millions dead in the barbaric chaos of rioting and fire—

Blythe might be the only living city in the world. If the rest of the world were thriving but had chosen to cast the U.S.A. out of the community of civilized peoples, it could not be worse. They were all beyond the reach of help. Except for what they could give each other.

"You've put me in an impossible situation. You know this book belongs in the Library at Blythe. So does Ray."

"Take it, Doc! Take it!"

The temptation was great: a priceless relic, and a young, pretty wife for the asking. *Can she really be attracted to me, or am I just a ticket out of here?*

Slowly he shook his head. Robbing his host, no matter how noble the reason, would cost him his reputation in the community, regardless of the fact that he was one of the precious few doctors left. And since medical science had been bombed back to ancient Greece, he couldn't take care of the sick without his reputation. And the sick had to come first, even before the School.

"Go see how Marylou's doing. Come and get me any time if there's a problem—check to make sure she's getting that fluid poured into her. She could still die from this, you know."

"Oh, Doc!" She gave him a big hug, but spared him the necessity of refusing a kiss. "I could love you, I really could. I'll make Ray give you the book in the morning."

She left before Mallin's resolve collapsed.

The sight of that saddle made Mallin's butt ache, but he heaved himself into it without assistance. Cindy had carefully packed his bag and his case of freshly washed instruments, more proof of the kind of doctor's wife she would make. That Marylou was still alive ought to have been cause for rejoicing, instead of the silence of Mallin's leave-taking.

"Her fever's down a bit, Ray; a good sign. She's not out of the woods but there's nothing I can do that you can't. I'll stop by on my way back to Quartzite. Shouldn't be more than a few days."

"Thank you, Doctor Mallin. Have a good trip." Ray didn't offer his hand.

"You're making a big mistake. Let me take that book to Blythe. I'll donate it in your name. For generosity like that, you could probably get volunteers to come out here and work your mine for food alone."

" 'Probably'!" Ray spat. "I've had it up to here with 'probablies.' There aren't a whole lot of chances left in the world, Doc, and if there's one left for me and my family, I'm going to take it." He couldn't keep up the tough pose. "There *is* silver out here. Think of it, Doc, getting a real money economy started again, and I hear there's some people in Blythe who are actually getting electricity started. They'll *need* silver! This is important work, Doc, and I need this chance!"

As if you could do anything with silver ore even if you found any. "Have it your way, Ray. Since you've been hearing things from all over, have you heard that it's customary to gift the doctor who's worked to save your wife's life?"

"She's not saved yet! You said so yourself!"

"Ray, without me she would be dead, no question about it. With me, her chances are fifty-fifty. There's no guarantees, and you know that."

"I'll let you know how she does. Why don't you take Cindy? She's a nice prize. Very loyal, too."

"The way I was brought up, human beings can't be given as gifts." He picked up the reins. "So long, Ray."

Cindy came down the path from the house to where Mallin was getting ready to leave as Ray stalked back up and through the gate, not meeting her eyes.

She came up close to him. "Marylou's sleeping now. She's really been sweating a lot."

"Then pour more broth in her! And for God's sake don't let her lie there like a lump! You've got to get her breathing and coughing, and it'll hurt, but do it anyway." All his barking wasn't going to faze those bright eyes. Maybe I'm not just a passport. "You let me know if he so much as touches you."

"You'll have to stand in line. Bend down. I want to whisper something." Her kiss was gentle, and gave Mallin the startling discovery that he had hoped for it. "Come and visit after Marylou's better, okay?"

"Cindy, how could I resist?"

"Easily," she said, and smiled her perfect smile again.

169

Cleaning up in the kitchen, Cindy felt Ray's presence behind her, felt him calculating the difference between the satisfactions of beating her and the inevitable sequelae when it became widely known. He kept his hands to himself.

"That bastard," he said quietly. "I'd rather burn the damn book than let him have it for nothing."

It always made Mallin smile when Blythe came into view: medieval barbicans, Roman walls, Egyptian agriculture, and Sumerian solitude. The Thames, Tiber, Nile, Euphrates, or Colorado—it was all the same. And fools said the bombs would send us back to the Stone Age.

Inside what seemed like miles of high, thick rubblestone walls, Mallin could barely remember the appearance of prewar Main Street, the home of Every Franchise Known To Man. Not one relic of the age of electricity had survived. It was easy to find California Hall, the largest building in Blythe constructed since the war. There were defunct movie houses larger than California Hall, but just to be inside the huge fieldstone chamber gave a person the confidence that there really would be a future worth having.

The proceedings stopped as soon as he was recognized.

"It's Jeff!" several people shouted at once. Mallin almost looked around; nobody called him by his first name anymore.

"Hello friends. Did I miss anything important?"

Barbara Hovic, one of the two obstetricians, took him by the arm, and whispered in his ear. "It's worse than Before. The surgeons want to throw the psychiatrist out."

"Figures." He pulled his pack off his shoulders. "Got a present from one of our 'prominent citizens.' " He was about to show her when Herb Gold, the cardiologist who'd been elected chairman, rapped for attention.

"Good to see you, Jeff. That's everybody, so far as I know, in the entire Southwest valley. Twenty-two doctors in the entire known world. If we die, that's it, unless we all start training successors at once. Now, there's been a couple of proposals on how to do it. One is for each of us to take at least one apprentice—"

Jake Engrand, a surgeon, interrupted. "Are we supposed to

feed the snot-noses while they wander around with us, getting in the way? And if so, with what?"

"Apprentices have always worked for their living," Gold shot back. "You should be able to find all kinds of useful things for an extra pair of hands to do, without abusing them in the process."

"That'll go over big with these so-called apprentices. And where does the food come from?"

"We'll have to bring that up with the whole City. When we built the walls, the framers didn't resent feeding the rest of us. As for the apprentices' attitudes, I'm not worried. Life is different now for everybody. Children are less spoiled now. Less than you are, for example."

The guffaws stopped when Jake jumped up to shout: "Your university days are over, Gold! Have you actually done anything for any of your patients lately? Medicine is a joke! Look at our 'medical library' over there." He pointed to a small bench on which rested the first sixty pages of an old Merck manual, a well-worn copy of the Lange pocket edition of *Medical Practice*, and the volume of Hippocrates from the *Great Books of the Western World*. "What good are drug-treatment protocols when there aren't any drugs? Fluid-and-electrolytes when there aren't any I.V.'s?"

"God, Jake, don't you think we all know that? But if we keep what we know alive, maybe the time to get back to where we were will be shorter . . ."

"And how long is that?"

Ken Wong stood up. He was the oldest, almost seventy. "Jake, your frustration doesn't matter. We need students for three reasons: because we need to keep medicine alive in our heads as well as for the future, because young people are starting to ask us about it, and because our patients will have stronger faith in us if we have a medical school behind us. Doctor Gold, please continue." He sat down, the only one comfortable in the silence.

Mallin whispered to Barbara, "Has it been like this all along?"

She shook her head. "Jake's been heading this way a long time. Everybody's had a lot of deaths. He's taking it personally."

"—apprentices, but only after a core curriculum," Gold continued. "This means a lot more work for everybody. Does anybody here have an eidetic memory? Anybody? I thought not. Recovering our medical school days and memorizing them could be a lifetime job."

"Mr. Chairman?"

"Jeff? What is it?"

Mallin brought his pack up to the podium. "The recovery part might be hard, but some of you younger guys can work on that. I've brought a present from a man in Quartzite to the Medical Society, if that's what we are." He reached in and brought out the skull first, and got a round of laughter. "No, that isn't it. I found that on the road; thought the dentists might want to get in on this act. Look at this." He brought out a gleaming white rectangular block and reached up to set it on the chairman's table. "Two hundred sheets of brand-new paper!"

Everybody crowded forward to touch the smooth, faintly toothy surface, and possibilities exploded in every imagination.

"This is a gift, and if we want more, he's not unreasonable. We can make copies of the books and atlas, and record what we know, and build a real medical library out of what's in our heads."

Engrand turned to Mallin. "Did you say 'atlas'?"

Conversation stopped. Herb Gold came over. "Atlas of what, Jeff?"

Mallin thought of Ray Smith's arrogant face. Well, the patient didn't tell him. It wasn't under the seal of confidentiality. "I discovered a copy of Grant's *Atlas* last night. It's not mine. It belongs to the husband of a woman I took care of last night, on my way here."

"So where is it?"

"Stop frothing at the mouth, Herb. He wouldn't give it up. He wants to sell it." Angry noises burst all around him. "I explained everything. He has plans and he thinks that this is the only—"

Two of the younger doctors came forward. "Where does he live, Jeff?"

"I don't think I like the sound of that."

"We've committed ourselves to busting our asses for our community, our world, and this selfish—"

"It would be a tremendous leg up to have anatomy already recorded instead of having to do all those dissections over and over again—"

"Damned ingrate! Maybe we ought to get the constables to go over there and—"

"Just boycott him, wait till he needs—"

"Why didn't you just bargain with him: you take care of his wife, he gives you the book?"

"HOLD IT!" Mallin jumped up on the podium and stared into all the angry faces. "What in hell do you think you're doing? We need that book and it doesn't belong to us! That's it! You know, Jake's right. This isn't the university anymore. Why don't you take a look in that copy of Hippocrates instead of sneering at it? Outside of describing illness, draining pus, reducing dislocations, and holding hands, there isn't a whole lot we can do right now. So what else have we got but the Oath? Not much.

"There's a woman dying with an acute abdomen. What do you do? Haggle with her husband? Is that how you expect people to learn to respect us? We aren't miracle workers anymore. Let's face it, hand-holding is what we do best.

"We all made it through the Dark. But our profession didn't make it at all. We have to use what we can remember from the past, or we're fools. And the Oath is one of the best parts of that. And even if you don't believe it, it's still good policy." He looked around, suddenly feeling embarrassed. "I didn't mean to make a speech," he said, and jumped down.

The murmuring began slowly but didn't get very far before Mallin heard Herb Gold's voice: "—adjourn till tomorrow. We'd all better think about what Jeff Mallin's said today—" turning his remarks into internal politics. He was exhausted. Barbara Hovic came up and took his arm.

"You can sleep at my place," she said, and led him out.

It was another fabulous sunset, which brought memories of Frederic Remington paintings and the bombs over San Diego all mixed together. "It doesn't make a difference," Jeff mumbled.

"I don't know," said Barbara. "I think you turned a few heads around in there."

The riders had gone east through the main gate; Barbara told him hours later, when he finally awoke. They're not idiots, Mal-

173

lin reflected. Surely they've figured out who owns the book. He hated to go—his buttocks were just beginning to feel like a part of him again—but it wasn't more than a half a day to Ray Smith's place.

Cindy was grim and determined, and the oldest boy was white-faced as they dug the hole. No jolly children had come running down the path.

"They told us you weren't to blame," Cindy said. "Ray came out with a gun. He didn't like their offer and started shooting."

"What did they bring?"

"A six-pound steel pick and a bolt of cloth." Steady rhythm of shovel into rocky soil. "They took it."

"How's Marylou?"

"Worse. She has no idea Ray's dead."

"It's true. I didn't mean to mention the *Atlas*, it just slipped out. But I never said who owned it. When it got ugly, I talked to them."

"Philosophy."

"They might have just come in shooting and taken it."

She stopped, leaned on her shovel, and looked straight at him. "I really want to believe all that, Doc. I really do."

He came forward, almost afraid to come close to her. But he couldn't keep his hands from reaching out and touching her shoulders. "I really want you to believe it, too."

A man dead, children deprived of a father, survival even more precarious than usual for half a dozen people. All because of a slip of the tongue.

He felt his heart pounding as he waited for her judgment, suddenly knowing that he wanted his loneliness to be over, wanted to share his secrets with her, wanted her to be with him, to be the doctor's wife she wanted to be. How foolish, he thought to himself. She's young enough to be my daughter. But it was no laughing matter.

When she spoke, the edge was out of her voice. "Get a shovel," she said, and he knew that he had found a partner for his sudden family and all the hard work ahead.

HORATIUS AT THE BRIDGE
Thomas Babington, Lord Macaulay

EDITOR'S INTRODUCTION

Unusual for anthologies, the *There Will Be War* series generates a large amount of reader correspondence, all of which we try to answer. (Any letters of comment can either be sent to us care of the publisher or to Jerry Pournelle, 3960 Laurel Canyon Blvd., Suite #372, Studio City, CA 91604.) Sometimes our readers direct us to favorite stories, or as in this case, poems that we have overlooked.

Dear Sir,
. . . Many of the stories and articles from [*There Will Be War*] Volume I through VII have been read and re-read, as they've been passed among my friends.

Your poetry selections for the series have not yet included one of my favorite poems, which depicts the role that the Soldierly Virtues had in founding the Republic of Rome. I have enclosed a copy of the text to "Horatius" from Lord Thomas Babington Macaulay's *Lays of Ancient Rome*. The version I know by heart is from "One Hundred and One Poems." . . . There is also some material from the preface of the novel *Perchance to Dream* written by your friend, the late Mack Reynolds.

I'm certain there is a more comprehensive version of the poem available somewhere. By now it's probably all in the public domain, since Lord Macaulay died in 1859 and the only version I know was published in 1958. In the meantime I have incorporated the passages from the preface to Mack Reynolds's story, along with some text of my own to provide continuity. . . .

Alas, the version he sent was missing many of its verses. Fortunately I didn't have to use it. Horatius was one of the lessons in my sixth grade reader from Capleville Consolidated. In those days we had two grades per room, and thirty pupils per grade. The teachers had only two-year normal-school degrees; but we all learned to read, and we read great literature. I still have a copy of my sixth-year reader, and I still remember having to memorize portions of Horatius: ". . . spake brave Horatius,/The Captain of the Gate:/'To every man upon this earth/Death cometh soon or late./And how can man die better/Than facing fearful odds,/For the ashes of his fathers,/And the temples of his gods . . .' "

Our modern schools no longer have two grades per room, but they seem more interested in the inane activities of Dick and Jane and their idiot dog Spot than in the West's heroic past. Indeed, I suspect that a good half our present-day teachers, despite having four-year college degrees, have never even heard of Thomas Babington, Lord Macaulay . . .

Rome had seven kings. The first was Romulus, the Founder; but later Rome fell under the rule of the Etruscans, and their last king was Tarquin the Proud. His son, Sextus, attempted seduction of a Roman matron of good family. When Sextus was rebuffed, he and his father had the lady killed; whereupon the Romans rose up and threw out both father and son, replacing the king with Consuls elected for one year terms.

Tarquin fled to his relatives, and enlisted the aid of Lars Porsena, King of Clusium, and a number of other heroes and allies, who marched on Rome.

Incidentally, the tradition was that the hero who led the uprising against the Tarquins was an ancestor of Brutus, whose family was thereafter particularly watchful lest any Roman try to become king; which is why, a few hundred years later, the historical Brutus turned on Julius Caesar.

They used to teach those things in public schools, at least in the rural South . . .

—————————————— ·|· ——————————————

— 1 —

Lars Porsena of Clusium
  By the Nine Gods he swore
That the great house of Tarquin
  Should suffer wrong no more.
By the Nine Gods he swore it,
  And named a trysting day,
And bade his messengers ride forth
East and west and south and north,
  To summon his array.

— 2 —

East and west and south and north
  The messengers ride fast,
And tower and town and cottage
  Have heard the trumpet blast.
Shame on the false Etruscan
  Who lingers in his home,
When Porsena of Clusium
  Is on the march for Rome.

— 3 —

The horsemen and the footmen
  Are pouring in amain
From many a stately market place;
  From many a fruitful plain;
From many a lonely hamlet,
  Which hid by beech and pine,
Like an eagle's nest, hangs on the crest
  Of purple Apennine.

— 4 —

The harvests of Arretium,
  This year old men shall reap;

177

This year, young boys in Umbro
  Shall plunge the struggling sheep;
And in the vats of Luna,
  This year, the must shall foam
Round the white feet of laughing girls
  Whose sires have marched to Rome.

— 5 —

There be thirty chosen prophets,
  The wisest of the land,
Who always by Lars Porsena
  Both morn and evening stand.
Evening and morn the Thirty
  Have turned the verses o'er,
Traced from the right on linen white
  By mighty seers of yore.

— 6 —

And with one voice the Thirty
  Have their glad answer given:
"Go forth, go forth, Lars Porsena;
  Go forth, beloved of Heaven;
Go, and return in glory
  To Clusium's royal dome;
And hang round Nurscia's altars
  The golden shields of Rome."

— 7 —

And now hath every city
  Sent up her tale of men;
The foot are fourscore thousand,
  The horse are thousands ten.
Before the gates of Sutrium
  Is met the great array.
A proud man was Lars Porsena
  Upon the trysting day.

— 8 —

But by the yellow Tiber
  Was tumult and affright:

From all the spacious champaign
   To Rome men took their flight.
A mile around the city,
   The throng stopped up the ways;
A fearful sight it was to see
   Through two long nights and days.

— 9 —

And droves of mules and asses
   Laden with skins of wine,
And endless flocks of goats and sheep,
   And endless herds of kine,
And endless trains of wagons
   That creaked beneath the weight
Of corn sacks and of household goods,
   Choked every roaring gate.

— 10 —

Now, from the rock Tarpeian,
   Could the wan burghers spy
The line of blazing villages
   Red in the midnight sky.
The Fathers of the City,
   They sat all night and day,
For every hour some horseman came
   With tidings of dismay.

— 11 —

To eastward and to westward
   Have spread the Tuscan bands;
Nor house nor fence nor dovecote
   In Crustumerium stands.
Verbenna down to Ostia
   Hath wasted all the plain;
Astur hath stormed Janiculum,
   And the stout guards are slain.

— 12 —

I wis, in all the Senate,
   There was no heart so bold,

But sore it ached, and fast it beat,
 When that ill news was told.
Forthwith up rose the Consul,
 Up rose the fathers all;
In haste they girded up their gowns,
 And hied them to the wall.

— 13 —

They held a council standing
 Before the River Gate.
Short time was there, ye well may guess,
 For musing or debate.
Out spake the Consul roundly:
 "The bridge must straight go down;
For, since Janiculum is lost,
 Naught else can save the town."

— 14 —

Just then a scout came flying,
 All wild with haste and fear;
"To arms! to arms! Sir Consul,
 Lars Porsena is here."
On the low hills to westward
 The Consul fixed his eye,
And saw the swarthy storm of dust
 Rise fast along the sky.

— 15 —

And nearer fast and nearer
 Doth the red whirlwind come;
And louder still and still more loud,
From underneath that rolling cloud,
Is heard the trumpet's war note proud,
 The trampling and the hum.
And plainly and more plainly
 Now through the gloom appears,
Far to left and far to right,
In broken gleams of dark-blue light,
The long array of helmets bright,
 The long array of spears.

Fast by the royal standard,
　O'erlooking all the war,
Lars Porsena of Clusium
　Sat in his ivory car.
By the right wheel rode Mamilius,
　Prince of the Latian name;
And by the left false Sextus,
　That wrought the deed of shame.

But when the face of Sextus .
　Was seen among the foes,
A yell that rent the firmament
　From all the town arose.
On the housetops was no woman
　But spat towards him and hissed;
No child but screamed out curses,
　And shook its little first.

But the Consul's brow was sad,
　And the Consul's speech was low,
And darkly looked he at the wall,
　And darkly at the foe.
"Their van will be upon us
　Before the bridge goes down;
And if they once may win the bridge,
　What hope to save the town?"

Then out spake brave Horatius,
　The Captain of the Gate:
"To every man upon this earth
　Death cometh soon or late.
And how can man die better
　Than facing fearful odds,
For the ashes of his fathers,
　And the temples of his gods,

"And for the tender mother
  Who dandled him to rest,
And for the wife who nurses
  His baby at her breast,
And for the holy maidens
  Who feed the eternal flame,
To save them from false Sextus
  That wrought the deed of shame?

"Hew down the bridge, Sir Consul,
  WIth all the speed ye may;
I, with two more to help me,
  Will hold the foe in play.
In yon strait path a thousand
  May well be stopped by three.
Now, who will stand on either hand,
  And keep the bridge with me?"

Then out spake Spurius Lartius,
  A Ramnian proud was he:
"Lo, I will stand at thy right hand,
  And keep the bridge with thee."
And out spake strong Herminius,
  Of Titian blood was he:
"I will abide on thy left side,
  And keep the bridge with thee."

"Horatius," quoth the Consul,
  "As thou sayest, so let it be."
And straight against that great array
  Went forth the dauntless three.
For Romans in Rome's quarrels
  Spared neither land nor gold,
Nor son nor wife, nor limb nor life,
  In the brave days of old.

Now while the Three were tightening
  Their harness on their backs,
The Consul was the foremost man
  To take in hand an ax;
And Fathers, mixed with Commons,
  Seized hatchet, bar, and crow,
And smote upon the planks above,
  And loosed the props below.

Meanwhile the Tuscan army,
  Right glorious to behold,
Came flashing back the noonday light;
Rank behind rank, like surges bright
  Of a broad sea of gold.
Four hundred trumpets sounded
  A peal of warlike glee,
As that great host, with measured tread,
And spears advanced, and ensigns spread,
Rolled slowly towards the bridge's head,
  Where stood the dauntless Three.

The Three stood calm and silent,
  And looked upon the foes,
And a great shout of laughter
  From all the vanguard rose;
And forth three chiefs came spurring
  Before that deep array;
To earth they sprang, their swords they drew,
And lifted high their shields, and flew
  To win the narrow way.

Aunus from green Tifernum,
  Lord of the Hill of Vines;
And Seius, whose eight hundred slaves
  Sicken in Ilva's mines;
And Picus, long to Clusium

Vassal in peace and war,
Who led to fight his Umbrian powers
From that gray crag where, girt with towers,
The fortress of Nequinum lowers
    O'er the pale waves of Nar.

— 28 —

Stout Lartius hurled down Aunus
    Into the stream beneath;
Herminius struck at Seius,
    And clove him to the teeth;
At Picus, brave Horatius
    Darted one fiery thrust,
And the proud Umbrian's gilded arms
    Clashed in the bloody dust.

— 29 —

Then Oenus of Falerii
    Rushed on the Roman Three;
And Lausulus of Urgo,
    The rover of the sea;
And Aruns of Volsinium,
    Who slew the great wild boar,
The great wild boar that had his den
Amidst the reeds of Cosa's fen,
And wasted fields and slaughtered men,
    Along Albinia's shore.

— 30 —

Herminius smote down Aruns;
    Lartius laid Ocnus low;
Right to the heart of Lausulus
    Horatius sent a blow.
"Lie there," he cried, "fell pirate!
    No more, aghast and pale,
From Ostia's walls the crowd shall mark
The track of thy destroying bark.
No more Campania's hinds shall fly
To woods and caverns when they spy
    Thy thrice-accursèd sail."

But now no sound of laughter
　　Was heard among the foes.
A wild and wrathful clamor
　　From all the vanguard rose.
Six spears' lengths from the entrance
　　Halted that deep array,
And for a space no man came forth
　　To win the narrow way.

But hark! the cry is Astur;
　　And lo! the ranks divide;
And the great lord of Luna
　　Comes with his stately stride.
Upon his ample shoulders
　　Clangs loud the fourfold shield,
And in his hand he shakes the brand
　　Which none but he can wield.

He smiled on those bold Romans,
　　A smile serene and high;
He eyed the flinching Tuscans,
　　And scorn was in his eye.
Quoth he, "The she-wolf's litter
　　Stands savagely at bay;
But will ye dare to follow
　　If Astur clears the way?"

Then, whirling up his broadsword
　　With both hands to the height,
He rushed against Horatius
　　And smote with all his might.
With shield and blade Horatius
　　Right deftly turned the blow.
The blow, though turned, came yet too nigh;
It missed his helm, but gashed his thigh.

The Tuscans raised a joyful cry
  To see the red blood flow.

He reeled, and on Herminius
  He leaned one breathing space;
Then, like a wild-cat mad with wounds,
  Sprang right at Astur's face.
Through teeth, and skull, and helmet,
  So fierce a thrust he sped,
The good sword stood a handbreadth out
  Behind the Tuscan's head.

And the great Lord of Luna
  Fell at that deadly stroke,
As falls on Mount Alvernus
  A thunder-smitten oak;
Far o'er the crashing forest
  The giant arms lie spread;
And the pale augurs, muttering low,
  Gaze on the blasted head.

On Astur's throat Horatius
  Right firmly pressed his heel,
And thrice and four times tugged amain,
  Ere he wrenched out the steel.
"And see," he cried, "the welcome,
  Fair guests, that waits you here!
What noble Lucumo comes next
  To taste our Roman cheer?"

But at his haughty challenge
  A sullen murmur ran,
Mingled of wrath and shame and dread,
  Along that glittering van.
There lacked not men of prowess,
  Nor men of lordly race;

For all Etruria's noblest
  Were round the fatal place.

— 39 —
But all Etruria's noblest
  Felt their hearts sink to see
On the earth the bloody corpses,
  In the path the dauntless Three.
And from the ghastly entrance
  Where those bold Romans stood,
All shrank, like boys, who unaware,
Ranging the woods to start a hare,
Come to the mouth of the dark lair
Where, growling low, a fierce old bear
  Lies amidst bones and blood.

— 40 —
Was none who would be foremost
  To lead such dire attack;
But those behind cried "Forward!"
  And those before cried "Back!"
And backward now and forward
  Wavers the deep array;
And on the tossing sea of steel,
To and fro the standards reel;
And the victorious trumpet peal
  Dies fitfully away.

— 41 —
Yet one man for one moment
  Stood out before the crowd;
Well known was he to all the Three
  And they gave him greeting loud,
"Now welcome, welcome, Sextus!
  Now welcome to thy home!
Why dost thou stay, and turn away?
  Here lies the road to Rome."

— 42 —
Thrice looked he at the city;

187

Thrice looked he at the dead;
And thrice came on in fury,
    And thrice turned back in dread;
And, white with fear and hatred,
    Scowled at the narrow way
Where, wallowing in a pool of blood,
    The bravest Tuscans lay.

— 43 —

But meanwhile ax and lever
    Have manfully been plied;
And now the bridge hangs tottering
    Above the boiling tide.
"Come back, come back, Horatius!"
    Loud cried the Fathers all.
"Back, Lartius! back, Herminius!
    Back, ere the ruin fall!"

— 44 —

Back darted Spurius Lartius;
    Herminius darted back;
And, as they passed, beneath their feet
    They felt the timbers crack.
But when they turned their faces,
    And on the farther shore
Saw brave Horatius stand alone,
    They would have crossed once more.

— 45 —

But with a crash like thunder
    Fell every loosened beam,
And, like a dam, the mighty wreck
    Lay right athwart the stream;
And a long shout of triumph
    Rose from the walls of Rome,
As to the highest turret tops
    Was splashed the yellow foam.

— 46 —

And like a horse unbroken,

When first he feels the rein,
The furious river struggled hard,
    And tossed his tawny mane,
And burst the curb, and bounded,
    Rejoicing to be free;
And whirling down in fierce career,
Battlement, and plank, and pier,
    Rushed headlong to the sea.

— 47 —

Alone stood brave Horatius;
    But constant still in mind,
Thrice thirty thousand foes before,
    And the broad flood behind.
"Down with him!" cried false Sextus,
    With a smile on his pale face.
"Now yield thee," cried Lars Porsena,
    "Now yield thee to our grace."

— 48 —

Round turned he, as not deigning
    Those craven ranks to see;
Naught spake he to Lars Porsena,
    To Sextus naught spake he;
But he saw on Palatinus
    The white porch of his home;
And he spake to the noble river
    That rolls by the towers of Rome.

— 49 —

"O Tiber! Father Tiber!
    To whom the Romans pray,
A Roman's life, a Roman's arms,
    Take thou in charge this day!"
So he spake, and speaking sheathed
    The good sword by his side,
And with his harness on his back
    Plunged headlong in the tide.

50

No sound of joy or sorrow
  Was heard from either bank;
But friends and foes in dumb surprise,
With parted lips and straining eyes,
  Stood gazing where he sank.
And when above the surges
  They saw his crest appear,
All Rome sent forth a rapturous cry,
And even the ranks of Tuscany
  Could scarce forbear to cheer.

But fiercely ran the current,
  Swollen high by months of rain;
And fast his blood was flowing,
  And he was sore in pain,
And heavy with his armor,
  And spent with changing blows.
And oft they thought him sinking;
  But still again he rose.

"Curse on him!" quoth false Sextus;
  "Will not the villain drown?
But for this stay, ere close of day,
  We should have sacked the town!"
"Heaven help him!" quoth Lars Porsena,
  "And bring him safe to shore;
For such a gallant feat of arms
  Was never seen before."

And now he feels the bottom;
  Now on dry earth he stands;
Now round him throng the Fathers
  To press his gory hands;
And now, with shouts and clapping,
  And noise of weeping loud,

He enters through the River Gate,
  Borne by the joyous crowd.

— 54 —

They gave him of the corn land,
  That was of public right,
As much as two strong oxen
  Could plow from morn till night;
And they made a molten image,
  And set it up on high,
And there it stands unto this day
  To witness if I lie.

— 55 —

It stands in the Comitium,
  Plain for all folk to see;
Horatius in his harness,
  Halting upon one knee;
And underneath is written,
  In letters all of gold,
How valiantly he kept the bridge
  In the brave days of old.

— 56 —

And still his name sounds stirring
  Unto the men of Rome,
As the trumpet blast that cries to them
  To charge the Volscian home;
And wives still pray to Juno
  For boys with hearts as bold
As his who kept the bridge so well
  In the brave days of old.

— 57 —

And in the nights of winter,
  When the cold north winds blow,
And the long howling of the wolves
  Is heard amidst the snow;
When round the lonely cottage
  Roars loud the tempest's din,

And the good logs of Algidus
  Roar louder yet within;

— 58 —

When the oldest cask is opened,
  And the largest lamp is lit;
When the chestnuts glow in the embers,
  And the kid turns on the spit;
When young and old in circle
  Around the firebrands close;
When the girls are weaving baskets,
  And the lads are shaping bows;

— 59 —

When the goodman mends his armor,
  And trims his helmet's plume;
When the goodwife's shuttle merrily
  Goes flashing through the loom,—
With weeping and with laughter
  Still is the story told,
How well Horatius kept the bridge
  In the brave days of old.

FEAR AND SURVIVAL
Reginald Bretnor

EDITOR'S INTRODUCTION

In past volumes of *There Will Be War* we have published a number of fine essays by Reginald Bretnor, the author of *Decisive Warfare*. Reg Bretnor, who lives in Oregon, is also a survivalist of some note. In this piece he gives us a plan for surviving Armageddon.

———————————— ▪▮▪ ————————————

WE LIVE IN A WORLD IN WHICH IT IS WISE TO BE AFRAID—BUT where it is extremely *un*wise to be afraid without understanding the meaning and the function of fear, something many of us have never been taught, and have to learn—if we ever do learn it—for ourselves. How many of us, for example, can remember scolding voices saying, "Johnny, you mustn't be afraid. *Big* boys like you aren't afraid. *They're* brave!" As though fear were an abnormality which could simply be outgrown or else suppressed by a firm act of will instead of being understood and rationally reacted to—which paradoxically is the only effective way to exorcise it.

Primitive fear is a simple thing. It causes adrenalin to shoot into the system so that you can run away or, alternatively, fight more desperately. Your senses—or your imagination—tell you there's danger. Instantly, psychosomatically, you feel fear. At that point, if you cannot evaluate rationally and practically, you can end up doing such silly things as running from a gopher snake, or trying to swat the wasp in your car at seventy-five mph, or spending half your waking life learning how to break bricks in two with karate chops, or any one of a myriad other things inappropriate to the danger in question. Fear has become your master, rather than your useful servant.

Today's World: Safer and More Dangerous

In many ways, the world is safer than it ever has been. Science and technology have virtually eliminated a great many of the natural perils which have beset man throughout history—those of childbirth, those of many once-prevalent, once-deadly diseases, those caused by vagaries of climate; and even in the case of those that have not been eliminated, we now have the know-how to cope more successfully. Powerless though we may be against earthquakes, tornadoes, tidal waves, and new strains of bacteria or viruses, we can recover from them, and repair damage done, much more effectively than could our ancestors.

For all this there has been a price to pay!

Because we live in a cleaner, safer world, we tend to forget how dangerous it can be!

And because we have become so dependent on the immensely complicated, interlocking systems of research, production, supply and communication which maintain the safety we enjoy, few of us retain the skills and the resourcefulness to cope, even marginally, with the dangers we have half forgotten, to say nothing of the new, unprecedented, and often even more deadly dangers to which our sciences and technologies have given birth, superweapons of all sorts, environmental pollutions of every kind, previously unknown mutations of insect species and disease organisms.

The greater the danger, or potential danger, the greater the dependency—and the greater, too, the subconscious awareness of danger, that awareness which fear inhibits most of us from confronting and analyzing. (A very good example is that muddy thinking—aided by hostile propagandists—with which so many people have reacted to a perfectly legitimate fear of nuclear weapons. The "reasoning" goes something like this: nuclear weapons are awesome and dangerous; nuclear power plants operate on the same principles; therefore nuclear power plants are as frightening as the weaponry. And so we have campaigns against nuclear power—but *always* against American nuclear power, never against Russian, never against Japanese or Pakistani or whatever.)

"We have nothing to fear but fear itself," said Winston Churchill, addressing a Great Britain faced by the seemingly overwhelming power of the enemy. Today, perhaps, we should restate the truth of this: "We have nothing *more* to fear than fear itself," for fear suppressed generates a feedback, an amplification, a constant crippling tension, often to the point where the original peril—real enough in itself—is lost sight of, and the practical reactions demanded by it forgotten.

Survival Models

Our present psychological climate is generating some strange models for those of us who are determined to survive and who cannot quite believe that our personal and family survival can be entrusted entirely to government. Foremost, or at least most visible, of these we can perhaps term the Sylvester Stallone Model, in which our hero performs prodigies, not only of valor, but of ferocity, thereby demolishing an enemy whom, in real life, we unhappily did not defeat. This is an easy one to fall for, for once we fall for it we can largely forget such practicalities as organization, supply, coolness of judgment, and our own vulnerability. (I am reminded of a story in one of the national news magazines in which, at one of their training camps, the PLO demonstrated their ferocity—and presumably their military effectiveness—by tearing live chickens and rabbits apart with their teeth. Had the rabbits been armed with Galils and trained to use them, this would indeed have been impressive. As it was—well, it did demonstrate vividly the difference between raw, purposeless violence and *controlled force*. Another example might be the difference between the thoroughly frightened soldier with his eyes closed spraying the landscape with full automatic fire and the rifleman, or machine-gunner or whatever, so well trained and with such self-confidence that he can go into a firefight with his eyes open, and open in every sense of the word.)

I hope I have conveyed the idea that, in my opinion, the gung-ho ferocity model—while it probably has its place in the training of certain special troops—is *not* an optimum ideal for the survivalist. Therefore let us consider one which I think is.

The Swiss Model

I recently read a book by John McPhee entitled *La Place de la Concorde Suisse*.[1] (No, it is not in French, but takes its title from the historic meadow where, almost seven hundred years ago, the first three Swiss cantons declared their unity and their independence—something which has been maintained, often against terrible odds, ever since.) McPhee is an excellent writer, and much of the book originally was published in *The New Yorker*, which occasionally comes up with something really refreshing. (They once printed an exhaustive study of why, in Tokugawa Japan after the Shogunate sealed the country off from the rest of the world, the samurai almost completely abandoned firearms, which had attained an unprecedented ascendancy, for the sword.)

McPhee went to Switzerland and, with the cooperation of Swiss military authorities, took part in a Swiss army exercise. He met the soldiery of Switzerland who—like the militia in the days of Washington and Jefferson—literally *are* the people. In a nation of less than seven million, six hundred and fifty thousand men can be mobilized in less than forty-eight hours, fully armed, trained, equipped. (If we could do the same, we could field about twenty million.) Weapons are kept at home; so is a ready supply of ammunition. Every pass, every railroad bridge, every mountain highway is mined; every point vulnerable to invasion is covered by artillery ready and waiting; jet fighters, their pilots adept at close mountain flying, lurk in hidden caverns behind otherwise useless airstrips. Supplies are stockpiled against every conceivable contingency. And an impressive degree of protec-

---

[1] John McPhee, *La Place de la Concorde Suisse*, Farrar/Straus/Giroux, New York, 1984.

tion against nuclear attack has been prepared, not just for the army, but for everyone, in every village, every city.

As for a regular army—yes, Switzerland has one. It numbers *one-half of one percent* of the armed forces, almost all technicians and instructors. The officer corps in general is not "regular," and consequently there is not, in Switzerland, the tremendous psychological and social gap between the professional military and the mass of conscripts that has existed in most major European nations, which so disturbed our Founding Fathers, and which has led to some damned odd ways of thinking. (For instance, why was it that the Italian General Giulio Douhet believed civilian morale would collapse almost immediately under mass bombardment? And why did he formulate an entire doctrine of air warfare based on this? And why was it so long believed—against all the evidence of London and Canterbury, Hamburg, Dresden, Tokyo? Incidentally, this has not been true of Europe only. Contempt for the citizen soldier, and especially for the citizen officer, has only too often been obvious in our own press, again against the evidence of war—there must be quite a number of newsmen who never heard of King's Mountain, or the 442nd Combat Team, or Nathan Bedford Forrest.)

The Swiss are an immensely practical people. They do not, for instance, believe in "mutual deterrence." In deterrence, yes, very definitely. They are determined to deter anyone from invading Switzerland, and so they have adopted the Porcupine Principle. You roll yourself into a ball and show your quills.[2] And their quills are by no means half-sharpened substitutes simply because they are a militia. Like the Israeli army, which took them for its model, they may not be full-time soldiers, but they are fully competent. Like the Israelis, who have done very nicely against enemies who outnumber them enormously, the Swiss are certain to make life very uncomfortable for any invader.

To the Swiss, survival is a way of life.
Joseph Stalin hated them.

---

[2]General Daniel Graham's "High Frontier" defense system could do something similar for us by drastically reducing our vulnerability to nuclear attack.

I wish every survivalist would read John McPhee's book. It is not long. It is beautifully clear. In it, you come to understand the soldiers of Switzerland and their officers. You learn how Swiss industry and business support the army and those who belong to it, and of the positive, healthy role the army plays in the life of the country. And you realize, of course, that the Swiss are afraid of war, because of its destructiveness, because of the agonies it brings in its wake, and because of the threat it would be to their ancient freedom, their democracy, their civilization.

They are afraid as any sane people would be afraid—but they are not panicked by fear, stunned by fear, or whipped by fear into reliance on ferocity and displays of violence.

There are many lessons we can learn from the Swiss and Switzerland:

The most important, to my mind, is that, ideally, the entire nation should be dedicated to survival, not just certain official elements, nor yet a minority of far-seeing citizens. We would have been strengthened immeasurably had we never fallen for the hollow promise of "mutual deterrence" and "mutually assured destruction" (MAD) and dismantled what little beginning we had made in building a civil defense system. Again, we would be strengthened immeasurably if we could develop a much closer relationship between the regular armed forces and National Guard and the citizenry as a whole, a relationship more closely resembling that which pertained in the days before the federalization of the Guard, when the states were more directly responsible for their militias. Just as the Swiss nation-in-arms is a guarantee against chaos and collapse in the event of a worst-case situation, so could our armed forces be were we to rebuild and strengthen our militias. Not only would we be better prepared against all-out attack, but we also would be far better off where natural disasters are concerned— something our sciences and technologies still cannot protect us against.

The main argument against such a reconstruction of our state and local militias would, of course, be a financial one. Where the hell are we going to get *that much money*? We are so used to everything military being hideously expensive that we cannot even entertain the idea of possibly making do—that a lot of obsolete weapons are still highly effective, and definitely better than none, and that the same goes for tools, transport, communications. Again, we have become used to the idea that men will not fight well unless they are well and promptly paid. That is not true. Some of the finest, bravest fighting men the world has ever seen have fought for next to nothing, for their families, their neighbors, their nations, for abstract causes, or just for the hell of it. The men of the Swiss army are paid almost nothing by our standards, but their corporate employers are sensible enough and patriotic enough to continue their salaries when they are on active duty.

Certainly it is late in the day for us to be considering any such fundamental changes in our society, but consider them we should, for if we fail to do so we may find ourselves with no society at all or one changed out of all recognition by our enemies.

Consider Switzerland. Basically, most Swiss are French or German speakers; some speak Italian as their basic tongue; a very few, a Latin dialect called Romansch. Yet they are a united country, and in that lies much of their strength, for there is strength in unity and in disunity nothing but the seeds of disaster. In the United States today, we have active among us men and forces whose primary purpose is to divide us against each other—and whose primary weapon is unreasoning fear—and I would not hesitate to gamble that somewhere behind each of them, no matter what doctrine they profess, there is Communist connivance and Russian money. As an example, let us take two nations which, not many years ago, were known as the Switzerland of the Near East and the Switzerland of South America: Lebanon and Uruguay. Lebanon fell into chaos, with a dozen feuding sects and parties killing each other, mostly with Iron Curtain weapons. Uruguay was forced into repression and tyranny by deliberate and persistent terrorist action seeking to destroy the sound democracy which had existed there. Do any of us, survivalists or not, want to see the United States follow in their footsteps?

We should, of course, be concerned for the survival of ourselves and our families, but like the Swiss we should also be concerned with the survival of our towns and cities, our states and our nation, our institutions and our freedoms.

Who knows what persuasion and patient effort might still accomplish on the local level?

THE BERENDT CONVERSION
John Brunner

EDITOR'S INTRODUCTION

> While you are reading these words four people will have
> died from starvation, most of them children.
> —Paul Ehrlich
> *The Population Bomb*

Thus opens Paul Ehrlich's *The Population Bomb*.

"It seems to me, then, that by 2000 A.D. or possibly earlier, man's social structure will have utterly collapsed, and that in the chaos that will result as many as three billion people will die. Nor is there likely to be a chance of recovery thereafter. . . ."

Thus closes a popular article by Dr. Isaac Asimov, perhaps the best-known science writer in America.

It would not be hard to multiply examples of doom-crying among science fiction writers, or, for that matter, the American intelligentsia. There are scores of stories and articles describing life in these United States after the year 2000 as poor, nasty, brutish, and short—although hardly solitary as Hobbes would have it.

Much of this doomsaying springs from four original sources which are endlessly requoted: *Global 2000: Report to the Presi-*

dent, Ehrlich's *The Population Bomb,* and two outputs from MIT: *World Dynamics* and *The Limits to Growth.* All are essentially mathematical trend projections, with the MIT studies employing complex and highly detailed computer models.

Strangely, intellectuals, including science fiction writers, have a lot of confidence in these economic models, although they offer us very little in the ability of social or physical scientists to save us. It's almost impossible to overestimate the influence of these books even twenty years after most of them were written. Writers make predictions based upon them; teachers quote them endlessly, or worse, quote secondary and tertiary sources which draw their ideas from them.

The result is that these works and the view they represent have become "conventional wisdom" for the young. Doom is "in the air," so to speak; a great part of our younger generation is convinced that no matter what we do, no matter how much we discover or learn, we are finally and inevitably doomed. If Isaac Asimov says we are finished, then what hope have we?

Yet—are we doomed? Surely the works which generated that view deserve analysis. Let's look at the models of doom. Back in March, 1972, Dennis and Donella Meadows published *The Limits to Growth.* This highly influential book grew out of research sponsored in 1970 by a group of wealthy industrialists and academics who called themselves "The Club of Rome." In contrast to the notion of progress, a view of history that had dominated Western intellectual thought throughout the previous 150 years, *The Limits to Growth* predicted an unending and probably unavoidable series of disasters: vast upswings in population punctuated with massive die-offs as we either ran out of resources, polluted ourselves to death, or otherwise ruined the planet.

Moreover, according to this view, there wasn't much we could do about the situation. Efforts to stave off one kind of a crisis would generally succeed only partially—and would create an even worse, and totally unavoidable, crisis of another kind.

Limits triggered a series of books and studies. It also inspired political movements based on the philosophy of "an era of limits." Phrases such as "appropriate technology" (those who wondered just who was for *inappropriate* technology were ignored), "limits," "soft paths," and "ecology" became widely known and were symbols of power. *The Limits to Growth* was probably very

202

influential in the election of Jimmy Carter as President; certainly the enthusiasts of the Club of Rome view of history believed that was true, just as they happily believed in his notion of a "national malaise."

The Limits to Growth was largely based on a single "systems dynamics world mode": a computer simulation developed at MIT by Professor Jay Forrester. This model is presented in considerable detail in Forrester's book World Dynamics (Wright-Allen Press, 1971, 2nd Ed., 1973). The world model consists of some 45 interconnected subsystems: typical subsystems are NRUR (Natural-resource-usage rate), DR (Death rate), POL (Pollution), CID (Capital investment discard), BR (Birth rate), etc., all of which are interactively connected: that is, agricultural investment increases agricultural output, which increases birth rate but also pollution; pollution decreases agricultural output; etc. The simulation output includes such things as total world population, total pollution, and something called Quality of Life (which, incidentally, peaked in 1940 according to the "standard" model).

By today's standards the world dynamics model may not be so impressive, but in 1970 it certainly was. It looked highly plausible, and furthermore, in those days there was a natural awe and respect for COMPUTERS; and perhaps even more for those who could persuade computers to do something useful. World Dynamics and more especially The Limits to Growth captured the imaginations of many respected social thinkers.

There were counter-arguments. I made some of them in a book called A Step Farther Out (Ace Books; it's still in print). Members of the faculty of the University of Sussex analyzed The Limits to Growth in a scholarly counterblast called Model of Doom. Herman Kahn's Hudson Institute published The Next 200 Years with a picture of the future nothing like what you found in Limits. However, in most academic institutions there was strong support for the conclusions and recommendations in Limits.

One thing was lacking in this debate: most of those doing the discussing, whether for or against The Limits to Growth, had no means of doing simulations of their own. Computers large enough to handle models of this complexity weren't all that widespread, and time on computers of any size wasn't easy to get. While (to Forrester's great credit) World Dynamics presents a thorough mathematical description of the world model, it doesn't give source code (other than in the language DYNAMO); and in those days few social scientists had means for producing computer programs in DYNAMO or any other language, even if they had access to suitable machines and compilers. Most of the analyses of *Limits* and *World Dynamics* models on which the book was based had to be done in words and on paper.

By 1978 that wasn't so true. By then it was possible to get source code in BASIC for the *World Dynamics* models. I wrote one myself. Running that program demonstrated quite dramatically just how sensitive the *World Dynamics* model was to a key pair of assumptions: that NR (National resources) was monotonically dwindling and did so at a rate proportional to CI (Capital investment); and that birth rate does not fall with increasing wealth.

Moreover, the model had no provision whatever for "resource substitution": although history shows that when a resource becomes scarce the price rises, and some other resource—often one not previously thought useful—is substituted. (The classic example is the use of coal after Britain's timber resources had been exhausted.)

What about *The Population Bomb*? First: the blurb that opens Ehrlich's book is clearly wrong. My copy was published in 1969, a year in which about 53 million people died from all causes. It takes four seconds to read the blurb, so for one person to die each second, 31.5 million—about sixty percent of all deaths—would have had to be from starvation.

Taking the UN cause-of-death statistics and being as fair as possible by including as "starvation" any cause related to nutrition—diphtheria, typhus, parasitical diseases, etc.—we get about a million, or some five and a half percent. Clearly Dr. Ehrlich is off by a factor of ten.

Actually, world agriculture is keeping up with population. At the Mexico City meeting of the American Association for the Advancement of Science in 1975, Dr. H. A. B. Parpia, the senior professional of the UN's Food and Agricultural Organization, told me that just about every country raises more than enough food to be self-sufficient. The food is grown, but sometimes not harvested; or if harvested, spoils before it can be eaten. In many countries vermin get more of the crop than the people; insects outeat people almost everywhere. The pity is that the technology to harvest and preserve enough for everyone exists right now.

I'm not saying there's any excuse for relaxing and saying hunger is a myth. It isn't. But simple food storage technologies, and research into non-damaging pesticides and pest-control methodologies, could stop famine in most of those parts of the world where that horseman still stalks the land. Other simple technologies—even mylar linings for traditional dung-smeared grain storage pits—would save lives.

We know how to do it; but we won't unless we're willing to try. We won't get anywhere sitting around crying "Doom!"

Yet according to Dr. Ehrlich's book, "the battle to feed all of humanity is over. In the 1970s the world will undergo famines—hundreds of millions of people are going to starve to death in spite of any crash programs embarked upon now."

Obviously that didn't happen; but the doomsayers' viewpoint—which did not stop agro-engineers from making efforts, despite the flat prediction that their efforts were useless—did invade our schools so successfully that a new generation of students believes in Doom as thoroughly as ever did a Crusader in the holiness of his cause.

The other side of the coin was expressed in the Hudson Institute's *The Year 2000*, which points out that the levels of rice yield per acre in India has not yet equaled what the Japanese could do in the twelfth century. Another analyst, Colin Clark, has shown that if the Indian farmer could reach the production levels of South Italian peasants, there would be no danger of starvation in India for a good time to come.

In other words, it doesn't even take Miracle Rice, fertilizers, and a high-energy civilization to hold off utter disaster in the developing countries. It only takes adding technology to traditional peasant skills—indeed, the kind of thing advocated by E. F. Schumacher in his *Small Is Beautiful: Economics As If People Mattered*. Showing people how to use mylar and simple non-persistent fungicides for food storage along with peasant agricultural methodology will hold the line against famine—for a while.

Moreover, we *have* new technologies. There *are* means for increasing protein production. More protein in childhood would cut back infant diseases like kwashiorkor and "red baby"; those diseases have the effect of permanently lowering adult IQ by about twenty points. What if the next generation of a developing country were "twenty IQ points" more intelligent? For many of the ignorant of the world are not stupid, but they may be *stunted*.

But the doomsters, like the following story, have an answer. If we help those people feed themselves, they'll only breed to famine again. Worse, they'll demand industry. They'll strip-mine phosphates and poison the seas (as shown by Cousteau in one of his films). What's the point of helping them? Doom is still around the corner.

————————————•┏•————————————

UNDER THE CLOUD-DARK SKY THAT PROMISED RAIN BY SUNSET: the noise of an approaching engine. Heads were turned. The soup-tanker was of course what everybody was looking forward to, but it couldn't possibly be here for at least another hour and would be later still if the crew had to beat off an attempted hijack. Anyhow, what was coming was a helicopter and those had been reserved since spring for moving people, not goods.

It was a bad time for the unexpected. Five wars were in progress over food.

Therefore soldiers' knuckles paled on the hands that held their guns. Many of them had seen service during hunger riots last year and the year before. Workers trudging down from the hills with burdens of miscellaneous vegetation reflexively glanced around in search of cover. In the supermarket car-park the non-working refugees reacted also, bar the handful who were too weak. But those were mostly children. This operation had an admirable record. Some days nobody died here at all.

The youngest of the five policemen whose job it was to keep order among the inhabitants of the car-park was proud of his contribution to this exceptional achievement. Before permitting himself to look up he took time to survey his charges. Most were sheltered by abandoned cars and delivery trucks; even the least fortunate were protected from wind and rain, if not from cold, by tents improvised out of plastic sheet and aluminium pipe. Now and then someone in a tent noticed that someone in a more substantial home was weakening and took advantage of the police's backs being turned to kick out the luckier neighbours. Once there had been an epidemic of such attacks and for a week more fatalities were due to murder than to hunger.

Not presently, however. And the young policeman had no opinion, private or public, concerning the latrine rumour which claimed that the protein content of the soup had been cut to increase fatigue and forestall another similar outbreak.

As soon as they realised the chopper was neither shooting nor being shot at, the refugees and workers slumped back in time to where they had been a moment earlier: the latter because payout was as distant as usual, the former—it could be read in their hostile eyes—because they feared more mouths were being brought, more empty bellies.

The soldiers would have done likewise but that the sergeant in charge of the assessment detail ordered them to stand to. The earliest-returning of the workers were coming up to the perimeter gate with their day's forages, demanding to be let pass along the barbed wire corridor into the supermarket, that horrible echoing cavern of a place where the only light came from holes blasted in the walls and meshed over against thieves, or cold refugees jealous that the soldiers and police should sleep under such solid cover.

The young policeman had often wondered what it was like to run that gauntlet at the end of a hard day: to face the scales, then the sonic testers employed to determine how much usable greenery, how much woody matter, and how much dirt and gravel made up the weight of each bag and basket, then let his hand be stamped with a code indicating what food he was to be allotted when the tanker pulled in with its loaf-nets sagging on either side.

Funny . . . As the summer wore to its end more and more of the workers seemed to be losing touch with reality, trying to deceive the assessors by hiding pebbles among the leaves and roots they could legitimately gain credit for, even though they must surely by now be aware that all such trickery was certain to be found out. Yesterday indeed a man who should have known better, being father of five children including a recent baby, had been fool enough to alter the *1* stamped on his hand to a *4* and in accordance with regulations had been refused any food at all.

It wasn't fair on the kids for him to have done that.

His eyes strayed to the hillside. To left, to right and also at his back, the slopes were littered with what had been handsome expensive homes before the ghetto-ghouls began their rampage through this valley. He tried to picture it as it had been five years earlier; failed, because as a kid he had never lived in nor even visited such a wealthy suburb; then tried not to visualise it as it inevitably would be after the winter and failed again. But for the frequent rain this land would already be shedding dust this fall as once it had shed leaves.

The helicopter settled on the patch where the soup-tanker ordinarily drew up, the most defensible spot. Alerted by radio, the commanding colonel and his adjutant were on hand. An armed private with the professionally paranoid air of a bodyguard jumped out, only condescending to salute after he had swept the vicinity with his suspicious gaze. Then an *important* passenger climbed down, encumbered with a bulging paunch, and shook the colonel's hand and marched off with him to the supermarket.

Among the refugees there had grown up a ritual to be performed on catching sight of anybody fat. Behind the wire a defiant old man demonstrated it, being himself as scrawny as a beanpole; he spat on the ground, trod on the spittle, turned his back with an over-shoulder scowl. To this the young policeman was directed to reply with a gesture towards his gun and a threatening glare, rehearsed again and again to render it maximally convincing and save the ammunition that would be wasted were he to have to shoot.

But the landing of the chopper had saved him from—from something. He had been on the edge of—of—of . . . It wouldn't come clear. He could, though, sense it would have been disastrous. (Maybe he himself would in a fit of craziness have spat on seeing how fat the visitor was?)

He did not even drop his hand to his holster. He simply stood and shivered, more from the narrowness of his escape from—from whatever it was he *had* escaped, than from the chill that harbingered the rain.

Who was this person, anyhow, who rated a slow, expensive, wasteful mode of transport like a chopper in times of planetary dearth? The machine's pilot, a lean man with a close-trimmed dark beard, had got out and stood a few feet away, stretching

208

himself limb by limb as he looked the scene over. The young policeman attempted to utter a greeting, pose a question . . . and abruptly couldn't. His mouth was watering incredibly. He had caught a scent so indescribably delicious it dizzied him. It awoke hunger that seemed to cry out from his very cells.

Hideously embarrassed, he gulped and gulped, hoping the bearded man would not notice. Seemingly he was more interested in the workers returning with their loads of greenstuff and the armed men lined up to receive them.

After a few moments he said, "Get much trouble with thieves, do you?"

The salivation was coming under control. (What *could* have triggered it?) "Not twice," the policeman managed to quote.

The pilot glanced at him as though surprised. "Hmm! It's long since I heard *that* crack! Must have been when the cows went on their involuntary seven-year diet . . . Still, I guess granary guards are much alike wherever and whenever."

The policeman let that pass without bothering about its meaning. Now that he could speak normally again, he preferred to put the question he had originally intended about the passenger.

"Government food chemist," the pilot answered.

The policeman essayed a joke. "Looks as though he tests his products on himself, doesn't it?"

A merely polite smile. "If you knew him you couldn't picture him being his own guinea pig . . . Oh-oh. Here it comes!"

Like stabbing needles the first drops of rain. In the car-park the refugees ducked under cover; workers lining up to be shepherded into the supermarket made what use they could of their bundled twigs and leaves.

"Inside, quickly!"

The policeman started. The pilot had scrambled back into his seat; now he was patting the place next to him, which had been occupied by the bodyguard. There were two more seats in back. One, the passenger's, was empty. In the other dozed a top sergeant, a man heavy-set without being fat, on whom the refugees would not have expended spittle, with great pouches under his eyes and sagging empty jowls that testified to his having lost much poundage since—since whenever. He snored occasionally.

"Come on!" the pilot urged. "The rain's doing half your work for you, isn't it?"

209

True, true. It dampened spirits as it wet the ground. He climbed three wide-spaced rungs and sat, pulling the door to behind him. At once his mouth flooded again. The same scent was in the air, far stronger.

"It's no fit way for a human being to end the day's work," the pilot muttered. He was staring as the workers formed a tidy line between the spikes of barbed wire and of bayonets. "To sweat from dawn to dusk, creep homeward folded double by your load, be told there's too much dirt and grit in it, half rations for your family tonight . . . *And* it's making more desert when we need less."

The policeman had heard that sort of talk before. But when people were starving by the tens of millions it was no time for fancy fits of conscience. Just so long as they were kept alive.

"You got a patch of dirt on your face," the pilot said after a pause. "Right cheekbone."

The policeman almost raised his hand to rub before he remembered. "Oh, that. No, it isn't dirt. I guess I bruised it somehow."

"Ah-hah?" The pilot scrutinised him. "Bruise easily, do you? Yes? Do your joints hurt?"

"Sometimes. Seems to be a thing going around."

"Be damned," the pilot said softly. "I knew the refugees were getting it, but I thought at least the guards . . . Here, boy." He reached under the instrument panel and produced a lunchbox previously hidden in shadow. The instant he opened it the delicious scent became unbearable.

"Boy?" the policeman bridled.

"Hell, if you're old enough to vote I'll personally eat the shit you've passed since your birthday. . . ." Taking from the box something brown and white, something pink, something round and red. Also a knife.

"Should give you an orange or a lemon," the pilot said musingly. "Don't have any by me, though. . . . What's 'going around,' as you call it, is something we've known the cure for since about the eighteenth century—scurvy. I recall at Alexandria it made the soldiers so listless they paid no attention when the enemy approached. Bad stuff. Here, eat this. Best be quick and not let any of the refugees see you with it." He held out a

swiftly-fashioned sandwich of bread and ham, and also a tomato.

"Are they real?" the young policeman breathed.

"I should live so long and grow so rich! Hell, no. These are
berendtised."

"All made out of—of . . . ?" With a gesture at the workers'
forage.

"Sure, but don't be put off. It's not rat-meat I'm giving you.
That's officer-grade food, four hundred fifty bucks' worth of
power to every pound. You won't taste the same again in a hurry . . . Mark you, when there's nothing else even rat-meat can
be tasty."

Taking the sandwich gingerly the policeman said, "I never
got that far down. Seen plenty that did, of course. Uh—where
were you reduced to rats?"

"Oh, there's nothing very special about rats. After the cats
and dogs are all gone . . . In Paris, though: that was something
else. We had some very strange meats when we cleared out the
Zoo—elephant, giraffe, even python . . . Say, eat up, will you,
instead of staring? It's not poisoned!"

The policeman opened his mouth and crammed it in, trying
to savour each crumb and morsel, failing because his hunger
was so deep, so keen.

"Oh, God," he said at length, and ran his tongue hopefully
around his lips to trap a last elusive drop of tomato juice. In
back, the sleeping sergeant shifted but didn't open his eyes.

The pilot closed the lunchbox and carefully put it away. There
was a little silence, but for the sound of rain. At last the policeman said, "I heard a story about Berendt. Is it true he killed
himself by jumping into his own food-converter?"

"It's true he killed himself. Whether he did it in that precise
way is just about impossible to find out. They prefer people not
to know they killed him."

"What? You just said he killed himself and now—"

"Did you never wonder what decided him?"

"Ah . . . Well, sure. It seems kind of odd he did it just when
he'd succeeded in his life's ambition, right?"

"Ambition," the pilot repeated thoughtfully. "Obsession may
have been more like it. The story goes he never talked or thought
about anything except his plan to save the world from famine."

"What—what drove him, do you think?"

"Heaven knows. Some people say his father had been eaten. Things like that did happen. It was a vicious winter. Of course it was just a Little Hunger, and at that it was in wartime. The Big Hunger hadn't more than started."

"Where was that?"

"Leningrad."

There was another pause. Now dusk and denser rain had almost veiled the late-returning workers. The soldiers, as wet and cold as their charges, were beginning to raise their voices and threaten to cuff with gun-butts.

"For whatever reason," the pilot resumed unexpectedly, "Yakov Berendt made the food converter his personal crusade. He had no scientific talent, so the first thing he had to do was make a fortune so he could hire top chemists and engineers and dietitians. It cost every penny he had just to build one pilot model. But when he had that, he had proof it could be done. He was able to borrow. Altogether he borrowed over twenty million. Produced the machine he'd always dreamed of. Drop in any kind of vegetation, even the poisonous kind, even the useless kind like straw and twigs, fit the right master-tape, and out would come good nourishing food. How could there be any more starvation when there was one of his machines in every village?"

"But there isn't," the policeman said, settling back comfortably in his seat and folding his hands on his stomach. It was amazing how full and sleepy that one sandwich had made him.

"Right. There isn't. With the Big Hunger looming larger by the day, the people who had loaned him the money to develop the converter branded him a crank and a lunatic and had him voted off his own company's board. Once they were in control they made sure the price of a Berendt converter was the highest the market could bear. No, there are not converters in every village. But there are in every smart restaurant and hotel. And some private homes, come to that. This guy I'm ferrying around: he has one." The pilot scowled into the gathering dark.

"But in any case," he added, "he was completely wrong to think his machine could save us."

"How's that again?" The policeman's eyes threatened to drift

212

shut; he forced the lids apart and forced himself to concentrate on what the pilot was saying.

"Proof is all about us. Like I said, this project and those like it are making more desert when we need less. There's nothing wonderful about being a villager, you know—what reason is there to think peasants would behave any differently from townsfolk? Just as your rich family in the big city buys dirt-cheap rubbish for the converter and puts on an expensive tape and eats the *haute cuisine*, so villagers would have been content to chuck in leaves and grass and the hell with actually planting anything. Who wants to break his back for corn and cabbages? Food from the converter is better than most of what you get from the ground; they choose only the very finest models to make up tapes from. Why, they've got to the stage now where they can duplicate vintage wines. The experts say they're more consistent than the original."

"I wouldn't know," the policeman muttered. "Never tasted wine . . . Say, you didn't finish telling me why Berendt committed suicide."

"It could have been because of what his partners planned to do with the converter; could equally have been because he suddenly realised his idea was stupid from the start. By the time he got the machine working it was already far too late. We were set for our population crash, one of the classic two-thirds degree. No point in arguing with laws of nature."

"Now wait a minute. Nature doesn't always rule us. We've changed the face of nature for a start. First time we ploughed a field, wasn't that going against nature?"

"If it was, it likely didn't work. Things like that succeed when you're working with nature, not against. Heard the news today?"

"Been on duty since dawn. No."

"There's civil war in Brazil. The people who accepted land grants in rain-forest areas and cleared them without realising that when you expose the ground it turns to a rock-hard crust which won't grow anything: they lost patience and took out after the bastards who sold them this bill of goods. A grenade killed the provincial governor and his senior aide last night; today the country's under martial law." The pilot stabbed the air with his forefinger. "What happened to those Brazilian farms: that's what

I mean when I talk about going against nature. You have to coax her, never drive her. And we're still animals for all our cleverness. Animals that outstrip their food supply suffer a population crash, and the rate is almost always two out of three. Rabbits. Lemmings. All kinds of animals. And us. And it's such a horrible state to be reduced to . . . I remember in India, where they had fourteen famines in ninety years. As the famine increased, men abandoned towns and villages and wandered helplessly. It was easy to recognise their condition: eyes sunk deep in the head; lips pale and covered with slime; the skin hard, with the bones showing through; the belly nothing but a pouch hanging down empty; knuckles and kneecaps showing prominently. One would cry and howl for hunger, while another lay on the ground dying in misery. Wherever you went, you saw nothing but corpses.''

The policeman shivered, though the cabin was snug and windtight.

"And it was bad in Skibbereen, too. That's Ireland. One village called South Reen seemed to be deserted when we went there with supplies of bread. So we looked in some of the houses—hovels, really. In the first, six famished and ghastly skeletons, to all appearances dead, were huddled in a corner on some filthy straw, their sole covering what seemed a ragged horse-cloth, and their wretched legs hanging about naked above the knees. I approached with horror, and found by a low moaning they were alive. They were in fever—four children, a woman, and what had once been a man . . .

"In another case my clothes were nearly torn off in my endeavours to escape from a throng of pestilence around, when my neck-cloth was seized from behind by a grip which compelled me to turn. I found myself grasped by a woman with an infant just born in her arms, and the remains of a filthy sack across her loins—the sole covering of herself and babe. The same morning the police opened a house on the adjoining lands which was observed shut for many days, and two frozen corpses were found lying upon the mud floor, half devoured by the rats . . .

"A mother, herself in fever, was seen the same day to drag out the corpse of her child, a girl of about twelve, perfectly naked, and leave it half covered with stones. In another house within 500 yards of the cavalry station at Skibbereen the dispen-

214

sary doctor found seven wretches lying, unable to move, under the same cloak—one had been dead many hours, but the others were unable to move themselves or the corpse."

"Well, if it's really a law of nature . . ." the policeman said, staring appalled at the pilot's calm face.

"Oh, I believe in the law all right. It doesn't say the two-thirds we're going to lose can't be the *right* two-thirds." He gave a harsh laugh. "Starting with people who starve others out of megalomania and greed. They'd be *no* loss. This guy, this food chemist I'm nursemaiding: he's like that. Reminds me a lot of John of Leyden. Real name was Bockelson but he preferred the short form. More like a king's name, I guess.

"And that was how he saw himself. Somehow he conned a gang of people in Münster into setting up a fantasy kingdom with him and his sidekicks at the top. Well, the Empire wasn't going to put up with that, so they set siege to the place and starved the defenders out. The self-styled king requisitioned all the food in the city and had all the horses killed. At all times the royal court ate well and had sufficient stocks of meat, corn, wine and beer for half a year. The rest were not so lucky. Every animal—dog, cat, mouse, rat, hedgehog—was killed and eaten and people began to consume grass and moss, old shoes and the whitewash on the walls, the bodies of the dead."

"Whitewash?" the policeman said incredulously.

"Oh, sure. People have been known to eat dirt; haven't you seen them? Even short of that, people put some funny things in their bellies. I remember on Guernsey they drank stuff made from parsnips and fruit leaves instead of tea. Smoked some peculiar things too. Made cigarettes out of dried potato peel—bramble leaves—rose-petals . . . even plain grass. Anything to stave off the pangs. Coming back from Moscow we boiled our boots and the leather harness left over after we'd eaten the horses, brewed something warm with the illusion of nourishment."

"I heard about people boiling boots," the policeman said. "Thought it was a joke."

"Not so funny when it happens to you," said the pilot. "Like I say, we'd finished the horses. Deprived of fodder and constantly exposed, they died in great numbers. Often men did not wait until the horses had fallen to devour them . . . A stray horse was instantly killed and dismembered almost living: unlucky

215

animal who moved a few steps away from his master . . . A lot of fights got started over who was to have what bit.''

Cold—unspeakable terrible cold—seemed to reach into the chopper. It was so completely numbing, one could not even shiver.

Eventually the policeman was able to say, "I get the feeling we here are—well, you'd have to call us lucky, I guess.''

"Sure. You're very lucky. Only thing apt to delay your daily rations is a bunch of people half out of their minds and armed with shotguns they have no more shells for. While in Africa . . . You said you didn't hear the news today?''

"Not yet.''

"Well, they had to ground the UN relief flights. Seems Zaïre got paranoid. Decided they aren't getting enough relief and all their neighbours are getting so much they're planning to trade it to Europe and buy arms in order to invade. So they dusted off their ground-to-air missiles—they got these good ones made in Switzerland—and started shooting down the UN planes. Pilots won't fly the missions any more, and do you blame 'em?''

"That's terrible!''

"Not so much terrible as typical. In L.A., you know, they'd put up a rick of oranges and apples, put gasoline over it and set fire to them. Vegetables were being destroyed and everything. To keep the price up. But there were great queues of guys in soup lines. Nobody had a dime.'' The pilot shook his head. "It's the 'I-don't-want-it-you-can't-have-it' syndrome. See it all the time in spoiled kids.''

"I guess maybe it's as well Berendt did away with himself,'' the policeman said. "Whether he jumped into his converter or not. If he was alive he'd be the world's most disappointed man.''

He hesitated. "Funny, you know. Talking to you makes me think about him as a person for the first time. Always before I've had this impression of him as—well, close to a saint. Spent his whole life for the sake of others and it isn't his fault his dream never came true.''

From the back of the cabin, a snorting noise. They looked behind and found the sergeant was awake.

"I've been listening to you, Jacobson,'' he said, pushing his blocky torso upright. "Spinning these crazy lies to someone

216

who's no more than a kid—it's disgusting. Hear me? What you said about Ireland: it's not true. I got family in Ireland and they just wrote me and said you can buy butter without a ration card. Natural butter! Can't do that here, can you? Does that sound like starvation?'' Aside to the policeman. ''And I just saw this TV report about Paris, too. And they are *not* burning food in L.A.— lies, all of it!''

The pilot winked sidelong at the policeman, who was bewildered.

''As for Berendt!'' The sergeant leaned forward, hands on the back of the pilot's seat and clenching tight as though he would rather have gripped the other's throat. ''Berendt did *not* jump into his own machine and there is *not* a little of him in everything that comes out of a converter and it's a load of blasphemous nonsense. I wish you weren't civilian personnel—I'd like to sort you out the way you deserve.''

With a final glare he slumped back and concluded, ''Out with you, boy. You've had enough of this bastard's yarn-spinning.''

Confused, the policeman opened the door to the rain and jumped down. Approaching were a group of men under an umbrella: the food chemist, an escorting officer and the bodyguard.

''They're coming back!'' he called to the pilot, who also clambered down.

And said very softly, almost without moving his lips but contriving to make himself heard perfectly: ''So maybe Yakov Berendt didn't wind up in a food-converter. But I'll tell you who did. The guy I used to fly around before this one. And soon's I get the chance he'll be the next.'' With ever so slight an inclination of the head. ''Like I said, we need to make sure it's the right two-thirds of mankind we dispose of. Thanks to Berendt we have the means to make them useful for a change. Tell people that. Tell people you can trust.''

He clapped the younger man on the shoulder, then went on loudly, ''Did everything go off all right, sir?''

''Perfectly, thank you, Joseph,'' said the important passenger. ''Though it took longer than I expected. I hope you weren't too bored.''

''Not at all, sir,'' said the pilot. ''Not at all.'' And made to help the fat man up the ladder.

For several minutes after the chopper had taken off the policeman was in a kind of daze. Extraordinary images kept flashing through his mind: some ludicrous, like a pan full of boots being boiled, and others ghastly, like an emaciated child licking a whitewashed wall.

And that parting remark. To be taken seriously? Surely it must be some sort of sick joke!

He was recalled to the present by the roaring noise of the soup-tanker as it ground to a halt among cheers from refugees and soldiers alike. It was a tradition to signal its arrival in that fashion. Automatically the young policeman started to join in.

And checked.

He looked at the bulky tanker with the loaf-nets dangling from it, thought of the grass and leaves and twigs and roots it would carry in those nets when it left here and returned to its base in the nearest city.

Thought of what would happen to that greenstuff. Thought of tomato juice on his chin, bread, ham . . . and then of the greyish quarter-loaf he would receive at supper, gritty in texture, under its sour crust more hole than crumb. That, and a bowl of the invariable watery broth in which floated a few anonymous vegetables. It was a common game to make bets on their identity. There was never meat, of course. It cost too much.

After a while he started wondering whom he could trust enough to tell about the Berendt conversion.

EDITOR'S AFTERWARD

But is doom around the corner, even without a marvel to turn weeds and stubble into nourishing food?

The best answer is that historically people haven't done it. When nations reach a high level of technology—and of infant survival—the fertility rate falls. The U.S. appeared to be an exception to that with the World War II "baby boom," but now that swiggle in the fertility rate has passed. The girls born in 1944 are 45 now, through their child-bearing period, and the number of girls born per fertile girl in the U.S. has fallen to an all-time low, despite the success of films like *Baby Boom* and *Three Men and a Baby*. So low has it dropped that now one occasionally hears economists advocate bonuses for larger families! The same is true of other industrialized nations, regardless of religion or socio-economic system. Populations of wealthy nations do *not* rise without limit.

Yet—in our schools and colleges and universities straight and unadulterated Malthusianism is taught and learned and has become "conventional wisdom."

THE CONTRACT
Don Hawthorne

EDITOR'S INTRODUCTION

Previously in these pages we have presented exploits of "The Iron Angel," a giant Russian steam locomotive pressed into service during the last days of the next war.

The Soviet Union, after a disastrous attempt to gain mastery over Western Europe and the Middle East through military conquest, has been defeated by a coalition of nations in the bloodiest and most costly war in human history. Denied its tremendous nuclear advantage by a vigorous and effective Strategic Defense Shield, the U.S.S.R. was prepared for yet another of the vicious wars of attrition that no other nation but she could survive and win.

Alas, the very faction which brought this war upon the Soviet people, a reactionary Committee for State Security dissatisfied with the performance of the Defense Forces, unleashed an extremely effective biological weapon: *Yo-Devyatnatsat*, binary biological agent "A-19," or as it has become known to the rest of the world, the *Gas Bug*.

The Gas Bug is an organism which metabolizes petroleum-derived fuels. Such a tailored organism is already under extensive testing by several of the world's major oil companies as an aid to combating oil spills, such as occurred on the *Exxon Valdez*.

The designers of the Gas Bug had a far different purpose in mind: An invading army (whatever its motives or justifications for them), utterly dependent upon petroleum-derivative fuels for its advances, would be stopped dead in its tracks should those fuel stocks be destroyed. The defenders, on the other hand, prepared for the use of such an organism and with access to immunizers against its effects, would be free to operate mechanized units with freedom in an otherwise infantry-only combat environment.

The perfect plan—unless the organism mutates to metabolize crude oil, as well.

With the loss of virtually the entire world's stocks of fuel, the major industrialized nations of the earth suffered the transportation equivalent of a stroke. Overnight entire economies ground to a halt; the world began to slip into a long night.

Such a chain of events, violent as they are, are no less likely because of *perestroika*, *glasnost*, or the less well publicized *demokratizatsiya* now chipping away at the monolithic facade of Soviet Communism. Indeed, resistance and resentment of these vital programs may make such a scenario more likely than any sane person would like to ponder.

In the April 10th, 1989, issue of *Time* magazine, the editor of *Ogonyok* magazine, Vitali Korotich, presented this grim prophecy for the Soviet Union should *glasnost* end: "I will be destroyed, and we will be left a hungry, stupid, terrible country with a big army—a very dangerous country."

One lesson of history is that the noblest causes have the most intractably evil opponents—*glasnost* is no exception, suffering all the more since its strongest detractors are not external foes of the nation, but committed patriots, convinced that their motherland stands on the brink of ruin because of the perceived excesses of *perestroika* and *glasnost*.

It is very dangerous to be standing close to anyone, or anything, on a precipice. The men of the Red Army Combat Engineers who commandeered the "Iron Angel" have done so in an attempt to put as much distance as possible between themselves and those of their countrymen who, rather than pull their nation back from that abyss by working together, are instead rushing headlong into it.

However, these Combat Engineers of the Red Army have been

at war for a long time, and not all the lessons they have learned have been bloody ones.

————————————— ■¸■ —————————————

> Here, in the waves and the troughs of the plains
>   Where the healing stillness lies,
> And the vast, benignant sky restrains
>   And the long days make wise—
> Bless to our use the rain and the sun
>   And the blind seed in its bed,
> That we may repair the wrong that was done
>   To the living and the dead!

—Rudyard Kipling
The Settler

"DON'T LEAVE ME, LYOSHA."

Chilled, Aleksei Aleksandrovitch Rostov pulled the covers tighter about his shoulders. He and Lilia were in their compartment aboard the *Krasnaya Strela*, the overnight express train from Moscow to Leningrad. They were both junior officers in the Soviet Army, so their coinciding leaves had been sheer good fortune, but this private sleeper cabin on the "Red Arrow" had been a wedding present from Rostov's commanding officer, Colonel Ivan Podgorny.

"*Nyet*, Lilia," he murmured, reaching for her in the darkness. "Don't talk foolishness; I will never leave you." But instead of her warmth his hand met the wall of the tiny bunk they had fallen into the night before, both of them full of laughter, vodka and hopes. He turned and, despite an odd apprehension at the idea, tried to open his eyes. Where *was* Lilia? Was that her, standing by the samovar, next to the window?

"*It wouldn't be right, Lyosha,*" she continued. Her pet name for him made him smile, as always, but her next words replaced it with a frown of puzzlement: "*Suschenko is everywhere, now.*"

"Suschenko?" he said aloud, his voice still thick with sleep. That was a place, he knew; a place he had been to recently. But it wasn't on the Red Arrow's route. They were going straight to Leningrad, for their honeymoon.

Despite that strange conviction that he should stay where he

222

was—sleeping, safe and happy—Rostov found himself standing by the samovar. *What is a samovar doing in our cabin?*

"Lilia?" He suddenly noticed that the room itself was much larger than he remembered, and now even the darkness could not conceal its lavish fittings: a liquor cabinet, a large desk, bookshelves, a sofa; even a water closet . . .

And finally, at last awake, he found himself listening to the rhythmic pounding of the wheels as they struck the parallel joins of the rails beneath. There was a warm wetness spreading down his arm, and with it a dull ache that nearly matched the one in his heart.

Yes, I have been to Suschenko recently. He took a napkin from the setting by the samovar and pressed it to the freshly opened bullet wound in his arm, watching the linen go from ghostly white to the blackness of blood in the dark. *And I am on a train, but we are not going to Leningrad.*

Rostov sat down on the desk and looked out the window into the backlit indigo of a pre-dawn sky. The room was stifling hot, and his tears disappeared into the tracks of sweat from his brow.

And Lilia was never here . . .

The radiotelephone on his desk began warbling, its power light a red eye winking in time. As he reached for it, the bloody napkin fell unnoticed to the floor. "Rostov here."

"Izvinite, Kapitan." Trainman Gyrich, rescued from the KGB in Moscow and now *de facto* leader of the conscript locomotive engineers who kept the train running, had to shout over the background noise of the engine cab; the radiotelephone, an excellent copy of a West German design, sometimes worked too well.

"Sorry if I woke you, Captain."

"That's all right, Comrade Trainman; something wrong?" Rostov's voice was as dead as his optimism. There was nearly *always* something wrong with this train.

"No, Captain, a town; we should be coming to it in another twenty minutes."

Rostov was instantly awake, fully alert. *"Spaceeba,* Comrade Gyrich, thank you. Stop us, please. I'll have some of my men move out ahead of us and reconnoiter."

Rostov entered the duty station number for Sergeant Dyatlov in the forward passenger cars, where the on-duty squad was posted. The sergeant had his men out and moving up the tracks in good time, a few waving at Rostov through the windows of the command car as they passed.

They crave the action, he thought, watching them move by in the quickening gray autumn dawn. *They need to be busy. Running seems to suit them no better than it does me.*

Two weeks ago, he and Colonel Podgorny had conceived the theft of this train to escape to Alliance lines in the West with all their men and their stocks of Immunizer against the Gas Bug, the biologic that metabolized petroleum fuels. They had an American intelligence officer in tow who would act as their liaison, and were themselves remnants of a crack unit of the Soviet Army, the Fifth Guards Armored Engineers. It was a dangerous plan, but it held more hope for their future than remaining in the Soviet Union. To do so was to live at the whim of the KGB, which had seized the reins of power on the collapse of the government, and begun the summary liquidation or annexation of all regular Army units.

Two weeks. Can it really have been only two weeks? Rostov found the thought hard to credit, for in that time, nearly every aspect of their plans had gone horribly wrong. Podgorny was dead, killed in the escape from Moscow, along with more than a dozen of their men. They were reduced to running this diesel-fired steam locomotive on a bastardized wood alcohol mixture which was already giving them difficulties. Worst of all, a KGB patrol had caught them back at Suschenko and nearly blown them off the tracks. The light tanks of the Committee for State Security had been beaten off or destroyed, but not before tearing up their planned escape route in the process, and forcing them to take so many switchbacks to avoid other ruined lines that they were now deeper into Old Soviet territory than ever. They had yet to find a single trace of the Alliance forces that had invaded the U.S.S.R. in retribution for the "Global War of Liberation," and there was now no telling when, or even if, they would ever escape the twenty-two-million-square-kilometer graveyard that had once been the Soviet Union.

Rostov was seized with a conviction so strong he almost cried out; the conviction that he was tired of running, tired, and something else.

Ashamed.

But they must not know that, he thought as he watched the last of the patrol disappear into the morning fog, and the first of the train's perimeter guards take up their positions. *I gave my word, to them and to Colonel Podgorny, that I would get them to safety in the West. Those were my orders, and my conscience does not enter into the matter.*

He put on his uniform, and sat at the desk to await Dyatlov's report.

An hour after full dawn, Rostov had the reconnaissance report. He was still at his desk in the command car, and with him were the five men he was coming to think of as his "staff": Lieutenant Zorin, formerly a Senior Sergeant but, like Rostov, promoted by a grateful reservist Colonel back in Suschenko; Blaustein, the unit's medical officer; Trainman Gyrich and his own assistant, the Lithuanian conscript named Pilkanis; and the American Naval Intelligence officer, Captain Martin Wrenn. The six men stared at the object on the desk while Dyatlov finished his report.

"How many of these"—Rostov indicated the thing that looked like a wreath of dried apricots—"have you and your men found, Sergeant?"

"Several dozen, sir. Most are nailed up on lampposts or doorways." Dyatlov's voice was low. Like most Russians, mutilation horrified him. It was not so much the act they found abhorrent as its implication of the stain of *nekulturny* on the part of the culprit. A lack of culture was the personal dread of every Russian. "Plus the ones the old fellow was—" He couldn't finish.

Rostov held up a hand in reassurance. "And you say he is the only person left alive there?"

"*Da, Kapitan,* just the old man. And he is incoherent. I wanted to bring him back for Comrade Blaustein to treat, but he won't leave." Dyatlov licked his lips, slightly sick. "*Kapitan* Rostov, do you think soldiers did this?"

Rostov flashed a look to the American, Wrenn, then back to Dyatlov. "No, Sergeant, I don't."

Dyatlov's eyes widened in horror. "*Nyet, Kapitan* Rostov! *Polkovnik* Wrenn"—Dyatlov used the formal Russian Naval rank—"please forgive me. I did not mean to imply—" He turned back to Rostov. "Sir, I was thinking of the KGB."

225

The tension eased, and Rostov considered that. *Was it possible? Could they do that to their own countrymen?* He almost smiled. *What am I saying?* he thought bitterly. *Haven't they had enough practice?*

"First let's talk to this old man. The rails into town are intact?"

Dyatlov nodded.

"Good. Take Surgeon Blaustein with you and stay with this fellow, try to calm him down."

"At once, sir." Dyatlov saluted and went to the door where he turned back before leaving. "I am sorry I could not find out more, *Kapitan*," he said, then went out and down to the stairs to the railbed.

Dyatlov's souvenir from the town lay on the sack he had brought it in, and Rostov used a pen to pull the bag closer. Since the war had slowly ground to a halt, the conditions of life in the ruins of the Soviet Union had deteriorated very quickly, he knew. But even so . . .

"Some crazy bastards in this world, Aleksei," Zorin said quietly. "But even the KGB doesn't usually stoop to this sort of thing."

Rostov looked up briefly from the string of human ears lying on the table. Even allowing for dehydration, it was obvious to everyone that many of the ears were very, very small. *Don't they, Mikhail?* he thought.

"What was it Dyatlov said? That he was sorry he couldn't find out more?" Rostov shook his head, sweeping the sack and its grisly souvenir into a wastebasket which he would later burn entirely.

"I am not sorry at all."

There were over a hundred armed men on the train Rostov had led out of the battle-torn ruins of Moscow. All were veterans of at least two years of war. Some, like Zorin, had been fighting since the beginning. Most of them were thus convinced that there was very little left in the world that could shock, or offend, or even surprise them. They were wrong.

The great locomotive moved slowly into the town, troops advancing before it in a skirmish line, carefully picking their way among the debris. What buildings remained standing bore gap-

226

ing holes, fire-blackened walls, or great smears of rusty brown that no one could mistake for rust.

Rostov stood in the hatch of the locomotive's celestory roof alongside their American intelligence officer "guest," and inspected the destruction with the practiced eye of the combat veteran.

There was ample evidence of small arms fire, and what looked like damage from grenade shrapnel, but not enough of either to explain the obvious slaughter that had occurred here.

"The blood," Wrenn said. "It looks like they gathered buckets of it and threw them against the walls."

Rostov nodded. "This was not a battle; it was butchery. And it was meant to be seen as such."

They left the engine and headed for the relatively intact building where Comrade Surgeon Blaustein would be examining the old man Dyatlov had found this morning. Along the way they saw bodies, but it was not until they had gone several dozen meters into the town that they saw the tableaux. Nothing in Dyatlov's report had prepared them for those.

Corpses were everywhere, every age and both sexes; men, women and children simply cut down where they stood. Wrenn knelt to examine one of them; the mutilation that had resulted in the "necklace" found by Dyatlov had been thorough, but Wrenn's attention had been drawn by something else. Along the back of one body—the father, likely, as the other two were a woman and child—a great wound had parted the spine and cracked one shoulder blade. He looked up at Rostov. "Pretty obviously an edged weapon; I'd say a cavalry saber, maybe something even heavier."

"*Christus.*" Rostov shook his head. Having been shown, he began to look more closely at the other dead, and saw that very few had been shot. Most were cruelly hacked. "What the devil did they use here? Axes, swords, knives . . ."

"Looks like a spear over here, Captain." One of the men tried to call out, but his voice faltered.

Then Rostov saw the hoofprints.

God save us, it's like something out of the history books. His mind reeled at the implication of mounted cavalry slaughtering a town.

Butchery indeed, Rostov thought, seeing some new atrocity

227

with every step deeper into this place. An isolated town, horse-men, the slaughter of innocent civilians; it reminded him of something he had heard once, but, not entirely to his regret, he could not place it.

Many of the dead had been hung from poles, or were hanging upside down in doorways where they had been nailed by their heels. The worst were on the steps of the local Political Committee headquarters. Here a dozen decapitated corpses had been placed sitting up with each other's heads nestled in their laps. One of the men abruptly vomited into the gutter, and Rostov envied him the release. For himself, the horror could not be purged so easily; each new sight of the atrocities that had been visited upon this town burned itself into his brain beside the image of the last.

He turned away from the steps. "That's enough. I want to see this old man." He went directly to the building opposite, where *Leytenant* Mikhail Zorin waited for him, standing guard.

"You are all right, Aleksei?" The big man's voice was quiet, gentle, steady.

Rostov nodded. "He is in there?"

"Yes. Blaustein managed to get a sedative into him." Zorin grabbed Rostov's arm as the younger man began to move by him. "Aleksei, don't be harsh with him. He is an old man. He used to be the Chief Political Administrator of this entire district. I think he is not sane anymore."

Rostov looked back over his shoulder, once. "I believe you."

He was sitting by a stove where Comrade Surgeon Blaustein had started a fire. It did little to warm the drafty room, but the old man in shirtsleeves did not seem to notice. Looking at him, Rostov remembered something Podgorny had told him once: No matter how bad you thought things were, they could always get worse. The old man was wearing half a dozen necklaces of human ears. He was staring at the floor between his feet where a smear of moisture darkened the wood.

Tears, Rostov realized. The old man's eyes poured them forth in a steady stream of grief.

"Captain Rostov." Blaustein rose and spoke to him in a low voice. "This is Sergei Josefovitch; I couldn't get his last name out of him."

"What in the name of all that's holy are those *things* doing

228

around his neck?'' Rostov could barely keep from shouting in rage.

"He won't let me touch them." Blaustein gestured to the open doorway and the scene beyond. "He seems to think that whoever did that will come back and kill the rest of the townspeople if they find out he's not wearing them as he was ordered to."

"*Ordered* to?" Then it hit him: "The rest of the townspeople? But . . ."

Blaustein shook his head. "His mind is gone, Captain. He is convinced that there are still survivors out there."

"You are sure there are not?"

"You haven't been to the other side of the town, I take it."

Rostov shook his head, and Blaustein finished: "It is even worse there."

The old man had become aware of Rostov's presence, and now he was staring at the gleaming white shoulder boards of a Captain of Engineers. "You are an officer." He said it simply, sounded almost satisfied; it was a pronouncement, not an observation. "You will take care of this business now."

Rostov crossed the floor to the old man and sat down next to him. "What business is that, Sergei Josefovitch?"

"This, all this. We surrendered our weapons, just as you ordered us to, all our weapons and ammunition. The invaders of the *Rodina* are defeated, that is what you said; their fuel has been destroyed by a triumph of Soviet Military Science. We have no need for self-defense weapons now, the government is firmly back in control of the situation, you will provide security for the rebuilding of the State."

Rostov and Blaustein shared a look; both of them knew KGB rhetoric when they heard it. "How long ago, Sergei Josefovitch?" Rostov pressed gently. "How long ago were your weapons collected?"

Sergei Josefovitch shook his head, seemingly in pain. "Ah; a week? Yes, one week before—" His tears, which had nearly subsided as he began speaking, now resumed, accompanied by two brief, wracking sobs. "Before the bandits came. They demanded food, but you had commandeered all of our surplus. Then they demanded weapons and ammunition, but we had already . . . We gave it all up, of course."

He looked at Rostov in utter bewilderment. "They killed."

229

He might have said "It rained" for as much effect as the words seemed to have upon him. But suddenly his face cleared, and he seemed lucid, almost cheerful as he resumed in a brisk, down-to-business tone. "But then they stopped killing, only a few, those few who resisted; an example had to be made, they said. And now you are here, and you will provide us the security you promised." He reached into his back pocket and from it drew a crumpled sheet of paper which he flourished before Rostov.

The young Russian officer took the note and unfolded it, smoothing the wrinkles to read the typed words. There were spots of dried blood across one corner, but none of the wording was obscured. It was a written notification that the forces of State Security, under the regional command of Political Recovery Group Four, would provide all security and protection for the town of Iamskoy—the name of the town had been written into a space left blank for it—for which consideration said town would provide all necessary supplies as determined by the commander of said Political Recovery Group, Captain Boris Yablomov, KGB.

"It is a contract," Sergei Josefovitch said, and the simple faith in his old man's voice sent a chill through Rostov on hearing it. "It is legal and binding, your Captain Yablomov assured us so."

"*My* Captain—" Rostov began, choking back a sob of his own, but the old man didn't hear. He had stood and shuffled to the window, blind to the carpet of unburied dead outside.

"Now that you are here, the rest of the citizens of Iamskoy can come out of hiding."

And before Blaustein or Rostov could stop him, he threw the window open and began shouting into the streets for the citizens to assemble. "Everyone, everyone can come out now! The army is here, and they will protect us." He slipped through the door and went past Zorin into the middle of the street, oblivious to the bodies he stepped on or over as he went. "It is safe, now. Only a few of us have died, just those two or three, just . . ."

Each time he approached one of Rostov's men, they jumped back as from an adder. But once the madman had moved on, the soldier would turn away to hide his own tears. One or two simply sat down on the spot and wept, or cursed, or walked away from the square, trying to find some place that was not

230

filled with the sight or the smell of the madness that had happened here.

The old man was suddenly alone in the middle of the square, waving his arms, shouting joyously; spittle flew from his lips as he exhorted his fellow citizens to greet their protectors, their deliverers. With a sudden snarl, he tore the wreaths of ears from his shoulders, sending petals of flesh flying everywhere. Soldiers who had seen and lived through years of the most brutal combat cowered at the prospect of being hit by the things.

"Come out, citizens! We are safe now; the forces of progress are intact, the socialist millennium is here! We are safe now." Sergei Josefovitch fell to his knees atop a body, lost his balance and dropped to one side in the bloody dust. "Safe . . ."

Zorin had rushed over to help the old man up, but when he reached him he only looked back at Rostov. "He is dead, Aleksei."

Rostov stood in the doorway, holding the contract the KGB had given the old man. He folded it carefully and put it into his pocket.

"Let us get the hell out of here."

Iamskoy changed everything for the men of the *Iron Angel*. Forward patrols, previously dispatched only when a town was indicated on the maps, now became the order of the day. Zorin and Rostov prepared duty rosters for the rotation of patrols, releasing a few light vehicles and the immunized fuel they would require for the job of reconnoitering, protecting the locomotive's flanks and confirming the condition of the tracks ahead.

During the briefing for the first patrol, Rostov told Sergeants Aliyev and Dyatlov to be sure to end with sweeps to the rear as they returned, in case any pursuit might be catching up with them.

"Or in case any of those bandit pricks get sloppy," Aliyev amended quietly.

Dyatlov smiled like a wolf and added: "So we can send back some 'volunteers' for a little party."

Rostov had pretended not to hear the comment, but inwardly his heart leapt. *Iamskoy did more than sicken them; it outraged them, as much as it did me . . . Well, and why not?* Until that moment, he had not realized that the thoughts and doubts which

231

had come to bedevil him might also be worrying at the minds of his men. Thoughts of defecting, thoughts of leaving his country and countrymen to the always inept care of the KGB and the tender mercies of the bandits that now ravaged both at will; thoughts of running away, while still in the uniform of the defenders of the *Rodina* . . .

Second thoughts.

It was the fourth day away from the butchery at Iamskoy, and Rostov was in the command car with Lieutenant Zorin, Surgeon Blaustein, and the American Captain Wrenn. The latter two played chess at the corner table while Zorin and Rostov continued the seemingly endless task of picking an intact route through the dense maze of the old Soviet rail network.

"The last patrol reports that all these lines to the south"—Zorin indicated an arabesque of light blue with a brief wave of his hand—"are intact." He looked up at Rostov with a rueful smile. "As *Polkovnik* Wrenn says, 'That is the *good* news.' The bad news is that, according to Trainman Gyrich, none of those lines can bear the weight of this locomotive. The safety margins are not even close."

"Then what might be clear running to Alliance lines in the south is denied us," Rostov said, "at least here." Despite himself, he could not keep a thin tone of relief—or was it a crazy sort of satisfaction?—out of his voice. He sighed heavily to imply a disappointment he could not bring himself to feel, and turned the map for a better view.

Tracing their route since leaving Moscow, he came to Suschenko, passed through it to Iamskoy and on to their present position. According to the map, a switchyard was up ahead; they were waiting for Aliyev's report on its condition now. Turning, not south from the switchyard, but northeast, Rostov's eye followed the line of the tracks, continuing a roughly circular path established by the curve of their route thus far. It ended back at Suschenko, having passed through almost two dozen towns and enclosing an area holding at least that many more, all of those on spur lines from the main track. He did not trace this route with his fingers, but Zorin had not been watching his hands.

"What are you thinking, Aleksei Aleksandrovitch?" the big man asked in a quiet voice.

Rostov blinked and smiled. "Hm? Ah, nothing, Mischa. Well, perhaps nothing."

Perhaps everything, he added to himself. The radiotelephone was going off, and Rostov found himself answering with less annoyance than usual; it would likely be Aliyev, and with this plan taking shape in his mind, Rostov was eager for the reconnaissance reports of the patrols.

"Rostov here." He activated the desk speaker as he answered.

"Aliyev, Captain. The switchyard is intact; no damage to the lines, but there are quite a few empty cars that might be in the way."

"Gyrich will be able to confirm that," Blaustein said without looking up from the game before him; his bishop was exposed to exploit a possible weakness regarding Wrenn's left flank.

Rostov nodded, thinking that they might even want to take on an extra car or two; several of theirs had been lost during their escape from Moscow and the firefight at Suschenko, and the ones remaining were crammed to their roofs full of supplies or Rostov's men. "Anything else, Sergeant?"

"Da, Kapitan." Aliyev sounded uncomfortable. "There are people here, sir. Farmers."

Rostov frowned. "Refugees?"

"No, sir. They have brought a large part of their grain harvest here. Captain Rostov, they yoked themselves to carts like oxen and dragged it here." Aliyev paused long enough that for a moment Rostov thought the connection had been broken, until the sergeant added: "They say that they have been waiting here two days for transport."

Rostov turned to look at his companions. The burly lieutenant's face was impassive, Blaustein's eyebrows were marching up to where his hairline had once been, but Wrenn simply looked over his shoulder once and turned back to the chess board before him.

"What should I tell them, Captain Rostov?"

Rostov kept his tone light, despite his excitement. "Tell them they are in luck. We should be there in"—he checked the map again, unnecessarily—"one hour. Rostov out."

Blaustein made a sound of disgust, and Rostov went to inspect the game. Wrenn had sprung a trap, and the surgeon's lines lay in ruin.

"I should resign this game," Blaustein muttered, checking his watch. "We'd still have time for another."

Wrenn looked up at Rostov, and his eyes said that his question had nothing to do with chess: "Is that what you think, Captain?"

The American knows, Rostov thought. *Not that it was hard to reason it out. But will he help? Can I trust him?* And deeper, in that most Russian part of his soul, the old unwanted question: *Can I afford to trust him?*

"No," Rostov answered after a moment. "Comrade Surgeon Blaustein should castle."

Wrenn considered the board for a moment. "Perhaps you're right. It does open up a few possibilities. But it leaves him a very slim chance of actually winning, or even forcing a draw. There is such a thing as knowing when to quit."

"That depends on the game," Rostov corrected him. "But it's not exactly what soldiers are paid for."

Rostov collected a slightly perplexed Zorin and left the command car. First things first: Gyrich would need to know about the switchyard, and Rostov wanted to be in the locomotive's roof hatch when they got there. He sent Zorin off with orders to deploy the men to fighting stations along the length of the train, then went on alone to the engine. As he passed along the outside catwalk, the frigid morning air cut through his uniform. He made a mental note to break out winter greatcoats from the stocks they had captured along with this train—and found himself wishing for an early, heavy snow.

Committed to his plan, he now sought anything which might delay their leaving Russia. The longer they stayed, the greater his idea's chances for success.

Staying, after all, was the whole idea.

The switchyard lay under a light morning fog. Stark outlines against a dawn sky of icy gray, dozens of boxcars stood silently on tracks and sidings in a Stonehenge of rolling stock.

Rostov had read about Stonehenge in school. *They drank blood there, once* . . . Which brought his mind back, inevitably, to Iamskoy.

He called down to Gyrich in the cab below: "*Stoy*, Comrade Trainman Gyrich. This is close enough, *spaceeba*."

234

Rostov looked at the tracks surrounding them; Aliyev and his men had formed a semicircle with the train at their backs. Before them, in groups of three and four and scattered throughout the yard, stood the farmers Aliyev had reported.

"*Gospodi pomilui,*" Rostov whispered. " 'Farmers,' Aliyev said." These men belonged in the fields, all right; but they would have looked less out of place hanging from poles to frighten away the crows than they would working the land. Gaunt and hollow-eyed, every one of them seemed to be looking right at him. But their gazes were not accusing, only weary; those eyes had seen more than Rostov could ever hope to surprise them with. They were the eyes of brutalized children, ready for the next betrayal, resigned to the next inevitable blow.

You don't get that look from invaders, Rostov thought bitterly. *That kind of disappointment starts very much closer to home.* It was in the way they looked, not at him, but at his uniform.

It suddenly struck him that these emaciated survivors yet had a surplus of grain; these were people who could at least make some living off the land, and yet they still looked weeks beyond their last decent meal. He wondered what the survivors in the cities must look like, and the thought rose up, impossible to avoid: *I suppose it would depend on what they have been eating . . .*

He went quickly down the ladder into the engine cab, where Zorin stood, putting his arm through the sling of an assault rifle with the grace of a man putting on a favorite coat. "*Mischa,* what is our food situation like?"

"Several months' rations for the men, plus that lot of stuff we got from Suschenko."

"Enough to spare some for these farmers, then."

Zorin paused, then: "*Da,* Aleksei, I am sure there is more than enough to share with them. And with the next group of civilians we run into, and perhaps the next group after them. Beyond that, and I am not joking"—he raised a finger at Rostov's widening smile—"beyond that we will have difficulty."

"Good. See that they get some of it. Am I that obvious, by the way?"

"*Lyosha,*" Zorin said in a low voice, and Rostov's smile died, "we have known each other for four years, now. When I was a

235

Starshi Serzhant and you were still my *Leytenant*, it was my job to anticipate your needs. I did not lose that ability when we received these field promotions from that old reservist in Suschenko."

"I see. And what is it you think I need now, old friend?"

Zorin buttoned his coat and set his helmet at a jaunty angle, lightening the moment. "*I* think you need a drink, Aleksei; it looks to me like you have already found a purpose."

"Don't you think it's a purpose we could all embrace? Even you?"

Zorin produced one of his trademark *papirosi*, went to Gyrich's hotplate, and lifted the teapot, leaning forward to light the cigarette. When he looked back up at Rostov, his eyes were half-lidded against the smoke. "I don't know yet, Aleksei. Purposes, causes: these are dangerous things to embrace. When it comes to letting you go, they are worse than women."

"Let's not talk about them, then. Let's talk about feeding these people, and any others we run into."

"You'd better start taking food in trade as well, then," Zorin said offhandedly, "like you did at Suschenko. We're not a bottomless bowl, after all."

"Splendid idea, *Mischa.*" Rostov sounded so pleased that Zorin sensed he had been trapped, but he was not sure exactly how until Aleksei came over and clapped a hand against his shoulder. "We can trade our materials and food for those of towns along our way, and carry their surplus on ahead for them, as well. I will be sure to let the men know it was your idea." He turned to the trainmen, who, their backs turned and their eyes intent on their instruments, still, he knew, had ears.

"Comrade Gyrich, you might want to have your people check out the lay of this switchyard. We'll probably need to shunt some of those cars about and hitch up one or two of them, and none of my men have any idea how to go about it. But take as many of them as you require if you need help."

Gyrich nodded, and Rostov headed for the door.

Zorin waited a moment before following, watching his young commander descend the steps to the railbed.

A week ago I'd have said what you needed was your wife back, Aleksei, but I'm not sure that is true any longer. The thought

236

troubled Zorin, but he could not have said why, and in a moment he left the engine cab.

Behind them the two senior trainmen, Gyrich and Pilkanis, shared a look.

"Now what, do you suppose?" Pilkanis asked the older man quietly. "I thought this was to be a three-day dash to freedom in the West. It's two weeks now, and I can't see as how we're much better off than we were when running this monster for the KGB."

Gyrich did not look up. "You are alive to complain about it, eh?"

Pilkanis' eyes narrowed behind his steel-rimmed spectacles. "Yes. So far. I still am not convinced that we haven't traded one master for another."

Gyrich kept his back to the younger man, hiding his humorless, knowing smile. *What did you expect*, boychik? *This is Russia* . . .

The farmers came from the collective of Volodyin, which Rostov recognized as one of the names on the route he had traced earlier. Their headman was a wiry, hunger-aged fellow named Semenov, who met Rostov at the foot of the ladder and traded introductions with more than a trace of suspicion in his voice.

"So," Semenov began, rubbing his hands together against the chill, "we have come according to instructions." He produced a manifest and handed it to Rostov. "Seventeen tonnes of grain for State economic purposes, plus three of flour and grain for the transporting troops, to be transported by your unit." He looked over Rostov's shoulder at the behemoth P-38 as it sat, softly hissing, on the tracks. "Probably a bit larger than we need," Semenov finished quietly.

"Your pardon, Comrade Semenov." Rostov spoke without looking at the manifest. "But there are one or two irregularities to be dealt with."

"Of course," Semenov said simply. *Aren't there always?*

"For one, I do not think that our train is the one you were expecting."

Semenov's look of suspicion turned to one of disappointment that Rostov had not come up with something more original. "I see. Then what is required to convince *your* train to carry our grain?''

''Where is it supposed to go?''

At that question, so casually asked, Semenov's suspicion returned. *What was this? Was this KGB lackey a fool, or far smarter than he appeared? Is this all an act to add some new outrage to these bitter contracts they shove down our throats and call it an "amendment"?*

''Volodyin's grain supplies the livestock collective of Almanikan,'' Semenov said as he would to a man with an empty vodka bottle and a loaded gun. ''Upon arrival of this shipment, Almanikan will release compensation in the form of beef cattle and several draft animals—mules, most likely—to Volodyin so that we can work our fields again in the spring.''

''How did you work the fields for this harvest?'' Rostov asked.

''We had vehicles, plenty, and good ones. And plenty of fuel. Then one day the tractors stopped running, right in the middle of the fields. The gauges read ''full,'' but we thought they must be broken, so we took petrol out to refuel them, and when we did, out came stuff that looked like pond scum and smelled like shit.'' Semenov spat onto the gravel of the railbed, seeing blood in his sputum for the second time today; he wondered if he had not ruptured something vital by towing that cart. ''Anyway, a week or so later, a truckload of KGB came tearing through, telling us all the war was over, that Soviet military science had defeated the invaders with a weapon that stopped their tanks dead in their tracks. That was how we learned about the Gas Bug: when they came through and issued us our contract.''

The moment he'd mentioned the contract, Semenov regretted it; the young officer's eyes narrowed and he thrust out his hand. ''You have this contract with you? Let me see it.''

Semenov produced the paper and watched while Rostov compared it to a similar document from his own pocket. He did not appear to be pleased.

''Comrade Semenov, my men will be inspecting the rails now; setting switches, shunting these idle cars and connecting others, that sort of thing. You and your men can get some hot food from our mess. When we've finished we'll load your grain.'' Semenov reached for the contract, but Rostov held it back. ''I'm keeping this,'' he said.

238

Keeping, Semenov thought. *And not "for a while"; just "keeping."* "Excuse me, Captain, but you said there were other 'irregularities'?"

"What? Oh, yes. Regarding your manifest, the quantities set aside for us." He handed Semenov the manifest back. "There's twice as much there as we need. Take the rest back or pass it on to Almanikan as you wish. *Leytenant* Zorin will show you to the mess car."

Now utterly mystified, Semenov simply went with the big lieutenant to gather up the rest of the Volodyin *kolkhozniki* and get some hot food.

Rostov walked through the switchyard, thinking. The sun was above the horizon and slipping behind an overcast sky of hammered lead; for now the morning light shone on ground fog, too weakly to burn it off, illuminating it instead.

This will be the test, Rostov thought as he moved among the cars. The fog hid the tracks and ties from view, but he took no special care in choosing his path. Indeed, he was hardly aware of the danger. *I will need to see how the men feel. Helping the people of Suschenko was not a problem, that town was along the way. But this; this requires a commitment.*

He took the two contracts from his pocket and compared them: Captain Boris Yablomov, Political Recovery Group Four— whatever the hell *that* was. Rostov wondered if the people of Volodyin had also been required to surrender their weapons, and if whatever bandits had struck Iamskoy were even now on their way there. If so, then this KGB fellow Yablomov had a great deal to answer for.

He thrust the papers into his pocket and hurried back toward the train.

They all do.

The men had formed up into three rough groupings that might generously be called "platoons," there being at least a sergeant front right in the ranks of each. Before them and to one side were Surgeon Blaustein and Captain Wrenn, along with Trainmen Gyrich, Pilkanis, and three of their assistants. Rostov and Zorin were up on a flatcar, facing the assembly.

The day had gone suddenly, bitterly cold, and Rostov had seen to it that the men were issued the heavy winter greatcoats from the stocks seized with the train. They were not the right service branch, of course; engineer's insignia for the field were trimmed in black, with white shoulder boards for officers, and these coats bore the bright red shoulder boards of two-year conscripts, along with the gold Cyrillic initials "CA," for "Soviet Army." Hardly the flashy cut Rostov's men were used to. They were, after all, remnants of a crack unit of combat engineers.

So, in the end, socialism has proven to be the great leveler, after all, Rostov thought. Socialism and winter, for the coats were very warm, and Rostov was only too happy to be wearing one himself.

He was surprised at his own feelings about the address he had summoned the men to hear. He had expected to be apprehensive, even fearful, and for one moment as he looked down at them, he very nearly was. Then, unsure himself of what he intended to say, he opened his mouth and began with a phrase that he doubted was even his own. Although it sounded oddly familiar, he could not think of where he had heard it.

"Soldiers of the *Rodina*," he had begun, and then the words came out: "Suschenko is everywhere, now."

The men watching him were quiet, attentive. A glance at the American showed none of the wariness Rostov had expected. *Perhaps he is with me on this after all,* he thought, although there was not a very great deal the American could do about it if he was not.

"Since leaving Moscow, our original purpose has been frustrated time and again. By ruined track, or track which will not bear the weight of our locomotive. But also by enemy action. Not the enemy fought so long and so hard against, not an enemy from outside our borders, but our own countrymen, serving under command of the KGB."

No low murmur went through the men; this was no mob, after all, but the survivors of an elite military unit. But their eyes told Rostov that they were in grim agreement with him.

"These *are* the enemy now. There is no invading Alliance any longer, and if there is still any such group of soldiers out there, surely they are struggling for survival even as we are. They cannot have any fuel or other supplies to spare for attacking.

240

This is no more than what we have all known in our hearts for more than a year: The War is over."

And at that there was a reaction from the men; a clearing of brows, a shifting of feet in the cinders of the switchyard. Upon hearing an *officer* speak those previously treasonous words, they became Truth. More, in the minds of men who had grown up in the blindly reactionary Soviet Union of the last twenty years, the words became *Safe*, a concept always far more important to Russians than mere Truth.

"But the fighting has not stopped," Rostov said, and the eyes before him said they knew this was so. And they asked a question: *What are you going to do about it?* Well, he was about to tell them.

"It has not stopped, comrades. One hour in Iamskoy told us that. One hour in the ruins of a town that could never have seen the face of a single Alliance soldier, so deep was it in friendly territory." He let the word hang in the air like a curse: *friendly*.

"And besides, what was done there was not the work of soldiers." He added a grim fighting man's jest that pleased the men without amusing them: "Not even Turkish soldiers.

"No," Rostov continued, "only bandits could have done such a thing. And only *Russian* bandits at that. Only we are capable of treating our people that way, and we all know it. Butchery, mutilation, families cut down together: these are things that terrify us, that disgust us, that every civilized citizen abhors. They are our greatest terrors, and only we know them well enough to use them against one another. Even the Fascists could not do so well what was done there. They were brutal and efficient; the history books tell us so. But no history book will ever tell what happened in Iamskoy.

"Only we will know. Only we will remember what was done, and by whom."

Rostov sat on his haunches and laced his fingers before him, looking over the men as he went on; not one did not have a look that said he was remembering Iamskoy. "So. You have all heard about the 'contract' we took from the old man there. KGB promises of protection, and the conditions to be met to ensure that protection. Well, we who know the KGB would have expected no better protection than Iamskoy got." Here a few men did laugh, but it was a hollow sound, bitter. Rostov acknowledged it and went on.

"Just so. But now we find these farmers from the Volodyin collective, a *kolkhoz* not far from here. Comrades, these men *dragged twenty tonnes of grain here*, from Volodyin, yoked to their carts like animals. Over a century of advancement, and what have we come to in the end? The people who work the land do not even rate as peasants, but as beasts of burden. Their only 'protection' comes not from the Army, but must be bought from petty *apparatchiks* strutting about as if they deserved the uniforms they wear, and that promise of protection a hollow lie." Rostov felt Wrenn's eyes on him, and met the American's gaze; it was an encouraging smile he saw there.

"Comrades, I am sorry. But this is not why I put on this uniform."

The men were utterly still now, and Rostov felt himself close to a thinner edge than the side of the flatcar. In the next ten seconds, they would either tear him limb from limb, or . . . well, it was the *or* that drove him on to the finish.

"We helped the people of Suschenko. We might have helped those of Iamskoy. I believe we should help those of Volodyin, and yes, of Almanikan, and of the hundreds of other towns and villages we might reach with this locomotive. I am staying in Russia, comrades. This train can carry you all on to the West, and although we are still a military unit, if that is your wish, I understand, but—"

But he was not heard; the men had sent up a cheer that drowned him out.

While it was going on, he looked back to Wrenn. The American very nearly astonished him with a thin smile; for a moment, Rostov almost expected him to wink, but the moment passed as the shouting died down.

As he looked back at them, he saw to his surprise that, to a man, they seemed elated at the news, and he wondered for a moment how he could have missed all the signs of the last two weeks. They, like he, had not been leaving because they wished to, but because no other place could be any worse. They, like he, had forgotten that, when things were at their worst, their countrymen needed them most.

"All right, then," he told them. "Comrades, I do not know

when, if ever, we will find our way out of these ruins to safety. But I want us to be *home* when we do. Now let's get this grain loaded. Dismissed.''

Loading the grain was warm work, but the greatcoats stayed on. The day was turning colder, and half the men in the unit predicted snow before dark.

The grain went into one of the empty boxcars which Gyrich and Pilkanis had salvaged from the switchyard, linked together and coupled forward of the engine. The reconnaissance squad moved out ahead on motorcycles, only this time they were also accompanied by the unit's single remaining armored car, a battered BRDM-11 which their chief mechanic, Senior Sergeant Myakov, had seemingly resurrected from the dead. Rostov watched the turret pass by the window of the command car as he sat at the desk, talking with Semenov.

''You really aren't with the KGB, then?'' Semenov had lost none of his suspicion; his questions were now aimed at discerning just what Rostov's game really was.

Rostov shook his head. ''No, *Gospodin* Semenov, we are not.'' His use of the pre-socialist honorific in place of ''comrade'' was a habit of his when dealing with the elderly. ''And we are not bandits. We are Soviet Army Combat Engineers.''

''Hm. I see.'' Semenov sipped at the tea Rostov had produced from the samovar. ''You live well for soldiers.''

''We've been fortunate enough to remain alive at all.'' Rostov thought about Colonel Podgorny, who had died giving his men a chance to escape the ruins of the Soviet Union. *Am I betraying him? Or might he have chosen this path himself, in the same circumstances?* Podgorny after all had not seen Iamskoy.

Dimly, Rostov listened to the sounds of men working: hammers on metal, arc welders, shouted commands. Even as the train was getting underway, the men were continuing to fortify her, building defensive positions for machine guns, armored firing pits for snipers. Even the unit's only remaining tank, lashed securely to a flatcar, was idling, charging the batteries that ran its turret and fire control systems. This train had been caught unawares once. The next time they were attacked, Rostov thought, she would provide a nasty surprise for someone.

''*Zhelezniy Angel,*'' Semenov said abruptly.

243

"Eh? What was that?"

"Iron Angel," the *kolkhoznik* repeated. "I saw it written on the sides of the locomotive. What is it supposed to mean?"

Rostov smiled, thinking of the huge red and gold words painted up there in letters almost three meters high. "It was a name given to us by an old woman in Suschenko. A christening, if you will."

"And the men's names underneath it?" Semenov watched the smile drift off the younger man's face.

"Casualties. The men who have died since we took—took over this assignment."

Semenov noticed the hesitation, and began to form his own ideas about this Rostov and his men and their train, so conveniently filled with all manner of military supplies. "There's a box painted around the names," he added.

"Yes, I know." Rostov frowned, puzzled. "What about it?"

Semenov shrugged. "It just seems odd. But I suppose it's good to be able to paint a box around the names of your dead. As if you won't have to add to the list."

The words chilled Rostov: *As if.*

"Tell me, *Gospodin* Semenov, what were some of the other conditions of this 'contract' Captain Yablomov gave you?"

"Nothing special, really. This Yablomov was in command of something called a 'political recovery group.' Pretty obvious what *that* is supposed to do. Anyway, they're supposed to provide security and protection for the area, so—" Semenov caught himself; he had not intended to tell this part, but Rostov finished it for him.

"So, perhaps to avoid any 'accidental confrontations' or 'misunderstandings,' you had to surrender any weapons you had in the town."

Semenov nodded, suddenly afraid; the lives of everyone in Volodyin now depended on this soldier's decency. It was a condition Semenov had never felt comfortable counting on.

But the young man simply turned and looked out the window; the train had started to move at last. "We have a great deal of surplus weaponry aboard this train. *Leytenant* Zorin will see to it that the weapons you lost are replaced."

"I don't understand."

Rostov turned back to him, and Semenov was struck by the

244

haunted look on this young man's face. "You heard me mention Iamskoy when I spoke to my men earlier?"

"Yes. I know Iamskoy; some of our people have relatives there."

"I am sorry, *Gospodin* Semenov. I have something to tell you about Iamskoy."

Rostov spoke as gently as possible. The headman for the Volodyin *kolkhoz* was silent for a long time after he finished.

The truth was that Semenov did not trust himself to speak without sobbing. By the time he did, the train had picked up speed; he stared out the window as he spoke, watching the meaningless landscape flow by outside. There was no craft in his tone now, no irony. He trusted Rostov, finally. Trusted him with the absolute faith of utter despair. "How did we come to this?"

"Sir?"

Semenov continued as if he hadn't heard. "I remember watching the Cosmonauts step out onto the surface of Mars, and plant the Banner of Heroes for the two missions that were lost before them. And these were *our* Cosmonauts, *Russians*. Not Americans, none of those tag-alongs from the Liberated Zones, nor even Cubans, or those treacherous East German parasites." Semenov's hands shook so badly that the teacup rattled when he put it down.

"Now look at us," he went on in a whisper. "The mightiest nation on earth, a fucking ruin. How did we come to this?"

Rostov thought he knew, but he could not bring himself to tell Semenov. *We did it the same way we established those Liberated Zones; once known as "Western Europe." The same way we went to Mars; alone among nations, we were willing to pay the price to put men there. We did it the same way we have done everything, even Iamskoy: one body at a time.*

No, he could not say that to Semenov. Not because it was cruel, only because it was the truth. A harmless lie to hold it back, a merciful *pokazuka*.

After a while, Semenov left to rejoin his fellow *kolkhozniki* in the passenger car that had been set aside for them. Rostov remained in the command car, alone, looking out the window and thinking about the Cosmonauts.

* * *

245

Almanikan was several hours away when Rostov called the meeting in the command car. The night had passed without event; as usual, they had stopped, the patrols unable to guarantee the safety of the track in the dark. With first light they had resumed speed, and the meeting began shortly after.

Wrenn and Blaustein were seated back at the chess table, but no game was in progress; Rostov had noticed that Blaustein's king lay on its side from the last game. Evidently castling had not helped after all, but Rostov did not believe in omens. Across the desk from Rostov were Trainmen Gyrich and Pilkanis, and seated by the door was Lieutenant Zorin.

"I know how the men feel about this," Rostov began without preamble, "but I want to know how all of you feel as well." He looked at Gyrich and Pilkanis in turn. "Particularly you, Comrade Trainmen." He glanced at the American. "And you, *Polkovnik* Wrenn."

The American raised an eyebrow. "Technically speaking, Captain Rostov, I am a prisoner of war. And if you want to be really cold about this, recall that my original arrangement was with your commanding officer, Colonel Podgorny, who is now dead. So what I think doesn't actually count for a whole hell of a lot."

Rostov nodded. "That may be true, but let us come back to it. Comrade Trainmen, I want to use this train to help as many civilians as possible, but I have no delusions about our ability to use it without your cooperation."

Pilkanis almost laughed. "I feel much the same way about my neck, Captain."

Gyrich turned to the younger man with a scowl. "That's enough of that, Marik. If we were still with that KGB lunatic Serafimov, by now we'd be a week dead." He turned back to Rostov. "We're not stupid enough to consider sabotage, Captain Rostov; but some of the crew have been wondering if you ever intended to go to the West at all."

The words seemed to fit into an empty notch in Rostov's mind; hadn't he wondered the same thing himself, lying awake at night, dreaming of Lilia? "That was Colonel Podgorny's intention for us, Comrade, but he died in the battle to take this train from the KGB. I have until now had every intention of following through with his wishes to get us to safety in the West."

246

" 'Until now,' " Blaustein put in. "You mean until Iamskoy."

"Perhaps even before, at Suschenko. Because there we saw that 'safety' is a relative term. *Is* the West any safer than here? I do not think so. In any case, there is a more important consideration. Has it occurred to anyone here that we have a certain responsibility to the people of these towns? Not just those of us in uniform, but you, Comrade Surgeon, a doctor. You, Comrade Trainmen; in a world where everything is falling apart, you are men who can keep *trains* running. Even you, Captain Wrenn."

Wrenn frowned. "How's that again?"

Rostov's smile was warm. "A 'prisoner of war,' you said. True enough, but the war is over. An enemy once, but an enemy of the State, not of the people. The very worst arm of that State now rules those people. You yourself said that the aim of the Alliance was to prevent that very thing from happening. Could you really do that from the West? Once there, would you even care to try?"

"Perhaps I would just like to go home, Captain Rostov," Wrenn answered quietly. "As you said, the war is over."

"You are forgetting something, Captain Rostov." Pilkanis cut in with a voice like ice. "Comrade Trainman Gyrich was drafted into the Ukrainian Nationalist Brigades. I am not Ukrainian. I am Lithuanian. And I was a volunteer."

There was a long silence before Rostov asked: "And do you really hate us that much?"

"In point of fact, Captain Rostov, I do. Not your men, very much, nor you, at all. But I saw things very much like Iamskoy in my own homeland before being captured, and as such I have very little concern for preventing such things from happening to Russians. Sorry, but that is how it goes."

Rostov nodded. "I see. Then do you wish to leave us now, and take your own chances, or will you stay with us until we reach more neutral ground?"

Pilkanis shook his head with a wintry smile. "I am a patriot, Captain Rostov. I am not a fool. Besides, it may be that we will never reach neutral ground. Either through mishap, or design."

Rostov turned to the other Trainman. "Comrade Gyrich; a draftee? Then where do you stand?"

"*Pfah!* 'Free Ukrainian Republic,' they said. What does that

247

mean? That land was bought with the blood of my fathers, and their fathers and their fathers before them. It was ours, whoever said they ruled us, what did we care? I am a *Trainman*, by God. The trains are what I always loved, all I ever wanted. Some men take to the sea, some to the land." He looked out the window, suddenly embarrassed at his emotionalism. "*This* was my calling."

They all turned at the sound of a short, easy laugh from Wrenn. " 'McAndrews' Hymn,' " he said, then raised a hand in deference. "Sorry. A poem by Rudyard Kipling. I guess the chief apologist for the British Empire wouldn't exactly be required reading in Soviet schools." He looked around at them and quoted: " 'Lord, Thou has made this world below the shadow of a dream—' "

" 'An' taught by time, I tak' it so—exceptin' always Steam.' " Gyrich finished quietly with a fair Scots burr, bizarre in its embrace of his Russian words. "I know the poem, Captain Wrenn. It is a favorite of mine."

Wrenn nodded, chastised. "I should have known. Kipling is a poet of soldiers and working men the world over, after all."

"Trainman Pilkanis," Rostov said, "you may leave us at any time you feel it is convenient for you, or safe. We will provide you with any equipment you might need and as much food as you can carry. Agreed?" Pilkanis nodded, once, and Rostov finished: "The same applies to all of you."

Rostov turned back to Wrenn. "Although, Captain Wrenn, I hope you will stay to put in a good word for us should we contact any of your countrymen who are unaware that the war is over. Comrade Surgeon Blaustein, I know I speak for the entire unit when I say it is my sincere wish that you remain with us."

"I am a Russian, Aleksei Aleksandrovitch," Blaustein said simply. "I am already home."

The meeting broke up, Gyrich and Pilkanis returning to the engine, Blaustein to the car where he was overseeing the construction of a permanent medical facility. Wrenn waited to speak to Rostov and Zorin.

"Do you know what you're getting into?" he asked as Rostov poured tea for the three of them. He pulled Rostov's maps forward and began reading off town names. "Suschenko, Iamskoy, Volodyin, Almanikan." Visualizing the same curve Rostov had,

248

he continued. "After that Opustoschenia, Leninakan—only a few hundred thousand of those in Russia, I guess—Byiero . . . looks like about two dozen before we come back to Suschenko."

"Your point, Captain Wrenn?" Rostov asked politely.

"You'll be visiting these places, getting to know the people in them, working with those people, for those people. You will be, in a word, *responsible* for them."

"What is wrong with that?"

"You have a *train*, Captain Rostov. And all those towns to link in trade, and tap for resources. Some will have manufacturing capabilities; that means spare parts for your equipment, consumer goods for your men. You have the dominant, maybe the only, unit of heavy transport for hundreds of kilometers, in an environment where the internal combustion engine is as dead as the dinosaur. You're in better shape than half of the world's major nations—including Russia—were at the start of the Industrial Revolution. You have a cadre of well-trained, well-armed, motivated combat veterans who can pass on much of that training to qualified civilians, and who, by the way, in addition to being first-rate fighters, also just happen to be as widely skilled in civil engineering as they are in the combat variety. In short, you have Roman legionnaires."

Rostov laughed out loud. "Well, and why not? We Russians always thought of our country as the third Rome, after Constantinople; our society is descended, not from the Western European heritage, but the Byzantine."

Wrenn nodded, smiling too. "You're talking about the past. I'm talking about the future. Empires have been built with very little more resources than you have right now. More often than not, even less. I'm just curious as to just exactly what *sort* of empire *you* intend to build."

Rostov's face held its wide grin. "Is that all you Americans ever think about, Captain Wrenn?"

Wrenn made a staying gesture. "Be careful, Aleksei Aleksandrovitch. You are going to get an empire whether you like it or not. But how long it lasts will depend on how well it functions; and the basic function of this sort of empire, an empire linked by transport, is going to be *what* is transported, and how. Face it, Rostov." Wrenn folded his arms on the desk before him.

"You are going to have to become a rail baron, and that means a good capitalist."

And for that conversation, at least, Wrenn had the last word.

The *Iron Angel* moved at a leisurely pace through a thickening snowfall. Almanikan was only an hour away, and Rostov wanted to be there before dark, especially after hearing the reconnaissance report. It had been Dyatlov's turn again, and he had, so to speak, hit the jackpot. The rails into Almanikan were intact, there were people moving about the buildings, the livestock were in holding pens where Semenov had said to look for them.

And there was a KGB light reconnaissance vehicle and three men with green shoulder boards in the town as well. Dyatlov had made out all the details through his field glasses, then brought the report back to Rostov personally. And based on his description of them to Semenov, one of the men was Yablomov.

Rostov had sent Dyatlov's and Aliyev's squads out to flank the town, keeping Zorin and the main force aboard the train, then given the order to move in.

He felt it odd that there was no excitement, no apprehension at capturing and confronting this Yablomov; only curiosity.

He simply could not imagine what the man would have to say for himself.

Boris Yablomov pulled the blanket over his head to shut out the noise of someone pounding on his door. These stupid peasants thought they could wake him at any hour of their choosing to air grievances that couldn't be helped anyway. He had spent the morning trying to raise Political Recovery Group One with no success, the afternoon finding a decent place to spend the night, and the early part of the evening moving out the belongings of the family from whom he'd commandeered this wretched hut. Now, only an hour after dark, he had barely got to sleep when the pounding began.

Groping in the dark for his sidearm, he finally found the belt and put it on—he was sleeping fully clothed against the cold—then opened the door a crack to keep the chill out.

The moment the bolt was thrown, the door crashed in, propelled by the biggest, meanest-looking conscript Yablomov had ever seen. Yablomov was sent reeling back to sit down, hard, on the floor. By the time he rose again, four strangers in uniform were in his room, all wearing conscripts' greatcoats, and all armed.

"What's going on?" Yablomov asked in a tight voice; he was smart enough to put his hand nowhere near his holster. "Those are conscript shoulder boards; they're obsolete. What branch are you men?"

One of them, a fair-haired young man with the bearing of an officer, gestured for Yablomov to sit down. "You are Boris Yablomov, Political Recovery Group Four?" he asked reasonably.

Yablomov relaxed, but only a little. These men must be the transport unit from Volodyin. Strange that he had not heard their trucks. "Yes, I am *Captain* Yablomov. You are late."

The young officer shared a look with the big man who'd shoved the door open. "Ah. I thought we'd got here just in time. No matter. We were held up at Iamskoy."

"Iamskoy? What the devil were you doing there? The only thing to pick up there is vulture bait."

"You know about Iamskoy, then?"

"I know it took those stupid bandits five days to get there instead of two, as they'd promised, and six hours to do the work that a single Special Section squad could do in one." Yablomov had been gathering his things from around the room and stuffing them into a rucksack as he spoke. "I'd given up getting out of this place before dawn, but with your trucks, we—" Yablomov felt himself gripped by the hair and lifted up and back, then slammed into the wall. For a moment he thought the big man had gone crazy, but when he twisted his head around he saw that it was the younger fellow with the fair hair who had him. "*Christus!* You crazy bastard, what the hell do you think you're doing?" Instinctively, his hand went for his pistol, but his captor was faster, removing the Makarov from its holster with his left hand, wincing as he did so.

"You are telling me that you left Iamskoy to be protected by *bandits*?" Rostov was shouting now, livid with rage. "Didn't you know what could happen, what *would* happen?"

"Protected?" Yablomov tried to free himself, to no avail. "What are you talking about? Iamskoy was to be pacified, as an object lesson; why the devil do you think we confiscated their weapons?"

251

And Rostov let him go. He took a step back from the KGB man, staring at him, open-mouthed as much in wonder as in shock. "*Streltsy,*" he said after a moment. "That's what Iamskoy reminded me of, but I couldn't remember then . . ."

"Of course, '*Streltsy,*'" Yablomov said. "That's the project code name. Weren't you briefed before you left *Novaya Moskva*?"

"Aleksei," Zorin asked quietly, "what does '*Streltsy*' mean?"

Rostov spoke as if he were sleepwalking. "The *Streltsy* were raiders, hand-picked by Ivan the Terrible; they roved the land, sacking villages at random, at will. Wherever they went, they left only corpses."

"What? In God's name, *why*?" Zorin had killed more men in combat than years he'd lived, but this was something beyond even his experience.

"To keep order, Comrade, *that's* why." Yablomov went back to gathering his things, keeping a close watch on Rostov as he did so. "State Security cannot be everywhere. The bandits can't either, but the fear they instill can. With fear comes dependency on a protector, and with dependency comes loyalty. That is how Russia has functioned for centuries."

Rostov simply stared at him. Yablomov was no older than he, perhaps younger. He spoke without a trace of cruelty or even coldness; his manner was so prosaic as to seem almost bored. All that had happened to Iamskoy, and God alone knew how many other towns and villages, was to him not an outrage, but only a tactic.

"Once that loyalty is firmly rooted in the populace again"—Yablomov zipped the rucksack closed with a flourish, and put on a pair of glasses—"State Security can begin the rebuilding of the Soviet in earnest." He looked at Rostov a moment, and put a hand on his shoulder. "Look, I can imagine what you must have thought at first, but don't worry about it. It's necessary, and it's for the best if an example of a few can serve a multitude."

Rostov nodded. "Yes. I do see. And of course, there are always more peasants."

"Well, 'peasants' is a bourgeois concept, but yes, that's essentially it." He blinked, looking around the room at them. "Well? Something else?"

252

Rostov produced the Iamskoy contract and held it out for Ya-blomov to see.

The KGB man blinked again, looking at the form. "You found that in Iamskoy?"

"Yes. It says that State Security will provide protection for the citizens of Iamskoy; it's a contract."

"What of it?" Yablomov's eyes narrowed. "I don't see any reason to have subordinates questioning State Security opera-tions. Or assaulting me. I think we'll take this up with PRG One the next time we check in." He held his hand out. "I'll take my pistol back, now."

Rostov raised the weapon and pointed it at the KGB man's face.

Yablomov was ready to swear he had seen artillery pieces with smaller-bore diameters, when he suddenly realized his mistake. "You are not KGB."

"Christus," Zorin said, reclaiming his personal favorite ex-pression of exasperation, "this *apparatchik*'s a regular rocket scientist."

A light seemed to go on behind Yablomov's eyes, and he al-most smiled. "Of course; you're in with another *Streltsy* unit. I should have guessed. You gave me quite a start for a moment there. Sorry if I—"

Rostov was shaking his head.

Yablomov felt every ounce of strength go out of his legs; part of him thought it miraculous that he was still standing at all. He tried to swallow and found he could not. "Then who—"

"Bring them in," Rostov said.

Zorin opened the door, and Dyatlov came in with Semenov and the headman of the Almanikan collective. "Did you hear?" Rostov asked them.

"Everything," Semenov said simply; the other man spat in disgust.

"Comrades," Yablomov began, "this is a grave error. You are not qualified to judge State policies. You are civilians, and as such—"

Rostov cut him off again. "But we are not civilians, Captain Yablomov." He opened the greatcoat with his free hand, expos-ing the collar tabs of an Army Combat Engineer. "And while you in the KGB have very little interest in the welfare of the people, we take it very seriously, indeed.''

Rostov lowered the pistol and crossed the room to Semenov and the Almanikan *kolkhoznik*. ''Whatever you gentlemen think is best, *Gospodin* Semenov.''

The older man squinted in concentration. ''I'm not trying to dodge the responsibility, Captain, but shouldn't this be handled according to military law or something?''

Rostov looked back at Yablomov, who was being quietly relieved of his rucksack and other equipment by the two troopers who'd entered with him and Zorin. ''Those rules only apply to soldiers, *Gospodin*. This man is not one of us.''

''You are renegades.'' Yablomov had suddenly found his voice. ''You are walking dead men, you know that. All armed forces personnel who have not reported for induction into KGB Ground Forces are declared criminals. You and all your men are Enemies of the State.''

Rostov looked at Yablomov a last time. Here was the creature they had planned to leave Russia to. These were the inheritors: people who could murder whole armies of their own men and women, kill husbands and wives, butcher towns, leave their countrymen to bandits, and sanction murder and mutilation. People who could cut the ears off children. They were the inheritors of the earth.

Better to leave it to the roaches than to men who could do all this and not be horrified by their own horror. It struck him that only the most well-meaning individual could commit such unspeakable atrocities. Soldiers might be brutal, even savage, but they lived in a black and white world of kill or be killed. Rostov was not a terribly sophisticated man, but neither was he a stupid one. He could see that only politicians and civilians with power, only people who truly loved their fellow man, only they made the Iamskoys of the world possible.

''An Enemy of the State,'' Rostov repeated. ''I am grateful, at least, for that.'' He went out the door and into the swirling clouds of snow.

By morning, Almanikan had her grain, the men of Volodyin had their livestock, and the *Rodina* had six inches of fresh snowfall. This was the second of the year, and this one would not melt; the air had the brittle feeling of true winter as they made ready to return Semenov and his men, along with their livestock, to Volodyin.

The Almanikan collective had presented the men of the *Iron Angel* with six sides of beef—less than a third of the KGB's usual "requirement," they told Rostov. Not to be outdone, Semenov had insisted Rostov's men keep the extra tons of flour and meal originally reserved for the KGB. The men were already planning a feast; field rations aboard the *Iron Angel* were plentiful, but getting dull. There was an official election gearing up to find a full-time cook for the unit.

Gyrich had shown the men of this morning's patrol how to check for track integrity under half a foot of snow; one of his assistants had gone with the patrol this morning as an advisor.

My men are learning their first trick of the Trainman's trade, Rostov realized. *In time they will have to learn them all, I suppose.* He was unable to suppress a smile of pride. *My men,* he had thought.

The patrol had moved out half an hour ago; now it was the *Iron Angel*'s turn. Rostov stood on the railbed looking up at the garish letters on the locomotive's sides. They should have been almost comical up there, a bright red and gold target, a six-meter-long bull's-eye for an enemy, an invitation to attack by KGB troops or their bandit lackeys. They should have been comical, but they were not. Rostov had yet to put a name to all the emotions those words stirred in him, but he did know that amusement was not among them.

And anyway, that's not entirely correct. Those words are not an invitation to attack. They are a challenge to battle, and that is a very different thing.

He climbed up the ladder into the engine, then up into the celestory roof hatch of the cab. He loved this seat, despite the cold. There was plenty of warmth from the cabin below, and he still wore the conscript greatcoat with its thick winter lining. He would need both; it had started snowing again.

And he loved it for the view. Or rather, at the moment, in spite of the view. Fifteen feet away, silhouetted against the white winter morning sky, were three dangling scarecrows that until last night had been Yablomov and his two aides. Their steam-powered field car was now on a flatcar, lashed securely along-side one of the Engineers' original vehicles. Spoils of war.

Rostov tried to feel some pity for the KGB men, some sense of regret. But he had no room in his heart for compassion for them. It was too full of Iamskoy.

The headman of the Almanikan *kolkhoz* had arrived on the platform to see them off, and he waved up at Rostov with a grin. "Godspeed, *Kapitan* Rostov," he shouted, his other hand gripping the shoulder strap of an AK-90 assault rifle. "We'll keep the track in repair over the winter."

"*Spaceeba*, Comrade. We'll try to be back before spring."

"I want to believe you, *Kapitan*," the man said with a wide smile, "but I'd feel better if I knew we had a contract."

Rostov remembered the outrage he'd felt at those worthless, even treacherous pieces of paper foisted on these people by Yablomov, and doubtless by others like him, probably all over Russia. He suddenly smiled, and taking one of his shoulder boards between thumb and forefinger, he lifted it and leaned forward so the man on the platform could see the bright red bar with the large gold letters "CA," the Cyrillic characters for the words "Soviet Army."

"We do," he said, then gave a brief signal to Gyrich.

The *Iron Angel* moved out into the light snowfall, and was soon lost from sight.

THE BODYGUARD
Vernon W. Glasser

EDITOR'S INTRODUCTION

It is possible that we'll muddle through without a world war. It's also possible that we won't; which leads us to the question: What can city dwellers do to be prepared for That Day?

First: Whether things come apart from war or economic collapse with consequent riots, it's pretty clear that we can't stay in our cities. There's some chance of it, of course: It's not necessarily the case that the Soviets will strike all our major cities, and some neighborhoods can be defended against looters and rioters; but the likelihood is high that most of us will have to abandon the city to go live elsewhere.

And thus we have two problems: where to go, and what to do when we get there.

Where to go? Some small place that can sustain itself; a small town, probably in the middle of ranching and/or agricultural country. That's been discussed many times before.

What will we do there?

That gets more complex. Much of what I've seen in print seems to imply that if you're a "survivalist," you'll somehow be different—and more welcome—than a "locust" or a looter; and clearly that isn't necessarily so. How are survivalists different from random looters? They may be willing to do their share. But how will anyone know that?

What sets survivalists, or survivors, apart must be what they bring with them.

And what's that?

Possibly trade goods. Although the late Mel Tappen used to come down hard on "gadget collector" survivalists, it is at least theoretically possible to accumulate items that will become scarce and in demand After Armageddon, and to use them to secure oneself a place to stay. Certainly one ought to be prepared.

Still, it's also possible to do everything right and yet lose the trade goods. Sure, part of what is accumulated will be weapons; but a strong man armed is not necessarily safe. There can be stronger men who are better-armed and more skillful. I've heard a lot of fairly tough dudes say things like "you collect gold, I'll collect guns, and guess which one of us will end up with both the gold and the guns . . ."

One response to that is to become part of a survival company; but even if you're part of a well-organized group, you've still got to have something to trade. Why would a survival company want you?

There is something valuable that can't be stolen: skills. Not just skill with weapons. Sure, it's nice to be a crack shot and be able to draw that weapon *fast*, but most of us are never going to be champions in combat-pistol competition, and anyway, I don't have to tell you to learn how to use any weapons you collect. I was thinking of skills useful before and after That Day.

Take communications as an example. Whatever the mechanism of collapse, there are going to be a lot of electronics floating around, and every community is going to need some kind of communications system. If you know how to cobble up two-way communications from what's likely to be left after the Fall, you have a very salable skill. Moreover, you're not threatening anyone.

It won't hurt to be able to invent, fix and install burglar alarms and other security equipment. In general, the more you know about electronics, the more welcome you're likely to be wherever you go. But note that I'm talking about hands-on practical work, technician-level stuff, not engineering.

Transportation will also be important. Time was, every kid had a jalopy that he understood perfectly, having taken it down to its constituent parts and put it back together again. That doesn't happen now. Maybe it would make sense to buy your teenager something he can keep running—and to learn a lot of it yourself. Not just how to change spark plugs (which, I must admit, takes a *lot* of skill when you're dealing with some of the new cars), but how to replace a broken axle, and how to make do with ill-fitting parts cannibalized from a wreck. This can lead to learning metalwork and machining in general, abilities that will certainly be useful after things come apart.

There are many such skills: chemistry, pharmacology, medicine. Or become an expert on food preservation: canning, salting, drying, smoking . . .

The point is to learn something useful now that will also earn you a place among the survivors. And the interesting part is that the city dweller has a much better chance of learning such skills.

Cities have the libraries and bookstores, to begin with. It's much easier to acquire the tools of your new trade in a city with a lot of specialty stores. Mostly, though, the best schools are also likely to be in cities. Los Angeles has a dozen community colleges with excellent night schools, as well as centers like Everywoman's Village. There's almost nothing you can't learn from highly qualified instructors, and at reasonable costs—and if you choose your "survival" skill carefully enough, it will be useful to you even if things don't come apart. Look at the money you can save if you really know cars, or electronics.

Even better: If enough of us go out and learn how to keep things working, maybe they won't come apart at all . . .

———————————•¦•———————————

I GOT INTO THIS BECAUSE OF THAT BUSINESS WITH THE ATOM Master, who turned out to be nothing more than a crazy old man living in the Ruins. He thought he was one of the Old Men, and called himself the Atom Master, and claimed he could blow everyone up. Of course, he could do no such thing. I went into the Ruins and brought him out, just a crazy sick old man. It got me some notoriety, because the other boys of the Bodyguard weren't too anxious to poke around in the Ruins and maybe catch a case of radiation.

I've been a Bodyguard for five years. Not that I like the work

259

so much, but it's a good living. We're the only organized group this side of the mountains, almost two hundred of us, and without us the Chief wouldn't last very long. That's why we're called the Bodyguard, and we are all guarding the same body, the Chief's.

So one day a couple of months after that Atom Master affair, I got a summons from the Chief himself. I'd met him personally only once before, when I was hired, though naturally I'd seen him often in parades, and once had been part of the horseback squad that pulled his car.

You don't waste any time when the Chief sends for you. I put on my best deerskin shirt with the fancy fringes, and went directly to the Fort. This is an old stone building, pretty well crumbled, and I believe the Old Men had used it for a military purpose. The Chief lives there with his wives, and also uses it as a headquarters. Although it is not in the best repair, it is strong enough to repel almost any kind of attack.

Some of the other Bodyguards were lounging around the outside stairs, and I said hello to them. Then I went in, and up another set of stone stairs, to the Official. The Official was supposed to have only one door, though I'd heard some of the boys hint that there was a secret exit from inside. A guard with a hatchet was standing before the door, and I recognized him. It was Billy Garth. I didn't like him much.

"The Chief wants to see me," I said.

"Well, if it isn't the Atom Master," he said. "The tough boy. You got a mark?"

I showed him my summons, the usual hunk of clay stamped with a seal.

"Go ahead," he said, "and leave your gun behind. I'll hold it for you."

"Nothing doing," I told him. "My gun is one of the twelve or fifteen left in the whole Valley, and maybe in the world for all I know. If I ever let it out of my hands, I'd never get it back." We looked at each other for a minute, and I could see his hand getting tight on the hatchet. I said, "Don't be a fool, Billy. I may give you trouble."

"All right, tough guy," he said uglily. "Get going."

I opened the door, looking as casual as I could but being

260

careful not to turn my back to Billy, and stepped into the Official.

The Chief is a man of about fifty, big, with gray hair and a very watchful look. He has a gun, too, of a different make than mine, and he lets the word get around that he possesses several boxes of bullets. He was wearing a real cloth shirt, and a cap with a shiny visor. Sitting on the arm of his chair was Norma, one of his wives, a short dark woman with a lot of jewelry. They both looked up when I came in.

"I know you," said the Chief. "Tom Hunter. I never forget a name."

"You wanted to see me, Chief?" I said.

"Sure," he said. "Norma, this is the boy who went into the Ruins after that crazy madman."

She smiled sulkily but said nothing, and I guess she wasn't supposed to answer, because the Chief went right on without waiting for her to say a word.

"I got a job for you, Tom," he said. "A big job that pays good—if you bring it off all right."

"I'm working for you," I said.

"Can you read, Tom?" he asked.

"No."

"I can't either," he returned heartily. "That makes us both the same kind of man. I can't read, and I never saw the reason why I should, either."

I knew that was a lie. The Chief could read, all right, but he preferred to keep it quiet. As for myself, I have nothing against reading. My father could read, and offered to teach me when I was a boy, but I guess I was too busy learning the other things that a man needs if he is going to stay alive.

"Reading can be dangerous, Tom," the Chief went on, acting as if he were the best friend I had in the world. "A lot of trouble comes from reading. Here in Sacramento we've got a fine country, with a thriving town and satisfied farmers. Never any trouble, except from agitators. And when we catch an agitator, what do we find? Why, every time, he's some fool who's been secretly reading a book he dug up out of a hole. Ain't that right?"

"Sure," I said.

"How do you feel about these trouble-makers, Tom, and their holler about learning how to make machinery and stuff?"

"Look," I said, "I told you before, I'm working for you. You furnish my keep, and I've got no complaint with the quality of it. So I don't have to have any opinions. Tell me the job and I'll do it."

Norma smirked, and leaned down to whisper in the Chief's ear. He listened intently, his shrewd eyes never leaving me. "All right, Tom," he said at last. "I want you to find a man, and bring him back to me if possible. But I want him alive. He has to be alive. If he dies, you do too."

"Who is he?" I asked.

"His name is Johnson. He's another one of these agitators I've been telling you about. A slim redheaded guy with a squint."

That reminded me. I'd heard about Johnson. He was a farmer in the southwest border, not too far from the Ruins. He had been making a nuisance of himself by urging everyone to learn reading, and had also been trying to organize some of the other farmers against the Chief. Of course, that is rebellion, and cannot be overlooked; so I hadn't been too surprised to hear, one fine day, that Johnson disappeared. However, these things took place a good year ago, and I never suspected that the redhead might still be alive.

"I thought he was dead," I said.

"Did you?" said the Chief. "Must be somebody else you're thinking about. This Johnson is alive, all right. I believe he went into the Ruins. He's working there, plotting against me, and that means against you, too. Now you know what you have to do."

If the Ruins do not frighten me as much as they do others, it's because I'm not superstitious. My father brought me up to believe only what I tested myself, and consequently I have no faith in mysterious radiations in the air, which can't be seen or felt, but nevertheless cause death. And if I keep quiet about that opinion, it's because I have learned that it does not pay to oppose the beliefs of other men unless there is a definite, practical reason for it. I felt no qualms, therefore, about going into the Ruins, but at the same time I knew that finding a man in that maze of broken buildings was not an easy task.

"How much time have I got?" I asked him.

"Whatever you need."

I figured I'd better get going right away. The Chief always tries to sound very generous about everything, but I knew he'd want results quickly. If I didn't produce, someone else would. He hadn't told me what the payoff would be, and I knew better than to ask him, but in a thing like this the reward if any is determined by the way you do your job.

When I left the room, Norma was whispering in the Chief's ear again, her eyes on me, and he was listening carefully and nodding. Sooner or later I'd be able to guess what she was telling him.

I went to the stables and got my best horse, a gray, named Nick because one ear had been nicked by an arrow in a tax brush with the whisky distillers. The blacksmith was pounding at his anvil nearby, and stopped to wave at me.

"Got me a lot of new iron, Tom," he called.

"Where'd you get it?"

"Dug up some machinery near the Old Men's highway. Plenty knives and horseshoes soon."

I told him to save some for me, because I might be needing new equipment when I came back. I put a bedroll on Nick, and a good spear in the saddle socket. My gun was in the shoulder holster, and I had a very fine knife almost eighteen inches long in the blade. I don't carry a bow, because I'm a poor shot, and I prefer to stick to weapons I can handle better than other men, not worse. Then I started off at a canter to the southwest.

It was my intention to start my search at the old Johnson place, which I understood had been abandoned since shortly after the redhead disappeared. It seemed to me that he'd had a family, but I had no idea what may have happened to them. Because I had assumed his disappearance was due to the action of the Chief, it was natural to assume also that his family had been murdered. That's the way the Chief works; he tries to take no chances.

Riding through the countryside, I noticed that the burned areas were getting harder to spot. Nature was coming back, like my father always said it would. Even when I was a boy the burned areas were already green during the rains, and now the shrubbery, and young trees, were beginning. The Wars of the

Old Men took place when my grandfather was a boy and I am told that, at that time, the skies were dark with smoke for months in a row.

It is not possible to doubt that the Old Men had wonderful things. Their relics are everywhere, like the Chief's car which once supposedly could travel under its own power. Then, take the buildings; many are faced in part with stone which simply is unobtainable anywhere around here. It must have been transported from a quarry in the mountains, and the nearest source of good stone for building is at least a two-days' ride. My father, who was a very keen man and also, of course, had learned much from his father, said that the Old Men were highly skilled in the making of vehicles which propelled themselves. They also had flying machines, and a form of communication over great distances.

The agitators, as the Chief calls them, claim that we could have such things again if everyone learned to read the old books. That may be so. However, I don't feel that it's any of my business.

When my father died he gave me two good things. One was the gun, which he had received from his father, and which he told me would ensure my independence so long as I used it only as a last resort, and carefully hoarded the thirty-three bullets remaining. I have used the gun four times in six years, and have twenty-nine bullets left. It marks me as a man apart, a man who carries potential death.

The other thing he gave me was advice. He said that I lived in a world of animals, and must govern myself accordingly. He said that animals could be either friends or enemies, and that even a friendly animal might turn on one suddenly. He said that I must try to make myself more than an animal, so that I would not be governed by passion alone. He said that a man could always control an animal, because a man thought and an animal only felt.

He gave me this advice because he was afraid for me, and wished no harm to come to me. I was a grown man when he died, but even to the end he would worry about any little scratch I received, or pat my shoulder as though I were still a little boy.

The old Johnson place is near the low range of hills which protects the Valley from the area of the Ruins, all around the

264

Bay. It was late the next day that I got there, though I rode fairly steadily. A farmer in the vicinity pointed the place out to me, keeping his distance pretty well when he noticed my Bodyguard badge.

I dismounted a good distance away and, taking advantage of whatever cover there was, circled the house cautiously. It wasn't deserted. There was smoke coming from the chimney, and a saddled horse was standing in the yard. I moved closer, got inside the rickety fence, edged over to the window, and looked in.

I knew what Norma had been whispering to the Chief. She'd told him to send someone else along, to check on me. Billy Garth, whom I'd last seen standing guard before the Chief's door, was inside now. Also, there was a red-haired girl about twenty years old, kind of skinny but still good-looking enough. Billy had the girl tied up in a chair. The smoke was coming from the chimney because Billy was heating his knife, and I knew what he intended to do to the girl with it.

I figured I could take a chance on a bullet. Taking my gun out of the holster, I leaned it on the window sill. "Don't bother heating that any more," I said.

The girl jerked her head around and looked at me. She wasn't gagged, but she didn't say anything. There was a big red mark across her face, and I figured she'd been slapped around some.

Billy turned slowly to look at me, the red-hot knife in his hand. "Well, look who's here," he said. "The tough kid. Took your time getting here, didn't you."

"Put the knife away," I said. "You might burn yourself." I watched him closely, because I don't trust Billy.

He just kept looking at me with his little red eyes. "You can't hit anything with that gun," he said.

"Sure not," I said. "Drop the knife, Billy."

He waited a little longer, and then sullenly dropped it point down into the floor, the wood smoldering at the contact. "You're safe," he snorted. "Got the nerve to come in now?"

I came in through the window, watching him. When I was inside, I put my gun back in the holster. "The Chief send you?" I asked.

"He thought maybe you needed some help."

"Why did you come here straight, instead of meeting me on the road?"

Billy picked up his knife and walked over to the corner where a bucket of water stood. He plunged the blade in the water several times, to cool it. "Never occurred to me," he said. "Were you lonesome?"

I wasn't going to get anything out of him. I turned my attention to the girl tied in the chair. "Who are you?" I asked.

She didn't say anything, just looked at me with eyes that almost scorched my jacket. However, the red hair made it obvious; she was one of Johnson's family, maybe his daughter. I took out my knife, went over, and cut the cords that tied her. It didn't change her expression; she just rubbed her wrists and ankles, and let her eyes spit hate at me.

"You don't have to look at me like that," I said. "Seems to me you owe me a favor."

"I don't owe a Bodyguard anything," she whispered.

Billy laughed. His knife was cool, and he stuck it back in its scabbard. "You should ha' come a little later," he said. "She'd tell me where the old man is, all right, after she crawled around on her wrists and ankles for a while."

"You hear him," I said to the girl. "You want me to turn you over to him again, or will you tell us where Johnson is?"

She was scared. She seemed to draw up into herself. "I don't know," she said. "I don't know where he is."

"You're his daughter, aren't you?"

"Yes."

"What are you doing here?"

"I've been living in the woods," she explained rapidly. "Pa's been gone a year now, nobody knows where he is. I came back to look around kind of, and see if it was safe to live here again."

"Whereabouts in the woods you been living?"

"Just around."

"Your father's hiding out in the Ruins, isn't he?"

"I don't know what you're talking about," she said.

I turned to Billy. "How'd you find her?" I asked.

He grunted. "I came down here to look the place over, same as you did. The old man is probably right around the neighborhood, living with one of these farmers. Anyhow, I see this girl sneakin' around in the house, so I grabbed her. Does that give you any ideas, bright boy?"

"You think Johnson's hiding out near here?" I asked him.

"Sure."

"Why?"

"A smart kid like you should be able to figure it out himself. Where else would he go?"

"For one thing," I said, watching the girl closely, "he might go into the Ruins. He believed in reading, so he'd go some place where there were a lot of books. He'd do that because he'd figure the books would show him how to get rid of the Chief."

It seemed to me the girl was trying too hard to look indifferent. I thought perhaps I was on the right track. We talked some more but got nowhere, except that I found out her name was Molly. She calmed down considerably after she was sure no one was going to burn her hands and feet off, but she stuck to her story about not knowing where Johnson was.

As it was getting late, I went out to get my horse, and stabled him in the old barn. I guess only Molly got much sleep that night, because both Billy and I were lying awake listening to each other's breathing. Maybe the Chief thought Norma'd given him a good idea, sending Billy to watch me, but it didn't seem so smart to me.

In the morning I brought down a couple of rabbits with my slingshot, and we had a good breakfast. There is no shortage of game in the Sacramento Territory. In the hills of the east, where I was raised, a good man with a spear can bring down a buck almost for the asking.

Then I put Molly on my horse behind me, and we started out for the Ruins. Billy Garth was sulky, but he came along; I could see that he was afraid of radiations. I kept watching Molly for signs of the same fear, but, as she showed none, I concluded that she really had been living in the Ruins with her father, and living there had learned the radiations were only superstition.

When you get to the top of the hills just this side of the Bay, you can see the beginnings of the Ruins. It is a breathtaking sight; thousands and thousands of houses, all of them just shells. I could see that Billy was sweating, so I took a lot of pleasure in riding forward steadily.

From the crest of the ridge there is a steady slope down to the Bay. We could see the brightly shining waters, and across them the site of San Francisco, another of the cities of the Old Men.

We could even see where the bridges had once jutted out from the shore. I said to the girl, "What was the name of this place, just below us?"

"I don't know," she said.

"Won't hurt you any to tell me," I answered. "I'd just like to know."

She paused. Though skinny, as I have said, she was somehow attractive. Her eyes were greenish and her skin was fair. "It was called Berkeley," she said. "That's what I was told. The Old Men had a lot of wonderful things here."

"For instance?"

"Books," she hesitated. "My f— People I know said there were just thousands of books buried here."

"Can you read?" I asked her.

"Yes," she said challengingly. "I don't care who knows it, either."

"That's all right," I said. "It's no skin off my back if you can read. Whereabouts did you say these books were buried?"

She saw where I was leading, then, and with a furious look turned her face away.

I heard a loud laugh from Billy Garth, who had been riding a little behind. "She's smarter'n you," he jeered. "How about it, tough guy? Ain't you tired yet, or do I heat up my knife and do it my way?"

I didn't answer. Billy suddenly spurred his horse alongside and laid hold of the bridle. "O.K., Hunter," he said. "You're so smart. You figure on poking around in these Ruins forever, looking for an old fool who only has to duck behind a wall to hide?"

"Get your hand off," I said.

"I've gone as far into this death trap as I'm going!" he snarled. "We've got the answer right here in this girl. We don't have to look for her old man. We just string her up by the thumbs in a nice prominent place, and let her holler a while, and *he'll* come to *us*. If you had half the nerve—"

I struck his hand off the bridle. He roared and lunged at me, clawing for his hatchet. I caught his wrist and twisted the hatchet out of his grasp. It fell on my horse; I could see the blood gush as the beast screamed and shot forward. All three of us, Molly,

268

Billy and I, fell to the ground in a heap. Something hit my head and that was all I knew for some time.

I woke up not wanting to. From the way it hurt to breathe, I knew I must have a couple of cracked ribs. And when I raised my hand to my face, it came away sticky with blood. With a good deal of effort, I managed to sit up and prop myself against a tree bole. My head was buzzing, and it was a few minutes before my eyes could focus.

What puzzled me was, that I was still alive. When the fall knocked me out, Billy doubtless had given me a going-over, but why hadn't he killed me? He had taken my gun, but my knife was still in its sheath. I had to get up and move; I knew if I just lay there I would soon be too stiff and weak to help myself.

After a couple of failures, I got to my feet, and my head cleared. I examined the tracks on the ground, and got a better idea of what had happened. Billy had been scuffling with Molly, she had broken away, run, and he had followed her. He had just been too busy to kill me, or perhaps had thought me already dead.

With my knife, I cut strips off my deerskin jacket, and bound my chest as well as I could. It helped some. Then, since my horse was gone, I started off on foot down the slope and into the Ruins, following the tracks.

By the position of the sun, I judged I had been unconscious for about two hours. Since Billy was mounted and I was not, I had no hope of overtaking him quickly, but I figured I would do it eventually.

The Ruins were beginning in earnest, now, and I lost Billy's tracks on the hard surface of an old road. It seemed to me that he would not go much farther down the slope, for fear of Radiations. I determined therefore to wait for developments, since Billy would have to make his presence known in some way if he intended to use Molly as bait for her father.

It was late afternoon by now. I ate some strips of the morning's rabbit, which I had shoved into a pocket. Then I climbed to the shattered roof of a small building nearby, and lay down behind the low parapet which surrounded the roof. From this position I had a fairly good view of the surrounding territory, merely by raising my head. It felt good to lie down and rest; my chest hurt with every breath, and my head throbbed.

With the coming of twilight, I began to watch very carefully. At last I saw the first flicker of a fire about half a mile south. I got going the best I could, sliding off the road and racing toward the south as fast as my painful chest would let me. I had to get there first.

The remains of a tower stood in a clearing. There were no building ruins within at least one hundred yards. Rubble from the tower itself made it very easy to climb to the highest point, about twenty feet above ground. Here, at the top, Billy Garth had built a huge fire. Sprawled at his feet, but plainly visible, was Molly. Her hands and feet were bound.

I found a good point of vantage, and settled down comfortably to wait. It wasn't long before I saw definite signs that someone was moving about in the perimeter of the Ruins. I advanced quickly, but at that I was almost too late.

"Hello!" came a voice out of the shadowy buildings. "What do you want, you up there with the fire?"

Billy Garth roared back, "I got something to trade!" He bent, seized Molly by the hair, and dragged her erect. "Look!" he boomed. "I got a redheaded girl named Molly. She's been beat up some. Maybe she'll get beat up some more!"

There was a pause, and then the newcomer's voice came again, hoarse and strained. "What do you want?"

"A trade!" shouted Billy gleefully. "One redheaded girl, in reasonable good shape, breathing anyhow, to trade for a red-headed dog named Johnson!"

I had rounded the last building now, scrambling in my haste, and saw the stranger at last. It was Johnson all right; there was no doubt of it.

"Let the girl go," Johnson was saying. "Let me see her walk away, and I'll give up."

"You don't make no deals with me," said Billy. "I make the deals. See?" He swung his hand heavily against the girl, knocking her down. "You got nothing to make deals about, Johnson. The Chief wants you. If you give up now, or not, we'll get you. But if you don't show in a hurry, I start kicking your girl's ribs into a busted basket!"

"I'll come," sobbed Johnson.

I moved forward quickly. Before Johnson had a chance to step out of the shadows, I was on him. The weight of my body knocked him flat on his face, stunning him. I whipped a cord around his wrists. Then I lifted him to his feet, and he stood groggily, facing me. He was a tall man, thin, not so young anymore, and he looked as though he hadn't eaten well for a while.

"Tricked!" he said thickly, as soon as he could talk. "You Bodyguards—"

"Keep quiet and you won't get hurt," I told him. I took out my knife and put it in his ribs. "Now move out into the light, and stop when I tell you to."

He walked, or rather staggered, a few steps into the flickering light thrown by the fire. I walked close behind him, my knife point ready. I saw Billy Garth make a gesture of surprise when he recognized me, and draw my gun out of his belt.

The girl saw us too, and struggled to her knees. "Go back, Pa!" she wailed. "Run! Run!"

I halted Johnson, and called up to where the others were. "You're through, Billy," I said. "I've got Johnson. I'll kill him before I'll let you have him, and the Chief wants him alive. Throw down my gun, Billy."

He swore at me.

I said, "It's no use, Billy. You never shot a gun in your life. You can't possibly hit me. Throw down the gun."

"You haven't got the nerve to kill him," he said.

I grabbed Johnson by the hair and pulled his head back. I put my knife across his throat. "Throw down the gun," I said.

Billy hesitated and then, with a curse, hurled the gun to the foot of the broken tower. He scrambled down the slope of rubble and vanished into the dark at a dead run. A moment later I heard the hoofbeats of his horse.

Johnson was almost fainting. I got my gun, then climbed to the tower and cut the girl loose. She was in bad shape. I helped her down to the ground and she stumbled to her father, holding on to him and kissing him.

"You wouldn't have killed him, would you?" she said to me.

"I don't know," I answered.

"He's a Bodyguard," rasped Johnson. "What are you going to do with Molly? That other one offered to trade her for me."

271

"He was kidding," I said. "You didn't really believe him, did you?"

"No," he admitted reluctantly. "But I thought . . . if there was a chance—"

The girl wept. She looked homely with tears running down her face, and her eyes and cheeks puffy with bruises. "You should have stayed away, Pa," she said. "You never should have come."

Johnson turned to me again. "What are you going to do with us?" he said.

"I have orders," I told him. "I work for the Chief, and I carry out orders. He told me to bring you back to him alive, and that's just what I'm going to do. But he didn't say anything about the girl. As soon as I figure it's safe, she can go. I don't care where she goes, and I'll see that she has a chance to get clear."

They stared at me. "You mean that?" asked Johnson slowly.

"Of course I mean it," I said irritably.

They didn't say any more, but only clung to each other. Then Johnson showed us where we could find fresh water, and we made a camp. He led us to food, too, the canned food of the Old Men, which was plentiful in the Ruins. All together, he was as little troublesome a prisoner as I ever took.

"Aren't you afraid to eat this food?" he asked me, when I had opened several cans with my knife.

"Why?"

"Radiations."

I smiled. "I don't believe in radiations," I said.

He shook his head gravely. "They're real. Very terribly real."

"Then you shouldn't be alive," I pointed out. "You've been living here for a year."

"This area," said Johnson, "and most of the other outlying districts as well, were destroyed by ordinary bombs. If you can use a word like 'ordinary' for bombs that do so much mischief. So the radiations are not present everywhere. Over there"—he pointed out towards the Bay—"on the other side of the water, where the main city stood, the radiations are probably still present, though nowhere near as bad as they used to be. People no longer really understand what radiations are, what they do. So

272

they keep away from all ruins, superstitiously. And that's a pity, because there is so much to be learned here.''

"Books?" I said.

"Yes."

"What can you learn from them?"

"Everything. How to make buildings like these, how to live like the Old Men lived, do as they did—"

"Not interested," I said.

"Don't you want to have those things again?"

I got impatient. "I never had them, so I don't miss them. My father said never to want anything I couldn't have. And now I'm going to get some sleep."

Molly came over. Without saying a word, she began to rebandage my chest. She did a good job, and I felt much better. Then, "What's your name?"

"Tom Hunter."

"All right, Tom. You're a hard man and a Bodyguard. But you helped me twice, even though you intend to turn my father over to the Chief. I won't ask you why you helped me, or why you have to take Pa to die."

"My father said—"

"I know. Your father said. Now your chest should feel better, if you give it some rest."

Though we all had apparently come to friendly terms, I did not neglect to tie up both of them securely for the night. I wanted to sleep without listening for hostile movements.

In the morning we started the long walk to Sacramento. I was stiff and sore, but the mild exercise and the warm sun combined to loosen my bruised muscles. We walked together, more like three friends than anything else, and Johnson talked very frankly to me.

He told me that he had known how to read since he was a boy. Living close to the Ruins, he had explored them for a long time, and had stumbled on a huge collection of books in a place near to the broken tower where I captured him. The things he read in these books inflamed his desire to know more, to dispose of our corrupt Chief, and to set the community on a track which would bring it back some day to the achievements of the Old Men. There was actually, he said, a secret organization among

273

the farmers of Sacramento Territory; the Chief knew it quite well, but dared not try to punish all involved because the disaffection was so widespread.

I, too, knew, of course, that the Chief was far from popular. That was why the Bodyguards existed. The news of a secret organization explained why the Chief was so concerned about Johnson, and why he wanted him alive.

Johnson said also that Molly had been working with him, to the extent of acting as liaison between the farmers and himself. She had been on one of her periodic trips into the Territory when Billy Garth found her.

"You shouldn't tell me this," I said.

"I think I should."

"Why?"

"Because you're on the wrong side in this struggle, Tom Hunter, and I believe you'll realize it soon."

I shrugged. "Your side may be wrong, too. You want to bring back the Old Men. You're like that crazy old man who called himself the Atom Master. What did the Old Men do that was so good? They built things and then smashed them. My grandfather was a little boy then. The sky was black and fires shot out of the earth like fountains. They learned how to do that from the books. What good are the books if that was the final use for them?"

Johnson protested that I didn't understand. Maybe I don't. I never read the books, I don't know what they say. Maybe there are books that tell people how to be good to each other, too.

It was on the morning of our third day of travel that I saw the horsemen approaching over the meadows. From their formation and the way they rode, I knew them to be Bodyguards. I was worried for Molly. She should have left long ago, but insisted on coming along as far as possible. I looked for a place where she might hide, but it was too late. Farmhouses were visible but distant, and the fringe of trees that marked the Big River was half a mile away.

There were five horsemen, and they reined in before us. I recognized the leader, big Joe Wentworth.

"Don't reach for anything, Hunter," said Joe. "You're covered."

I hadn't made a motion. "Why should I reach?" I said. "What's up?"

"This Johnson?" asked Joe.

"Yes. What's the trouble?"

"I got my orders, Hunter. The Chief sent me to bring you in, and Johnson, too, if he was with you." He looked at me levelly for a moment. "I might as well tell you, Tom. The Chief wants this guy Johnson alive, but he told me to finish you off if you make any trouble."

The picture was plain. Too plain. Billy Garth had returned, and told some interesting story.

"You won't have any trouble," I said. "What kind of a story did Billy tell?"

"Beats me. It's none of my business. Now, Tom, I'll have to ask you for your gun. We'll get it from you one way or the other, and it's better this way. You know me, and I promise I'll return it to you."

"I'll take your word for it, Joe," I said. Bitterly, I took the gun out of its holster and handed it to him. I gave him my knife, also.

He took both, and turned to Molly. "This girl," he said. "Who is she?"

"Never saw her before," I said. "She lives in that house over there, she says." I waved my hand toward a distant farmhouse. "We just came across her a few minutes ago."

Joe Wentworth looked at her. "She's got red hair," he said. "Like Johnson."

"Lots of people have red hair," I said.

"How about it, Johnson?" asked Joe. "You know this girl?"

"No," said Johnson.

"I think you guys are both liars," said Joe. "But the Chief didn't say anything about a girl. He said you and Johnson. And I got you and Johnson. That should be enough blood to drink for one day. All right, let's get going!"

Johnson and I were swung up, each behind one of the riders, and we galloped off. I turned my head and saw Molly stand watching us for a moment, then turn and run in the direction of the farmhouse.

Walking had been easier on my ribs than riding. By the time we got to the Fort, I was badly shaken up. I expected to be taken

275

in to the Chief, but instead I was thrown into one of the strong-rooms of the cellar, with Johnson. I made no fuss about it; there's no use complaining about something you can't help.

I sat there for two days with Johnson. He tried to thank me for not giving Molly away, but I cut him off short. I wasn't too sure why I'd done it. And I suspected that, by that impulse, I might have put a noose around my neck. "That's your trouble," I told myself. "You're too squeamish. You should have killed Billy Garth when you first put a gun on him through the window of the old Johnson place."

Finally they came for us and marched us upstairs, into the Official. I got the feeling that something was wrong. The men who brought us looked as though they had been fighting recently. One had a bandaged arm. They were surly and silent, not what I would have expected. I asked them what the trouble was, but they said nothing. They brought us into the Official and stood by the door, inside.

The Chief sat behind his desk, looking sour. Norma was on the arm of his chair, as though she hadn't even moved since last I saw her. Joe Wentworth leaned against the wall, his face dark, and I wasn't at all surprised to see Billy Garth, who stood near the Chief with one hand on the hatchet in his belt. He was grinning slyly.

The Chief examined us critically, while Norma whispered in his ear like a black bird perched on his shoulder. "So you two men been working together," he said at last. "No wonder you didn't mind going into the Ruins after the Atom Master, Hunter. You had friends there, eh?"

I didn't answer.

"Then when I sent you for Johnson, that was right up your tree. Only you didn't intend to get him. You just figured on warning him."

"Ask Joe Wentworth," I said. "Ask him where I was going when he arrested me."

"Yeah, yeah," said the Chief. "You might have been going anywhere. Besides, I think maybe Joe is a liar, too." He darted an angry glance at Wentworth, who looked blacker than ever. "Because you had a girl with you, and Joe let her go. Didn't you, Joe."

"You didn't say nothing about a girl," responded Joe sturdily.

The Chief leaned back and was whispered to some more. Then, "That was Johnson's daughter. You didn't know that, did you? The hell you didn't. You let her get away to stir up these fool farmers."

I said, "He didn't know it was Johnson's daughter. I knew, but I told him it wasn't."

I was standing before his desk. The Chief is a big man, but he moved faster than I have ever seen anyone move. In a single motion he rose from his chair, plucked his gun from his belt, and hit me across the face with the barrel. I didn't even have time to duck. I landed on the floor, blood streaming from a face still puffy since my encounter with Billy Garth near the Ruins. Even with the pain, I couldn't help noticing Norma's malicious smile.

I climbed to my feet and let the blood drip. "You shouldn't have done that," I said. "Now, watch out for me."

"You!" said the Chief. "Watch out for you! You renegade!" He was white with rage. "You let the girl go, and now every blasted farmer in the Valley has ridden into town yelling for Johnson!"

Norma grabbed his arm, as though to stop him from saying too much. He shook her off. "Thirty Bodyguards dead!" he bellowed. "I shouldn't ha' done that to you, hey? Spying for this redheaded bookworm, and you tell me to watch out for you!"

Johnson spoke up. "This man found me for you, but he found me too late. Whether or not you kill me now doesn't matter. The date for this action was set a month ago. You're through, Chief."

The Chief sat down and looked at him coldly. Norma perched on the arm of the chair again, and put her hand on his shoulder. She bent and whispered to him.

"Since you think you know so much about it," said the Chief, "I'll tell you something you don't know. We're going to wipe out your whole lousy crew. I'm going to fix you up right now, both of you, just as pretty as I can make you. Then I'll hang what's left of you outside the window, for your friends to see."

It got very quiet in there. I began to understand what was happening. Some kind of revolt had started, all right, and the

277

Chief was hard-pressed. He might yet even be beaten. I felt a little hope. There could be a way out. I looked around at the room, at the Chief, at Billy, at Joe Wentworth, at the two guards standing by the door. Joe had my gun in his belt, and only the Chief had another.

"Well, Joe," I said, "seems to me you got something you promised to return to me."

The Chief leaned forward. "We'll start now," he said. I felt my elbows clamped from behind by one of the guards. Johnson was held the same way.

"All right, Billy," said the Chief. "You can start in on your friend Hunter. Joe, I want you to muss up Johnson."

I heard noises outside, and shouting. I figured that if I could stay alive for a few minutes more, I might have a chance. Billy approached me, grinning all over. He was going to like this. I kicked back hard and twisted forward at the same time, feeling my broken ribs stab me like knives. I got one arm loose just in time to deflect Billy's first punch, which glanced off the side of my head but hurt me anyhow. I got my other arm loose and shook off the guard just in time to receive another blow full in the face. It knocked me sprawling into the corner.

I saw Billy coming at me, and tried to get up in time to avoid his feet. I wasn't sure I'd manage. Then something flew through the air and landed against my chest with a thump. It was my gun!

"I near forgot to return it," said Joe calmly.

With a cry of fear, Billy Garth snatched at his hatchet. He didn't draw it. I shot him through the head, and he fell in a heap before me.

Too much happened, too fast. The Chief missed with his first shot, and never had a chance to try again. Joe Wentworth and I, together, beat him to death. I put a bullet through Norma myself, while she ran screaming for the door. I forgot about the two guards until I noticed that Johnson was holding them off, very nicely, with the Chief's own gun. Then, when it was over, when my head cleared and I could see the blood and bodies, I was sick, while big Joe Wentworth watched me solemnly.

So that was the end of the big revolt. There was no more fighting after Joe and I dragged the bodies downstairs, out in the

278

front of the Fort, and nailed them to the door. That was Johnson's idea; he said it would give notice, and it did.

The Chief was dead, and so the Bodyguards had no leader; but Johnson was alive, and he had all the farmers Molly had gathered. The result was easy to see.

It was two weeks later that I stood in the Official again. The blood had been washed off the floor, but it seemed to me that I could still smell it. The room was different in another way, too, because now Johnson sat in the big chair, and Molly stood beside him.

"I wish you'd change your mind, Tom," said Johnson.

"I'm going," I said.

"We could use you."

"You've got Joe Wentworth," I said. "He's better than I am. You've got a gun now, too." I pointed at the Chief's gun, which he was wearing.

"But you could help, Tom," said Johnson. "We can get a new world started here. We're not the only people left alive in this continent. There must be other groups, many groups, across the mountains to the east. We can join them all together, get a Nation like the Old Men had."

"Let him alone, Pa," said Molly. She came over and put her hands on my shoulders. Her face wasn't bruised anymore, and she was very good-looking, though she was skinny as ever. "Your chest feel all right now, Tom?"

"Sure," I said. "I can travel fine."

"What's the trouble, Tom?" said Johnson. "You know how much we'd like your help in this. We've got a lot to do. Set up schools, set up proper authority, see that sound laws are made, explore the Ruins—"

"Look," I said, "I quit being a Bodyguard when the Chief swiped me across the face with a gun barrel. By any other name, it's still Bodyguarding you want me for. I've got nothing against you, Johnson. You won't order any killings just for the fun of it. But I don't go for your ideas."

"What ideas?"

"You think we had trouble because we had bad government. You think good government will make people better. I don't see it that way. The trouble is not bad government, but just government itself. With the wrong kind of people, no government can do any good. With the right kind of people, you don't need government at all.

"You think you can get the right kind of people by starting from the government end, and telling them to go to school, and putting out Bodyguards to walk the fields and keep people straight. I think you've got to start from the other end, forget the Old Men and the way they worked things, forget about organizations and just start raising people right. Like my father wanted to raise me, to be a man and not an animal.

"Johnson, you want to bring back the days of the Old Men, but I'm glad the Old Men are gone, and I hope they never come back. I had enough killing right here, in this room. I'm not interested in any more, for any purpose."

I ripped my gun out of its holster and threw it on the table before Johnson. "Here," I said, "keep this one until the books teach you to make some more."

"I'm sorry," said Johnson. "I'm really sorry."

I turned around and went out, down the stairs and into the sunshine. The air smelled good. I saw that Molly had followed me.

"That's the longest speech I ever heard you make," she said.

"The last, too."

"Where are you going now?"

"East. To the mountains. Where I used to live with my father."

"You got a wife there, maybe?"

"No. You got somebody?"

"No."

We looked at each other, and then we both began to laugh.

280

THE PALACE AT MIDNIGHT
Robert Silverberg

EDITOR'S INTRODUCTION

Robert Silverberg has been at the forefront of science fiction writers during a long and distinguished career. In this excellent story he shows us an After Armageddon setting that is typical of—and could happen only in—California . . .

———————————————**¦ ¦**———————————————

THE FOREIGN MINISTER OF THE EMPIRE OF SAN FRANCISCO WAS trying to sleep late. Last night had been a long one, a wild if not particularly gratifying party at the baths, too much to drink, too much to smoke, and he had seen the dawn come up like thunder out of Oakland 'crost the bay. Now the telephone was ringing. He integrated the first couple of rings nicely into his dream, but the next one began to undermine his slumber, and the one after that woke him up. He groped for the receiver and, eyes still closed, managed to croak, "Christensen here."

"Tom, are you awake? You don't sound awake. It's Morty."

The undersecretary for external affairs. Christensen sat up, rubbed his eyes, ran his tongue around his lips. Daylight was streaming into the room. His cats were glaring at him from the doorway. The little Siamese pawed daintily at her empty bowl and looked up expectantly.

281

"Tom?"

"I'm up, I'm up! What is it, Morty?"

"I didn't mean to wake you. How was I supposed to know, one in the afternoon—"

"*What is it*, Morty?"

"We got a call from Monterey. There's an ambassador on the way up and you've got to meet with her."

The foreign minister worked hard at clearing the fog from his brain. He was thirty-nine years old and all-night parties took more out of him than they once had.

"You do it, Morty."

"You know I would, Tom. But I can't. You've got to handle this one yourself. It's prime."

"Prime? What kind of prime? Like a great dope deal? Or are they declaring war on us?"

"How would I know the details? The call came in and they said it was prime, Ms. Sawyer must confer with Mr. Christensen. It wouldn't involve dope, Tom. And it can't be war, either. Shit, why would Monterey want to make war on us? They've only got but ten soldiers, I bet, unless they're drafting the Chicanos out of the Salinas *calabozo*, and—"

"All right." Christensen's head was buzzing. "Go easy on the chatter, okay? Where am I supposed to meet her?"

"Berkeley."

"You're kidding."

"She won't come into the city. She thinks it's too dangerous over here."

"What do we do, kill ambassadors and barbecue them? She'll be safe here and she knows it."

"I talked to her. She thinks the city's too crazy. She'll go as far as Berkeley, but that's it."

"Tell her to go to hell."

"Tom, Tom—"

Christensen sighed. "Where in Berkeley will she be?"

"The Claremont, at half past four."

"Jesus," Christensen said. "How did you get me into this? All the way across to the East Bay to meet a lousy ambassador from Monterey! Let her come to San Francisco. This is the Empire, isn't it? They're only a stinking republic. Am I supposed to swim over to Oakland every time an envoy shows up and

282

wiggles a finger? Some bozo from Fresno says boo and I have to haul my ass out to the valley, eh? Where does it stop? What kind of clout do I have, anyway?''

"Tom—"

"I'm sorry, Morty. I don't feel like a goddamned diplomat this morning."

"It isn't morning anymore, Tom. But I'd do it for you if I could."

"All right. All right. I didn't mean to yell at you. You make the ferry arrangements?''

"Ferry leaves at three-thirty. Chauffeur will pick you up at your place at three, okay?''

"Okay," Christensen said. "See if you can find out any more about all this and have somebody call me back in an hour with a briefing, will you?''

He fed the cats, showered, shaved, took a couple of pills, brewed some coffee. At half past two the ministry called. Nobody had any idea what the ambassador might want. Relations between San Francisco and the Republic of Monterey were cordial just now. Ms. Sawyer lived in Pacific Grove and was a member of the Monterey Senate and that was all that was known about her. Some briefing, Christensen thought. He went downstairs to wait for his chauffeur. It was a late autumn day, bright and clear and cool. The rains hadn't begun yet and the streets looked dusty. The foreign minister lived on Frederick Street just off Cole, in an old white Victorian with a small front porch. He settled in on the steps, feeling wide awake but surly, and a few minutes before three his car came putt-putting up, a venerable gray Chevrolet with the arms of imperial San Francisco on its doors. The driver was Vietnamese or maybe Thai. Christensen got in without a word, and off they went at an imperial velocity through the practically empty streets, down to Haight, eastward for a while, then onto Oak, up Van Ness past the palace, where at this moment the Emperor Norton VII was probably taking his imperial nap, and along Geary through downtown to the ferry slip. The stump of the Bay Bridge glittered magically against the sharp blue sky. A small power cruiser was waiting for him. Christensen was silent during the slow dull voyage. A chill wind cut through the Golden Gate and made him huddle into himself. He stared broodingly at the low rounded East Bay hills, dry and

283

brown from a long summer of drought, and thought about the permutations of fate that had transformed an adequate architect into the barely competent foreign minister of this barely competent little nation. The Empire of San Francisco, one of the early emperors had said, is the only country in history that was decadent from the day it was founded.

At the Berkeley marina Christensen told the ferry skipper, "I don't know what time I'll be coming back, so no sense waiting. I'll phone in when I'm ready to go."

Another imperial car took him up the hillside to the sprawling nineteenth-century splendor of the Hotel Claremont, that vast antiquated survivor of all the cataclysms. It was seedy now, the grounds a jungle, ivy almost to the tops of the palm trees, and yet it still looked fit to be a palace, hundreds of rooms, magnificent banquet halls. Christensen wondered how often it had guests. There wasn't much tourism these days.

In the parking plaza outside the entrance was a single car, a black-and-white California Highway Patrol job that had been decorated with the insignia of the Republic of Monterey, a contorted cypress tree and a sea otter. A uniformed driver lounged against it. "I'm Christensen," he told the man.

"You the foreign minister?"

"I'm not the Emperor Norton."

"Come on. She's waiting in the bar."

Ms. Sawyer stood up as he entered—a slender dark-haired woman of about thirty, with cool green eyes—and he flashed her a quick, professionally cordial smile, which she returned just as professionally. He did not feel at all cordial.

"Senator Sawyer," he said. "I'm Tom Christensen."

"Glad to know you." She pivoted and gestured toward the huge picture window that ran the length of the bar. "I just got here. I've been admiring the view. It's been years since I've been in the Bay Area."

He nodded. From the cocktail lounge one could see the slopes of Berkeley, the bay, the ruined bridges, the still imposing San Francisco skyline. Very nice. They took seats by the window and he beckoned to a waiter, who brought them drinks.

"How was your drive up?" Christensen asked.

"No problems. We got stopped for speeding in San Jose, but

284

I got out of it. They could see it was an official car and they stopped us anyway.''

"The bastards. They love to look important."

"Things haven't been good between Monterey and San Jose all year. They're spoiling for trouble."

"I hadn't heard," Christensen said.

"We think they want to annex Santa Cruz. Naturally we can't put up with that. Santa Cruz is our buffer."

He said sharply, "Is that what you came here for, to ask our help against San Jose?"

She stared at him in surprise. "Are you in a hurry, Mr. Christensen?"

"Not particularly."

"You sound awfully impatient. We're still making preliminary conversation, having a drink, two diplomats playing the diplomatic game. Isn't that so?"

"Well?"

"I was telling you what happened to me on the way north. In response to your question. Then I was filling you in on current political developments. I didn't expect you to snap at me like that."

"Did I snap?"

"It sounded like snapping to me," she said.

Christensen took a deep pull of his bourbon and water and gave her a long steady look. She met his gaze imperturbably. She looked annoyed, amused and very, very tough. After a time, when some of the red haze of irrational anger and fatigue had cleared from his mind, he said quietly, "I had about four hours sleep last night and I wasn't expecting an envoy from Monterey today. I'm tired and edgy, and if I sounded impatient or harsh or snappish, I'm sorry."

"It's all right. I understand."

"Another bourbon or two and I'll be properly unwound." He held his empty glass toward the hovering waiter. "A refill for you, too?" he asked her.

"Yes. Please." In a formal tone she said, "Is the Emperor in good health?"

"Not bad. He hasn't really been well for a couple of years, but he's holding his own. And President Morgan?"

"Fine," she said. "Hunting wild boar in Big Sur this week."

285

"A nice life it must be, President of Monterey. I've always liked Monterey. So much quieter and cleaner and more sensible down there than in San Francisco."

"Too quiet sometimes. I envy you the excitement here."

"Yes. The rapes, the muggings, the arson, the mass meetings, the race wars, the—"

"Please," she said gently.

He realized he had begun to rant. There was a throbbing behind his eyes. He worked to gain control of himself.

"Did my voice get too loud?"

"You must be terribly tired. Look, we can confer in the morning if you'd prefer. It isn't *that* urgent. Suppose we have dinner and not talk politics at all and get rooms here, and tomorrow after breakfast we can—"

"No," Christensen said. "My nerves are a little ragged, that's all. But I'll try to be more civil. And I'd rather not wait until tomorrow to find out what this is all about. Suppose you give me a précis of it now, and if it sounds too complicated, I'll sleep on it and we can discuss it in detail tomorrow. Yes?"

"All right." She put her drink down and sat quite still, as if arranging her thoughts. At length she said, "The Republic of Monterey maintains close ties with the Free State of Mendocino. I understand that Mendocino and the Empire broke off relations a little while back."

"A fishing dispute, nothing major."

"But you have no direct contact with them right now. Therefore this should come as news to you. The Mendocino people have learned, and have communicated to our representative there, that an invasion of San Francisco is imminent."

Christen blinked twice. "By whom?"

"The Realm of Wicca," she said.

"Flying down from Oregon on their broomsticks?"

"Please. I'm being serious."

"Unless things have changed up there," Christensen said, "the Realm of Wicca is nonviolent, like all the neopagan states. As I understand it, they tend their farms and practice their little pagan rituals and do a lot of dancing around the maypole and chanting and screwing, and that's it. You expect me to believe that a bunch of gentle goofy witches is going to make war on the Empire?"

286

She said, "Not war. But definitely an invasion."

"Explain."

"One of their high priests has proclaimed San Francisco a holy place and has instructed them to come down here and build a Stonehenge in Golden Gate Park in time for proper celebration of the winter solstice. There are at least a quarter of a million neopagans in the Willamette Valley and more than half of them are expected to take part. According to our Mendocino man, the migration has already begun, and thousands of Wiccans are spread out between Mount Shasta and Ukiah right now. The solstice is only seven weeks away. The Wiccans may be gentle, but you're going to have a hundred fifty thousand of them in San Francisco by the end of the month, pitching tents all over town."

"Holy Jesus," Christensen muttered, and closed his eyes.

"Can you feed that many strangers? Can you find room for them? Are the people of San Francisco going to meet them with open arms? Is it going to be a festival of love?"

"It'll be a fucking massacre," Christensen said tonelessly.

"Yes. And the witches may be nonviolent but they know how to practice self-defense. Once they're attacked, there'll be rivers of blood in the city, and it won't all be Wiccan blood."

Christensen's head was pounding again. She was absolutely right—chaos, strife, bloodshed. And a merry Christmas to all. He rubbed his aching forehead, turned away from her and stared out at the deepening twilight and the sparkling lights of the city on the other side of the bay. A bleak bitter depression was taking hold of his spirit. He signaled for another round of drinks. Then he said slowly, "They can't be allowed to enter the city. We'll need to close the imperial frontier and turn them back before they get as far as Santa Rosa. Let them build their goddamned Stonehenge in Sacramento if they like." His eyes flickered. He started to assemble ideas. "The Empire might just have enough troops to contain the Wiccans by itself, but I think this is best handled as a regional problem. We'll call in forces from our allies as far out as Petaluma and Napa and Palo Alto. I don't imagine we can expect much help from the Free State or from San Jose. And of course Monterey isn't much of a military power, but still—"

"We are willing to help you," Ms. Sawyer said.

"To what extent?"

"We aren't set up for much actual warfare, no, but we have access to our own alliances from Salinas down to Paso Robles, and we could call up, say, five thousand troops all told."

"That would be very helpful," said Christensen.

"It shouldn't be necessary for there to be any combat. With the imperial border sealed and troops posted along the line from Guerneville to Sacramento, the Wiccans won't force the issue. They'll revise their revelation and celebrate the solstice somewhere else."

"Yes," he said. "I think you're right." He leaned toward her and said, "Why is Monterey willing to help us?"

"We have problems of our own brewing—with San Jose. If we are seen making a conspicuous gesture of solidarity with the Empire, it might discourage San Jose from proceeding with its notion of annexing Santa Cruz, don't you think? That amounts to an act of war against us. Surely San Jose isn't interested in making any moves that will bring the Empire down on its back."

"I see," said Christensen. She wasn't subtle, but she was effective. Quid pro quo, we help you keep the witches out, you help us keep San Jose in line, and all remains well without a shot being fired. These goddamned little nations, he thought, these absurd jerkwater sovereignties, with their wars and alliances and shifting confederations—it was like a game, it was like playground politics. Except that it was real. What had fallen apart was not going to be put back together, not for a long while, and this miniaturized *Weltpolitik* was the realest reality there was just now. At least things were saner in Northern California than they were down south where Los Angeles was gobbling everything, but there were rumors that Pasadena had the bomb. Nobody had to contend with that up here. Christensen said, "I'll have to propose all this to the defense ministry, of course. And get the Emperor's approval. But basically I'm in agreement with your thinking."

"I'm so pleased."

"And I'm very glad that you took the trouble to travel up from Monterey to make these matters clear to us."

"Enlightened self-interest," Ms. Sawyer said.

"Mmm. Yes." He found himself studying the sharp planes of her cheekbones, the delicate arch of her eyebrows. Not only was she cool and competent, Christensen thought, but now that the business part of their meeting was over, he was coming to notice that she was a very attractive woman and that he was not as tired as he had thought he was. Did international politics allow room for a little recreational hanky-panky? Metternich hadn't jumped into bed with Talleyrand, nor Kissinger with Indira Gandhi, but times had changed, after all, and—no. *No.* He choked off that entire line of thought. In these shabby days they might all be children playing at being grownups, but nevertheless, international politics still had its code, and this was a meeting of diplomats, not a blind date or a singles-bar pickup. You will sleep in your own bed tonight, he told himself, and you will sleep alone.

All the same he said, "It's past six o'clock. Shall we have dinner together before I go back to the city?"

"I'd love to."

"I don't know much about Berkeley restaurants. We're probably better off eating right here."

"I think that's best," she said.

They were the only ones in the hotel's enormous dining room. A staff of three waited on them as though they were the most important people who had ever dined there. And dinner turned out to be quite decent, he thought—seafood, calamari and abalone and sand dabs and grilled thresher shark, washed down by a dazzling bottle of Napa chardonnay. Even though the world had ended, it remained possible to eat very well in the Bay Area, and the breakdown of society not only had reduced maritime pollution but also had made local seafood much more readily available for local consumption. There wasn't much of an export trade possible with eleven national boundaries and eleven sets of customs barriers between San Francisco and Los Angeles.

Dinner conversation was light, relaxed—diplomatic chitchat, gossip about events in remote territories, reports about the Voodoo principality expanding out of New Orleans and the Sioux conquests in Wyoming and the Prohibition War now going on in what used to be Kentucky. There was a bison herd again on the Great Plains, she said, close to a million head. He told her what he had heard about the Suicide People who ruled between San Diego and Tijuana and about King Barnum & Bailey III who governed in northern Florida with the aid of a court of circus freaks. She smiled and said, "How can they tell the freaks from

289

the ordinary people? The whole world's a circus now, isn't it?''
He shook his head and replied, "No, a zoo," and beckoned the
waiter for more wine. He did not ask her about internal matters
in Monterey, and she tactfully stayed away from the domestic
problems of the Empire of San Francisco. He was feeling easy,
buoyant, a little drunk, more than a little drunk; to have to
answer questions now about the little rebellion that had been
suppressed in Sausalito or the secessionist thing in Walnut Creek
would only be a bringdown, and bad for the digestion besides.

About half past eight he said, "You aren't going back to Monterey tonight, are you?"

"God, no! It's a five-hour drive, assuming no more troubles
with the San Jose highway patrol. And the road's so bad below
Watsonville that only a lunatic would drive it at night. I'll stay
at the Claremont.''

"Good. Let me put it on the imperial account."

"That isn't necessary. We—"

"The hotel is always glad to oblige the government. Please
accept their hospitality."

Ms. Sawyer shrugged. "Very well. Which we'll reciprocate
when you come to Monterey."

"Fine."

And then her manner suddenly changed. She shifted in her
seat and fidgeted and played with her silverware, looking awkward and ill at ease. Some new and big topic was obviously
about to be introduced, and Christensen guessed that she was
going to ask him to spend the night with her. In a fraction of a
second he ran through all the possible merits and demerits of
that and came out on the plus side, and had his answer ready
when she said, "Tom, can I ask a big favor?"

Which threw him completely off balance. Whatever was coming, it certainly wasn't what he was expecting.

"I'll do my best."

"I'd like an audience with the Emperor."

"What?"

"Not on official business. I know the Emperor talks business
only with his ministers and privy councillors. But I want to see
him, that's all." Color came to her cheeks. "Doesn't it sound
silly? But it's something I've always dreamed of, a kind of ad-
olescent fantasy. To be in San Francisco, to be shown into the

imperial throne-room, to kiss his ring, all that pomp and circumstance—I want it, Tom. Just to *be* there, to *see* him—do you think you could manage that?''

He was astounded. The facade of cool, tough competence had dropped away from her, revealing unanticipated absurdity. He did not know what to answer.

She said, ''Monterey's such a poky little place. It's just a *town*. We call ourselves a republic, but we aren't much of anything. And I call myself a senator and a diplomat, but I've never really been anywhere—San Francisco two or three times when I was a girl, San Jose a few times. My mother was in Los Angeles once, but I haven't been anywhere. And to go home saying that I had seen the Emperor—'' Her eyes sparkled. ''You're really taken aback, aren't you? You thought I was all ice and microprocessors, and instead I'm only a hick, right? But you're being very nice. You aren't even laughing at me. Will you get me an audience with the Emperor for tomorrow or the day after?''

''I thought you were afraid to go into San Francisco.''

She looked abashed. ''That was just a ploy. To make you come over here, to get you to take me seriously and put yourself out a little. The diplomatic wiles. I'm sorry about that. The word was that you were snotty, that you had to be met with strength or you'd be impossible to deal with. But you aren't like that at all. Tom, I want to see the Emperor. He does give audiences, doesn't he?''

''In a manner of speaking. I suppose it could be done.''

''Oh, would you! Tomorrow?''

''Why wait for tomorrow? Why not tonight?''

''Are you being sarcastic?''

''Not at all,'' Christensen said. ''This is San Francisco. The Emperor keeps weird hours just like the rest of us. I'll phone over there and see if we can be received.'' He hesitated. ''It won't be what you're expecting.''

''In what way?''

''The pomp, the circumstance—you're going to be disappointed. You may be better off not meeting him, actually. Stick to your fantasy of imperial majesty. Seriously. I'll get you an audience if you insist, but I don't think it's a great idea.''

''Can you be more specific?''

''No.''

"I still want to see him. Regardless."

"Let me make some phone calls, then."

He left the dining room and, with misgivings, began arranging things. The telephone system was working sluggishly that evening and it took him fifteen minutes to set the whole thing up, but there were no serious obstacles. He returned to her and said, "The ferry will pick us up at the marina in about an hour. There'll be a car waiting on the San Francisco side. The Emperor will be available for viewing around midnight. I tell you that you're not going to enjoy this. The Emperor is old and he's been sick and he—he isn't a very interesting person to meet."

"All the same," she said. "The one thing I wanted, when I volunteered to be the envoy, was an imperial audience. Please don't discourage me."

"As you wish. Shall we have another drink?"

"How about these instead?" She produced an enameled cigarette case. "Humboldt County's finest. Gift of the Free State."

He smiled and nodded and took the joint from her. It was elegantly manufactured, fine cockleshell paper, gold monogram, igniter cap, even a filter. Everything else has come apart, he thought, but the technology of marijuana is at its highest point in history. He flicked the cap, took a deep drag, passed it to her. The effect was instantaneous, a new high cutting through the wooze of bourbon and wine and brandy already in his brain, clearing it, expanding his limp and sagging soul. When they were finished with it, they floated out of the hotel. His driver and hers were still waiting in the parking lot. Christensen dismissed his, and they took the Republic of Monterey car down the slopes of Berkeley to the marina. The boat from San Francisco was late. They stood around shivering at the ferry slip for twenty minutes, peering bleakly across at the glittering lights of the far-off city. Neither of them was dressed for the nighttime chill, and he was tempted to pull her close and hold her in his arms, but he did not do it. There was a boundary he was not yet willing to cross. Hell, he thought, I don't even know her first name.

It was nearly eleven by the time they reached San Francisco.

An official car was parked at the pier. The driver hopped out, saluting, bustling about—one of those preposterous little civil-service types, doubtless keenly honored to be taxiing bigwigs around late at night. He wore the red-and-gold uniform of the imperial dragoons, a little frayed at one elbow. The car coughed and sputtered and reluctantly lurched into life, up Market Street to Van Ness and then north to the palace. Ms. Sawyer's eyes were wide and she stared at the ancient high-rises along Market as though they were cathedrals. When they came to the Civic Center area she gasped, obviously overwhelmed by the majesty of everything, the shattered hulk of Symphony Hall, the Museum of Modern Art, the great domed enormity of the City Hall, the Hall of Justice and the Imperial Palace itself, awesome, imposing, a splendid many-columned building that long ago had been the War Memorial Opera House. A bunch of imperial cars were parked outside. With the envoy from the Republic of Monterey at his elbow, Christensen marched up the steps of the palace and through the center doors into the lobby, where a great many of the ranking ministers and plenipotentiaries of the Empire were assembled. "How absolutely marvelous," Ms. Sawyer murmured. Smiling graciously, bowing, nodding, Christensen pointed out the notables, the defense minister, the minister of finance, the minister of suburban affairs, the chief justice, the minister of transportation, and all the rest. At midnight precisely there was a grand flourish of trumpets and the door to the throne room opened. Christensen offered Ms. Sawyer his arm; together they made the long journey down the center aisle and up the ramp to the stage, where the imperial throne, a resplendent thing of rhinestones and foil, glittered brilliantly under the spotlights. Ms. Sawyer was wonderstruck. She pointed toward the six gigantic portraits suspended high over the stage and whispered a question, and Christensen replied, "The first six emperors. And here comes the seventh one."

"Oh," she gasped—but was it awe, surprise, or disgust?

He was in his full regalia, the scarlet robe, the bright green tunic with ermine trim, the gold chains. But he was wobbly and tottering, a clumsy staggering figure, gray-faced and feeble, supported on one side by Mike Schiff, the imperial chamberlain, and on the other by the grand sergeant-at-arms, Terry Coleman. He was not so much leaning on them as being dragged by them. Bringing up the rear of the procession were two sleek, pretty boys, one black and one Chinese, carrying the orb, the scepter and the massive crown. Ms. Sawyer's fingers tightened on Christensen's forearm and he heard her catch her breath as the Emperor, in the process of being lowered into his throne, went boneless and nearly spilled to the floor. Somehow the imperial chamberlain and the grand sergeant-at-arms settled him properly in place, balanced the crown on his head, stuffed the orb and scepter into his trembling hands. "His Imperial Majesty, Norton the Seventh of San Francisco!" cried Mike Schiff in a magnificent voice that went booming up into the highest balcony. The Emperor giggled.

"Come on," Christensen whispered, and led her forward.

The old man was really in terrible shape. It was weeks since Christensen last had seen him, and by now he looked like something dragged from the crypt, slack-jawed, drooling, vacant-eyed, utterly burned out. The envoy from Monterey seemed to draw back, tense and rigid, repelled, unable or unwilling to go closer, but Christensen persisted, urging her onward until she was no more than a dozen feet from the throne. A sickly-sweet odor emanated from the old man.

"What do I do?" she asked in a panicky voice.

"When I introduce you, go forward, curtsy if you know how, touch the orb. Then step back. That's all."

She nodded.

Christensen said, "Your Majesty, the ambassador from the Republic of Monterey, Senator Sawyer, to pay her respects."

Trembling, she went to him, curtsied, touched the orb. As she backed away, she nearly fell, but Christensen came smoothly forward and steadied her. The Emperor giggled again, a shrill horrific cackle. Slowly, carefully, Christensen guided the shaken and numbed Ms. Sawyer from the stage.

"How long has he been like that?" she asked.

"Two years, three, maybe more. Completely insane. Not even housebroken anymore. You could probably tell. I'm sorry. I told you you'd be better off skipping this. I'm enormously sorry, Ms.—Ms.—what's your first name, anyway?"

"Elaine."

"Elaine. Let's get out of here, Elaine. Yes?"

"Yes. Please."

She was shivering. He walked her up the side aisle. A few of the other courtiers were clambering up onto the stage now, one with a guitar, one with a juggler's clubs. The imperial giggle pierced the air again and again, becoming shrill and rasping and wild. The royal levee would probably go on half the night. Emperor Norton VII was one of San Francisco's most popular amusements.

"Now you know," Christensen said.

"How does the Empire function, if the Emperor is crazy?"

"We manage. We do our best without him. The Romans managed it with Caligula. Norton's not half as bad as Caligula. Not a tenth. Will you tell everyone in Monterey?"

"I think not. We believe in the power of the Empire and in the grandeur of the Emperor. Best not to disturb that faith."

"Quite right," said Christensen.

They emerged into the dark clear cold night.

Christensen said, "I'll ride back to the ferry slip with you, before I go home."

"Where do you live?"

"The other way. Out near Golden Gate Park."

She looked up at him and moistened her lips. "I don't want to ride across the bay in the dark alone at this hour of the night. Is it all right if I come home with you?"

"Sure," he said.

She managed a jaunty smile. "You're straight, aren't you?"

"Sure. Most of the time, anyway."

"I thought you were. Good."

They got into the car. "Frederick Street," he told the driver, "between Belvedere and Cole."

The trip took twenty minutes. Neither of them spoke. He knew what she was thinking about—the crazy Emperor, dribbling and babbling under the bright spotlights. The mighty Norton VII, ruler of everything from San Rafael to San Mateo, from Half Moon Bay to Walnut Creek. Such is pomp and circumstance in imperial San Francisco in these latter days of Western civilization. Christensen sent the driver away and they went upstairs. The cats were hungry again.

"It's a lovely apartment," she told him.

"Three rooms, bath, hot and cold running water. Not bad for a mere foreign minister. Some of the boys have suites at the palace, but I like it better here." He opened the door to the deck and stepped outside. Somehow, now that he was home, the night was not so cold. He thought about the Realm of Wicca, far off

295

up there in green, happy Oregon, sending a hundred fifty thousand kindly Goddess-worshiping neopagans down here to celebrate the rebirth of the sun. A nuisance, a mess, a headache. Tomorrow he'd have to call a meeting of the cabinet, when everybody had sobered up, and start the wheels turning, and probably he'd have to make trips to places like Petaluma and Palo Alto to get the alliance flanged together. Damn. Damn. But it was his job, wasn't it? Someone had to carry the load.

He slipped his arm around the slender woman from Monterey.

"The poor Emperor," she said softly.

"Yes. The poor Emperor. Poor everybody."

He looked toward the east. In a few hours the sun would be coming up over that hill, out of the place that used to be the United States of America and now was a thousand thousand crazy fractured fragmented entities. Christensen shook his head. The Grand Duchy of Chicago, he thought. The Holy Carolina Confederation. The Three Kingdoms of New York. The Empire of San Francisco. No use getting upset—much too late for getting upset. You played the hand that was dealt you and you did your best and you carved little islands of safety out of the night. Turning to her he said, "I'm glad you came home with me tonight." He brushed his lips lightly against hers. "Come. Let's go inside."

WINTERGATE II:
THE WAR OF THE WORLDS
Russell Seitz

EDITOR'S INTRODUCTION

During a talk with Russell Seitz, an old friend who has spent the last five years doing much to de-mythologize nuclear winter, I mentioned we were doing a book on After Armageddon. When I asked him to do a piece on the myth of nuclear winter for the book, he responded: "I'll do better than that; I'll recommend a story too. 'Torch' by Christopher Anvil, the first published work—fiction or non-fiction—to describe a nuclear winter."

Herewith is Russell to tell you all about it himself:

━━━━━━━━━━━━━━ •¦• ━━━━━━━━━━━━━━

WE LIVE ON IMAGES; FIVE SEASONS AGO WE SAW ON TELEVISION the dark dawning of a new apocalypse on prime time: "Nuclear Winter." It seemed to combine the glint of hard science with the gloom of Icelandic saga.

Last fall, a chilling *Time* essay, "Cloudy Crystal Balls," reminded us that "Climatologists regularly issue confident warnings about impending atmospheric disasters. The secret of their wizardry: sophisticated computer models . . ." In 1983 a group of scientists (known as TTAPS) modeled "what would happen if the U.S. and the Soviet Union fought a nuclear war. Their conclusion: the dust and smoke . . . would blot out enough sunlight to plunge the land into a 'nuclear winter.' ''

"It is the Halloween preceding 1984, and I deeply wish that what I am about to tell you were only a ghost story, only something invented to frighten children for a day. But, unfortunately, it is not just a story." "After more than two months, minimum temperatures of fifty-three degrees below zero are reached—temperatures characteristic of the surface of Mars." ". . . named after and consecrated to the Lord of the Dead. The original Halloween combines the three essential elements of the TTAPS scenario: fires, winter and death."

Just days after Carl Sagan recited these grim lines, Canadian listeners were startled to tune into a voice coldly intoning, "Of course, the people who are not directly affected by the war in the tropical area are now freezing to death in large numbers . . . We are beginning to get reports of starvation and a great deal of thirst because the surface waters are frozen almost everywhere." It wasn't Vincent Price, just Sagan's sidekick Paul "Population Bomb" Ehrlich doing a little consciousness-(and hair-)raising on CBC Radio. But these words on the eve of 1984 have proven Orwellian.

For, as *Time* relates, Sagan's one-dimensional model "ignored such key factors as winds, oceans and seasons. When [National Center for Atmospheric Research (NCAR) Scientists] Stephen Schneider and Starley Thompson ran [a] three-dimensional computer model, they found that the winter would be more like a 'nuclear autumn.' " Since his "war" scenario kills hundreds of millions outright, one must agree with Schneider: this briefer "nuclear autumn is not going to be a nice picnic . . . watching the leaves change color." But where are the snows of yesteryear?

Long before NCAR exorcised the Dark Emperor's new shroud, Sagan asked, "What else have we overlooked?" A curious answer has emerged, stripping "nuclear winter" of its most urgent claim to our attention: its very novelty. Sagan says, "For me it began in 1971 with the exploration of the planet Mars." He noted when a "dust storm stirred that cold and darkness were spreading over the planet." Yet for some, it began when *Contact*'s author was a teenage science fiction fan.

Back in 1954, cooling of the Earth by a dusty thermonuclear

war was analyzed in Senate testimony by the father of computer science, John von Neumann, who presciently pegged that threat's magnitude to be roughly one degree of cooling. Smoke was studied too, but the media focused on the fatal fallout far downwind—remember *On the Beach*? The Geiger counters' ominous clicks drowned out all talk of twilight at noon. The von Neumann effect just wasn't ready for prime time.

But in 1957, Christopher Anvil published a Walpurgis Night's tale entitled "Torch" in *Astounding Science Fiction*. The story begins with a bang-up Russian May Day celebration, as a monstrous H-bomb test shatters an enormous Siberian oil field, igniting a smoky inferno. Anvil uses the old *War of the Worlds* broadcast's format. His "wire service" sound bites relate "the *Cold* War":

St. Paul, Minn., May 10th—A light powdering of black flecks has been reported in snow that has fallen.

Washington, May 15th:—The Senate Committee on the May Bomb met today . . . Senator Keeler: "Gentlemen, what's going on over there?" General Maxwell: . . . "The air is full of soot . . . There's a severe cold wave in the north."

Tokyo, July 2nd—The Smog Belt is reported extending itself southward . . . the unseasonable cold will swell the mounting casualty list still further.

Moscow, December 3rd—Winter . . . seems to be taking hold with a vengeance. Temperatures of a hundred degrees below zero are being reported from many regions.

Washington, December 10th— . . . Bundled in heavy overcoats, the senators listened: "The smaller particles remain aloft and screen out part of the sun's radiation. It's a good deal as if we'd moved the Arctic Circle down."

Science fiction writers often wade in where (to their mutual credit) scientists fear to tread. But as science progresses and facts accumulate, good models tend to drive the bad out of circulation. Stephen Schneider observed that "Carl's idea was brilliant—he proposed an invasion from Mars." And so he did—on Halloween. The very day that Orson Welles's 1938 broadcast struck fear into the credulous hearts of his lawful prey.

But what of today's computerized warnings of ozone depletion and the Greenhouse Effect? Whatever its cause, the Antarctic ozone hole is neither a media event nor a mirage in a machine. It is not chagrin over the antics of "nuclear winter's" advocates that is making scientists in Antarctica look a bit red in the face, but more ultraviolet light than is healthy. *This is no model*; there really *is* something new under the baleful midnight sun: sunburned penguins.

Many and subtle are the Spirits of the Air, hard to summon, harder still to exorcise. So when the Wizards of NCAR conjure us to keep a genuine Imp named Chlorine securely bottled, we should take heed. For theirs is no astounding tale of the Lord of Darkness's looming shadow. But a fair warning against the day when searing ultraviolet rays can bleach through the tattered sky and fall earthward like bright Lucifer in his pride. That is their lesson to us this winter, and this time they are not just crying wolf on All Hallows' Eve. For we have already unleashed on the fragile stratosphere things that go bump in the light.

TORCH
Christopher Anvil

Moscow, April 28th—Official sources here have revealed that the firing of a huge intercontinental ballistic missile is scheduled for the annual Soviet May Day celebration.

New York, May 1st—Seismologists report violent tremors occurring shortly after 8:00 a.m. G.M.T. this morning.

Washington, May 1st—The Soviet May Day missile is suspected here to have been the first of the new "groundhog" type, capable of penetrating underground shelters. But no one here will comment on certain rumored "strange characteristics" of the blast.

New York, May 2nd—Seismologists report repeated tremors, apparently from the site of the blast of May 1st. One noted seismologist states that this is "most unusual if the result of a bomb explosion."

Moscow, May 2nd—There is still no word here on the May Day blast. All questions are answered, "No comment."

New York, May 3rd—Seismologists report tremors of extraordinary violence, occurring shortly after 1:00 a.m., 1:35 a.m., and 1:55 a.m., G.M.T. this morning.

Washington, May 3rd—The Atomic Energy Commission this morning assured reporters there is no danger of the world "taking fire" from recent Soviet blasts.

Chicago, May 3rd—The world may already be on fire. That is the opinion of an atomic scientist reached here late this evening—"if the initial blast took place in the presence of sufficient deposits of light or very heavy metals."

Los Angeles, May 3rd—The world will end by fire on May 7th, predicts the leader of a religious sect here. The end will come "by the spreading of fiery fingers, traveling at the speed of light from the wound in the flesh of the Earth."

Tokyo, May 4th—A radioactive drizzle came down on the west coast of Honshu, the main Japanese island, last night. Teams of scientists are being rushed to the area.

New York, May 4th—Stocks fell sharply here this morning.

Paris, May 4th—A correspondent recently arrived here from the Soviet Union reports that rumors are rife in Moscow of tremendous flames raging out of control in Soviet Siberia. According to these reports the hospitals are flooded with burned workers, and citizens east of the Urals are being recruited by the tens of thousands to form "flame legions" to fight the disaster.

London, May 5th—The British Government today offered "all possible assistance" to Moscow, in the event reports of a great atomic disaster are true.

New York, May 5th—Seismologists report repeated tremors, from the site of the shocks of May 1st and 3rd.

Tokyo, May 6th—A heavy deposit of slightly radioactive soot fell on Honshu and Hokkaido last night.

Moscow, May 6th—There is no comment yet on the May Bomb or on British, French and Italian offers of aid.

New York, May 7th—Seismologists here report tremors of extraordinary violence, occurring shortly after 8:00 p.m. G.M.T. last night.

Washington, May 7th—A special Senate committee, formed to consider the atomic danger in the U.S.S.R., announced this morning that it favors "all reasonable aid to the Russians." The committee chairman stated to reporters, "It's all one world. If it blows up on them, it blows up on us, too."

Washington, May 7th—The Atomic Energy Commission repeated its claim that the earth could not have caught fire from the recent Russian explosions.

Tokyo, May 8th—Japanese fishermen to the northeast of Hokkaido report the waters in large areas black with a layer of radioactive soot.

New York, May 8th—Seismologists report repeated tremors from the region of the severe shocks of May 1st, 3rd, and 7th.

Washington, May 9th—The United States has offered special assistance to Soviet Russia, but the latest word here is that no reply has been received.

Washington, May 9th—Responsible officials here indicate that if no word is received from Moscow within eighteen hours, and if these shocks continue, a special mission will be sent to Russia by the fastest military transportation available. "We are not," said one official, "going to stand around with our hands in our mouths while the world disintegrates under our feet."

Seoul, May 9th—It is reported here that the radioactive soot that plastered Japan and adjacent areas has fallen even more heavily in North Korea. The Communist Government is reportedly trying to pass the soot off as the work of "Capitalist spies and saboteurs."

Washington, May 9th—The United States government has reiterated its offer to the Soviet Union of "prompt and sympathetic consideration" of any requests for aid.

New York, May 10th—Seismologists here report repeated tremors from the region of the earlier shocks.

Moscow, May 10th—It has been impossible to reach any responsible official here for comment on Western offers of assistance.

London, May 10th—The British Government today urgently recommended that the Soviet Union seriously consider Western offers of assistance.

Washington, May 10th—No word having been received here from Moscow, an experimental Hellblast bomber sprang from her launching rack bearing a nine-man mission to Moscow. Word of the mission's departure is being sent the Russians by all channels of communication. But it is said here that if no permission to land is given, the Hellblast will attempt to smash through to Moscow anyway.

Tokyo, May 10th—Another load of soot has been dumped on Japan today. This batch is only slightly radioactive, but scientists are not happy because they do not know what to make of it.

Seoul, May 10th—Riots are reported in Communist North Korea as the "black death" continues to rain down from the skies. It is not known whether the soot has caused actual death or merely panic.

St. Paul, Minn., May 10th—A light powdering of black flecks has been reported in snow that has fallen near here in the last twenty-four hours.

Moscow, May 11th—A United States Hellblast bomber roared out of the dawn here today bearing a nine-man mission. The mission was greeted at the airfield by a small group of worn and tired Russian officials.

Minneapolis, May 11th—Scientists report only a trace of radio-activity in the "tainted snow" that fell near here yesterday. The scientists reiterate that the radioactivity is not present in danger-ous amounts.

Tokyo, May 11th—Considerable deposits of radioactive soot and ash landed on Japan yesterday and last night. Japanese scientists have issued warnings to all persons in the affected areas. The Japanese Government has delivered a severe protest to the Soviet embassy.

Hong Kong, May 11th—Reports here indicate the Chinese Com-munist Government is making representations to Moscow about the soot-fall following the Russian May Day blast. According to these reports, the North Korean Government is being over-whelmed with the people's angry demands that the Russians cease "dumping their waste on their allies."

New York, May 12th—The American mission that arrived here yesterday has disappeared into the Kremlin and has not been seen or heard from since.

Washington, May 12th—The United States Government reports that it is now in close contact with the Soviet Government on the situation in Siberia.

Seoul, May 13th—It is reported here that the government of Communist North Korea has issued a twelve-hour ultimatum to the Soviet Union. If the dumping of fission products continues beyond that time, North Korea threatens to break off relations and take "whatever other measures prove to be necessary."

Paris, May 13th—Repeated efforts by the French Government have failed to produce any response from Moscow. French atom scientists have offered to travel to the Soviet Union in a body if their services can be of any use.

Washington, May 14th—A Soviet request for American aid was received here early this morning. Reportedly, the Russians asked for ten thousand of the largest available bulldozers or other earth-moving vehicles, equipped with special high-efficiency filters for the air-intake mechanisms.

London, May 14th—The British Government reports receiving a request for large numbers of specially-equipped earth-moving vehicles. Red tape is being cut as fast as possible, and the first consignment is expected to leave tomorrow. However, there is still no explanation of what is going on in the Soviet Union.

Washington, May 14th—A special meeting of the Senate committee investigating the May Bomb is scheduled for tomorrow, when the American mission is expected to return.

New York, May 15th—Repeated tremors are reported here from the region of the severe shocks of May 1st, 3rd, and 7th.

Washington, May 15th—The Senate Committee on the May Bomb met today, and questioned members of the American mission that had just returned:

> *Senator Keeler:* Gentlemen, what's going on over there?
> *Mr. Brainerd:* They're in a mess, Senator. And so are we.
> *Senator Keeler:* Could you be more specific? Is the . . . is the earth on fire?
> *Mr. Brainerd:* No. It's not that, at least.
> *Senator Keeler:* Then there's no danger—
> *Mr. Brainerd:* The earth won't burn up under us, no. This thing was set off atomically, but it goes on by itself.
> *Senator Keeler:* What happened?
> *Mr. Brainerd:* They tried out their groundhog missile on May Day. They had a giant underground shelter built, and they wanted to show what the groundhog would do to it. The idea was to show there was no use anyone building shelters, because the Russian groundhog could dig right down to them.
> *Senator Keeler:* Did it?
> *Mr. Brainerd:* It did. It blew up in the shelter and heated it white hot.
> *Senator Keeler:* I see. But why should that cause trouble?
> *Mr. Brainerd:* Because, unknown to them or anyone else,

Senator, there were deep deposits of oil underground, beneath the shelter. The explosion cracked the surrounding rock. The oil burst up through the cracks, shot out into the white-hot remains of the underground chambers, and vaporized. At least that's the explanation the Russians and Dr. Dentner here have for what happened. All anybody can *see* is a tremendous black column rising up.

Senator Keeler: Do you have anything to add to that, Dr. Dentner?

Dr. Dentner: No, that about covers it.

Senator Keeler: Well, then, do any of my colleagues have any questions? Senator Daley?

Senator Daley: Yes, I've got some questions. Dr. Dentner, what's that black stuff made of?

Dr. Dentner: Quite a number of compounds: carbon monoxide; carbon dioxide; water vapor; saturated and unsaturated gaseous hydrocarbons; the vapors of saturated and unsaturated non-gaseous hydrocarbons. But the chief constituent seems to be finely-divided carbon—in other words, soot.

Senator Daley: The world isn't on fire?

Dr. Dentner: No.

Senator Daley: The oil fire can't spread to here?

Dr. Dentner: No. Not by any process I can imagine.

Senator Daley: All right, then, I've got a crude idea. Why not let them stew in their own juice? They started this. They were going to scare the world with it. O.K., let *them* worry about it. It'll give them something to do. Keep them out of everybody's hair for a while.

Senator Keeler: The idea has its attractions, at that. What about it, Doctor?

Dr. Dentner: The fire won't spread to here, but— Well, General Maxwell has already considered the idea and given it up.

Senator Daley: Why's that?

General Maxwell: Set up an oil furnace in the cloakroom and run the flue in here through that wall over there. Then light the furnace. That's why.

Senator Daley: The stuff's going to come down on us?

307

Dr. Dentner: It seems probable. There have already been several light falls in the midwest.

Senator Daley: I thought it was too good to work. O.K. then, we've got to put it out. How?

Dr. Dentner: They've already made attempts to blow it out with H-bombs. But the temperature in the underground chambers is apparently so high that the fire reignites. The present plan is to push a mass of earth in on top of it and choke out the flame.

Senator Daley: Don't they have enough bulldozers? I mean, if it's that simple, why don't they have it out?

Dr. Dentner: It's on a large scale, and that produces complications.

General Maxwell: For instance: the air is full of soot. The soot gets in the engines. Men choke on it.

Mr. Brainerd: The general effect is like trying to do a day's work inside a chimney.

General Maxwell: And the damned thing sits across their lines of communications, dumping heaps of soot on the roads and railroad tracks, and strangling anyone that tries to get past. The trains spin their wheels, and that's the end of that. It's a question of going way around to the north or way around to the south. There's a severe cold wave in the north, so that's out. They're laying track to the south at a terrific pace, but there's a long way to go. What it amounts to is, they're cut in half.

Senator Daley: It seems to me we ought to be able to make a buck out of this.

Mr. Brainerd: It's a temptation; but I hate to kick a man when he's down.

Senator Daley: ARE they down?

Mr. Brainerd: Yes, they're down. The thing is banging their head on the floor. They're still fighting it, but it's like fighting a boa constrictor. Where do you take hold to hurt it?

Senator Daley: Just back of the head.

Mr. Brainerd: That's the part they can't get at. Meanwhile, it crushes the life out of them.

General Maxwell: The idea is, to fight the main enemy. If they don't beat it, we'll *have* to. And it will be a lot harder for us to get at it than it is for them. The idea is, to pour the supplies to them while they're still alive to use them. Otherwise, that volcano keeps pumping soot into the air and we get it in the neck, too.

Dr. Dentner: There's one more point here.

Senator Daley: What's that?

Dr. Dentner: Neither their scientists nor I could understand why a stray spark hasn't ignited the soot. It must be an explosive mixture.

General Maxwell: If that happens, it will make World War II look like a garden party.

Mr. Brainerd: Like a grain-elevator explosion a thousand miles across.

Senator Daley: Well— All right, that does it. What do they need?

Mr. Brainerd: We've got a list here as long as your arm for a starter.

Senator Daley: Then let's get started.

Senator Keeler: Let's see the list. And I'm not sure the rest of this shouldn't be secret for the time being.

Senator Daley: Right. Let's see what they want first.

New York, June 8th—The first ten shiploads of gangtracks, bores, sappers, and hogger mauls raced out of New York harbor today on converted liners, bound for Murmansk. A similar tonnage is reported leaving San Francisco for Vladivostok tonight.

Tokyo, June 14th—The evacuation of another one hundred square miles of Honshu Island was completed early today.

Hong Kong, June 27th—Reports reaching here from Red China indicate that the Chinese Communist Government is moving its capital south from Beijing to Nanking. Relations between Red China and the Soviet Union are reported extremely bad.

New York, June 28th—According to the U.N. Disaster Committee meeting here this morning, over three billion dollars worth of supplies has thus far been poured into the U.S.S.R. in Operation Torch.

Tokyo, July 2nd—The Smog Belt is reported extending itself southward. Officials here fear that this, combined with the unseasonable cold, will swell the mounting casualty list still further.

Seoul, July 9th—Severe fighting is reported between the North Korean People's Army and Russian troops defending the border region south of Vladivostok.

New York, July 18th—Three specially-built high-speed dual-hull transports left here this morning bearing three Super-Hoggers of the Mountain-Mover class.

London, July 23rd—The furnaces of Britain's yards and factories are blazing as they have not in three generations, to finish the last four sections of the huge Manchester Snake, which will be shipped in sections to France and assembled for its overland trip to the Soviet Union. Work has been aided somewhat here by the unusually cool summer weather.

Skagway, Alaska, August 2nd—The Pittsburgh Mammoth rolled north past here at 2:00 a.m. this morning.

Nome, August 5th—The Bering Bridge is almost complete.

Moscow, August 6th—The 20th, 21st, and 40th Divisions of the Soviet 2nd Red Banner Flame Army marched in review through Red Square today before entraining for the East.

Nome, August 8th—The Pittsburgh Mammoth crushed past here at dawn this morning. Crowds from up and down the coast, their faces hidden behind gas masks and soot shields, were on hand to see the Mammoth roll north toward the Bering Bridge. Tank trucks in relays refueled the giant.

Headquarters, Supreme High Command of the Soviet Red Banner Flame Legions, September 21st—Final Communique: The campaign against the enemy has ended in victory. Nothing remains to mark the site save a towering monument to the bravery of the Soviet citizen, to the supreme organization of the war effort by the high officials of the Soviet Government, and to the magnificent output of Soviet industry. Help also was received from countries desiring to participate in the great Soviet effort, which has resulted in this great victory. Work now must be begun with unhesitating energy to return the many brave workers to their peacetime stations.

London, September 22nd—The consensus here seems to be that naturally we cannot expect credit, but it is at least a relief to know the thing is over.

Washington, September 22nd—After talking with a number of high officials here, the general feeling seems to be: After this, we are to go back to the Cold War?

Moscow, December 3rd—Winter here seems to be taking hold with a vengeance. Temperatures of a hundred degrees below zero are being reported from many regions that normally do not record even remotely comparable readings till the middle of January. It looks by far the severest winter on record. Coming after all the trouble this spring and summer, this is a heavy blow.

Ottawa, Canada, December 8th—The cold here in Canada is unusually severe for this time of year.

Washington, December 10th—The Senate Committee on the Russian May Bomb explosion reconvened briefly to hear expert testimony today. Bundled in heavy overcoats, the senators listened to testimony that may be summed up briefly in this comment by a meteorologist:

"No, Senator, we don't know when these fine particles will settle. The heavier particles of relatively large diameter settle out unless the air currents sweep them back up again, and then we have these 'soot showers.' But the smaller particles remain aloft and screen out part of the sun's radiation. Presumably they'll settle eventually; but in the meantime it's a good deal as if we'd moved the Arctic Circle down to about the fifty-fifth degree of latitude."

When asked what might be done about this immediately, the experts suggested government aid to supply fuel to people in the coldest locations, and it was urged that fuel stockpiles be built up now, as unexpected transportation difficulties may arise in the depths of winter.

Underground Moscow, December 17th—The Soviet Government is reported making tremendous efforts to house millions of its people underground. Much of the equipment used in fighting the Torch is fitted for this work, but deep snow and the severe cold have hamstrung the transportation system.

New York, January 15th—National Headquarters of the Adopt-A-Russian Drive has announced that their drive "went over the top at 7:00 tonight, just five hours before deadline."

Prince Rupert, Canada, January 22nd—Three polar bears were reported seen near here last Friday.

Washington, February 3rd—Scientists concluded today that things will get worse before they get better. Settling of the particles is slow, they say, and meanwhile the oceans—"the great regulator"—will become colder.

New York, March 10th—Heavily dressed delegates of the former "Communist" and "Capitalist" blocs met here today to solemnly commemorate the ending of the so-called "cold war"—the former ideological phrase—in the strength of unity. The delegates agreed unanimously on many measures, one of them the solemn pledge to "Remain united as one people under God, and to persevere in our efforts together till and even beyond the time when the *Cold* War shall end."

BRINGING HOME THE BACON
Eric Oppen

EDITOR'S INTRODUCTION

On the surface, anyway, we appear to be entering a new phase of *rapprochement* with the Soviet Union—if Mikhail Gorbachev's words are to be believed. As I write this the headline of *The Christian Science Monitor* reads "In March to the Polls, Soviets Tread on Taboos." This is not the first time a Soviet premier has promised more than he intended to deliver—remember detente . . .

At the International Institute for Strategic Studies annual conference, the Right Honourable George Younger, Secretary of State for Defence of Great Britain, had some important words to say about the current state of relations between East and West:

> The Western Alliance has itself seen many changes and borne many strains since 1958. In the late 1950s the United States' nuclear capability so far surpassed that of the Soviet Union that the "tripwire" strategy could form the basis of Western deterrence. But the continual development of the Soviet Union's military capability meant that the strategy had to change, particularly to ensure that the American nuclear "umbrella"—so vital a guarantee for the nations of

Western Europe—could continue to be relied upon. This it did, and "Flexible Response," which now underpins our strategy, has served the Alliance since 1967.

The internal cohesion of NATO, and its consistent and unmistakable determination to act firmly to protect its security interests, have been major strengths in facing the Soviet threat. Ever since its formation, NATO has been faced by a potential adversary which has maintained a military establishment far greater than the need for its defense, armed and organized for swift, offensive operations, and which, by its actions, has shown it has no compunction about using force to achieve its political ends. It has constantly maneuvered to undermine the unity of NATO and to encourage a decoupling of the United States from Europe. For many years, while building up its own military might, it sought to promote campaigns by groups in the West which would have weakened NATO's military posture.

Yet, now the Soviet Union says that it no longer requires military superiority, and that its forces will adopt a defensive rather than an offensive posture. It says that it accepts the need for asymmetrical cuts in force levels to reflect existing imbalances, and it says that it does not seek to drive wedges between the members of NATO. Has the leopard changed its spots?

I am reminded of a story about Prince Metternich at the Congress of Vienna. He was woken by his valet in the middle of the night. The valet said: "Sir, the Russian Ambassador has died in his sleep." Metternich pondered for a moment and said: "I wonder what was his motive for doing that."

I know a number of people accuse NATO of displaying the same attitude as Metternich to the changes now taking place in the Soviet Union. Let me make our position clear. We welcome these changes, and we wish Mr. Gorbachev every success. But common prudence dictates that we do not allow ourselves to be seduced into a premature sense of optimism about what the future may bring. Our experience of dealing with the Soviet Union over many years entitles us to suspect its motives. After nearly ten years of bluff, bluster and obstruction in the INF negotiations—tactics intended to maintain its superiority in this class of weapon—the U.S.S.R. at last signed an agreement on terms very similar to those proposed by the United States in 1981.

We hope that the INF Agreement will pave the way for further agreements which will enhance the security of Europe. The achievement of fifty-percent reductions in the strategic arsenals of the two super-powers, the elimination of disparities in conventional forces in Europe, and a complete ban on chemical weapons—which have caused such carnage in the Gulf War—are our goals. But the overwhelming Soviet superiority in the conventional and chemical areas remains a major barrier to enhanced stability in Europe. Until the current imbalances in conventional forces have been redressed and a ban on chemical weapons achieved, it would be inappropriate to turn again to negotiations on further reductions in nuclear weapons in Europe.

We hope that the Soviet Union, by its actions, can convince us that the changes flowing from *glasnost* and *perestroika* will be far-reaching and permanent. But so far we have seen no evidence of any significant changes in Soviet military posture or a reduction in the resources devoted to military spending. In the absence of firm evidence about the future development of the Soviet Union, we must base our responses on our experience so far. The lessons we draw from our experience of dealing with the Soviet Union since the end of World War II are that negotiation is more likely to bear fruit if it is backed up with firmness, and that effective arms control is the product of painstaking and patient negotiations, not quick and extravagant declarations . . .

━━━━━━━━━━━━━━ ▪▮▪ ━━━━━━━━━━━━━━

TOM PETERSON STUCK HIS HEAD OUT OF HIS SLEEPING BAG AND a cold drizzle stung his cheeks. In the first dim light of dawn, not much could be seen. Squirming regretfully out of his warm sleeping bag, he scratched his ribs, wondering absently how a hot shower would feel.

As his eyes adjusted to the gloom, he slipped on his boots.

When the Soviets had invaded, he had fled to the hills with a pair of worn-out tennis shoes on his feet. When the soles finally fell off, he had scrounged a "new" pair of boots from a dead Soviet paratroop officer. The same officer had also "donated" the warm sleeping bag he was regretfully rolling up.

Shivering and yawning, Tom wandered over to a small fire, where several shadowy figures were patiently coaxing the coals back to life. Their breath left streamers in the cold air. A small radio was quietly playing music, as the rest of the partisans were awakening.

"—That was 'Polovtsian Dances' from *Prince Igor*, by Aleksandr Borodin. Now, the latest news.

"Soviet liberation forces in the State of Kansas report unprecedented success in extirpating the counter-revolutionary bandit groups found resisting the People's Government of the United States. The people of Kansas spontaneously demonstrated in gratitude to the Soviet liberation forces.

"From the front, the People's Army command has released a bulletin stating that reactionary forces sustained a crushing defeat near the site of Albuquerque. Several enemy armored units were reported destroyed by the People's Army of the United States, the Mexican Liberation Army, and elements of the glorious Soviet armed forces.

"The People's Government of the United States regrets to announce that the promised increase in rations will not take place, due to the necessity of disciplinary action against the reactionary elite of Iowa and Illinois. Exploiters, know that the workers demand bread, not excuses! The toilers' just wrath cannot be held off forever!"

"Sounds bad for the folks in Iowa and Illinois," grunted Tom. Snapping the radio off, he walked over to the fireside, rubbing his hands over the flames. "Speaking of rations, what's for breakfast?"

"One pan of squirrel stew." Tom became aware of the aching hunger that was his constant companion. It was so familiar that he had almost ceased to notice it.

Bill Rockwell, the leader of the partisan band, looked around. "Andy, Christine, go get Crow and Jill. Crow's up the north path with the Hunter's Ear and Jill's on the south path with those night-vision goggles. Tell them to get back here. We're moving

316

out today, back to the National Forest. The fog and drizzle should cover us. Tom, we'll meet you by the Big Rock.''

"You want me to go hunting?"

"Yeah. Take Jane along. She's the best shot we've got."

"Now, just a minute!" Tom stood up angrily. "Jane may be a good sniper, but she's too damn bloodthirsty for this! Remember the time she almost got us caught because she couldn't resist the temptation to kill just one more Russian? On this kind of trip, I want someone who's able to understand that we aren't out looking for a fight!''

Jane Cole stood up, afire with indignation. "You'll never let me live that down, will you, Tom? One little mistake, and a person's no good! I have all the self-control I need!''

The look in her eyes made Tom step back. "Look at yourself. You're fingering that rifle of yours as if you'd like to use it on me right now!''

Jane gave Tom a startled look, hefting the sniper rifle as though she were only then aware of it. She sighed, and the indignation seemed to run out of her. "You have a point. Maybe I am over-enthusiastic. I also know you're in charge of hunting. If it'll make you feel better, I'll promise to do just what you tell me. Friends?" She smiled tentatively.

"Friends. Be ready to leave in an hour. Bring your rifle, too, but only in case we run into Ivans. I'm going to use my crossbow and hunting slingshot.''

An hour later, Tom and Jane were alone on the path. The rest of the guerrillas had disappeared into the gloom a few minutes ago, laden with their weapons and gear. Jane waited silently, her bow over her shoulder and rifle in hand.

Tom cocked an eyebrow sardonically. "Don't we look like regular ragpicker's children?''

Jane looked at him, then down at herself. The sight of their ragged, mud-stained combinations of American civilian and Soviet military clothes forced her to grin. Before the invasion, she had always dressed as well as her parents could afford.

"Don't think the rabbits will think any the worse of us because we don't dress well.''

Tom was pleased to see a twinkle in her eye. Hefting his crossbow, he set off into the mist, Jane at his heels.

An hour later, Tom and Jane were resting in some bushes at

317

the top of a ridge. In the distance, the town of Franklin, Colorado was just visible through the persistent mist and drizzle.

Jane looked disconsolately into her game bag, as though she hoped the two scrawny rabbits had multiplied. Tom wished aloud that the ranchers had let the partisans know that the Soviets were confiscating most of their livestock.

"Don't blame the ranchers, Tom. We insisted that they not contact us, for their own safety. Ours, too. What they don't know, they can't spill."

"Yeah. But that doesn't take the knot out of my gut like a nice, juicy steak or lambchop would."

In the distance, a helicopter's thuttering could be heard. Tom and Jane instinctively drew farther back into the bushes. In the Occupied Zone, there were no friendly choppers.

Shortly, the helicopter dropped out of the low-lying clouds. From his vantage point in the bushes, Tom watched as it followed the railroad right-of-way into the valley below the ridge.

As the noise faded in the distance, Tom heard another sound, one that puzzled him. He glanced at Jane, to meet an equally puzzled look.

"It sounds like—" Curiosity overwhelming him, Tom wormed forward under the bushes to the lip of the ridge, where he could see the railroad tracks.

Up the rails came a huge flock of sheep. Baaing and bleating, they straggled up the railroad right-of-way. Jane squirmed her way to Tom's side, getting out her binoculars.

"Looks like the Russkies have some help to herd their stolen sheep." Behind the herd walked several green-uniformed figures. Their baggy clothes and the hats they wore made it impossible to determine sexes and ages, but their red armbands marked them for what they were.

"The Red Militia!" Jane snarled. Soon after the Soviet armies had landed, they had started to recruit the idlers, petty crooks and juvenile delinquents of the areas they held. Under the leadership of the few pro-Soviet Americans to be found, the Red Militia had speedily earned a foul reputation.

Jane raised her rifle, aiming it at the Militiamen. Tom grabbed her shoulder. "You damned fool, do you want to let the world know we're here? I know the Red Militia raped you, but this

318

isn't the right time to take them. Let's see where they're taking those sheep. *Now!*''

Jane didn't dispute Tom's decision. Keeping out of sight of the railroad, they started through the bush in the direction the sheep had gone.

"God damn it!" cursed Jane, picking herself up after a loose stone sent her sprawling. Once she was back on her feet, she carefully checked her rifle to make sure that it hadn't been damaged by her fall.

At last, the two partisans heard the bleating of sheep ahead. Keeping under cover, they crept silently through the bushes and trees to the edge of a meadow. In the pasture, a huge flock of sheep were milling around.

The helicopter was lifting off, and Tom could see the old Colorado National Guard markings on the sides, under the clumsy paint job. As it passed them, heading for the Red Militia base in Franklin, Tom and Jane shrank back into the bushes.

As soon as the helicopter left, the Red Militia began opening boxes. Tom whistled softly under his breath and passed Jane the binoculars.

"Look at those steaks! The Reds sure aren't hurting for food like the people in Franklin! When was the last time you ate steak?"

"Too long ago. My God, they've got more beer there than at the last fraternity kegger I went to!"

"What do you expect, Tom? With the kind of recruits they get in the Red Militia, you should be expecting this sort of thing. On the other hand, I've got a good mind to write to the Soviet governor in Denver and report this bunch of layabouts!"

Tom was surprised. Jane's sense of humor was sporadic at best, and was usually much darker. The only time since the Invasion he had seen her laugh out loud was when she had been amused by the antics of an East German soldier who had drunk a bottle of vodka heavily laced with strychnine.

The Red Militia stuffed themselves with steaks, washed down with liberal amounts of beer. When the food was gone, they kept drinking, until they staggered around, throwing mud at each other.

One Red Militiaman didn't participate in the party. He watched disapprovingly as his comrades grew drunker and drunker. He cradled an M-16 across his knees.

"Damn," Jane whispered in Tom's ear. "There's one in every crowd, isn't there? That guy's one of the true believers. The son-of-a-bitch! This job'd be so easy if he weren't along!"

Before too long, the Red Militiamen were stretched out on the grass, snoring. One lay in a puddle of his own vomit, sleeping peacefully. Only the zealot still stood, trying futilely to sober them up.

Tom made a decision. "Jane, I'm going down there and poach some sheep. If we had the band here, I'd want to kill those traitors and steal the herd. For now, I'd be satisfied just to get some *real* meat." Before Jane could reply, Tom moved down toward the edge of the herd. Over his shoulder, he said: "Sight in on Dudley Do-wrong there, and if he makes one false move, waste him."

A fine fat ewe was grazing on the edge of the herd. Tom's broad-bladed hunting quarrel thunked into her neck, knocking her down soundlessly. There was little bleating from the other sheep, so Tom reloaded his crossbow and sighted in on his next target.

Three kills later, the sheep were aware that something was wrong. The smell of blood in the air was making them nervous. They were milling around, baaing and shying away from Tom's kills.

"KA-RACK, KA-RACK, KA-RACK," came from behind Tom. He looked up, to see the one sober Red Militiaman coming at him, fumbling to load his M-16 as he came. Abandoning his cover, Tom rose, aiming his crossbow at the traitor's chest. The quarrel sang out, hit dead on target, and bounced off.

Frozen with horror, Tom stared openmouthed as the Red Militiaman raised his rusty M-16. In one part of his mind, he coolly noted: *He's got a goddamn bulletproof vest on, that's why Jane couldn't take him out.* Meanwhile, his hands were automatically reloading his crossbow. The Red Militiaman smiled nastily and squeezed the trigger of his rifle. Nothing happened.

For a second, they stared at each other unbelievingly. Tom snapped out of it first, throwing away his useless crossbow and running toward the Militiaman, tackling him around the waist.

Coming to grips with his enemy, Tom quickly realized, had

been a mistake. The Militiaman was much better fed than he was, and much stronger. Tom's only assets were his greater skill and desperation. While the Militiaman clawed at his face and rained wild, ineffective blows on his body, Tom concentrated on getting his fingers around the bastard's throat.

As they rolled in the mud, cursing and straining, Tom heard the Militiaman's voice, hissing: "Fascist bastard! You won't get away with this, you—" Tom's fingers found his throat, squeezing frantically.

Finally, the Militiaman's face turned an odd color, his eyes rolled and bulged, and he ceased struggling. For a few seconds, Tom continued throttling him, unwilling to trust the obvious.

"Come on! We've got to get out of here!" hissed Jane, coming out of the bushes with her rifle over one shoulder. "Well, are you just going to stand there? Let's get these sheep under cover, butcher them, and take care of these traitors! They might awaken any minute!"

Jane pulled out her hunting knife. Tom blanched at the look in her eyes.

"Why not let me take care of the traitors? Buck fever's no disgrace, but you need time to get over it. Besides, you're a lot better at field-butchering animals than I am. You butcher those sheep, and I'll do the rest."

Tom had hidden the dead sheep under the brush and was gutting one expertly when Jane reappeared. She had a contented look in her eyes and was meditatively wiping blood off her knife.

"Here, Jane, bear a hand. Be sure to trim so that we carry only the best meat back. By the way, did you see that rifle?" Tom jerked a thumb at the Red Militiaman's M-16. "Crud in the chamber, more crud in the barrel, and springs rusted clear through. I was going to smash it, but we can cannibalize it later."

Hours later, they were a few miles from the Big Rock, loaded with mutton, when a horribly familiar thuttering noise surrounded them.

For a moment, the two partisans couldn't figure out just where the chopper was coming from. The mountains around them reflected sound so bewilderingly that there was no way to tell where the chopper was. Tom looked up to see if he could locate it. No such luck.

Stumbling under the weight of their packs of meat and weapons, Tom and Jane abandoned the game trail. They scrambled downslope toward a large grove of trees, arriving in the middle of a mini-avalanche of loose pebbles.

Over a ridge came the same helicopter they had seen before. The bubble canopy was transparent enough that Tom could see the two men inside as they scanned the ground.

Jane had her rifle up, and was trying to sight on the helicopter.

Tom hissed: "You damn fool, what do you think you're doing? They'll spot us!" The helicopter abandoned the trail and swung over sideways to take a closer look at the grove.

A gun muzzle poked out of the helicopter. A puff of smoke and the roar of a shotgun announced that the danger of being spotted was real. Pellets spattered against the trees, to the left of Tom and Jane's position.

Jane's rifle bucked and roared. The co-pilot dropped his shotgun and screamed, throwing himself across the pilot's lap. Startled, the pilot jerked the helicopter away from the grove, then lost control. Slipping farther and farther sideways, the helicopter drifted helplessly toward the side of a mountain.

Emerging from their hiding place, Tom and Jane watched in fascination. "Always said those things weren't safe," commented Jane, deadpan.

"Trouble with using amateur talent," Tom answered.

A rending crash and explosion echoed from across the valley. Jane grinned. "Ding, dong, the no-good Reds are dead."

Tom smiled back. "Come on, those sheep won't just sit there until we get back. Besides, our buddies're hungry."

As the sun was setting behind the clouds, Tom and Jane arrived at the Big Rock. Tom glanced around as he unstrapped his pack. Jane's sister Christine was sewing a patch on a ragged pair of camouflage pants. Andy Sanders and "Crow" Lawrence were cleaning a Kalashnikov. Bill Rockwell was clipping his whiskers with a pair of scissors, and Jill O'Hara was poring over a demolition manual. The radio was tuned to the same Soviet propaganda station as it had been that morning. Tom basked for a moment in the quiet domesticity of the camp.

"Hey, everybody!" Jane called out. "We brought home the

bacon, or in this case, mutton. There's lots more, but we'll need help to get it.''

Jill O'Hara tore herself away from her demolition manual with an effort. ''You two were gone a long time. Anything unusual happen?''

Tom and Jane exchanged looks. ''Nothing unusual, Jill.''

JOURNALS OF THE PLAGUE YEARS
Norman Spinrad

EDITOR'S INTRODUCTION

In many ways Norman Spinrad's "Journals of the Plague Years" is the most frightening story in this collection—thanks to our public health officials' neglect of the most dangerous disease since the Bubonic Plague. At least the medieval city fathers faced with the Black Death had the excuse of ignorance of disease and germ theory. What excuse do our public safety officials have? No excuses really, just fear of offending political voting blocs, which keep them from exercising even the most trivial duties of their office—such as tracking secondary contacts. God forbid they carry out their office; the possibility of quarantine sets them quivering under their desks.

Thus, here we stand with our collective heads in the sand while this terrible pestilence has time to incubate and mutate into perhaps more virulent forms—ones that could possibly be carried by mosquitoes or other insects, or even contaminate the air we breathe. That's unlikely, but it's not impossible; no more unlikely than other disasters we do prepare for.

Herewith the new Journals of the Plague Years . . .

It was the worst of times, and it was the saddest of times, so what we must remember if we are to keep our perspective as we read these journals of the Plague Years is that the people who wrote them, indeed the entire population of what was then the United States of America and most of the world, were, by our standards, all quite mad.

The Plague virus, apparently originating somewhere in Africa, had spread first to male homosexuals and intravenous drug users. Inevitably it moved via bisexual contact into the population at large. A vaccine was developed and for a moment the Plague seemed defeated. But the organism mutated under this evolutionary pressure and a new strain swept the world. A new vaccine was developed, but the virus mutated again. Eventually the succession of vaccines selected for mutability itself, and the Plague virus proliferated into dozens of strains.

Palliative treatments were developed—victims might survive for a decade or more—but there was no cure, and no vaccine that offered protection for long.

For twenty years, sex and death were inextricably entwined. For twenty years, men and women were constrained to deny themselves the ordinary pleasures of straightforward, unencumbered sex, or to succumb to the natural desires of the flesh and pay the awful price. For twenty years, the species faced its own extinction. For twenty years, Africa and most of Asia and Latin America were quarantined by the armed forces of America, Europe, Japan, and the Soviet Union. For twenty years, the people of the world stewed in their own frustrated sexual juices.

Small wonder then that the Plague Years were years of madness. Small wonder that the authors of these journals seem, from our happier perspective, driven creatures, and quite insane.

That each of them found somewhere the courage to carry on, that through their tormented and imperfect instrumentalities the long night was finally to see our dawn, *that* is the wonder, that is the triumph of the human spirit, the spirit that unites the era of the Plague Years with our own.

—Mustapha Kelly
Luna City, 2143

I was gunfoddering in Baja when the marks began to appear again. The first time I saw the marks, they gave me six years if I could afford it, ten if I joined up and got myself the best.

Well what was a poor boy to do? Take my black card, let them stick me in a Quarantine Zone, and take my chances? Go underground and try to dodge the Sex Police until the Plague got me? Hell no, this poor boy did what about two million other poor boys did—he signed up for life in the American Foreign Legion, aka the Army of the Living Dead, while he was still in good enough shape to be accepted.

Now you hear a lot of bad stuff about the Legion. The wages suck. The food ain't much. We're a bunch of bloodthirsty killers too bugfuck to be allowed back in the United States fighting an endless imperialistic war against the whole Third World, and our combat life expectancy is about three years. Junkies. Dopers. Drooling sex maniacs. The scum of the universe.

For sure, all that is true. But unless you're a millionaire or supercrook, the Legion is the best deal you can do when they paint your blue card black and tell you you've Got It.

The deal is you get the latest that medical science has to offer and you get it free. The deal is you can do anything you want to the gorks as long as you don't screw up combat orders. The deal is that the Army of the Living Dead is coed and omnisexual and every last one of us has already Got It. We've all got our black cards already, we're under sentence of death, so we might as well enjoy one another on the way out. The deal is that the Legion is all the willing meat-sex you can handle, and plenty that you can't, you better believe it!

Like the recruiting slogan says, "A Short Life but a Happy One." We were the last free red-blooded American boys and girls. "Join the Army and Fuck the World," says the graffiti they scrawl on the walls about us.

Well that too, and so what?

Take the Baja campaign. The last census showed that the black card population of California was entitled to enlarged Quarantine Zones. Catalina and San Francisco were bursting at the seams and the state legislature couldn't agree on a convenient piece of territory. So it got booted up to the Federal Quarantine Agency.

Old Walter T., he looks at the map, and he sees you could maintain a Quarantine line across the top of the Baja Peninsula with maybe two thousand SP troops. Real convenient. Annex the mother to California and solve the problem.

So in we go, and down the length of Baja we cakewalk. No sweat. Two weeks of saturation air strikes to soften up the Mexes, a heavy armored division and two wings of gunships at the point, followed by fifteen thousand of us zombies to nail things down.

What you call a fun campaign, a far cry from the mess we got into in Cuba or that balls-up in Venezuela, let me tell you. Mexico was something like fifty percent Got It, their armed forces had been wiped out of existence in the Chihuahua campaign, and so it was just a matter of three weeks of leisurely pillage, rape, and plunder.

The Mexes? They got a sweet deal, considering. Those who were still alive by the time we had secured Baja down to La Paz could choose between deportation to what was left of Mexico or becoming black card citizens of the state of California, Americans like thee and me, brothers and sisters. Any one of them who had survived had Gotten It in every available orifice about 150 times by us zombies by then anyway.

Wanna moralize about it? Okay, then moralize this one, meat-fucker:

The damn Plague started in Africa, didn't it? That's the Third World, ain't it? Africa, Latin America, Asia, except for China, Japan, and Iran, they're over 50 percent Got It, ain't they? And the It they Got keeps mutating like crazy in all that filth. And they keep trying to get through with infiltrators to give *us* the latest strain, don't they?

The Chinese and the Iranians, they *kill* their black-carders, don't they? The Japs, they deport them to Korea. And the Russians, they nuked themselves a cordon sanitaire all the way from the Caspian to the Chinese border.

Was I old Walter T., I'd say nuke the whole cesspit of infection out of existence. Use nerve gas. Fry the Third World clean from orbit. Whatever. They gave us the damn Plague, didn't they? Way we see it in the Army of the Living Dead, anything we do after that is only a little piece of what the gorks got coming!

Believe me, this poor boy wasn't shedding any tears for what we had done to the Mexes when the marks starting coming out just before the sack of Ensenada. Less still when they couldn't come up with a combo of pallies that worked anymore, and they shrugged and finally told me it looked like I had reached Condition Terminal in the ruins of La Paz. Like I said, when I first Got It, they gave me six years, ten in the Army of the Living Dead.

Now they gave me six months.

I shot up with about a hundred milligrams of liquid crystal, chugalugged a quart of tequila, and butt-fucked every gork I could find. Think I blew about ten of them away afterward, but by then, brothers and sisters, who the hell was counting?

Walter T. Bigelow

Oh yes, I knew what they say about me behind my back, even on a cabinet level. Old Walter T., he was a virgin when he married Elaine, and he's never even had meat with his own pure Christian wife. Old Walter T., he's never even stuck it in a sex machine. Old Walter T., he's never even missed the pleasures of the flesh. Old Walter T., he'd still be the same sexless eunuch even if there had never been a Plague. Old Walter T., he's got holy water for blood.

How little they know of my torments.

How little they know of what it was like for me in high school. In the locker room. With all those naked male bodies. All the little tricks I had to learn to hide my erections. Knowing what I was. Knowing it was a sin. Unable to look my own father squarely in the eye.

Walter Bigelow found Christ at the age of seventeen and was Born Again, that's what the official biography says. Alas, it was only partly true. Oh yes, I dedicated my life to Jesus when I was seventeen. But it was a cold, logical decision. It seemed the only means of controlling my unwholesome urges, the only way I could avoid damnation.

I hated God then. I hated Him for making me what I was and condemning me to hellfire should I succumb to the temptations

328

of my own God-given nature. I believed in God, but I hated Him. I believed in Jesus, but how could I believe that Jesus believed in me?

I was not granted Grace until I was twenty.

My college roommate Gus was a torment. He flaunted his naked body in what seemed like total innocence. He masturbated under the bedclothes at night while I longed to be there with him.

One morning he walked into the bathroom while I was toweling myself down after a shower. He was nude, with an enormous erection. I could not keep my flesh from responding in kind. He confessed his lust for me. I let him touch me. I found myself reaching for his manhood.

He offered to do anything. My powers of resistance were at a low point. We indulged in mutual masturbation. I would go no further.

For months we engaged in this onanistic act, Gus offering me every fleshly delight I had ever fantasized, I calling on Christ to save me.

Finally, a moment came when I could resist no longer. Gus knelt on the floor before me, running his hands over my body, cupping my buttocks. I was lost. His mouth reached out for me—

And at that moment God at last granted me His Grace.

As his head lowered, I saw the Devil's mark upon the back of his neck, small as yet, but unmistakable—Karposi's sarcoma.

Gus had the Plague.

He was about to give it to me.

I leaped backward. Gus was an instrument of the Devil sent to damn my flesh to the Plague and my soul to everlasting torment.

And at last I understood. I saw that it was *the Devil*, not God, who had tormented me with these unwholesome urges. And God had let me suffer them as a test and a preparation. A test of my worthiness and a preparation for this moment of revelation of His Divine Mercy. For had He not chosen to show me the Sign that saved me from my own sinful nature at this eleventh hour?

That was when I was granted true Grace.

I sank to my knees and gave thanks to God. *That* was when I was Born Again. *That* was when I became a true Christian. That

329

too was when I was shown my true calling, when the vision opened up before me.

God had allowed the Devil to inflict the Plague on man to test us, even as I had been tested, for to succumb to the temptations of the flesh was to succumb to the Plague and be dragged, rotting and screaming, to Hell.

This was the fate that Jesus had saved me from, for only the Sign He had shown me had preserved me from death and eternal damnation. My life, therefore, was truly His, and what I must use it for was to protect mankind from this Plague and its carriers, to save those I could as Jesus had saved me.

And He spoke to me in my heart. "Become a leader of men," Jesus told me. "Save them from themselves. Do My work in the world."

I promised Him that I would. I would do it in the only way I could conceive of, through politics.

I became a prelaw major. I entered law school. I graduated with honors. I found, courted, and married a pure Christian virgin, and soon thereafter impregnated Elaine with Billy, ran for the Virginia State Assembly, and was elected.

The rest of my life is, as they say, history.

Linda Lewin

I was just another horny spoiled little brat until I Got It, just like all my horny spoiled little friends in Berkeley. Upper-middle-class family with an upper-middle-class house in the hills. My own car for my sixteenth birthday, along with the latest model sex interface.

Oh yes, they did! My mom and dad were no Unholy Rollers, they were educated intellectual liberal Democrats, they read all the literature, they had been children of the Sexy Seventies, they were realists, they knew the score.

These are terrible times, they told me. We know you'll be tempted to have meat. You might get away with it for years. Or you might Get It the first time out. Don't risk it, Linda. We know how you feel, we remember when everyone did meat. We know this is unnatural. But we know the consequences, and so do you.

And they dragged me out on the porch and made me look out

across the Bay at San Francisco. The Bay Bridge with its blown-out center span. The pig boats patrolling the shoreline. The gunships buzzing about the periphery like angry horseflies.

Meat City. That's where you'd end up, Linda. Nothing's worth that, now is it?

I nodded. But even then, I wondered.

I had grown up with the vision of the shining city across the Bay. Oh yes, I had also grown up knowing that the lovely hills and graceful buildings and sparkling night lights masked a charnel house of the Plague, black-carders all, 100 percent. We were told horror stories about it in sex hygiene classes starting in kindergarten.

But from about the fifth grade on, we told ourselves our own stories too. We whispered them in the ladies' room. We uploaded them onto bulletin boards. We downloaded them, printed them out, wiped them from memory so our parents wouldn't see them, masturbated over the printouts.

As porn went, it was crude, amateurish stuff. What could you expect from teenage virgins? And it was all the same. A teenager Gets It. And runs away to San Francisco. Or disappears into the underground. And, sentenced to death already, sets out to enjoy all the pleasures of the meat on the way out, in crude, lurid, sensational detail. And of course, the porn sheets all ended long before Condition Terminal was reached.

But I was a good little girl and I was a smart little girl and the sex interface my parents gave me was the best money could buy, not some cheap one-way hooker's model. It had everything. The vaginal insert was certified to five atmospheres, but it was only fifty microns thick, heated to blood temperature, and totally flexible. It had a neat little clit-hood programmed for five varieties of electric stimulation and six vibratory patterns. I could wear the thing under my jeans, finger the controls, and never fail to come, even in the dullest math class.

The guys said that the interior lining was the max, tight and soft and wet, the stim programs the best there were. But what did they know? Who among them had ever felt real meat?

Oh yes, it was a wonderful sex interface my parents gave me to protect me from the temptations of the meat.

And of course I hated the damned thing.

Worse still when the guy I was balling with it insisted on

331

wearing *his* interface too. Yech! His penile sheath in my vaginal insert. Like two sex machines doing it to each other. I remember an awful thing I did to one wimp who really pissed me off. I took off my interface, made him take off his, inserted his penile sheath in my vaginal insert, activated both interfaces, and made him sit there with me watching the two things go at each other without us for a solid hour.

And then there came Rex.

What can I say about Rex? I was eighteen. He was a year younger. He was beautiful. We never made it through two interfaces. I'd wear mine or he'd wear his and we'd go at it for hours. It was wonderful. We swore eternal love. We took to telling each other meatporn stories as we did it. This was it, I knew it was, we were soul mates for life. Rex swore up and down that he had never done meat and so did I. So why not . . .

Finally we did.

We took off our interfaces and did meat together. We tried out everything in those meatporn stories and then some. Every orifice. Every variation. Every day for two months.

Well, to make the usual long sad story short and nasty, I had been telling the truth, but Rex hadn't. And I had to learn about it from my parents.

Your boyfriend Rex's Got It, they told me one bright sunny morning. He's been black-carded and they've dropped him in San Francisco. You and he never . . . you didn't . . . because if you did, we're going to have to turn you in, you know that, don't you?

Well of course I freaked. But it was a cold slow-motion freak, with everything running through my head too fast for me to panic. I had a whole month till my next ID exam. I knew damn well my card would come up black. What should I do? Let them drop me in San Francisco and go out in a blaze of meatfucking glory with Rex? Yeah, sure, with the lying son of a bitch who had killed me!

I thought fast. I lied up and down. I threw an outraged temper tantrum when my parents suggested maybe I should go in for an early check. I convinced them. Or maybe I just let them convince themselves.

I found myself an underground doc and checked myself out. Got It. I drifted into the Berkeley underground, not as difficult as you might think for a girl who was willing to give meat to the secret Living Dead for a few dollars and a few more connections. I learned about how they kept ahead of the Sex Police. I learned about the phony blue cards. And I made my plans.

When I had hooked enough to score one, I got myself a primo counterfeit. As long as I found myself a wizard every three months to update the data strip, it would show blue. I could stay free until I died, unless of course I got picked up by the SP and got my card run against the national data bank, in which case I would turn up null and it would all be over.

I hooked like crazy, three, four, five tricks a day. I piled up a bankroll and kept it in bills. The day before I was to report for my ID update, I got in my car to go to school, said the usual goodbye to my parents, and took off, headed south.

South to Santa Cruz. South to L.A. South to anywhere. Out along the broad highway to see what there was to see of California, of what was left of America, out along the broad highway toward the eventual inevitable—crazed, confused, terror-stricken, brave with fatal knowledge, determined only to have a long hot run till my time ran out.

Dr. Richard Bruno

They used to call it midlife crisis, male menopause, the seven-year itch, back when it wasn't a condition to which you were condemned for life at birth.

I was just about to turn forty. I had dim teenage memories of quite a meaty little sex life back at the beginning of the Ugly Eighties, before the Plague, before I married Marge. Oh yes, I had been quite a hot little cocksman before it all fell apart, a child of the last half-generation of the Sexual Revolution.

When I was Tod's age, fifteen, I had already had more real meat than the poor frustrated little guy was likely to get in his whole life. Now I had to watch my own son sneaking around to sleazy sex parlors to stick it into sex machines, and don't think I was above it myself from time to time.

Marge, well . . .

Marge was five years younger than I. Just young enough to never have known what the real thing was like, young enough to remember nothing but condoms and vaginal dams and the

333

early interfaces. Oh yes, we had meat together in the early years, before it finally resulted in Tod. Poor Marge was terrified the whole time, unable to come. After Tod was born, she got herself an interface, and never made love again without it.

Marge still loved me, I think, and I still loved her, but the Plague Years had dried her up sexually, turned her prudish and sour. She wouldn't even let me buy Tod an interface so he could get it from a real girl, if only secondhand. His sixteenth birthday is more than time enough, she insisted shrilly every time we fought about it, which was frequently.

Naturally, or perhaps more accurately unnaturally, all my libidinal energies had long since been channeled into my work. It was the perfect sublimation.

I was a genetic synthesizer for the Sutcliffe Corporation in Palo Alto. I had already designed five different Plague vaccines for Sutcliffe that made them hundreds of millions each before the virus mutated into immunity. I was the fair-haired boy. I got many bonuses. I had my own private lab with little restraint on my budget. For a scientist, it should have been heaven.

It wasn't.

It was maddening. A new Plague strain would appear and rise to dominance. I'd strip off the antigen coat, clone it, insert its genome in a bacterium, and Sutcliffe would market a vaccine to those who could afford it, make hundreds of millions in six months. Then the next immune strain would appear, and it would be back to square one. I felt like a scientific Sisyphus, rolling the dead weight of the Plague uphill, only to have it roll back and crush my hopes every six months.

Was I taking my work a bit too personally? Of course I was. My "personal life" consisted of the occasional interface sex with Marge, which I had long since come to loathe, watching my son sneaking around to sex machine parlors, and the occasional trip there myself. My "personal life" had been stolen from me by the Plague, by the Enemy, so of course I took my work personally.

I was obsessed. My work *was* my personal life. And I had a vision.

Cassette vaccines had been around for decades. Strip down a benign virus, plug in sets of antigens off several target organisms, and hey, presto, antibodies to several diseases conferred in a single shot.

Why not apply the same technique to the Plague? Strip one strain down to the core, hang it with antigen coats from four or five strains at once, and confer multistrain immunity. Certainly not to every mutation, but if I could develop an algorithm that could predict mutations, if I could develop cassette vaccines that *stayed ahead* of the viral mutations, might I not somehow be able eventually to force the Plague to mutate out?

Oh yes, I took the battle personally, or so I admitted to myself at the time. Little did I know just how personal it was about to become.

John David

No sooner had we finished mopping up in La Paz than my unit was airlifted up to the former Mexican border as part of the force that would keep it sealed until the SPs could set up their cordon. Through the luck of the draw, we got the sweetest billet, holding the line between Tijuana and San Diego.

They kept us zombies south of the former border, you better believe they didn't want us in Dago, no way they would let us set foot on real American soil, but meatfucker, you wouldn't *believe* the scene in TJ!

Back before the Plague, the place had been one big whorehouse and drug supermarket anyway. For fifteen years it had been a haven for underground black-carders, Latino would-be infiltrators, black pally docs, dealers in every contraband item that existed, getting poorer and more desperate as the cordon around Mexico tightened.

Now TJ found itself in the process of becoming an American Quarantine Zone, and it was Bugfuck City. Mexicans trying to get into Dago on false passports and blue cards. Wanted Americans trying to get out to anywhere. False IDs going for outrageous prices. Pussy and ass and drugs and uncertified pharmaceuticals and armaments going for whatever the poor bastards left holding them could get.

And the law, such as it was, until the SPs could replace the Legion, was *us*, brothers and sisters. Unbelievable! We could buy anything—drugs, phony blue cards, six-year-old virgins, you name it—or just have what we wanted at gunpoint. And money hand over fist, I mean we looted everything with no law but us to stop us, and did heavy traffic in government arms on top of it.

Loaded with money, we stayed stoned and drunk and turned that town into our twenty-four-hour pigpen, you better believe it! No one more so than me, brothers and sisters, with those marks coming out, knowing this could be my last big night to party.

I scored half-a-dozen phony blue cards and corroborating papers to match. I stuffed my pockets with money. I shot up with every half-baked pally TJ had to peddle, and they had everything from Russian biologicals to ground-up nun's tits in holy water. If this was my Condition Terminal, I was determined to take as much of the world with me as I could before I went out. I meat-fucked myself deaf, dumb, and blind and must've Given It to five hundred Mexes in the bargain.

Then they started phasing in the Sex Police. Well, as you might imagine, there was no love lost between the Army of the Living Dead and the SPs. Those uptight Unholy Rollers took any opportunity to snuff us. Looters were shot. Meatfuckers caught in the act were executed. And of course, brothers and sisters, the Army of the Living Dead gave as good as we got and then some.

We'd kill any of the bastards we caught on what remained of our shrinking turf. We'd get up kamikaze packs and go into their turf after them. When we were really loaded, we'd catch ourselves some SP assholes and gang-bang them senseless. Needless to say, we weren't into using interfaces.

Things got so out of hand that the Pentagon brought in regular airborne troops to round us up. That little action took more casualties in two days than the whole Baja campaign had in three weeks.

When they started dropping napalm from close-support fighters, it finally dawned on those of us still around that the meatfuckers had no intention of rounding us up and shipping us to the next theater. They were out to kill us all, and they were probably working themselves up to tactical nukes to do it.

Well, we weren't the Army of the Living Dead for nothing. I don't know where it started or who started it. It just seemed to happen all at once. Somehow all of us that were left stuffed our loot in our packs, armed ourselves with whatever we could lay hands on, and suddenly there was a human wave assault on the border.

It was the bloodiest ragged combat any of us ever saw, crazed zombies against gunships, fighters, and tanks. How many of the bastards did we get on the way? More than you might imagine, better believe it, we were stoned, drunk, in a berserker rage, and we were now the Living Dead twice over, with Double Nothing to lose, triple so for yours truly.

How many of us got through? A thousand? Five hundred? Something to keep you from oversleeping, citizens. Hundreds of us zombies, our packs stuffed with money, false IDs and ordnance, over the border into San Diego, hunted, dying, betrayed by even the Army, with nothing left for kicks but to take our vengeance on *you*, meatfuckers!

And I was one of them. The meanest and the craziest, it pleases me to believe. Betrayed, facing Condition Terminal, with nothing left to do with what little was left of my life but bop till I dropped and take as many of you as I could with me.

Linda Lewin

I drove aimlessly around California for months, down 101 or the Coast Highway to Los Angeles, down 5 to San Diego, up to L.A. again, up 5 to the Bay Area, back around again, like a squirrel in a cage, like one of those circuit-riding preachers in an old Western.

I Had It. My days were numbered. I needed cash—for gas, for food, for a flop in a motel, for what pallies I could score, for updating the data strip on my phony blue card. I hooked wherever I could, using my interface always, for I swore to myself that I would never do to anyone what Rex had done to me. I didn't want to go to Condition Terminal with *that* mark on my soul.

Bit by bit, inch by inch, I drifted into the underground. You'd be surprised how many black-carders there were surviving outside the Quarantine Zones on phony IDs, a secret America within America, hiding within plain sight of the SPs, living by our wits and our own code.

We found one another by some kind of second sight impossible to explain. Pally pushers. ID wizards. Hookers just like me.

And not like me.

There were bars where we met to trade in pallies and IDs and information. You met all kinds. Pally dealers and drug dealers. ID wizards. Hookers like me, male and female, selling interface sex to the solid citizens. And hookers of the other kind.

Hookers selling meat.

It was amazing how many blue-carders were willing to risk death for the real thing. It was amazing how innocent some of them were willing to be. At first I refused to believe the stories the meatwhores told in the bars, cackling evilly all the time. I refused to believe that they were knowingly spreading the Plague and laughing about it. I refused to believe that blue-carders could be so stupid.

But they were and they could. And after a while, I understood.

There were people who would pay fantastic prices for meatsex with another certified blue-carder. There were clandestine meat-bars where they hung out, bars with ID readers. Pick up one of these fools, pop your phony card in a reader, and watch their eyes light up as the strip read out blue, no line to the national data banks here, not with the SPs raiding any such bar they could get a line on. And you got paid more for a quick meatfuck than you could earn in a week of interface hooking.

Sure I was tempted. There was more to it than the money. Didn't I long for meat myself? Wasn't that how I had Gotten It in the first place? Didn't these damn blue-card assholes deserve what they got?

Who knows, I might have ended up doing it in the end if I hadn't met Saint Max, Our Lady of the Flowers.

Saint Max was a black-carder. He carried his own ID reader around and he didn't worry about phony cards reading out blue.

Saint Max would give meat only to certified *black*-carders, and he would never refuse anyone, even the most rotted-out Terminals.

I was in an underground bar in Santa Monica when Saint Max walked in, and half-a-dozen people told me his story before I ever heard it from his lips. Saint Max was a legend of the California underground. The only real hero we had.

Max was a bisexual, male or female, it didn't matter to him, and he never took money. People fed him, bought him drinks, gave him the latest pallies, found him free flop, sent him on his way. "I am dependent on the kindness of strangers," Max used to say. And in return, any black-carder stranger could depend on kindness from him.

Max was old; in terms of how long he had survived with God knew how many Plague strains inside him, he was ancient. He had lived in the San Francisco Quarantine Zone before it was a Quarantine Zone. And he was a man with a mission. He had this crazy theory.

I heard it from him that night after I had bought him a meal and about half-a-dozen drinks.

"I'm a living reservoir of every Plague strain extant, my dear," he told me. "And I do my best to keep up with the latest mutations."

Max believed that all black-carders had a moral obligation to have as much meatsex with one another as possible. So as to speed the pace of evolution. In a large enough pool of cross-infected Plague victims the virus might mutate out into something benign. Or a multiimmunity might evolve and spread quickly. A pathogen that killed its host was, after all, a mal-adapted organism, and as long as it was killing us, so were we.

"Natural selection, my dear. In the long run, it's our species' only hope. In the long run, everyone is going to Get It, and it's going to get most of us. But if out of the billions who will die, evolution eventually selects for multiimmunity, or a benign Plague variant, the human race will survive. And for as long as all these pallies keep me going, I intend to serve the process."

It seemed crazy to me, and I told him so, exposing yourself to every Plague strain you could. Didn't that mean Condition Terminal would just come quicker?

Saint Max shrugged. "Here I am," he said. "No one's been exposed to as many Plague variants as me. Maybe it's already happened. Maybe I've got multiimmunity. Maybe I'm a mutant. Maybe there's already a benign strain inside me."

He smiled sadly. "We're all under sentence of death the moment we're born anyway, now aren't we, my dear? Even the poor blue-carders. It's only a matter of how, and when, and in the

339

pursuit of what. And like old John Henry, I intend to die with my hammer in my hand. Think about it, Linda.''

And I did. I offered Max a ride up the coast and he accepted and we ended up traveling one full slow cycle of my circuit together. I watched Max giving meat freely to one and all, to kids like me new to the underground, to thieves, and whores, and horrible Terminals on the way out. No one took Saint Max's crazy theory seriously. Everyone loved him.

And so did I. I paid my way with the usual interface sex, and Max let it be until we were finally back in Santa Monica and it was time to say goodbye. "You're young, Linda," he told me. "With good enough pallies, you have years ahead of you. Me, I know I'm reaching the end of the line. You've got the heart for it, my dear. This old faggot would go out a lot happier knowing that there was someone like you to carry on. Think about it, my dear, 'A Short Life but a Happy One,' as they say in the Army of the Living Dead. And don't think we're all not in it.''

I thought about it. I thought about it for a long time. But I didn't do anything about it till I saw Max again, till Max lay dying.

Walter T. Bigelow

After two terms in the Virginia Assembly, I ran for Congress and was elected. Capitol Hill was in a state of uproar over the Plague. National policy was nonexistent. Some states were quarantining Plague victims, others were doing nothing. Some states were testing people at their borders, others were calling this a violation of the Constitution. Some representatives were calling for a national health identity card, others considered this a civil rights outrage. Christian groups were calling for a national quarantine policy. Plague victims' rights groups were calling for an end to all restrictions on their free movements. Dozens of test cases were moving ponderously toward the Supreme Court.

After two terms watching this congressional paralysis, God inspired me to conceive of the National Quarantine Amendment. I ran for the Senate on it, received the support of Christians and Plague victims alike, and was elected by a huge majority.

The amendment nationalized Plague policy. Each state was required to set up Quarantine Zones proportional in area and economic base to the percentage of victims in its territory, said division to be updated every two years. Every citizen outside a Zone must carry an updated blue card. In return for this, Plague victims were guaranteed full civil and voting rights within their Quarantine Zones, and free commerce in nonbiological products was assured.

It was fair. It was just. It was inspired by God. Under my leadership it sailed through Congress and was accepted by three-quarters of the states within two years after I led a strenuous nationwide campaign to pass it.

I was a national hero. It was a presidential year. I was told that I was assured my party's nomination, that my election to the presidency was all but certain.

Linda Lewin

Saint Max had suddenly collapsed into late Condition Terminal. Indeed he was at the point of death when I finally followed the trail of the sad story to a cabin on a seacliff not far from Big Sur. There he lay, skeletal, emaciated, his body covered with sarcomas, semicomatose.

But his eyes opened up when I walked in. "I've been waiting for you, my dear," he said. "I wasn't about to leave without saying goodbye to Our Lady."

"Our Lady? That's *you*, Max."

"*Was*, my dear."

"Oh, Max . . ." I cried, and burst into tears. "What can I do?"

"Nothing, my dear . . . Or everything." His eyes were hard and pitiless then, yet also somehow soft and imploring.

"Max . . ."

He nodded. "You could give me one last meatfuck goodbye," he told me. He smiled. "I would have preferred a boy, of course, but at least it would please my old mother to know that I mended my ways on my deathbed."

I looked at his feverish, disease-ravaged body. "You don't know what you're asking!" I cried.

"Oh yes I do, my dear. I'm asking you to do the bravest thing you've ever done in your life. I'm asking you to believe in the

341

faith of a dying madman. On the other hand, I'm asking for nothing at all, since you've already Got It.''

How could I not? Either way, he was right. The Plague would kill me sooner or later no matter what I did now. I would never even know by how much this act of kindness would shorten my life span. Or if it would at all. And Max was dying. He had lived his life bravely in the service of humanity, at least as he saw it. And I loved him more in that moment than I had ever loved anyone in my life. And what if he was right? What other hope did humanity have? How could I refuse him?

I couldn't.

I didn't.

Afterward, as I held him, he spoke to me one last time. ''Now for my last wish,'' he said.

''Haven't I just given it to you?''

''You know you haven't.''

''What then?''

''You know, my dear.''

So I did. I had accepted it when I took his ravaged manhood inside my unprotected body. I knew that now. I knew that I had known it all along.

''Will you take up this torch from me?'' he said, holding out his hand.

''Yes, Max, I will,'' I promised and reached for the phantom object.

''Then this old faggot can go out happy,'' he said. And died in my arms with a smile on his lips.

And I became Our Lady. Our Lady of the Living Dead, as they were to call me.

John David

San Diego was crawling with SPs, and they probably would have sent in commando units to hunt us down, if they weren't so terrified of what would happen if the citizens were to find out that hundreds of us zombies were loose and on the warpath in the good old US of A.

And we were, meatfuckers, better believe it! Wouldn't you? Sooner or later they were going to get us all, and if they didn't, the Plague would, and in my case, sooner than later. So we scattered. I don't know what the others did, but me, I stayed drunk and stoned, and meatfucked as many of the treacherous blue-carders as I could lay my hands on. And tracked down all the pally pushers I could find. I don't even know what half the stuff I shot up was, but something in the mix, or maybe the mix itself, seemed to slow the Plague. I didn't get any better, but I seemed to stabilize.

But the situation in Dago didn't, brothers and sisters. It became one close call after another. Finally I got caught by a couple of stupid SPs. Well, those Unholy Rollers were no match for a zombie with my combat smarts. While they were running one of my phony cards through the national data bank and coming up null, I managed to kill the meatfuckers.

I picked my IDs off the corpses, but now the national data bank had me marked as a zombie on the run, and when they found these stiffs, they'd fax my photo to every SP station in the fifty states. The Sex Police took a real dim view of SP killers, and nailing me would be priority one.

I had only one chance, not that it was max probability. I had to disappear into a Quarantine Zone. San Francisco was the biggest, hence the safest. Also the tastiest, or so I was told.

So I snatched a car and headed north. How I would break *into* a Zone, I'd have to figure out later. If, by some chance, I managed to avoid the SPs long enough to get there.

Walter T. Bigelow

Congress set up the Federal Quarantine Agency to administer the National Quarantine Amendment. It would have enormous power and enormous responsibility. It was the wisdom of Congress, with which I heartily concurred, that it be entirely insulated from party politics. The director would be chosen in the manner of Supreme Court justices—nominated by the president, approved by the Senate, serving for life, removable only by impeachment.

After the president signed the bill, he called me into his office and pleaded with me to accept the appointment. It was my amendment. I was the only political figure who had the confidence of both Plague victims and blue-carders.

All that, I knew, was true. What was also true was that many

343

insiders blanched at the thought of a Bigelow presidency. This was the perfect political solution.

It was the most important decision of my life and the most difficult. Elaine had had her heart set on being First Lady. "You just *can't* let them take the presidency away from you like this," she insisted. Ministers and black-carder groups and politicians of my own party, some sincere, some otherwise, begged me to accept the lifetime directorship of the FQA. For weeks, they all badgered me while I procrastinated and prayed.

It seemed as if the voices of God and the Devil were speaking to me through my wife, party leaders, men of God, men of power, saints and sinners, battling for possession of my soul. But which was the voice of God and which the voice of Satan? Which way did my true duty lie? What did God want me to do?

Finally, I went on a solitary retreat into the Utah desert, into Zion National Park. I fasted. I prayed. I called on Jesus to speak to me.

And at length a voice did speak to me, in a vision. "You are the Moses I have chosen to lead My people out of the wilderness," it told me. "Have I not commanded you to become a leader of men? Those who would deny you power are the agents of the Adversary."

But then another stronger and sweeter voice spoke out of a great white light and I knew that this was truly Jesus and whose the first voice had really been.

"I saved you from the Plague and your own sinful desire in your hour of need," He told me. "I raised you up from the pit so that you might do God's will on Earth. As I gave up My life to save Man from sin, so must you give up worldly power to save the people from their dark natures. As God chose Me for My Calvary, so do I choose you for yours."

I returned from the desert to Washington and I obeyed. I put the thought of worldly glory behind me. There were those who snickered when I accepted this appointment. There were those who laughed when I told the nation that I had done it at the bidding of Jesus.

Even my wife told me I was a fool, and a breach was opened between us that I knew no way to heal. We became strangers to each other sharing the same marriage bed.

Oh yes, I paid dearly for my obedience to God's will. But while I may have lost my chance at worldly power and hardened my wife's heart against me, I remained steadfast and strong.

For God had saved me in that dormitory room with Gus and granted me Grace and salvation. And Jesus spoke truth to me in the desert in the presence of the Adversary and saved me again. And so in my heart I knew I had done right.

Dr. Richard Bruno

How could I have done such a thing? How could I, of all people, have been naïve enough to Get It from a meatwhore? As the ancient saying has it, a stiff dick knows no conscience, and they don't call a fool a stupid prick for nothing.

For my fortieth birthday, I got royally drunk and righteously stoned, and I demanded a special birthday present from Marge. Was it really too much to ask from one's own wife on the night of the rite de passage of my midlife crisis? Tender loving meat for my Fateful Fortieth? We were both blue-carders. Marge had hardly any sex life at all. The only times I had been unfaithful to her were with radiation-sterilized sex machines.

I was loaded and raving, but she was entirely irrational. She refused. When I attempted to get physical, she locked herself in the bedroom and told me to go stick it in one of my goddamn sex machines.

I reeled out into the streets, stoned out of my mind, aching with despair, with a raging fortieth-birthday hard-on. But I didn't slink off to the usual sex machine parlor, oh no; that was what Marge had told me to do, wasn't it?

Instead, I found myself one of those clandestine meatbars. To make the old long story modern and short, I picked up a whore. We inserted our cards in the bar's reader and of course they both came up blue. Off I went to her room and did every kind of meat I could think of and some that seemed to be her own inventions.

I staggered home, still loaded, and passed out on the couch. The Morning After . . .

Oh my God!

Beyond the inevitable horrid hangover and conjugal recriminations, I awoke to the full awfulness of what I had done. In my

345

present sober and thoroughly detumescent state, I knew all too well how many phony blue cards were floating around the meatbars. Had I . . . ?

I ran the standard tests on myself in my own lab for six days. On the sixth day, they came up black. When I cultured the bastard, it turned out to be a Plague variant I had not yet seen.

By this time I had prepared myself for the inevitable. I had made my plans. As fortune would have it, I had ten weeks before my next ID update, ten weeks to achieve what medical science had failed to achieve in twenty years and more of trying.

But I had motivation. If I failed, in ten weeks I would lose my blue card, my job, my mission in life, my wife, my family, and with no one to blame but myself. At this point, I wasn't even thinking about the fact that I was under sentence of eventual death. What would happen in ten weeks was more than disaster enough to keep me working twenty hours a day, or so at least it seemed.

And, crazed creature that I was, I had a crazy idea, one that, in retrospect, I saw I had been moving toward all along.

My work on cassette vaccines was already well advanced, so might it not be possible to push it one step further, and synthesize an *automatic self-programming* cassette vaccine? It might be pushing the edge of the scientific possible, but it was my only hope. A crazy idea, yes, but was not madness just over the edge from inspiration?

I stripped a Plague virus down to the harmless core in the usual manner. But I didn't start hanging on the usual series of antigen coat variants. I started crafting a series of nanomanipulators out of RNA fragments, molecular "tentacles."

What I was after was an organism that would infect the same cells as the Plague. That would seize any strain of Plague virus it found, destroy the core, and wrap the empty antigen coat around itself, much as a hermit crab crawls inside a discarded seashell in order to protect its nakedness from the world.

In effect, a killed-virus vaccine that could still reproduce as an organism, an organism continually reprogramming its antigen coat to mimic lethal invaders, that would use the corpses of the Enemy to stimulate the production of antibodies to it, a living, self-programming cassette vaccine factory within my own body.

346

The theory was simple, cunning, and elegant. Actually synthesizing such a molecular dreadnaught was something else again . . .

Linda Lewin

The story of what happened on Saint Max's deathbed became a legend of the underground. And whereas Max had been old and had long since outlived any rational expectations of survival, I was young, I appeared healthy, and so what I was risking was readily apparent.

Like Saint Max, Our Lady gave the comfort of her meat to anyone who asked her. I gave freely of my body to young black-carders like myself, to rotting Terminals, to every underground black-carder between.

Perhaps because I was young, perhaps because I was the first convert to Saint Max's vision daring enough to put it into practice, perhaps because I was so much more naïvely earnest about it than he had been, perhaps because I appeared to be in such robust health, there were those who believed in it now, who believed in me, in the Faith of Our Lady. If Saint Max had been our Jesus, and I was our Paul, now there were disciples to spread the Faith, no more than scores, maybe, but at least more than Christianity's original twelve.

Spreading the Faith of Saint Max and Our Lady. Gaining converts with our hope and our bodies as we wandered up and down California. The Plague strains would spread faster now. Millions might die sooner who might have lingered longer. But were we not all under sentence of death anyway, blue-carders and black-carders alike?

Millions of lives might be shortened, but out of all that death, the species might survive. We would challenge the Plague head-on, in the only way we could—love against despair, sex against death. We would force the pace of evolution and/or die trying.

And while we lived, we would at least live free, we would live, and love, and fight for our species' survival as natural men and women. Better in fire than in ice.

I had done as God commanded, I was doing His work, but the Devil continued to torment me. Elaine remained distant and cold, the Plague continued to spread despite my best efforts, and then, at length, Satan, not content with this, reached out and put his hand upon my Billy.

Billy, the son I had raised so carefully, the son who to my joy had Found the Light at the age of fourteen, began to act strangely, moping in his room at night, locking himself in the bathroom for suspiciously long intervals. I didn't need to be the director of the Federal Quarantine Agency to suspect what was happening; any good Christian father could read the signs.

I was prepared to find pornography when I searched his room one morning after he had left for school, but nothing could have prepared me for the vile nature of the filth I found. Photographs of men having meatsex with each other. With young boys. Photographs of naked young boys in the lewdest of poses. And, worse still, hideous cartoons of boys and girls having the most impossible and revolting intercourse with sex machines, automated monstrosities with grotesque vulvas, immense penile organs, done up to simulate animals, robots, tentacled aliens from outer space.

I reeled. My skin crawled. My stomach went cold. Worst of all, the Devil caused my weak flesh to become loathsomely aroused as all those terrible and tantalizing memories of Gus came rushing back between my legs to haunt me.

Revolted, appalled, shaking with outrage and confusion, I was forced to wait until the evening to confront him, and the Devil struck me a second blow in the office, for that was the day when the first reports of the Satanic cult of Our Lady of the Living Dead appeared in my electronic mailbox.

Of course I was aware that there were hundreds of thousands, perhaps millions, of black-carders living underground outside the Quarantine Zones on bogus blue cards, and spreading their filth among the innocent. We caught hundreds of them every week.

But this . . . this . . . this was Satan's masterstroke!

Out there in California was a woman, or perhaps several women, known as Our Lady of the Living Dead, clearly possessed by the Adversary and doing his work quite consciously, recruiting others into her Satanic cult, spreading his lies and the Plague in ever-wider circles.

Black-carders were openly offering their meat to their fellow black-carders, spreading multiple strains of Plague virus throughout the underground. Interrogations seemed to indicate that these slaves of Satan actually believed that they were the saviors of the species, that in some mystical manner they were speeding the course of evolution, that somehow out of their unholy and deadly couplings a strain of humanity would evolve that was immune to the Plague.

He is not the Prince of Liars for nothing. He had apparently quite convinced these poor doomed creatures of this one, cunningly using their despair-maddened lust and turning it against us all, giving them a truly devilish excuse to wallow in it until they died in the conviction that they were doing God's Work in the process.

And laughing at them and at me by causing his servant to wrap himself in the cognomen of the Mother of Jesus!

I gave the necessary orders. The stamping out of the cult of Our Lady was to be the SP's number one priority. Arrest these people. If any resisted, shoot to kill. Close as many meatbars as possible. And do it all as conspicuously as could be managed. Spread the fear of God's wrath and that of the SP among the denizens of the underground.

After a day like that, I was constrained to return home and confront Billy. There was denial, sobbing confession, promises of repentance, and strong penances set. I had done my patriotic duty and my fatherly duty. It had been hard, but I had done God's will and was as at peace as one could be under the terrible circumstances.

But Satan was still not finished with me. He seized Elaine, my good Christian wife, and caused her to launch into the most appalling tirade. "How can you be so hard-hearted?" she demanded. "Aren't things bad enough for young people growing up these days? At least you shouldn't try to keep Billy from a little safe masturbation."

"It's against God's law! Besides, you saw that revolting, unnatural—"

"Of course it's unnatural, Walter! What else can you expect

349

when the most natural thing in the world is the one thing none of us can do anymore!''

"Elaine—"

"If you were a real man, Walter T. Bigelow, if you were a real Christian, if you were a real loving father, you'd take the poor boy to a sex machine parlor and show him how to get some harmless release!''

I could hardly believe my ears for a long moment. This could not be Elaine! But then I understood. This insinuating blasphemy was coming from her lips, but my poor wife was only an instrument. The voice saying these awful things through her had identified itself by the very act of causing a good Christian woman to mouth them.

"I know you . . .'' I muttered.

"No you don't, Walter Bigelow, you don't know me at all!''

"Get thee behind me—"

"Have it your own way!'' she shouted. And she locked herself in the bedroom, leaving me to spend a sleepless night in the living room, praying to Jesus, demanding to know why He had so forsaken me in the presence of the Enemy.

John David

I made my way up the coast toward San Francisco real slowly, spending nearly a month in Los Angeles, which was big, and sprawling, and a hell of a town for a zombie to party in. There were plenty of meatbars, my latest batch of pallies seemed to be holding up real well, I was lookin' good, I had umpteen phony blue cards, and I was able to meatfuck myself near to exhaustion. It was almost too easy.

And then one night I found out why.

I let myself get picked up on the street by this sexy space case who told me she'd give me free meat if I was a *black*-carder, if you can believe that one. Well, she was beautiful, I was real stoned and in a kind of funny mood, so I shoved her into an alley, Gave It to her, and then announced my wonderful secret identity as a black-card-carrying zombie of the Army of the Living Dead, expecting to get my jollies watching her freak.

Only she didn't. She smiled at me. She fuckin' kissed me,

350

and she told me I was doin' the Work of Our Lady whether I knew it or not.

Say what? Say who?

And she told me.

She told me that whether I knew it or not, I was a soldier in a different army now, an army called the Lovers of Our Lady. Whose mission it was to have meat with as many people as possible in order to save the species, if you can believe *that* one, brothers and sisters! That somehow by all of us Giving as many strains of It to each other as we could, we might end up with multiimmune humans.

Believe it when they tell you L.A. is full of all kinds of weirdos, brothers and sisters!

But soon the weirdness began getting ominous. All of a sudden the SPs were swarming all over the meatbars like flies on horseshit, running every last customer they caught through the national data bank no matter how long it took. The underground safe houses were no longer so safe. They were grabbing people at random on the streets and blowing away anyone who showed any resistance. I mean, suddenly the Sex Police were real agitated.

I never did find out whether they were hot after me and my fellow zombies or what, I mean after a few close calls, there was clearly no percentage in sticking around to find out. Especially since the pallies were starting to wear off once more and I was getting to lookin' obvious and ragged. San Francisco was beginning to look like my best bet again after all.

I snatched me another car and headed north again, staying away from the population centers, meatfucking my way slowly up the center of California, following a kind of secret underground circuit.

It was real easy, once I got the hang of it and picked up on the stories. That weirdo back in L.A. had given me a good steer. All I had to tell these assholes was that I was doin' the Work of Our Lady and they'd do me anything.

It was arduous, but my little dreadnaught was ready with five days to spare, and it was even more elegant than my original concept. Like the Plague itself, it infected via the usual sexual or intravenous vectors, colonizing semen, blood, and mucous membrane. Unlike the Plague, however, it did not interfere with T-cell activity or production. Lacking an antigen coat, it was "invisible" to the host immune system.

As a retrovirus, it would write itself into host genomes, so that when it expressed itself during cellular reproduction, it would invade two more cells, a process that would continue until all suitable host cells were infected.

If an invading retrovirus should be encountered during the expression phase, it would destroy the active core and wrap itself in the "dead" antigen coat. If the host already had antibodies to these antigens, that variant would die. If not, it would eventually write itself back into a host genome, shedding the antigen "shell" in the process.

Thus, when a retrovirus invaded the host, the host bloodstream would become saturated with empty invader antigen coats, to which the host immune system would eventually form antibodies, conferring immunity to the invader precisely in the manner of a "killed virus" vaccine.

It not only conferred immunity to all strains of the Plague virus, it would automatically immunize the host against *all* retroviruses. And, like the Plague, it would spread via sexual contact.

That was what my molecular analysis predicted. It remained only to test the dreadnaught. But there was a stringent law against introducing into human hosts a live, genetically tailored organism capable of reproduction outside the lab, even for test purposes. It would take congressional legislation to allow me to begin human tests, and even then it could be years before the dreadnaught received FDA certification.

And I had only five days. In five days, I was up for ID card updating. If I tested out black, which I would, I would lose my job and be dumped unceremoniously into the San Francisco Quarantine Zone, and all would be lost.

I had only one chance to keep my blue card long enough to

see the whole process through. I myself would have to be my first test subject. If it didn't work, all was lost anyway. If it did— and I was convinced it would—no one ever need know that I had violated the FDA regulations.

So I injected myself with the dreadnaught culture. Three days later, my body was free of the Plague. I took some of my blood and exposed it to other Plague strains as well as a variety of other retroviruses. My dreadnaught killed them all.

I called Harlow Prinz, the president of Sutcliffe, and asked for a special meeting of the board of directors, at which I promised to present the greatest advance in medicine in the last fifty years and then some. I could all but hear him drooling.

The Nobel for medicine seemed a certainty.

And, seeing as how the dreadnaught would spread itself by sexual contact without the need for economically prohibitive mass inoculation, it could eliminate the Plague from the festering Third World as well, so a second Nobel, this one for peace, might not be beyond the bounds of possibility.

Walter T. Bigelow

Elaine refused to have interface sex with me at all. She refused to sleep in the same bedroom with me. She took to disparaging my manhood. Meals were undercooked, overcooked, slovenly prepared. Her housekeeping deteriorated. She kept insisting that I introduce Billy to the sex machine parlors and called my righteous refusal "un-Christian."

I no longer knew the woman I lived with. Elaine was now acting like a woman with a secret life, indeed like a woman hiding an adulterous relationship. Was it possible? How long had it been going on? Had she been making a fool of me all these years?

Of course I had the necessary resources to find out. I had her followed. But what the reports revealed was no human lover.

There were written accounts. There were still photos. There was even an ingeniously obtained clandestine video.

Elaine was a sex machine addict.

Almost every day when I was away at work, she visited one of several sex machine parlors, and stayed for at least an hour, engaging in machine sex perversions of which I had previously been unaware, which I had not even previously believed possible.

When I confronted her with the evidence, she defiantly admitted that she had been doing it secretly for years. "You just haven't been satisfying me, Walter."

"Adulteress!"

"*Adulteress?* Just the opposite! I've been doing it to *keep from becoming* an adulteress!"

"It's against God's law!"

"Show me anything in the scriptures against it!"

"It's the sin of Onan!"

"Good Lord, Walter, it's the Plague, can't you see that?"

"Of course I can see that! God is testing us, and you've failed Him."

"*I've* failed *Him*? Or has *He* failed *us*?"

"Blasphemy!"

"Is it?" she insinuated. "Can it be Jesus's God of Love who has taken natural love itself away from us and forced us into all these perversions? Look what's happened to us! Look what's happened to Billy! Where is God's Love in all that?"

"It's the Devil tormenting us, not God, Elaine!"

"That's what I'm telling you, Walter Bigelow! The Plague is the work of the Devil, not God. So anything that helps us survive Satan's torment—the interfaces, the sex machines—must be God's mercy. Jesus loves us, doesn't He? He can't want us to suffer any more than we have to!"

And then I knew for certain.

Not the Prince of Liars for nothing.

My Elaine had neither the evilness of spirit nor the cunning of mind to say these things to me. She was clearly possessed by the Devil.

Christian and husbandly duty coincided.

I placed Elaine under clandestine house arrest.

And began consulting exorcists.

Dr. Richard Bruno

They were all there—Harlow Prinz, the president of Sutcliffe, Warren Feinstein, the chairman of the board, and the entire board of directors. They all had dollar signs in their eyes as I began my presentation. They listened with rapt silence as I proceeded, a silence that grew rather ominous and eerie as I went on.

And the conclusion of my presentation fell into a deathly graveyard hush that seemed to go on forever. I finally had to break it myself.

"Uh . . . any questions?"

"This, ah, dreadnaught virus is a self-replicating organism? It will reproduce by itself outside the lab?"

"That's right."

"And it spreads like the Plague?"

"It can easily enough be made pandemic."

"Who has had access to this information?"

"Why, no one outside this room," I told them. "I did this one on my own."

Like a crystal suddenly dissolving back into solution, the hushed atmosphere shattered into a series of whispered cross-conversations. After a few minutes of this, Prinz snapped orders into his intercom.

"Security to lab twelve! Seal it off. No one in or out except on my personal orders. Get a decontamination team down there and execute Code Black procedures."

"*Code Black?*" I cried. "There's no Code Black in my lab! No pathogen release! No—"

"Shut up, Bruno! Haven't you done enough already?" Prinz shouted at me. "You've created an artificial human parasite, you imbecile! The FDA will crucify us!"

"*If* we report it . . ." Feinstein said slowly.

"Yes . . ." Prinz said.

"What are you going to do, Harlow?"

"I've already done it. We'll follow maximum Code Black procedure. Incinerate the contents of lab twelve, then pump it full of molten glass. We'll keep this an internal matter. It never happened."

"But what about *him*?"

"Indeed . . ." Prinz said slowly. "Security to the boardroom!" he snapped into his intercom.

"What the hell is going on?" I finally managed to demand.

"You've committed a very serious breach of FDA regulations, Dr. Bruno," Feinstein told me. "One that could have grave consequences for the company."

"But it's a monumental breakthrough!" I cried. "Haven't you heard a word I've said? It's a cure for all possible Plague variants! It'll save the country from—"

"It would destroy Sutcliffe, you cretin!" Prinz shouted. "Fifty-two percent of our gross derives from Plague vaccines, and another twenty-one percent from the sale of palliatives! And your damned dreadnaught is a *venereal disease*, man—it wouldn't even be a marketable product!"

"But surely the national interest—"

"I'm afraid you haven't considered the national interest at all, Dr. Bruno," Feinstein said much more smoothly. "The medical industry's share of GNP has been twenty-five percent for years, and the Plague is hard-wired into our economy; your dreadnaught would have precipitated a massive depression."

"And destroyed the whole raison d'être of our policy vis-à-vis the Third World."

"Thereby shattering the Soviet–Chinese–American–Japanese entente and rekindling the Cold War."

"Leading to a nuclear Armageddon and the destruction of our entire species!"

What monstrous sophistry! What sheer insanity! What loathsome utterly self-interested bullshit! They *couldn't* be serious!

But just then two armed guards entered the boardroom, and their presence suddenly forced me to realize just how serious the board really was. They were already destroying the organism. From their own outrageously cold point of view, their hideous logic was quite correct. The dreadnaught virus *would* reduce the medical industry to an economic shadow of its former self. Sutcliffe *would* fold. And their jobs and their fortunes would be gone. . . .

"Dr. Bruno is not to be allowed to leave the premises or to communicate with the outside," Prinz told the guards. They crossed the room to flank my chair with pistols at the ready.

"What are we going to do with him?"

How far would they really go to protect their own interests?

"Perhaps Dr. Bruno has met with an unfortunate accident in the lab . . ." Prinz said slowly.

My God, were they *deadly* serious?

"Surely you're not suggesting . . . ?" Feinstein exclaimed, quite aghast.

356

"The organism is being destroyed, we can wipe his research notes from the data banks, no one else knows, we can hardly afford to leave loose ends dangling," Prinz said. "You have any better ideas, Warren?"

"But—"

Did I panic? Did I become one of them? Was I acting out of ruthless self-interest myself, or following a higher imperative? Or all four? Who can say? All I knew then was that my life was on the line, that I had to talk my way out of that room, and the words came pouring out of me before I even thought them, or so it seemed.

"One million dollars a year," I blurted.

"What?"

"That's my price for silence. I want my salary raised to one million a year."

"That's preposterous!"

"Is it? You've said yourself that the survival of Sutcliffe is at stake. Cheap at twice the price!"

"Cheaper and safer to eliminate the problem permanently," Prinz said.

"Ye Gods, Harlow, you're talking about murder!" Feinstein cried. "Dr. Bruno's suggestion is much more . . . rational. He'd hardly be about to talk while we're paying him a million a year for his silence!"

"He's right, Harlow!"

"The other's too risky."

"I don't like it, we can't trust—"

"He'll have to agree to accept an appointment to the board," Feinstein said. "Meaning that he knowingly accepts legal responsibility for our actions. Besides, we're destroying the organism, aren't we? Who would believe him anyway?"

"Will you agree to Warren's terms?" Prinz asked me.

I nodded silently. In that moment, I would have agreed to *anything* that would let me get out of the building alive.

Only later, driving home, did I ponder the consequences of what I had agreed to, did I consider what on Earth I was going to do next. What could I possibly tell Marge and Tod? How could I explain our sudden enormous riches?

And what about my mission, my Hippocratic oath, my duty to suffering humanity? Those imperatives still existed, and the

357

decision was still in my hands. For what the board fortunately did not know was that the dreadnaught virus had *not* been completely destroyed. The sovereign cure for the Plague was still alive and replicating in my body. I was immune to all possible Plague variants.

And that immunity was infectious.

John David

I made my way up the coast to the Bay Area, and there I was stymied, brothers and sisters. I kept on the move—San Jose, Oakland, Marin County, and back again in tight little circles. The SPs were everywhere, they were really paranoid, they were rounding up people at random on the street, and it wasn't only the likes of me they were after.

The Word had come down from the usual somewhere to put the heat on. The SPs around the meatbars were tighter than a ten-year-old's asshole. Everyone they rousted got their cards run through the national data bank, I mean there were roadblocks and traffic jams ten miles long. People were disappearing wholesale. And the poop in the underground was that they were doing all this to come down as hard as they knew how on anyone "doing the work of Our Lady."

And that was me, brothers and sisters. I mean, I was determined to meatfuck anything I could anyway, and calling myself a "Lover of Our Lady" was not only the best come-on line anyone had ever invented, it was ready access to the safe houses that were opening up everywhere in response to the heat, to cheap and even free pallies, to the whole black-carder underground. For sure, I'm not saying that I bought any of that bullshit about sacred duty to evolve immunity into the species, but I sure dished plenty of it out when it made life easy.

But why did I stick around the Bay Area in the middle of the worst Sex Police action in the country when sooner or later I figured to get caught in a sweep? When I did, and my phony blue card came up null, they'd run a make on my prints and come up with my Legion record, and then they'd for sure flush me down their toilet bowl, you better believe it!

Well, for one thing, the marks were coming out again, I was beginning to get moldy and obvious, and here at least I had some chance of disappearing into the underground. And for another, I was getting weak and feverish and maybe not thinking too clearly.

And there was San Francisco, clearly visible across the Bay. Where the SPs never went. The only safe place for a wanted zombie like me. The only place I could bop till I dropped. Sitting there staring me in the face. Somehow, getting there had become a goal in itself, something I just had to do before I went under. What else was left?

But there was an impenetrable line of razor wire and laser traps and crack SP troops across the Peninsula behind it and a bay full of pig boats patrolling its coastline and enough gunships buzzing around it day and night to take Brazil. All designed to keep the meatfuckers inside. But just as effective in keeping the likes of me out.

No one ever got out of San Francisco. And there was only one way in. Your card came up black, and the SPs loaded you into a chopper and dumped you inside from five feet up. But if the SP ever got its meathooks on me, they'd punch my ticket for sure, and not for San Francisco, you better believe it!

The only other way in was a loner kamikaze run on the blockade, and that was even more certain death. Oh yeah, I knew I was deep into Condition Terminal now, but *that* spaced out yet, I wasn't!

Dr. Richard Bruno

What I did, for the time being, was nothing. I banked my new riches in a separate account and told Marge nothing. I showed up at the lab every day and puttered around doing nothing.

I staggered around in a trance like a moral zombie, hating myself every waking moment of every awful day. I had successfully performed my life's mission. I had conquered the Enemy. I could have been the Savior of mankind. I *should* have been the Savior of mankind.

Instead, all I could do was hide the secret from my wife and collect my blood money.

Would I have done it on my own? Would morality finally have been enough? Would I have ultimately been faithful to the oath of Hippocrates? I would never know.

My son Tod took the decision out of my hands.

One night the Sex Police showed up at our house with Tod in custody. He had been caught in a raid on a meatbar. His card had come up blue against the national data bank and he had passed a spot genome test that I had never heard of before, so they really had nothing to hold him for.

But they read Marge and myself the riot act. This kid was caught peddling his ass in a meatbar, we don't know how long he's been doing it, he claims it was his first time. He's blue now, but you know what the odds are. Get the horny little bastard an interface and scare the shit out of him, or he's gonna end up as Condition Terminal in San Francisco.

While Marge broke down and wept, I had my awkward man-to-man with Tod, poor little guy. "Do you realize what you've been risking?" I demanded.

He nodded miserably. "Yeah," he said, "but . . . but isn't it worth it?"

"Worth it!"

"Oh, Dad, you knew what it was like, flesh on flesh without all this damned metal and rubber! How could you expect me to live my whole life without ever having that?"

"It's your *life* we're talking about, Tod!"

"So what!" he cried defiantly. "We're all gonna die sooner or later anyway! I'd rather live a real life while I can than die an old coward without ever knowing anything but interfaces and sex machines! I'd rather take my chances and be a man! I'd rather die brave than live like . . . like . . . like a pussy! Wouldn't you?"

What could I possibly say to that? What would *he* say if he knew my wonderful and awful secret? How could I even look my own son in the eye, let alone continue this lying lecture? What could I possibly do now?

Only one thing.

If I was still too much of a cowering creature to save the world at the expense of my own life, at least I could contrive to save my son, and without alerting the powers at Sutcliffe in the process. And at least covertly pass this awful burden off to someone else.

Tod's plight had shown me the way and given me the courage to act.

A stiff dick might ordinarily know no conscience. But mine was the exception that proved the rule. It *was* my conscience now. *Use me*, it demanded. *Use me and let a Plague of life loose in the world.*

Linda Lewin

"I may be a meatwhore, but I'm not a monster!" I told him indignantly. "What you're asking me to do is the most loathsome thing I've ever heard!"

He had approached me in a meatbar in Palo Alto.

I had been spending a lot of time in such places lately, for here the Work of Our Lady was doubly important. For here bitter and twisted black-carders came with their phony blue cards to take sexual vengeance on foolish blue-carders. Every time I could persuade one of these wretches to take their comfort in me, I saved someone from the Plague. And every time I could persuade him afterward to do the Work of Our Lady instead of infecting more blue-carders, the ranks of the Lovers of Our Lady grew.

But Richard, as he called himself, was something different, the lowest creature I had ever encountered even in a place like this.

He wanted me to have meat with him, and then, a week later, to have meat with his own teenage son! And I could name my own price.

"What's so terrible about that?" he said ingenuously. "Your card will come up blue, won't it?" But his sickly twisted grin told me all too well that he knew the truth. Or part of it.

I knew what a chance I was taking. He could be undercover SP. He could be anything. But if I just refused and walked away, he'd only find another meatwhore with a phony blue card more than willing to take his money to do this terrible thing.

"I'm *her*," I told him. "I'm Our Lady of the Living Dead."

He didn't even know who Our Lady was or the nature of the Work we were doing. So I told him.

"And that's why I won't do what you ask. I only have sex with black-carders. I've Got It. And I'll give the Plague to you and your son. And so would any meatwhore you're likely to find. Don't you really know that?"

361

"You don't understand," he insisted. "How could you? You can't give me the Plague, no one can. I'm immune."

"You're *what*?"

And he told me the the most outrageous story. He told me that he was Dr. Richard Bruno of the Sutcliffe Corporation, that he had developed an organism that conferred immunity to all Plague variants. That he could infect me with it and make me a carrier. That's why he wanted me to have meat with his son, to pass this so-called dreadnaught virus to him.

"You really expect a girl to believe a line like that?"

"You don't have to believe anything now," he told me. "Just have meat with me now; you've already Got It, so you have nothing to lose. A week later, meet me here, and I'll take you to a doctor. We'll do a full workup. If you test out blue, you'll know I'm telling the truth. I'll give you fifty thousand right now, and another fifty thousand after you've had meat with Tod. Even if I'm lying, you're still a hundred thousand richer, and you've lost nothing."

"But if you're lying to me, I'll have given you the Plague!" I told him. "I won't risk that."

"Why not? I'm the one taking the risk, not you."

"But—"

"You *do* know what I'll do if you refuse, don't you?" he said, leering at me. "I'll just offer someone with less scruples the same deal. Even if I'm just a lying lunatic, you won't have saved anyone from anything."

He had me there. I shrugged.

"I've got a room just around the corner," I told him.

Dr. Richard Bruno

It was the best sexual experience I've ever had in my life, or at any rate since my teenage years, back before the Plague. Flesh on flesh with no intervening interface or rubber, and with no fear of infection either, the pure simple naked act as it was meant to be. And while some part of me knew that it was adultery, an act of disloyalty to Marge, a better and higher part of me knew that it was an act of loyalty to a higher moral imperative—to Tod, to suffering humanity—and that only sharpened my pleasure.

But I did feel shame afterward and not for the adultery. For *this*, this pure simple act of what was once quite ordinary and natural pleasure, was what I had the power to bring back into the world, not just for me and for her and for Tod, but for everyone everywhere. This was my victory over the Enemy. And what was I doing with it?

Nothing. I was taking a million dollars a year's blood money to hold my silence and, admittedly, to preserve my own life.

But now that I had already taken the first step upon it, a way opened up before me. I could hold my silence and keep taking the money, but I could spread the dreadnaught virus far and wide, via this cult of Our Lady and my own clandestine action.

The moral imperatives of the oath of Hippocrates and the fondest desire of any man coincided. It was my duty to have meat with as many women as I could as quickly as possible.

Linda Lewin

I hadn't even dared to let myself *want* to believe it, but oh God, it was true!

The underground doctor to whom Richard Bruno had taken me ran antibody tests and viral protein tests and examined blood, mucus, and tissue samples through an electron microscope.

There was no doubt about it. I was free of all strains of the Plague. Indeed, there was not a retrovirus of any kind in my body.

"Do you know what this means?" I cried ecstatically on the street outside.

"Indeed I do. The long nightmare of the Plague Years is coming to an end. We're carriers of life—"

"And it's our duty to spread it!"

"First to my son. Then to as many others as quickly as possible. We need to infect as many vectors as we can before . . . in case . . . so that no matter what happens to us . . . "

I hugged him. I kissed him. In a way, in that moment, I think I began to love him.

"When?" I asked him breathlessly.

"Tonight. I'll bring him to your room."

Dr. Richard Bruno

Tod was all hot sweaty excitement when I told him I was taking him to a real human whore. "Oh Dad, Dad, thank you . . ." he cried. But then he hesitated. "This girl . . . I mean, you're sure she's . . . you know . . ."

Now *I* hesitated. Between telling him the easy lie that I had found him a real blue-carder or telling him the whole improbable truth. I sighed. I screwed up my courage. I had lived too long with deception.

"It's really true?" Tod said when I had finished. "The dreadnaught virus? What they did at Sutcliffe? All that money?"

I nodded. "Do you believe me, Tod?"

"Well yeah . . . I mean I want to, but . . . but why haven't you told Mom? Why haven't you . . . you know, given it to her?"

"Would she have trusted me?"

"I dunno . . . I guess not. . . ."

"Do *you* trust me?"

"I want to . . . I mean . . ." He looked into my eyes for long moments. "I guess I trust you enough to take the chance," he finally said. "I'm the one that did all the talking about being brave, huh, Dad. . . ."

I hugged my son to me. And I took him to Linda Lewin's room. He entered tremulously but he stayed almost two hours.

Linda Lewin

I longed to shout the glorious truth from the rooftops, but when Richard told me the whole horrible story of what had happened at Sutcliffe, I had to agree that I should continue the Work of Our Lady as before, spread the dreadnaught virus as far and wide as possible among the unknowing before those who would stop us could find out what was happening. It was hard to believe that such greedy evil was possible, but the fact that I was cured and the world knew nothing about the dreadnaught proved the sad truth that it was.

Richard swore Tod to secrecy too, and together and separately the three of us began to spread the joyful infection around Palo Alto, telling no one.

Why did I stay in Palo Alto for two weeks instead of resuming my usual rounds up and down California, when in fact spreading the cure around the state as quickly as possible would have probably been wiser and more effective?

Perhaps I felt the need to be near the only two people who shared the glorious secret and the deadly danger of discovery. Perhaps I had fallen in love in a strange way with Richard, with this tormented, fearful, but oh so brave man.

More likely that I knew even then in my heart of hearts that this couldn't last, that sooner or later Sutcliffe would get wind of it and we would have to run. And when that happened, Richard and Tod would be helpless naifs without me. Only Our Lady would have the connections and road wisdom to even have a chance to keep them one step ahead of our pursuers.

Dr. Richard Bruno

Once again, what could I possibly tell Marge? The whole story, including the fact that my Hippocratic oath required me to have meat with as many anonymous women as I could? That I had our son similarly doing his duty to the species?

Obviously I had been inexorably forced step by step into such extreme levels of marital deception that there was no way I could now get her to believe the truth, let alone accept its tomcatting moral imperative.

Yet, tormented as I was by the monstrous series of deceptions I was forced to inflict upon my wife, I had to admit that I was enjoying it.

After all, no other men in all the world had the possibility of enjoying sex as Tod and I did. Meat on meat as it was meant to be, and not only free of fear of the Plague, but knowing that we were granting a great secret boon with our favors, that we were serving the highest good of our species in the bargain.

And I was cementing a unique relationship with my son. Tod and I became confidants on a level that few fathers and sons achieve. Swapping tales of our sexual exploits, but sharing the problem of how to recruit Marge to the cause too.

Or, at the very least, infect her with the dreadnaught. But Marge would never have meat with me. Nor would she willingly abandon monogamy. Sexually, psychologically, Marge was a child of the Plague Years, and even if she were to be convinced of the whole truth, she would never condone the need for my profuse infidelities, let alone agree to spread the dreadnaught in the meatbars herself.

In retrospect, of course, it was quite obvious that things could not really go on like this for long.

They didn't.

Tod got caught in an SP raid on a meatbar again.

But they didn't drag him home this time. Instead, the news came on the telephone, and it was Marge who chanced to take the call. Tod was being held at the Palo Alto SP headquarters. Other detainees had told the SP that he had been a regular. Black-carders had admitted having meat with him. He was undergoing testing now and his card was sure to come up black.

"Don't worry," I told her when she relayed this information in a state of numb, teary panic, "they'll have to let him go. He'll test out blue, I promise."

"You're crazy, Richard, that's plain impossible! You're out of your mind!"

"If you think I'm crazy now," I said, pouring her a big drink, "wait till I get drunk enough to tell you why!"

I gulped down two quick ones myself before I found the courage to begin, and kept drinking as I babbled out the whole story.

"Now let me give the dreadnaught to you," I woozed when I was finished, reaching out for her in a state of sloppy inebriation.

She shrieked, pulled away from me, ran around the living room screaming, "You animal! You're crazy! You've killed our son! Stay away from me! Stay away from me!"

How can I explain or excuse what happened next? I was drunk out of my mind, but another part of me was running on coldly logical automatic. If there could be such a thing as loving rape, now was the time for it. Marge was certain that I was a sinkhole of the Plague, and there was only one way I could ever convince her of the truth. I had to infect her with the dreadnaught, and I couldn't take no for an answer.

The short and nasty of it was that I meatraped my own wife, knowing I was doing the right thing even as she fought with all

366

her strength against me, convinced that she was fighting to keep herself from certain infection with the Plague. It was brutal and horrible and I loathed myself for what I was doing even as I knew full well that it was ultimately right.

And left her there sobbing while I reeled off into the night to retrieve Tod from the SP.

I was in a drunken fury, I was a medical heavyweight, I demanded that they run a full battery of tests on Tod and myself, and I browbeat the tired SP timeserver who ran them unmercifully. When they all turned out blue, I threatened lawsuits and dire political recriminations if Tod were not released to my custody at once, and succeeded thereby in deflecting his attention from the "anomalous organism" he had noticed in our bloodstreams long enough to get us out the door.

But the "anomalous organism" would be noted in his report. And Sutcliffe would be keeping close tabs on my data file, and there were certainly people on their end who would put one and one and one together. It was only a question of how much time it would take.

And we couldn't stay around to find out. We had to run. Tod, myself, Linda, and Marge. But where? And how?

We drove to Linda's and had to wait outside for half an hour till the man she was with left.

Linda Lewin

"There's only one place we can go," I told Tod and Richard. "Only one place we can hide where the SP can't come after us . . ."

"The San Francisco Quarantine Zone?" Richard stammered.

I nodded. "The SP won't go into San Francisco. There isn't a Fuck-Q alive who'd be willing to do it."

"But . . . *San Francisco* . . . ?"

"Remember, *we* have nothing to fear from the Plague," I told them. "Besides . . . can you think of anywhere where what we three have is more needed?"

"But how can we even *get* inside the Zone?"

I had to think about that one for a good long while. I had never even heard of anyone trying to get past the SP *into* San Francisco. On the other hand, neither had the SP. . . .

367

"Our best bet would be by boat from Sausalito. We wait for a good foggy night, then cross the Golden Gate through the fogbank in a wooden rowboat, no motor noise, no radar profile. The patrol boats stick in close to San Francisco and they're watching the coastline, not the Bay. The helicopters won't be able to see us through the fog even if they are flying. . . ."

"Sounds like risky business," Richard said dubiously.

"Any better ideas?"

Richard shrugged. "Let's go collect Marge," he said.

Dr. Richard Bruno

The three of us piled into Linda's car—they'd be looking for mine once they were looking for anything—and drove back to our house.

Marge was still in a state of shock when we got there. Even when she saw Tod, even when he and Linda backed up my story, she still couldn't quite believe me. She started to come around a bit when I showed her the enormous balance in my secret account.

But when I told her we had to flee to San Francisco, she fell apart all over again. There was no time for further persuasion. Richard, Linda, and I were forced to wrestle her into the car by brute force, with my hand clamped over her mouth to prevent her from screaming.

We drove around the rim of the bay to Sausalito, bought a rowboat, rented motel rooms, and waited.

The fog didn't roll in good and thick until two nights later. During these two days, with Tod and Linda and myself talking to her almost nonstop, Marge slowly came to believe the truth.

But accepting the fact that all of us had a moral duty to spread the dreadnaught in the only way possible was a bit more than she could swallow. She could accept it intellectually, but she remained emotionally shattered.

"I believe you, Richard, truly I do," she admitted as the sun went down on our last day in Sausalito. "I can even admit that what you're doing is probably the right thing. But me, I just can't. . . ."

"I know," I told her, hugging her to me. "It's hard for me

368

too. . . ." and I made tender love to her, meat on meat as it was meant to be, for what was to prove to be the last time.

That night a big bank of fog rolled in through the gap in the Golden Gate Bridge, a tall one too, that kept the gunships high above the San Francisco shoreline. It was now or never.

Tod hesitated on the pier.

"Scared?"

He nodded.

"Me too, Tod."

He clasped my hand. "I'm scared, Dad," he said softly. "I mean, I know we don't have much of a chance of making it. . . . But if anything happens . . . I want you to know that I wouldn't have it any other way. . . . We had to do what we did. I love you, Dad. You're the bravest man I've ever known."

"And I'm proud to have you for a son," I said with tears in my eyes. "I only wish . . ."

"Don't say it, Dad."

I hugged him to me, and then we all piled into the boat, and Tod and I began to row.

The currents were tricky and kept pushing us east and the going was tougher than I had anticipated, but we steered for the lights of the city and made dogged progress.

We couldn't have been more than five hundred yards from the shore when a spotlight beam suddenly pinned us in a dazzling circle of pearly light. "Rowboat heave to! Rowboat heave to!"

So near and yet so far! If the SP caught us, we were finished. We had no choice but to row for it.

We pulled out of the spotlight and zigged and zagged toward the shore while a motor roared back and forth behind us and the spotlight flitted randomly over the flat waters. The fog was quite thick, and they had trouble picking us up again.

When they finally did we were within two hundred yards of the shore. And then they opened up with some kind of heavy machine-gun.

"We're sitting ducks in this boat!" Tod shouted. "Got to swim for it!" And he dived overboard and down into the darkness of the waters under a hail of bullets.

Everything seemed to happen at once. The boat tipped as Tod dived, Linda rolled over the side, Marge panicked and fell overboard, the boat turned turtle—

And we were all in the cold water, swimming as far as we could under water before surfacing for air, catching quick breaths, swimming for our lives beneath a random fusillade of bullets and a skittery searchlight beam.

There was no room for thought or even fear as I swam for my life with aching lungs, no time or space to feel the horror of what was happening. Until, gasping for air, exhausted and freezing, I clawed my way up a rocky beach.

Out across the dark waters, the searchlight still roamed and the machine-gun fire still flashed and chattered. Linda Lewin crawled up beside me, panting and coughing. We lay there, not moving, not talking, not thinking, for a long time, until the gunboat finally gave up and disappeared into the fog.

Then we got up and searched the beach for at least an hour.

Tod and Marge were nowhere to be found.

"Maybe they made it farther up the beach," Linda suggested wanly.

But I knew better. I could feel the void in my heart. They were gone. They were gone, and I had killed them as surely as if the hand on the machine-gun trigger had been mine.

"Richard—"

I pulled away from her comforting embrace.

"Richard—"

I turned away from her and let a cold black despair roll like a fog bank into my mind, erasing all thought, and filling me with itself, wondering whether it would ever roll out again.

And hoping in that endless bleak moment that it never would.

John David

I suppose I knew it had to happen sooner or later, brothers and sisters, but at least I thought I'd be able to go down fighting and take some of the meatfuckers with me.

It didn't happen that way. They got me while I was asleep, would you believe it!

I was going downhill fast, I was feverish, weak, and I wasn't really thinking, I mean I was wandering the streets like an obvious zombie for real. I got picked up by some people whose faces I don't even remember who took me to an Our Lady safe house in Berkeley, where I passed out as soon as I hit the mattress.

Some meatfuckin' safe house!

I got woke up in the middle of the night by a gun butt in the back of the neck and another in my belly. They rounded everyone in the joint up and hauled us to the SP station. They ran everyone's cards against the national data bank.

Everyone but me. Me, they didn't have to bother, seeing as I was an obvious Condition Terminal and they had caught me with about a dozen assorted phony blue cards in my kit. Me, they just took my finger and retina prints and faxed 'em to Washington.

"Well, well, well," the SP lieutenant purred after no more than half an hour. "John David recently of the Legion, wanted for about ten thousand counts of murder, meatrape, and ID forgery, not to mention robbery, insurrection, border crashing, and treason. You're a bad boy, aren't you, John? But I'm real pleased to meet you. I get the feeling you're gonna get me a nice promotion. Tell you what, if you do, the night before they do you, your last meal's on me."

Walter T. Bigelow

Not content with possessing my wife, Satan pursued me to my office. First the blasphemous cult of Our Lady and then a series of anomalies in the San Francisco Bay Area that seemed to indicate that the national data bank had somehow been compromised.

It was common enough for phony blue cards to come up black against the national data bank. But it was unheard of for anyone caught with a forged blue card not to prove out black upon actual testing for the Plague, for of course it made absolutely no sense for someone with a valid blue card to use a forged one.

But it was happening around the Bay Area. There were almost a dozen cases.

And now this truly bizarre incident last night in the same locale. Four people in a rowboat had actually tried to run the Quarantine blockade *into* San Francisco! Two of them seemed to have actually made it.

When the bodies of the other two were fished out of the Bay, they proved to be Tod and Marge Bruno, the son and daughter of one Dr. Richard Bruno, a prominent genetic synthesizer with the Sutcliffe Corporation.

The local SP commandant was due for a promotion or at least a commendation.

He had run all three names through the national data bank. Tod Bruno had been caught in a meatbar sweep three days previously. Although many witnesses claimed he was an habitué, he had come out blue under a full spectrum of tests. The commandant had had the wit to dig deeper and found that some "anomalous organism" had been noted in the actual report.

Instinct had caused him to order the bodies of Tod and Marge Bruno to be given a thorough and complete autopsy down to the molecular level. And it was that report that put me on a plane for San Jose.

There was a strange "pseudovirus" written into both of their genomes. It shared many sequences with the Plague virus but resembled no known or extrapolated variant, and it had other sequences that could not have evolved naturally. The bodies had been dead too long to try to culture it.

An unknown "pseudovirus" in the bodies of the family of a prominent genetic synthesizer . . . It could only be one thing—an unreported Condition Black incident at Sutcliffe. And the ultimate handiwork of the Devil had been released—some kind of horrible artificial human parasite, a manmade Plague variant. We had two corpses that had been infected with it, and I was virtually certain that Bruno at least was also infected, and was alive somewhere in San Francisco.

What might happen in that cesspit of Satan was none of my affair, but Tod Bruno had been infected when he was picked up in a meatbar outside the Quarantine Zone, and he had passed through a full battery of tests and come out blue.

Meaning that this monstrous thing was invisible to all our standard Plague tests. What had the Devil wrought at the Sutcliffe Corporation?

As I flew westward, I had the unshakable conviction that I was flying toward some climactic confrontation with the Adversary, that the battle of Armageddon had already begun.

San Francisco was not what I had expected. I'm not sure what I had really expected, a foul Sodom of ruins and rotting zombies, maybe, but this was not it.

The streets were clean and the quaint buildings lovingly cared for. The famous old cable cars were still running and so were the buses. The restaurants were open, the bars were crowded, and there were cabarets and theaters. There were even friendly cops walking beats.

Food and various necessities were allowed in through the Daly City Quarantine Line and sterilized products allowed out, so the city did have an economy connected to the outside world. The place was poor, of course, but the people inside it held together to see themselves through. Food was expensive in the restaurants but artificially cheap in the markets. Housing was crowded, but the rents were kept low, and the indigent or homeless were put up in public buildings and abandoned BART stations.

Oh yes, there were many horrible Condition Terminals walking around, but many more people who could have easily melted into the underground life outside. And there was something quite touching about how all the temporarily healthy deferred to and showed such tender regard for the obvious Living Dead, something that reminded me of dear old Max.

Indeed his spirit seemed to hover over this doomed but fatalistically gay-spirited city. Of necessity, everyone was forced to be a Saint Max here, and although the Lovers of Our Lady did not exist as such, everyone here seemed to be doing the Work.

No one here had to worry about Getting It, or being carded, or picked up by the SP. All of that had already happened to all of them. So, while there were more open gays here than I had ever thought to see in my life, stranger still to say, there was less . . . perversion in San Francisco than anywhere else I had ever been.

No meatbars as such, for every bar was a meatbar. Hardly any sex machine parlors, for the people of San Francisco, already all under sentence of death, could give one another love freely, like what natural men and women must once have been. Even the obviously terminal had their needs tenderly cared for.

No place I had ever been seemed more like home.

373

Only the pall of Plague that hung over the city marred the sweetness of the atmosphere, and that seemed softened by the fogs, pinkened by the sunsets, lightened by the deathhouse gaiety and wistful philosophic melancholy with which the citizens confronted it. "Everyone's born under a death sentence anyway," went the popular saying. "Here at least we all know it. There is no tomorrow sooner or later, so why not live and love today?"

Uncertain of what to do next, I began doing the Work of Our Lady in the usual manner, offering myself to anyone and everyone, spreading the dreadnaught slowly, but unsure as to whether or when to spread the glorious news.

I would have been happy there—indeed the truth of it was that I *was* happy—even while I sorrowed for poor Richard.

Richard, though, was like a little child whom I had to lead around like a creature in a daze. All his energy and motivation seemed to have vanished with his wife and son. I could understand his grief and guilt, but this couldn't last forever.

"We've got work to do, Richard, glorious and important work," I kept telling him. "We've got to spread the dreadnaught among these people."

Mostly, he stared at me blankly. Sometimes he managed a feeble, "You do it."

After a few days of this, I decided that I could no longer wait for Richard to come around. I had to make the fateful decision on my own.

This spreading the dreadnaught by myself clandestinely was just too slow. If there were evil men out there intent on stopping the dreadnaught, they'd be tracking us down. I needed to infect thousands, tens of thousands, before they could act, and the only way that could happen would be if the people of San Francisco *knew* what they were spreading and set out to do it systematically.

First I began revealing myself as Our Lady to my lovers and in the bars, and there were enough people in San Francisco who had once done the Work on the outside—even some I had once known in my circuit-riding days—so that my claim gained credibility.

In one sense, the people of San Francisco had always been doing the Work of Our Lady, of Saint Max, but in another sense, the legend had never been central here. In San Francisco, the

374

people did the Work of Our Lady to please one another and themselves, not because they believed they were serving the species' only hope.

But then I began recruiting an army of Lovers of Our Lady and I did it by proclaiming the glorious truth.

That the shattered man I sheltered in my rooms was a great scientist and an even greater hero. That he had developed the dreadnaught organism. That through him I had been infected with the gift of life. That I could infect anyone I had meat with with the cure, that anyone I had meat with would also become infectious. That the Plague Years, through Richard Bruno's instrumentality and at horrible personal cost to himself, were now coming to an end.

That all we had to do was what we were doing already—love one another.

There were more skeptics than believers at first, of course. "Bring me your Terminals," I told them. "Let them have meat with Our Lady. When they're cured, the whole city will see I'm telling the truth."

Walter T. Bigelow

Satan himself seemed to be speaking through Harlow Prinz when I confronted him, laughing his final laugh, for what the president of Sutcliffe finally admitted under extreme duress was worse, far worse, than what I had originally feared.

Bruno had been working on some sort of Plague-killer virus. But he had been building it around a Plague variant and something went wrong. He had created instead a Plague variant that mutated randomly every time it reproduced. That was invisible not only to all current tests short of full-scale molecular analysis, but would *remain so* to anything that could be devised.

There *had* been a Condition Black, but only inside the lab, and there were plenty of reports to prove that Sutcliffe had followed proper procedure, as well as a mountain of legal briefs supporting the position that such internally contained Condition Blacks need not be reported to the SP.

"We had no idea Bruno was infected," Prinz claimed. "Isn't that right, Warren?"

Warren Feinstein, Sutcliffe's chairman, who had sat there silently all the while with the most peculiar expression on his face, fidgeted nervously. "No . . . I mean yes . . . I mean how can we be so sure he *was* infected . . . ?"

"The man's wife and son were infected, now weren't they, Warren?" Prinz snapped. "You heard the director. Extreme measures must be taken at once to contain this thing!"

"But—"

"Wait a minute!" I cried. "Surely you're not suggesting the man . . . had *meatsex* with his wife and . . . and his *son* knowing he was infected?"

"Let's hope so," Prinz said. "At any rate, we have no choice but to act on that assumption."

"What?"

"Because if he didn't . . ." Prinz shuddered. "If he didn't, then we may all be doomed. Because if Tod and Marge Bruno *weren't* infected sexually, then this new virus has to be what we've always feared most—a Plague variant that doesn't need sexual or intravenous vectors, an ambient version that spreads through the air like the common cold."

"Oh my God."

"You have no alternative, Mr. Director," Prinz went on relentlessly. "You must obtain the necessary authority from the president and have San Francisco sterilized at once."

"Sterilized?"

"Nuked. Condition Black procedure, admittedly on a rather extreme scale."

"That's monstrous, Harlow!" Feinstein shouted. "This is going too far! We've got to—"

"Shut up, Warren!" Prinz snapped. "Consider the alternative!"

Feinstein slumped over in his chair.

"If this thing *is* ambient, we're all doomed anyway, so what's the difference?" Prinz said in Satan's cold, insinuating voice. "But if it isn't, and if Bruno's spreading it in San Francisco . . ."

"You can't just kill a million people on the supposition that—"

"Shut up, Warren!" Prinz snapped. "You can't afford to listen to this sentimental fool, Mr. Director. You've got to be strong. You've got to do your duty."

My duty? But where did that lie? If I had the San Francisco

Quarantine Zone sterilized by a thermonuclear explosion, Bruno would be vaporized. And I had to have Bruno live for interrogation before I did any such thing, I realized. I had to know whether he had had meatsex with his wife and son. For if he had, then I would know the virus *wasn't* ambient, that there was hope. *Then* and only then could I have San Francisco sterilized with a clear conscience.

Then and only then would such an awful decision serve God and not the Devil.

I had to find someone willing to go into San Francisco and bring Bruno out. But where was I going to find someone crazy or self-sacrificing enough to do that?

John David

I was feeling pretty punk when two SPs dragged me into an interrogation room, handcuffed me to a chair bolted to the floor, and then split.

But I came around fast, you better believe it, when old Walter T. himself walked into the room and shut the door behind him!

The old meatfucker came right to the point.

"I've been looking for someone very special, and the computer spit your name out," he told me. "I've got a job for you. Interested?"

"You gotta be kidding. . . ."

"We're going to drop you in San Francisco. I want you to bring a man out."

"Say what?" Well shit, brothers and sisters, I could hardly believe my ears. I mean, even in my present Condition Terminal, my ears pricked up at *that* one. And old Walter T., he sure didn't miss it.

"Interested, aren't you? Here's the deal. . . ."

And he told me. An SP helicopter would drop me into San Francisco, where I was to snatch and hold this guy Richard Bruno. Every afternoon at three o'clock they'd have a chopper circle Golden Gate Park for an hour. When I had Bruno, I'd shoot off a Very pistol, and they'd pick me up.

"What do you want this guy for?" I demanded.

"You have no need to know," he told me.

I eyed him dubiously. "What makes you think I'll want to

377

come out?'' I mean, this dumb meatfucker was gonna throw me into my briar patch, but what could possibly make him believe I'd do his dirty work for him and deliver some poor bastard to the SP? Could he *really* be as stupid as he seemed? It didn't seem real likely.

"Because upon delivery of Bruno you'll be given a full pardon for all your capital crimes."

"Hey, look at me, man, I've got maybe a month left anyway."

"You can go back into the Legion. As a captain."

"As a captain?" I snorted. "Shit, why not a bird colonel?"

"Why not indeed?"

"You're really serious, aren't you?" Jeez, what a tasty run I could have as a fuckin' brigade commander. But . . . "But I'm a goner anyway. What difference is it gonna make?"

"The Legion is going into Brazil again even as we speak," he told me. "We can pump you up with the best military pallies and all the coke and speed you can handle. And drop you into Brazil with colonel's wings at the head of a brigade twelve hours after you deliver Bruno. A short life, but a happy one."

"Terrific," I said, studying old Walter T. carefully. This still didn't quite add up. He was holding something back, and I had a feeling I wasn't gonna like it. "But what makes you so sure I wouldn't prefer to spend that short happy life in San Francisco?"

Now it was Walter T.'s turn to study *me* carefully, then shrug. "Because unless you bring Bruno out, that could be a lot shorter than you think."

"Huh?"

"We're going to drop you into San Francisco anyway, so I might as well tell you the truth," Bigelow said. "I get the feeling nothing else is really going to motivate you, but *this* surely will."

He told me, and it did.

Bruno was some kind of genetic synthesizer. He had screwed up real bad and created a new Plague variant that was invisible to all the standard tests and just might be able to spread through the air.

"So we need to know whether Bruno is infected with something that could be spreading around San Francisco right now, something that we can only hope to stop by . . . shall we say, measures of the maximum extremity."

Well, brothers and sisters, I didn't need any promotion to bird colonel to figure out what he meant by *that*. "You mean nuke San Francisco, don't you?"

"Unless we have Bruno to examine and unless that examination reassures us that he hasn't been spreading this thing, we really have no alternative. . . . I'll give you two weeks. After that, well . . ."

"You nuke San Francisco with me inside it!"

Bigelow nodded. "I think I can trust you to do your honest best, now, can't I?" he said.

Well, what could I say to that? Only one thing, brothers and sisters. What I told old Walter T. next.

"I want the coke and the speed and the pallies *right now*. All I can carry."

"Very well," he said. "Why not? Anything you need."

"I don't have any choice, now, do I?"

"None whatever."

If I hadn't been cuffed to the chair, I would have ripped off the old meatfucker's arm and beaten him to death with it. But even then, I had to admire his style, if you know what I mean. Turn the bastard's card black, and old Walter T. would have been right at home with us, fellow zombies.

Linda Lewin

After the marks started to fade from terminal cases and black-carders started proving out blue on the simple tests the underground docs put together, the word began to spread faster, and so did the dreadnaught, and the Lovers of Our Lady began to spread the good news on their own in the streets and bars of San Francisco.

One day a delegation came to me and took me to a rambling old house high on a hill above Buena Vista Park that they called the House of Our Lady of Love Reborn. They installed me in quarters on the third floor and they brought Richard with me.

There I was surrounded by the Lovers of Our Lady. And so was Richard. He was surrounded by people who cared for him, who loved him, who knew what heroic deeds he had done, and at what terrible cost. Slowly, far too slowly, he began to react to his surroundings, to mutter haltingly of his guilt and despair.

379

But he still refused to join in the Work, for he found the mere thought of sex loathsome, no matter who offered themselves to him, including myself.

And the Work itself, though proceeding apace, was going far too slowly. How long did we have before the outside world learned the truth? Months? Weeks? Days? And what would happen then? Indeed, might it be in the process of happening already?

What I needed to do was infect all of San Francisco with the dreadnaught, so that when the outside world finally intruded, it would be presented with the truth and its massive proof as a glorious fait accompli—an entire city, a Quarantine Zone once completely black, now entirely free of the Plague.

Once, long before most of the people here were born, San Francisco had experienced a magical few months that was called the Summer of Love, a legend that still lived in the myth of the city.

So I conceived the notion of a Week of Love, a celebration of the dreadnaught and a means of quickly spreading it to all, a carnival of sex, a citywide orgy, a festival of Our Lady of Love Reborn.

And perhaps via such a manifestation and celebration of what he had brought back into the world, Richard too might be reborn back into it. . . .

John David

The pallies they shot me up with before they dropped me in San Francisco didn't seem to do much good, but the speed and coke sure did, brothers and sisters. I might look like Condition Terminal on its last legs, but I was riding high and burning bright on the way out, you better believe it!

I expected San Francisco to be weird and wild, something like TJ before the SP moved in on us, but this was something else again, weird for sure, but not exactly this zombie's idea of *wild*.

The city was like something out of an old movie—clean, and neat, and like you know *quaint*, like some picture postcard of itself, and I found I could have just about any kind of meat with anyone I wanted to just by asking for it, even looking like I did.

There were plenty of terminal zombies like me walking around and plenty more outrageous faggots, but these people were like so damned sweet and kind and nicey-nice to us on the way out it made me want to puke. I mean all this peace and sympathy sex and love pissed me off so bad I just about *wanted* to see Wimp City nuked, if you know what I mean.

But not, of course, with me in it!

Bigelow had it covered. I had no choice at all. I had to get my crumbling ass in gear and get my mitts on Bruno, on my only ticket out.

Dr. Richard Bruno

I can hardly remember what it was like inside that place of darkness or even precisely how and when I began to emerge from it. First there was a soft warm light in my cold blackness, and then I slowly began to take notice of my surroundings.

I was living in an ancient Victorian house high on a hill in San Francisco, a place that was known as the House of Our Lady of Love Reborn. Linda Lewin was living there with me, and I knew that she had been caring for me through my long dark night. As had many others. For this was a house of love and hope. It was a kind of a brothel, and a kind of church, and what was being spread here was my dreadnaught virus. And all those who came and went here loved me.

"Dr. Feelgood," they all called me. Not the creature who had brought his wife and son to death, but the man who had brought love back into the world.

"You've grieved long enough, Richard; Marge and Tod are gone, and they deserve your grief," Linda told me. "But you've also done a wonderful thing, and that deserves your joy. Come join the party now. See what they died for. See what you've brought back into the world! This is the Festival of Our Lady of Love Reborn, but it's the Festival of Dr. Feelgood, too."

And she and the Lovers of Our Lady took me on a tour of San Francisco, on a tour of the carnival, on a tour through an erotic wonderland out of long-lost dreams.

The whole city was partying—in the bars and the parks and

the streets. It was Mardi Gras, it was the feast of Dionysus, it was the Summer of Love, it was beautiful madness. Everyone was drunk and stoned and deliriously happy, and people were making love, sharing meat, openly everywhere—in apartments, in bars, right out on the streets.

They were celebrating Love Reborn in the very act of creating it. They were celebrating the end of the Plague Years as they brought it to an end with their joyful flesh.

"Do you understand, Richard?" Linda asked later, back at the House of Our Lady of Love Reborn. "Marge and Tod are dead and they never lived to see what they died for, and that's a sad thing, and you're right to mourn. But they didn't die in vain, they died to help you bring love back into the world, and if they're watching from somewhere, you can know they're smiling down on you. And if they're not, if there's no God or Heaven, well then, we're all we've got, and we can only take shelter in the living. Do you understand?"

"I'm not sure, Linda . . ." I murmured.

"Then let me help you to begin now," she said, holding me in her arms. "Come take shelter in me."

And, hesitantly at first, but with a growing strange peace in my heart, a warrior's peace, a peace that had become determination by the time we had finished our lovemaking, I did.

And afterward, I understood. Marge and Tod were gone and nothing I could do would bring them back, and that was a terrible thing. The Plague Years had in one way or another made monsters and madmen of us all, we had all been trapped into grievous mistakes, fearful, and frustrated, and loathsome acts, and nothing we did now could change that either. We had *all* been victims, and perhaps the lives of all of us who lived through the Plague Years could never be made whole.

But that dark night was ending and a new day was dawning, and we, and I, had to act to give it birth and protect it into its full maturity. My personal life had died back there in San Francisco Bay with Marge and Tod and I had nothing left but my duty to the Hippocratic oath.

And vengeance.

Nothing I could do would ever bring my family back or entirely erase my guilt in their deaths. But I could take my vengeance on Prinz, on Feinstein, on the Sutcliffe board, I could do

382

my part in seeing to it that their worst fears were realized, that the dreadnaught virus they had sought to destroy spread far and wide, saving suffering humanity while it destroyed the Sutcliffe Corporation in the process.

Thus would my part in the twisted nightmare of the Plague Years end with the ultimate perverse yet joyful irony:

Just and loving vengeance.

So tomorrow I will go forth into San Francisco and join the Week of Love. And tonight I am sitting here in the House of Our Lady and writing my story in this journal, which is now concluding. When it is finished, it will be sent to the president, to the head of the Federal Quarantine Agency, to the news services, to the television networks. Before you let them act against us or tell you that this is all an evil lie, demand that they go in and test the populace or at least a good sample for Plague. That's all I ask. Know the truth for yourself. Tell others.

And I promise it will set all of you free.

John David

I had good photos of Bruno, but you ever try tracking down one guy in a city of a million? Especially in a city that seemed to have gone completely apeshit. Everyone seemed to be drunk or stoned. People were having meat *everywhere* right out in the open, in the streets, in the parks, in alleys. Half-dead as I was, they were still shoving their meat even at the likes of me, babbling a lot of crazy stuff about how they were saving me from the Plague, as if anything could help me now!

I was goin' out fast, I was a mess of sarcomas and secondary infections, weak, and feverish, and half out on my feet, taking enormous doses of speed and coke just to keep going. But, fast as I was going, I still knew that this city was gonna go faster, and with me in it, unless I could deliver Bruno to the SP. I mean, one way I had maybe three weeks left, the other only ten days.

An extra eleven days of life may not seem like such a big deal to *you*, brothers and sisters, but it sure as shit would if *you* were the one who knew that was the best you had left!

Anyway, it was enough to keep me focused on finding Bruno, even spaced and stoned and dying and staggering around in the biggest orgy the world had ever seen. And I started grilling random people on the street and being none too gentle about it.

I was so far gone I must have beaten the crap out of half-a-dozen of them before it got through to me that the "Dr. Feelgood" the whole damn city was babbling about was the very guy I was looking for. Dr. Richard Bruno, the son of a bitch who had maybe let loose the worst Plague variant ever and who for sure was gonna get all these assholes vaporized, and me with them; and they were somehow convinced the bastard was some kind of hero!

Well, after I copped to that, it wasn't much sweat tracking the famous Dr. Feelgood down. All I had to do was follow my nose and all the talk about him through the bars and streets until I ran into someone who told me he was partying in a certain bar in North Beach right now.

I got there just as he was walking out with a good-looking momma on his arm and a dreamy smile on his lips. As soon as I saw him, I went into motion, no time or energy left for tactics or thought.

"Okay, Bruno, you son of a bitch, you're comin' with me!" I shouted, grabbing him by his right arm and whipping it behind his back into a half-nelson bring-along.

Half-a-dozen guys started to move in, but, far gone as I was, I still had that covered. I already had my miniauto out and waving in their faces.

"This guy's comin' with me, assholes!" I screamed. "Anyone tries to stop me gets blown away!"

Then everything seemed to happen at once.

Some jerk got brave and slammed into my knees from behind.

I kicked blindly backward, fighting for balance.

Bruno yanked himself out of the half-nelson.

A circle of angry meat closed in.

I started firing without caring at what, whipping the miniauto in fanning fire at full rock and roll.

"Dr. Feelgood" got himself neatly stitched up the back from ass to shoulder by high-velocity slugs.

Bruno folded as everyone else came down on me like a ton of bricks.

Next thing I knew, I had had the shit thoroughly beaten out of me, and two guys were holding me up by the shoulders, and

Bruno was down there on the sidewalk croaking and looking up at me.

"Why?" he whispered with blood drooling out of his mouth.

"Don't die, you stupid meatfucker!" I screamed at him. "You're my only ticket out of here!"

"Kill the bastard!"

"Tear him apart!"

I laughed and laughed and laughed. I mean, what else was there to do? "Go ahead and kill me, suckers!" I told them all. "I'm dead already and so are you, gonna nuke you till you glow blue!"

"Cut his heart out!"

Bruno looked up at me from the sidewalk with this weird sad little grin, almost peaceful, kind of, as his light went out.

"No . . ." he said. "No more . . . just and loving vengeance, don't you see . . . Marge . . . Tod . . . it's nobody's fault . . . take him . . . take him. . . ."

His voice started to fade. He coughed up more blood.

"Take him where, Richard?" a woman said, leaning over him.

"Take him to Our Lady . . ." Bruno whispered. "Let him take shelter in . . . in . . ."

His lips moved but no more sound came out. And that was the end of that.

Bruno was dead.

So was I.

And in ten days, so was San Francisco.

Linda Lewin

They brought Richard's body back to the House of Our Lady of Love Reborn and laid him out on a couch. Half-a-dozen Lovers of Our Lady were restraining a wild-eyed young terminal case and being none too gentle about it.

And they told me what had happened. And Richard's dying words.

Only then did I really look at his murderer. His body was a mass of sarcomas. His frame was skeletal. His eyes were red and wild.

"Why?" I asked him in a strange imploring voice that surprised even me.

"My ticket out of here before they drop the Big One Lady but it's all over now ain't it do your damnedest we're all dead zombies anyway brothers and sisters. . . ."

He wasn't making sense, nor would he, I knew then. This poor creature was no more responsible for his actions than Richard had been when Marge and Tod died. I had heard of this sort of thing before. Condition Terminals turning berserker on the way out, taking as many as they could with them. He too was a victim of the Plague, as were we all.

And I understood Richard's last words now too, perhaps better even than he had in the saying of them. His life had been in a sense over already, and all this poor creature had done was set his tormented soul free. I understood why he had forgiven his assassin, for in that act of forgiving, he had at last found forgiveness for himself for the deaths on his own hands, or so at least I prayed to whatever gods there be.

"What should we do with the bastard?"

"Kill him!"

"Tear his damn heart out!"

"No!" I found myself saying. "I'll do it for you, Richard," I whispered, and I took his murderer's hand. "He forgave you, and so must I."

"Go ahead and kill me, don't want your forgiveness, it don't mean shit, I'm a dead man already and so are you!"

"No, you're not," I told him gently. "Let me take you upstairs and give you the good news."

John David

And she did, though of course I didn't believe a word of it at the time, not even after Our Lady gave my disgusting dying flesh the gift of her meat. Not that I was exactly in any mental condition for deep conversation anyway.

But days later, when the sarcomas began to disappear and my head cleared, I knew that the whole damn story that Linda had told me over and over again was all true.

I mean, I had sure done my share of evil, but what those meatfuckers at Sutcliffe had done was enough to make a combat medic puke! I never had no use for Walter T. Bigelow—and less so after the number he had run on me—but I was willing to bet that the old meatfucker had believed what he told me about poor Bruno. Those Sutcliffe creeps must have fed him their line about Bruno to get him to nuke the evidence of what they had done out of existence. And the dreadnaught virus along with it! Just to line their own pockets and save their own worthless asses!

And oh shit, Bigelow still believed it!

"What day is this?" I asked Linda when my head was finally clear enough to realize what all this meant and what was about to happen.

It was two days till the Big Flash.

"You've given me the good news, now I've gotta give you the bad news," I told her. And I did.

I had never seen Our Lady break down and cry before, but now she did. "Then poor Richard died for nothing. . . . And everyone here is doomed. . . . And no one will even know. . . . And the Plague will go on and on and on. . . ."

While she was moaning and sobbing, I did some fast thinking. I still had the Very pistol, and that SP chopper was going to circle Golden Gate Park at three for two more days. I had the means to bring it down, and if I could take it . . .

"You gotta find me a guy who can fly a helicopter," I said.

Our Lady stared at me blankly. I shook her by the shoulders. "Hey, you gotta snap out of it, Linda, and listen to me! I got a way to get us out of here before they drop the Big One!"

That brought her around, and I laid it out for her.

It was simple, really. We'd dress the helicopter pilot up in a trench coat and a slouch hat or something so no one could see he wasn't Bruno until I got us aboard the SP chopper.

"I'll take care of the rest," I promised. "Probably be just a pilot and a copilot, piece of cake. Then you come aboard, and we take off like a big-assed bird for the Marin side, ditch the chopper, and disappear. You saved my life, now I'll save yours."

Linda Lewin

"But what about *San Francisco*?" I said. "We can't just . . ."

John shrugged. "San Francisco is gonna be nuked out of existence anyway," he said. "Nothing we can do about that, our asses is all we can save."

"But all these people . . . and the dreadnaught virus . . ."

"Look at it this way—at least there'll be you and me left to spread it. . . ." He leered at me wolfishly. "I'll do my part to spread it far and wide, you better believe it, sister!"

"We just can't leave a whole city to die!"

"You got any better ideas?"

I stared at this poor savage creature, at this killing machine, at this ultimate victim of the Plague, and I thought and thought and thought, and finally I did.

"We'll capture the SP helicopter," I told him. "But we won't just escape. We'll fly down to Sutcliffe—"

"And do what?"

"Capture Harlow Prinz and Warren Feinstein. Take them to Bigelow."

"Huh?"

"Don't you see? When they tell Bigelow the truth—"

"Why the hell would they do that?"

I did my best to imitate John David's own fiercest leer. "I think I can leave that one up to you, now can't I?" I said.

He stared at me as his face slowly twisted into the mirror image of my own. "Yeah . . ." he said slowly. "I think I could enjoy that. . . ."

He frowned. "Only this is getting mighty dicey, sister. I mean, grabbing the chopper should be no sweat, and if all we was doing was putting it down in Marin and disappearing on foot, our chances would be pretty good. But faking the radio traffic long enough to fly the thing to Palo Alto and snatching the Sutcliffe creeps and getting them to Bigelow . . . Hey, the SP ain't the Legion, but they ain't that far out to lunch either. . . ."

"We've got to try it!"

"We wouldn't have a chance!"

"What if we had a diversion?" I blurted. "A big one . . ."

"A diversion?"

My blood ran cold as I said it. It was monstrous. Thousands might die. But the alternative was a million dead for no good cause. And monstrous as it was as a tactic, it was still the only just thing to do. Morally or practically, there really was no choice. It was the only chance we had to save the city, and the people had the right to know.

"What do you think would happen if everyone in San Francisco knew what you've just told me?" I said.

"That they were all going to be nuked in two days? Are you kidding? They'd go apeshit! They'd—"

"Storm the Quarantine Line en masse? Swarm out into the Bay in hundreds of small boats? Try to get across the gaps in the bridges?"

"Jeez, it'd be just like TJ, only a thousand times bigger, the SP would have its hands full, we just might be able to. . . ."

He studied me with new eyes. "Hey, beneath all that sweetness and light, you're pretty hard-core, you know that, sister? I mean, using *a whole city* as a diversion . . ."

"These people have a right to know what's going to happen anyway, don't they, John?" I told him. "Wouldn't *you* want to know? This way, even if we fail, they get to go out fighting for something and knowing why. Better in fire than in ice."

Walter T. Bigelow

Satan held me on the rack as I waited fruitlessly for David to extract Richard Bruno from San Francisco. Three and four times a day Harlow Prinz called me to demand in shriller and shriller tones that I have the city nuked. Was this the voice of God or the voice of the Devil? What did Jesus want me to do?

And then Satan put my back to the final wall.

Reports started coming in to the Daly City SP station, where I had ensconced myself, that a huge ragtag flotilla of small boats was leaving the San Francisco shoreline. Fighting had broken out all along the landward Quarantine Line.

It was becoming all too apparent that I could procrastinate no longer.

Mobs with bridging equipment were swarming onto the San Francisco ends of the Golden Gate and Oakland Bay bridges. The whole city was trying to break out of the Quarantine Zone, and they couldn't all be stopped by conventional means. Only a thermonuclear strike could prevent the new and far deadlier Plague strain from entering the general populace now.

I was forced to put in my long-delayed fateful call to the President of the United States. . . .

389

I had wanted the Big Breakout to start sharply at three to make damn sure the SP chopper wasn't scared off, but Linda had told too many people, and the Lovers of Our Lady were out in the streets whipping things up for hours beforehand, and the action began to come down raggedly an hour early.

But the fighting was going on at the borders, not the center, and Golden Gate Park was just about empty. The SP chopper pilot must've been over the city already, or maybe he was the sort of righteous asshole who followed the last order no matter what.

For even with half the city already throwing itself against the Quarantine Line, the chopper appeared over the park right on the money at three sharp.

I fired off the Very pistol, and down it came. I stuck my miniauto conspicuously in our pilot's back and frog-marched him to the open chopper door.

As I had figured, there were only a pilot and a copilot in the cockpit. The moment we were inside, I jammed the muzzle of my piece into the back of the pilot's neck.

"Outside, assholes!" I ordered. "But strip first! One word out of either of you and I blow you away!"

"Hey—"

"What the—"

"I told you, no lip! Out of those uniforms! Move your asses!"

They took one look at the miniauto and another at me, and stripped down to boxer shorts and T-shirts muy pronto, you better believe it!

"Out, assholes. Better run till you drop, and don't look back!"

I booted them out of the chopper and fired a long burst over their heads as Linda climbed aboard, and they ran for the nearest bushes.

Then me and our pilot put on their uniforms, which I figured would come in mighty handy if we ever made it to Sutcliffe, and off we went.

The skies were empty as we headed south over the city at about three thousand feet, but things started getting hairy as we approached the Quarantine Line.

I could see ragged mobs of people moving toward the SP

positions below, the SP troops were using heavy machine-guns and some light artillery, and the air beneath us was thick with gunpowder smoke, through which I could see sparkles, laser-straight tracers, occasional explosions.

All hell was breaking loose on the ground, and the airspace below us was full of helicopter gunships making low, slow strafing runs with cannon and rockets.

But all the thunder and lightning and confusion made it easier for us in the end, seeing as we were one chopper out of many.

"Bravo five three seven Charlie, what the hell are you doing up there?" a voice screeched at us over the radio.

"Don't answer!" I told our pilot. "Take her down into the traffic!"

When we had dropped down into the cloud of gunships, I screamed into my microphone, "Motherfucking black-carder faggot bastards!" And fired off a few rockets.

"Hey, those are *our* people down there!"

"And *our* asses up *here!*" You just fly this thing, and let me worry about tactics, okay!" And I fired off a couple more blind shots into the confusion.

It worked like a charm. Every time we got static on the radio, I cursed and screamed like a good combat animal and fired a few random rockets at the ground and nobody challenged us as we threaded our way south over the combat zone.

Once we were well clear, we went back up to three thousand feet, and the only traffic we saw between Daly City and Palo Alto was a few more gunships heading north into the mess far below who probably didn't even see us.

We landed inside the Sutcliffe compound right in front of the administration building and sat there with our rotor whumping as company rent-a-cops poured raggedly out of the building and finally managed to get us surrounded.

"Stay here, and fer chrissakes keep the engine running," I told Linda and the pilot. And climbed out of the chopper to make like a modern major general.

"National Emergency!" I barked at the bozo in charge of the rent-a-cops. "Direct orders from Walter T. Bigelow, director of the Federal Quarantine Agency. He wants Harlow Prinz and Warren Feinstein in his headquarters half an hour ago, and we're here to get 'em!"

"Hey, I got no orders to—"

"Argue with Bigelow if you want to!" I snapped. I gave the sucker a comradely shrug. "But I don't advise it. I mean, there's already been some kind of screw-up over this with all the heat going on, and he ain't exactly being reasonable just now, if you get me."

"I don't take my orders from the SP!"

"Your funeral, pal," I told him, nodding toward the chopper. "I got orders to blow the shit out of this place if I meet any resistance, and there's five more gunships orbiting just over the ridgeline in case you got any dumb notions . . ."

"Hey, hey, don't get your balls in an uproar," the head rent-a-cop soothed much more politely, and trotted off into the building.

I waited there outside the chopper surrounded by rent-a-cops for what seemed like ten thousand sweaty years but couldn't have been more than ten minutes by the clock.

Finally the head rent-a-cop appeared with two middle-aged bozos. One of them seemed to be staggering toward me in a daze, but the other was the sort of arrogant in-charge son of a bitch you want to kill on sight.

"What's the meaning of this?" he screamed in my face. "I'm Harlow Prinz, I'm the president of this company, and I don't—"

"And I'm just Walter Bigelow's errand boy, but I don't take shit either," I told him. "Except of course from the boss man, and I got enough of that for being late already! So do us both a big favor and get into this chopper." I waved my miniauto.

" 'Cause if you don't, shit is about to flow downhill, if you get my meaning."

The wimpy type, who had to be Warren Feinstein, started to climb aboard, but that murdering meatfucker Prinz stood there with his hands on his hips looking suspicious. He took a good long look at my badly fitting uniform. "Let's see your papers," he said.

I brought up the muzzle of my piece and pointed it at his belly button. "You're lookin' right at 'em," I said.

"Harlow, for chrissakes, he *means* it!" Feinstein said, and hustled his ass into the copter.

Prinz moved slowly past me to the door and reluctantly started to board the chopper, but he must've spotted Linda when he peered inside and put it all together.

'Cause he suddenly aimed a sloppy kick at my nuts that missed the target but knocked me off balance, yelled, "Shoot! Shoot!" at his rent-a-cops, and broke and ran.

Furious as I was, I didn't blow my combat cool.

I leaped through the door, scattering the rent-a-cops with a long fanning burst as our pilot lifted the chopper, and flipped myself into the copilot's seat.

By this time we were about a hundred feet in the air, and heading straight up into the wild blue yonder.

"Hold it right here a minute!" I told the pilot.

The rent-a-cops were scattering for cover. Only a few of 'em had the balls to fire a few useless shots up over their shoulders and they plinked harmlessly off the chopper's armored belly.

Prinz was running for the administration building. I smiled. I lined the bastard up in my sights and savored it just for a moment. This, after all, was the son of a bitch who was willing to let the Plague take us all to line his own pockets. I had wasted more citizens than I could count, but this was going to be special. This was going to be primo.

"Thanks ever so much for making my day," I told Harlow Prinz as he reached the stairs leading up to the entrance. And I fired a single rocket.

A perfect shot. It hit him right in the base of the spine and blew him to dogmeat.

I went aft, where Feinstein was cowering against a bulkhead. I grabbed him by the neck with my left hand, squeezed his jaws open, and jammed the muzzle of my piece down his throat.

"You saw what I did to your buddy," I told him. "And knowing what I know about you sons of bitches and what you've done, you better believe I enjoyed it just as much as I'll enjoy wasting *you* if you don't do exactly what you're told. Get the message, meatfucker?"

Feinstein nodded and I pulled the gun barrel out of his mouth. And when I tossed his worthless ass onto the deck, he just lay there blubbering. "I *told* Harlow he was going too far, it's not my fault, it wasn't my idea. Bigelow will believe me, won't he, I swear I'll tell him the truth, I never thought, I never knew. . . ."

"He *better* believe you, meatfucker, or a lot of asses are gonna be grass," I told him. "And *you* better believe that you're gonna go first!"

Walter T. Bigelow

The station was in an uproar. The situation was growing graver by the minute. The mob had bridged the gap in the Golden Gate and fighting was raging on the Marin side of the span. Our gunboats were sinking scores of small craft loaded to the gunwales with black-carders, but all was chaos on the Bay; they couldn't establish or hold a line. The landward Quarantine Line was crumbling under human wave onslaughts.

There was no alternative. When I got the President on the line I was going to have to ask him to authorize an immediate nuclear strike against San Francisco.

But while I was waiting for my call to the White House to get through, there was a commotion in my outer office, and a moment later an SP captain burst inside.

"Warren Feinstein's outside, Mr. Director," he stammered. "There's . . . there's a girl with him who says she's Our Lady of Love Reborn . . . and there's a man holding him at gunpoint. Says he's gonna blow his head off if we make a move and—"

There was a further commotion in the outer office and then Feinstein was rudely thrown through the doorway by a man who held the barrel of a miniauto at the back of his neck, followed by a young girl, and half-a-dozen SP men with drawn pistols.

The man with the miniauto was John David, whom I had sent into San Francisco after Richard Bruno. And he was wearing an SP uniform.

"What's the meaning of this?" I demanded. "This isn't Bruno! How did you—"

"No shit!" David snarled, prodding Feinstein with his gun barrel. "Go ahead, tell the man, or I'll blow your worthless head off!"

Tears poured from the eyes of Sutcliffe's chairman as he blubbered out the most incredible and chilling story.

"Harlow *lied* to you, Bruno's virus wasn't an ambient Plague variant, it was a *cure* for all Plague variants, an artificial venereal disease—"

"A cure? But then why—"

"—that conferred total immunity—"

"If it was a cure, then why on Earth did you suppress it?" I shouted at him. "Why did you tell me—"

"It's a venereal disease!" Feinstein babbled. "Spreads by itself, nothing for us to market, it would have bankrupted Sutcliffe, brought on an economic depression, Harlow insisted—"

I could not believe my ears. I could not be hearing this. "You suppressed a total cure for the Plague to preserve your own profits? My God, Prinz kept trying to get me to nuke San Francisco *just to keep Sutcliffe solvent*?"

Feinstein shook his head. "By then it was too late, don't you see?" he moaned. "The whole thing had gone too far. I warned him, I swear I did, but he insisted that San Francisco *had* to be nuked to cover up what we'd done. . . ."

Feinstein seemed to pull himself together with an enormous effort. "But you can't do that now," he said much more coherently. "You won't do that now. I'm willing to take my medicine, even if it means spending the rest of my life in jail. Harlow was wrong, monstrously wrong, and I was weak, horribly weak. You can't nuke San Francisco. You can't kill millions of people. You can't destroy the dreadnaught virus."

Was this the truth, or was it Satan's greatest lie? Feinstein was, after all, speaking with a gun at his throat. And he was a self-admitted liar.

If this was the Devil speaking through him, and I believed Satan's greatest lie, I would infect the nation with a deadly new Plague variant that might destroy all human life.

But if God had chosen this unlikely instrument to reveal His truth at the eleventh hour and I *didn't* believe it, I would not only be responsible for the deaths of a million people, I would be responsible for destroying God's own cure for the Plague.

What was I to do? What could I believe? *Whatever* the truth was, Satan could not have devised for me a more perfect moral dilemma.

"The President on the line . . ." said a voice on my intercom.

No man should be forced to make such a decision. But I was. And I had to do it now. But I could not. There was only one thing that I could do.

There, in front of Feinstein, and David, and my own men,

and with the President of the United States waiting on the telephone, I sank unashamedly to my knees and prayed aloud.

"Please, Jesus, I know that this cup cannot pass from me," I prayed. "But grant me at least one mercy. Send me a Sign. Show me Your Countenance."

And God, in His infinite wisdom, answered my prayer, through the most unlikely of instruments.

The young girl stepped forward. "Let me help you," she said softly. She took my hand in hers and raised me to my feet. "Let me be your Sign," she said.

"*You?* You're—"

"Our Lady of Love Reborn—"

"—the blasphemous mouthpiece of Satan!"

"No, I'm not. Nothing speaks through me but the truth in an ordinary girl's heart, and I'm very much afraid," she said with the strangest gentleness. "But I know that this man is speaking the truth, and there's no one else. So I *have* to be your Sign, now don't I? In the only way I can."

"How?" I asked softly, wanting very much, in that moment, to believe. In Jesus. In God's Grace. In anything that would show me the truth.

Even in she whom I had believed to be my nemesis, even in Our Lady of Love Reborn, if she could make me.

"By placing my life in your hands," she said.

I locked eyes with Our Lady of Love Reborn. They were young and they were fearful, but there was a strength in them too that seemed timeless. She smiled the Madonna's smile at me. Or was this only what I was longing to see?

"There's a helicopter waiting outside. I'm going to go to it and fly back to San Francisco. If the city dies at your hand, so will I. Would Satan's mouthpiece do that, Walter Bigelow?"

"The President on the line . . ."

"You would do that?" I said. "You'd really do that?"

She nibbled nervously at her bottom lip. She nodded demurely. "You'll have to kill me right now to stop me," she said, letting go of my hand, and turning to confront the men blocking the doorway. "Will you tell these men to shoot me, Mr. Bigelow? Or will you let me pass?"

"Hey, Linda, you can't do that, we're safe here, don't be crazy!" I said, grabbing her by the arm.

The SP guards trained their pistols on us, looking to Bigelow for orders. I brought up my miniauto, flipped it to full rock and roll as conspicuously as I could, just daring the mothers to try it.

"I can, John, I must," Linda told me, and took two steps forward with me hanging on to her.

I turned to confront Bigelow. I could see that he *wanted* to believe. Wouldn't you?

What can I tell you, brothers and sisters? Maybe I figured Bigelow needed a final push. Anyway, how could I let her do this thing all alone? A short life, but a happy one, as we say in the Army of the Living Dead.

"Not without me, you don't," I said, taking her hand.

"The President on the line . . ."

I whipped the miniauto around and pointed it right at Bigelow's head. "I could blow you away right now," I told him. "And don't think I wouldn't enjoy it, meatfucker!"

Walter T. Bigelow looked straight into my eyes and didn't flinch. The bastard had balls, you had to give him that.

"But I won't," I told him. " 'Cause this old zombie believes her. And you've gotta believe her too."

"Make me," Walter T. Bigelow said softly. "I truly pray that you can."

"Then try *this*," I said. I smiled, I shrugged, and I threw the miniauto on the floor in front of him. "We're gonna walk out of here to that helicopter, and we're gonna fly back to San Francisco. You can clock us on radar."

I turned to face the pistols of the SPs. "Or you can have these bozos fill us full of holes—your choice, Bigelow," I said over my shoulder. "Of course then you'll never know, now will you?"

And hand in hand we walked toward the armed men blocking the doorway.

The guards' fingers tightened against their triggers.

The moment hung in the air.

"Let them pass," Walter T. Bigelow said behind us. "Praise the mysterious workings of the Lord."

397

And the two of them walked out of the room hand in hand toward the helicopter, toward San Francisco, toward their faith in the wisdom and mercy of God, which no true Christian, in that moment, could justly deny.

In all my life, no one had placed greater trust in me than this young girl and this savage young man.

A nimbus of clear white light seemed to surround them as they walked out the door, and there were tears in my eyes as I watched them go.

God could not have granted me a clearer Sign.

I sank once more to my knees and gave thanks for His infinite wisdom, His infinite mercy, for His presence in that room, in that moment, in my heart, for the Sign He had granted me in my ultimate hour of need.

The rest is, as they say, history, and this is the end of the story of my part in it.

I did not ask the President for a nuclear strike. Instead I told him what Feinstein had told me. And I issued an order for my troops to cease firing, to let those seeking to leave San Francisco pass as well.

There was much confusion afterward as hundreds of thousands of people poured out of the San Francisco Quarantine Zone. Congress called for my impeachment. I offered up my resignation. It was refused. Proceedings began in the House.

But as the hearings began, hundreds of escapees from San Francisco were rounded up, and all of them tested out blue. And the dreadnaught virus was found in all of their bodies.

So did the Plague Years end. And so too my public life. I became a national hero once more, and though there was no further need for a Federal Quarantine Agency or its director, I could no doubt have been elected to any office in the land.

But I chose instead to retire. And write this memoir. And go off on a long retreat into the desert with my family to try to understand the mysterious ways of God. And to reconcile with my wife.

And God granted us an easy reconciliation, for Satan had gone from her, if he had ever really possessed her, and she believed in me again.

398

"It was a true Christian act, Walter, and a brave one," she told me the night she took me once more into her arms. "God works in mysterious ways."

So He does. And perhaps the true wisdom is that that is all we can ever really know of the workings of His Will.

Did Satan send the Plague to torment us? Or did God send the Plague to chastise and test us?

If so, it was a terrible chastisement and a cruel testing. But so was the Great Flood, and the Ten Plagues, and the Forty Years in the Wilderness, and of course Jesus's own martyrdom on the Cross.

"Love thy neighbor as thyself," Jesus told us, and was crucified for it.

How could that be the Will of a God of Love?

How could the Plague Years be the Will of God either?

I don't know. I don't think I ever will.

And yet my faith is still strong. For God spoke to me in my greatest hour of need through the unlikely instrumentalities of a young girl whom I had believed to be Satan's daughter and a vicious creature who had certainly spent most of his life doing the Devil's work on Earth.

Such a God I will never understand.

In such a God I can only believe.

Such a God I can only love.

AFTERWARD
J.E. Pournelle

EVERY NOW AND THEN I GET TO WRITE A DIATRIBE. IT'S ONE OF my perks for doing this series. That's just as well, because I feel a speech coming on.

I'm sitting at the high table in the great hall of the Trusteeship Council of the United Nations. This is the room often referred to as the UN's "Independence Hall," since it was here that nearly half the UN membership was granted independence from mandates or colonial supervision. I'm about to make a speech. Meanwhile, two seats down from me, a Nobel Laureate is making his own speech, and it's about to drive me up the wall.

I suppose I'd better explain?

We got here by flying all night from Flagstaff, Arizona, where I was attending a meeting of the Board of Advisors of the Lowell Observatory on Mars Hill. We were whisked away from discussing the future of the institution that discovered the galactic red shift and the planet Pluto to the Flagstaff airport, thence by Twin Otter to Phoenix. Then came the redeye to Newark. It was a harrowing trip, and I am *not* in the mood to listen to a Nobel physicist cackle with absolute glee that cold fusion is impossible, "Fleischmann and Pons are idiots," and anyone who thinks they aren't idiots just doesn't know anything about science. Alas, that's just what I *am* hearing. Apparently my physicist colleague just can't stand the notion that a pair of chemists—chemists!—may have done something he thought impossible. It's all right, though. He doesn't think *anyone* in the United States knows anything about science.

As to why we're in the United Nations building, it was all arranged by Dr. Hans Janitschek, President of the United Nations Society of Writers. There are two panels this afternoon. The first was entitled "Earth My Beautiful Home: The Role of the Artist in Shaping the Environmental Future of Our Planet," and it was finished half an hour ago. The second, "Which Tomorrow: The Role of the Scientist in Choosing the Future," is just starting. The whole program was sponsored by Bridge Publications as part of the awards ceremony of their Writers of the Future contest, and no, I haven't the foggiest notion how they managed to get the UN Society of Writers to set this up for them.

I do know I'm listening to a speech that's got my teeth on edge. The only way to contain myself is to make these notes, and keep remembering that I get to speak last.

The earlier panel was depressing enough. A panel of artists, chaired by Dr. Charles Sheffield, who is both artist and scientist, seems pretty well convinced that we're bent on both mucking up the Earth and uglifying it, and if we've done very much good in the past twenty years, no one seemed eager to talk about it.

Now this speech. Our distinguished colleague has entitled his talk "The End of Science Fiction." What he's really hinting at is the end of science. The great discoveries have all been made. From here on in we'll only fill in details. And no, we're not going to the stars, nor even to the planets; that's all hogwash and wishful thinking. The reality is that here on Earth things are going from bad to worse.

My, he's eloquent. Our children don't know any science. They don't even know any history. In fact, they don't seem to know anything at all. Our politicians don't know anything either. We have no long-term goals, and we're incapable of having any. Our undergraduates are stupid, and so are our graduate students, whose places in our deteriorating schools are increasingly being taken by foreigners anyway. One wonders why the best and the brightest of the foreign students come here?

Thank heaven that's over. Now we hear Ed Gibson, astronaut,

and Yoji Kondo, NASA scientist. Both seem a bit subdued by what they've just heard. Dr. Kondo, in his usual quiet and reasonable way, pleads that there is indeed much we can do, and much we are doing; and the world is hardly a worse place now than when we were children. I can see why he would think that way. Yoji grew up in Japan during World War II. His wife Ursula grew up in Germany at the same time. They are now citizens of the United States, and they don't think the country is coming apart.

And it's shortly going to be my turn. What do I say?

The problem is that much of the depressing litany of condemnation was all true. We don't do a very good job of teaching science, at least not to the great majority of our students; and we do leap on many scientific frills and frauds with great joy. We are busily spending our children's inheritance on ourselves, and we invest precious little of it in anything that will have a long-term payoff for them.

Still in all, there's no situation so gloomy and depressing that, if looked at in just the right way, can't be made even gloomier and more depressing; which is what I've just heard, and now it's my turn.

We hear a lot about the coming global disaster. There's the "greenhouse effect," which may be warming the planet enough to melt the polar icecaps; if that happens the seas will rise from a few feet to, at the extremes, over a hundred feet. Even a small rise would finish off Venice and a number of coastal areas. All this from burning fossil fuels, which dump carbon dioxide into the atmosphere. CO_2 lets in short-wave, high-energy radiation—the ultraviolet end of the spectrum—but traps the re-radiation of long-wave infrared, otherwise known as heat. This isn't how a real greenhouse works, but it is a major reason the planet Venus got to be boiling hot. Clearly it's something to worry about—

Except that we don't really know. While global warming and the greenhouse effect are all the rage this year, I can recall not twenty years ago when the big concern was that the Earth was *cooling off*, and indeed there were some wondering if we weren't headed for another Ice Age. Incidentally, lest we get too complacent about that, it's now known that the last Ice Age came on rather suddenly: in fewer than forty years England went from being inhabited to under several feet of snow and ice.

Meanwhile, all the coal and wood we burn puts smoke particles into the atmosphere. They make the atmosphere more reflective. This cuts down on the heat coming in. I've heard quite distinguished climatologists argue that it's only the smoke up there that keeps the Earth as cool as it is . . .

We really don't know. But we'd better find out. More than that, once we do know, we'd better have the means to do something about it. It wouldn't take a great deal to do that, provided we invest now.

Next question. Is the global disaster required? And again we know the answer. Clearly it's not, so long as we act sensibly.

What's sensible?

Let me give an example of something that *isn't* sensible: a few weeks ago there was a spate of pronouncements from Stanford and Berkeley professors about the possible effects of cold fusion: to wit, it would be the worst thing that could happen to the world. Clean cheap energy would be a disaster. It would utterly wreck the "quality of life"—which, incidentally, has been going steadily down for the past forty years.

To which the only possible answer is, quality of life for whom? I suspect that many of those whose nations achieved independence, whose representatives now sit in the United Nations, do not believe their quality of life has been steadily falling. The millions who for the first time in history have discovered that you don't have to have ten children in order for two or three to survive; who have discovered that you don't have to die of malaria, or smallpox; the millions of children who don't have cavities because we now know about fluorides: I suspect they don't think quality of life is falling. I know they wouldn't think cheap clean energy was the worst thing that could happen.

The fact is that cold fusion doesn't matter. We can hope it's all true, but even if it isn't, there are other energy sources. They aren't free, but even the expensive ones are cheap compared to the billions we waste.

We know how to solve most of the world's problems. We've known for some time. We're not running out of energy, and we'll never run out of natural resources.

Ninety percent of the resources easily available to mankind

are not on this planet; but they are available, as soon as we decide to go get them.

So what? We don't look like we're going after them. Last summer marked the twentieth anniversary of Apollo, and it's been a long time since we lit a fire on the Moon.

What man has done, man can aspire to.

The problem with the doomsayers is that their horizons are too small. It may be that the United States has lost its goals and dreams. It may be that we're determined to spend our children's inheritance on ourselves and invest none of it. It may be that, having come so far, we'll quit. But we're not the whole human race.

Who chooses the future? Those who dream the future choose the future.

You can't predict the future, but you can invent it.

We have it in our power to survive the end of the Earth, even the end of the solar system. We have the power to do whatever needs doing to ensure the survival of the human species. We know how to do it, and it will be done.

By someone.

They may not speak English. They may not even speak Japanese, or Russian. Perhaps a nation which didn't exist until given independence right here in this hall.

We know the way. We have the designs. We can have the first of the new generation of spacecraft in under four years, and for less than we spend each year on tobacco subsidies. We can, or someone else can.

If we don't need the resources of the solar system, someone will. I'd like it to be us, of course. I think the best remedy to our education problem is to give the kids new hopes and new dreams; to stop talking about insoluble problems and talk instead of opportunities. If we've someplace exciting to go, we won't have much trouble getting kids to tool up to go there. And what could possibly be more exciting than the first steps toward a billion year future? America or another, someone will lead the way.

THE TOR DOUBLES

Two complete short science fiction novels in one volume!